There was a creak from downstairs. A wind started catching the door that led from the garage into the kitchen. Beckett must have left it open again. Let them try it, he thought. I can deal with a burglar at least. The wind moved the door a second time. In the silence, it sounded like the creaking timber of a ship lost somewhere far out to sea. There it was again. The sound, Beckett realised, was what he himself had become. A ghost ship, becalmed, adrift, waiting. Another long and sleepless night stretched out before Tom Beckett and he'd measure out every awful minute until, finally, the sickly grey light would trickle in through the gap in the curtains and tell him to rise again and begin the day.

'Did you?' Beckett asked the darkness. 'Did you know how much I loved you?'

Mark Peterson was born in London and studied Literature at the University of Essex. He then moved to Brighton and worked in PR and teaching before embarking on his writing career. He lives in Brighton with his wife and two children. *Flesh and Blood* is his first novel.

# FLESH AND BLOOD

## MARK PETERSON

| LIVEWIRE WARRINGTON | |
|---|---|
| 34143101242707 | |
| Bertrams | 12/03/2013 |
| AF | £7.99 |
| WAR | |

An Orion paperback

First published in Great Britain in 2012
by Orion
This paperback edition published in 2013
by Orion Books,
an imprint of The Orion Publishing Group Ltd,
Orion House, 5 Upper Saint Martin's Lane,
London WC2H 9EA

An Hachette UK company

1 3 5 7 9 10 8 6 4 2

A CIP catalogue record for this book
is available from the British Library.

ISBN 978-1-4091-3592-0

Typeset by Input Data Services Ltd, Bridgwater, Somerset

Printed and bound by CPI Group (UK) Ltd, Croydon, CR0 4YY

The Orion Publishing Group's policy is to use papers that
are natural, renewable and recyclable products and
made from wood grown in sustainable forests. The logging
and manufacturing processes are expected to conform to
the environmental regulations of the country of origin.

www.orionbooks.co.uk

*This book is for Claire*

# Acknowledgements

My heartfelt thanks go to Anna Webber at United Agents for spotting a bit of talent and sticking with it through thick and thin. At the University of Sussex, Irving Weinman and Dr Sue Roe nurtured that bit of talent and sent it back into the world better equipped. A big thank you to Craig Melvin and Araminta Craig-Hall for the warmth of their friendship and the extent of their encouragement. Thanks to the team at Orion: Natalie Braine, Julia Silk and an inspirational editor, Sara O'Keeffe, who saw this book through to publication at the same time as accomplishing a Very Special Project of her own. Thank you to Minter's helpers: Stephen, Martin and Paul, Elizabeth, Helen, Kristina, Julie and Laura. And special thanks to Margaret Bingham, who is the keeper of the faith. Finally, and most importantly, thanks to my supportive and loving wife and children, to my own flesh and blood: Siobhan, Kate and William.

# 1

### ...

The final racehorse entered the parade ring. In the fierce sunshine, its black flanks shone like water. All around it, people were moving, making their way over to watch the race from up in the stand, or hurrying to the Tote for a final punt. An announcer's voice carried over from the line of tannoys: 'The Mishon McKay Novice Stakes is up next, ladies and gentlemen, and what a great field it's attracted to Brighton this afternoon.' Trackside, first-time racegoers waved banknotes at the bookies' chalkboards, where the odds were changing in the blink of an eye. Amid the piped trumpets and excited chatter, a racehorse pranced nervously towards the starting line.

Behind the Tattersall, in the corner of the car park nearest the racecourse, a blue Mondeo was waiting. Detective Chief Inspector Tom Beckett sat sweltering in the driver's seat. Beside him was Detective Constable Vicky Reynolds. At twenty-four, Vicky was the youngest DC on Beckett's squad, and the only woman. Neither of them was thinking about the next race.

1

Beckett looked across at Vicky. 'You OK?' he asked.

Vicky nodded. The senior investigating officer for Operation Windmill, Tom Beckett was a hard taskmaster. Vicky stared at the red Alfa Romeo parked a hundred yards away, halfway down the middle row of cars. She glanced at the clock on the Mondeo's dashboard. 'He's half an hour late,' she said.

'Alan Day is always late,' said Beckett. 'It's in his nature. Like being an evil bastard is in his nature.'

There was a sudden crackle of static in Beckett's earpiece and a message from the surveillance unit came over the secure waveband. Alan Day was coming up the hill.

'What's he driving?' Vicky asked.

Another crackle, then the answer came: 'The Cayenne.'

A moment later, Day's enormous car entered the car park. The red Cayenne was Porsche's punchy version of the classic 4x4. As it prowled along the first rank of cars, its chunky wheels crunched over the exposed chalk. At the end of the line, it turned round. It drove back along the middle row, pausing only briefly in front of the puny-looking Alfa. Then it drove on, slotting into one of the few remaining spaces.

Ray Tyler got out of the Alfa Romeo. As the undercover police officer walked towards the Cayenne, he was trying to concentrate only on the throaty growl still emanating from its engine.

The driver's window of the Cayenne slid down and instantly Tyler recognised Alan Day's ugly, hyper-mobile features. Tyler's mouth was dry now and he could feel his body pumping adrenaline. 'All right, Al?' he asked.

'Good, mate,' Day answered from his lofty seat. He wasn't looking at Tyler. His shaven head was turned towards the windscreen of the Cayenne and the city of Brighton, laid out before him at the bottom of the steep hill.

Tyler hesitated. 'You sure, Al?' he asked.

Day shrugged. 'Just need to get well.'

Tyler ventured a smile. 'Don't we all, mate?'

Alan Day turned his face towards the undercover cop. 'Do we?' he snapped. 'Didn't fancy it the other night, then?'

Tyler looked down, shifting the position of his feet. 'On and off, y'know.' Day resumed his silent study of Brighton's teeming seafront. He seemed to be thinking something over. 'We all set for Wednesday, then?' Tyler asked.

Day sucked at his teeth. 'Not sure.'

'What's up?'

The fake Yardie accent rippled through Day's voice. 'It's a lot of chiva, man,' he said. Day was nineteen and white, but he spoke like a black man and he drove a fifty-grand car.

Tyler knew that something was wrong. He shifted his feet again. 'It's your call, Al. But the money's still sweet, yeah?'

'A lot of people asking questions.'

Tyler laughed unconvincingly. 'They would ask questions, wouldn't they? Like, I'm the new boy in town.' He hesitated, then gambled. 'But don't forget that I'm the one holding the cash, Al, and the money's not going to stay on the table for ever.'

Day stared Tyler in the face. 'But who are you, Ray?' Out of nowhere, a Tokarev pistol had appeared in the window of the Cayenne. 'Where you from, Ray? That's what I want to know.'

The last thing Tyler saw was the sneer on Alan Day's

face. There was a single sharp crack and a boom that filled the entire hillside. The high-velocity round lifted Tyler off his feet, smacking his shoulders back against the roofline of the car parked next to the Porsche. Tyler slid down the door, bloodying the paintwork, then slumped onto the stony ground.

Day threw the pistol onto the passenger seat and rammed the engine into reverse. The back wheels crunched over Tyler's outstretched legs at the same time as an unmarked police van screeched forwards to block the exit of the car park. Day saw his escape route closed off. The Cayenne roared backwards again along the line of cars, barely missing Vicky Reynolds, who had got out of the Mondeo to go to Tyler's aid.

Vicky stood over Tyler's body. The undercover officer was lying on his back, unmoving, a circle of blood spreading out from the massive gunshot wound in the side of his head. Vicky put her hand up to her mouth. 'Oh God,' she breathed. She stood there for a moment, rooted to the spot. Then she remembered she was mic'ed up. 'Day shot him in the face!' she cried.

Tom Beckett was still in the Mondeo. 'Take Day down!' he yelled as the Cayenne raced towards him along the line of parked cars. It swung round, raising up clouds of white dust that prevented the firearms officers from getting a clear sight. A single shot split the air nonetheless, but by now Day was heading for the top corner of the car park, where he'd spotted a gap next to the St John's Ambulance.

Alan Day's Cayenne bumped up onto the grass verge. In a moment, he'd be gone. One of his officers was down, and DCI Beckett was closest to the perp. Without waiting for

Reynolds, he floored the accelerator and gave chase.

In the parade ring, spooked by the gunfire, the black horse kicked and reared, tugging its reins free from the stable lad's outstretched hands. It skittered out of the enclosure, straight into the path of the speeding Cayenne. The gelding's forelegs buckled. The impact sent him up onto the bonnet of Alan Day's car before sliding him off again in a flail of broken limbs.

A moment later, two thousand amazed racegoers watched from the stand as the mighty Cayenne crashed through the white railings and out onto the hillside. Some of the spectators had heard the gunshots, but they'd mistaken them for nothing more alarming than a misfiring starting pistol. Now – as the bookies threw themselves off their boxes and a man yanked his daughter out of the way of the Porsche – everyone knew that something very bad had just happened.

Day's car crashed through both sets of railings and out onto the Downs. A few seconds later, the Mondeo joined it. The two cars sped along the hilltop. Day turned right, away from the houses, down towards the sea, the Cayenne ripping up the thin topsoil but keeping tight to the ground. Behind it, Beckett almost lost control of his plunging saloon, the Mondeo's backside slewing suddenly out to the left. The gap between the two cars began to widen again.

At the bottom of the hill, Day smashed through a metal barrier and screeched out onto Wilson Avenue. A horn blared as a van whacked up onto the kerb to avoid it, the wing clipping the back of the Cayenne, the nudge helping Day wheel-spin out onto the seafront road. There were more horns from the braking cars. Day ignored them. He regained control of the Cayenne and roared through the red traffic lights. In his rear-view mirror, Day could see the Mondeo threading its way through the vehicles lodged at odd angles around the junction.

Looking ahead again, Day saw, in the middle distance, traffic queuing all the way to the city centre. The black-yellow police helicopter had already appeared in the sky above the Palace Pier.

Day pulled out onto the wrong side of the carriageway and accelerated hard. The single column of cars coming out of the city began splintering before him. Closer to the Steine, the road began to narrow. Day could hear the wailing two-tones of the squad cars coming up the hill. 'Fuck it,' he spat out, taking his foot off the pedal and yanking the long, leather-bound handbrake. Its tyres screaming, the Cayenne spun round once, twice. The massive vehicle slid sideways across the road, toppling the bollards at a traffic island. Then it slammed into the door of a parked green-and-white taxi.

In the Mondeo, Beckett saw the cloud of glass fly up, heard the terrible, grinding thud of metal tearing into metal. He stood on his own brakes, stopping the Ford just a few feet from the collision.

Behind the smoked windows of the Cayenne, Day was still invisible. Beckett opened the door of his saloon. Noises returned to the scene around him: police sirens, the chuntering of the helicopter, the taxi's pointless alarm.

Beckett walked forwards. The cab driver had still been in the vehicle when Day hit it. The Cayenne's high bonnet had smashed straight into his head.

Suddenly, the driver's door of the Cayenne flew open and Day jumped down onto the road. Looking straight at Beckett,

6

he raised the Tokarev to fire. Beckett flinched, expecting the shot to come, but something made Day change his mind. Instead of firing, he turned and ran. Within seconds one of the narrow lanes leading off the seafront had swallowed him up.

Half an hour later, Tom Beckett was walking up the steps in front of the entrance to Kemptown Police Station. There was a television news camera pointing at his face and Beckett realised that Alan Day was no longer just a drug dealer. He was a celebrity.

Beckett strode inside the narrow, scruffy 1960s tower block. Someone had tried to tart up the reception area, sticking the Sussex Police insignia on the wall and installing a civilian behind a desk to answer phones. Very corporate, Beckett thought, walking straight past the lifts and smacking open the door of the stairwell. Like the building, DCI Tom Beckett was showing his age. He'd found his first grey hair and he'd noticed the beginnings of a paunch. It was the TV dinners he was eating. As Beckett climbed the stairs, though, it wasn't the salt in his veins that set his heart racing but the thought of Alan Day slipping through his fingers. Right now, most of the Windmill team were out on the streets, or upstairs in the Major Incident Room. They were working the phones, calling in favours, dishing out threats, pumping everyone they knew for the word about Alan Day's where-abouts. Beckett wanted to be with them, doing something, not walking into a meeting with Chief Superintendent Roberts.

On the third floor, Beckett's mobile rang. He grabbed it out of his pocket – perhaps this was the call about Alan

Day. Pressing the button, he barked his own name into the phone. It was the consultant doctor at the Royal County Hospital: on his arrival, Ray Tyler had gone straight into emergency surgery. Beckett stood still and listened to what the doctor had to say.

After a moment, he closed his eyes. This afternoon, Operation Windmill had turned to shit, but the news Beckett had just been given was the worst news of all. Tom Beckett was the SIO and it had been his decision to send Ray Tyler up against Alan Day armed with nothing more lethal than a radio microphone and a suitcase full of marked banknotes. On the landing of the stairwell, Beckett searched his mind for any prior indication, any reason to believe that Tyler's cover had been anything less than secure. There was nothing, nothing at all, but that didn't make it any easier.

On the phone, the consultant said something else.

'Sorry?' Beckett asked. 'Yeah, that's right – there's a wife.' Another question.

'No, I'll call her.' Beckett gazed out of the window of the stairwell. 'It's down to me.'

On the fifth floor at Kemptown Station, Detective Sergeant Minter was working in his office. Minter was the new boy. He'd only moved his things in a couple of days ago.

There was an electronic beep and the computer screen on Minter's desk flipped back to ExCal, the intelligence database deployed by SOCU, Brighton's Serious and Organised Crime Unit. Today was a good day because ExCal had only crashed the once.

The 5x5x5 intelligence forms from the racetrack shooting were coming in thick and fast, and Minter had recognised lots of things from Alan Day's Target Profile. There was the same cocksure personalised number plate on the Porsche Cayenne – RE5IN – and the pistol he'd used on Tyler had long been Alan Day's firearm of choice. The Tokarev might be surprisingly old-fashioned, but it packed a punch. Minter downloaded the latest 5x5x5 and read the brief paragraph on the screen. The uniformed officer he had sent to one of Alan Day's known addresses in Whitehawk was reporting that Trish Yates wasn't at her mum's house. Trish Yates was Alan Day's girlfriend, and she hadn't been seen all day. It was probably nothing, Minter thought. Just coincidence. But he knew that Russell Compton had taken hostages before. Minter picked up his mobile from the desk, composed a text to DCI Beckett and pressed send.

Minter was ambitious. He was twenty-seven years old – pretty young for a DS – and at Kemptown he had a lot to prove, having spent the last two years behind a desk up at Division, where he worked for Chief Superintendent Roberts. It had raised quite a few eyebrows when Minter took his detective exams and applied to join the Crime Squad.

Minter put down his mobile and glanced around the office. The bookcase on the side wall was neatly lined with rows of training manuals. Piled on the bottom shelf were copies of the three reports Minter had compiled last year for Chief Superintendent Roberts. He'd stowed them there just yesterday, uncertain of where else they should go but deciding not to shred them, which was what he really wanted to do.

On the whiteboard on the other wall, Minter had drawn a diagram of Russell Compton's heroin distribution network.

Pinned up in the middle of the spider's web was a recent colour surveillance photo of Russell Compton himself. It showed a tall, sandy-haired man getting out of a top-of-the-range Lexus. A handy amateur boxer in his youth, Compton was a big guy who dwarfed the side of the luxury car. Operation Windmill had been pressing Brighton's biggest, best-organised heroin franchise for over a year now and Russell Compton was the main target. He was the kingpin, the thirty-kilo man, and it was in order to make inroads into Compton's organisation that the undercover operation with Tyler had been set up. Compton shifted kilo after kilo of gear every single week, in Sussex and beyond, so it needed a lot of protection. Russell wasn't involved in the violence himself anymore – he had Alan Day to do that for him, among others – but everyone on SOCU knew exactly what he was capable of. One word from Russell Compton and someone got beaten or stabbed or shot, just like Ray Tyler had been.

On the diagram, lines radiated out from Compton's name and photograph like spokes running down from the hub of a wheel. At the end of each line, written up in red, the name of one of Compton's associates appeared, together with their designated function. Alan Day was the enforcer. In return for the discounted deals that Russell Compton gave him, Day provided the muscle needed to keep the seafront and the estate dealers in line. Apart from Day, Russell Compton ran a family business. His brother-in-law, Dave Gillespie, ran the stash houses, and his wife, Jacqui Compton, laundered the money.

Looking away from the whiteboard, Minter caught sight of a black lever-arch file hidden underneath the pile of intelligence reports on the side of his desk. He hesitated. He didn't really have time for that at the moment, but there was something about the Murder Book he just couldn't leave alone. As an intelligence analyst, Minter had top-level security clearance for his rank. He could go anywhere, look at anything, and it had been a relatively simple thing a couple of days ago to retrieve the cold case file from a long-forgotten corner of the archive in the basement of the Kemptown station. The victim's name was written on the spine of the Murder Book in felt-tip pen, along with the date of her death: *Anna May, 12 July 1995*. Minter opened the front cover. On top of the thick wedge of papers was a contemporaneous clipping from the *Evening Argus*, Brighton's local newspaper. In her black blazer with the crest on the pocket, Anna smiled out innocently from the front page. Minter recognised the shoulder-length hair, the open, good-natured expression and he touched the faded newsprint with the tips of his fingers. Anna would have been thirty one now, although for some reason Minter found that difficult to imagine. Last night, with his analyst's eye for detail, he'd read Anna's Murder Book. Like Operation Windmill, the investigation seventeen years ago lacked method, lacked rigour. Far too many clues had been overlooked and, as a result, too many lines of enquiry had run into the sand, but that wasn't really surprising since the SIO on both cases had been the same DCI. Minter's mobile drummed on his desk. Beckett had texted straight back: he was coming to see Minter now.

Concealing the Murder Book under all the 5x5x5s again, Minter looked back at the whiteboard. This was his priority now, he told himself, this and the murder of Ray Tyler. In the top left-hand corner of the whiteboard, in his neat, almost fastidious script, Minter had written the single word *Importer*, followed by a red question mark. Compton might be a thirty-kilo man, but as yet there was no indication he was bringing in the heroin himself. That meant Compton was buying from someone else in the UK. As far as Minter could see, however, no one on Windmill had ever bothered to ask who that might be. 'Who do *you* buy from, Russell?' Minter wondered aloud just before the door burst open and Beckett came into the room.

'I'm on my way to see Roberts,' Beckett said, glaring at the young DS. 'You've got one minute.'

Minter stood up. 'Trish Yates, sir.'

'Never heard of her.'

'She's Alan Day's girlfriend,' said Minter. 'Lives in Whitehawk.'

'So?'

Minter picked up the 5x5x5 from his desk. 'She's gone missing. An officer from East Brighton just sent this.'

Beckett ignored the intel report. 'Missing since when?'

'Since this morning.'

Beckett shrugged. 'It's the weekend. The girl could be anywhere.'

'I've checked, sir,' said Minter. 'Trish Yates waitresses in the Laines. She was supposed to turn up for work at two o'clock this afternoon, but she never showed. I tried the mobile number they gave me. No answer.'

Beckett stared at SOCU's newest recruit. Minter was keen, he'd give him that, but he wouldn't give him anything else. Not in a million years. 'I don't have time for this,' he said, turning round. 'Put it in an email, Minter.'

'Trish Yates has a daughter, sir,' Minter said quickly. It was just enough to stop Beckett in his tracks. The DCI turned back. 'A baby girl,' Minter added.

'Ten seconds left,' said Beckett.

'Trish was supposed to drop the little girl off this afternoon at the baby's grandmother. It was the gran who rang us. She's worried.'

Beckett thought about it for a moment. 'So you're thinking that Trish Yates and this baby of hers have been taken hostage by Russell Compton, to keep Alan's mouth shut once he's in custody.'

'Yes, sir. Russell's working the angles, like he always does.'

'I see,' said Beckett. He walked round the desk and took the intelligence report out of Minter's hand. Beckett screwed the piece of paper into a tight little ball. Staring at the younger man, he let it fall to the floor. It rolled a few inches along the new carpet.

Beckett followed it, taking another couple of steps towards Minter. The younger man was two or three inches taller than he was. With his neat, side-parted hair, he was good-looking, too. The new DS obviously worked out a lot, but Beckett knew he could take him. 'You're going to have to do a lot better than this, Minter. Alan Day's the original baby father. He's got three kids. Three kids we know about, at least. All of them have got different mums. You're the intelligence analyst. You figure it out for yourself. If Day doesn't give a shit about any of his offspring, why should Russell Compton? And why the fuck should we?'

There was a pent-up fury about Beckett that was making Minter nervous. 'I'm sorry, sir. It was just an idea.'

13

'I told you – I don't have time for ideas.' He left a beat of silence. 'Tyler's dead, Minter. It happened just now, in the hospital.' Beckett caught the fear in the other man's eyes. 'These guys don't fuck around, Minter. They've killed an officer. Scary, isn't it?' Beckett looked around the office, taking in the neat ranks of training manuals on the bookcase. 'You know, when I put in that request for another detective, I wanted someone who knew his way around the estates. Or at least someone with their own contacts on the seafront. Someone useful, Minter.'

'Sir,' said Minter, 'I was a PC in East Brighton. I know Whitehawk very well.'

'Yeah? And how long ago was that?'

Minter glanced down at the floor. 'Two years ago. But I asked for a transfer into SOCU twice. I want to work crime.'

Beckett snorted. 'So that's it, is it? I suppose it makes sense. I mean, whoever heard of a detective inspector without experience of major crime? Not even your mate Roberts would sign off on that one. Well, let me tell you something, Minter. We're not here for the sake of your career development.'

Minter tried again. 'I just want the chance to show what I can do.'

'Oh, yeah? Well, I know all about what you can do, Minter. I've heard about how good you are at mangling crime stats for Roberts.' Beckett looked up at the ceiling. 'What was it this year? Oh, yeah. Auto crime down by 2.3 per cent. Well, that was a hard fucking rain that fell, wasn't it?'

'Sir—'

14

'Listen, Minter,' said Beckett. 'My team has got the best clear-up rate in this entire fucking division. Now, I know that gets on Roberts's tits, but there it is. And not even *you* can slice and dice the numbers any other way. So the last thing I need is some jumped-up little tosser like you coming in here and telling me how to run things. Got it? And while we're at it, Minter, let me make something else very plain. You haven't got any friends in this station. No one at Kemptown is glad you're back. We all know the score. We all know what you did to Kevin.'

Minter was shocked. 'That panel was confidential.'

Beckett leaned in even closer. 'We're family, Minter, and family looks after its own. Remember that next time you're shuffling your fucking papers.'

Turning on his heels, Beckett marched out of the room.

At the top of St James's Street, Jimbob McFarland stopped outside an antiques shop. A large, gold-framed mirror was hanging in the window. Jimbob leaned closer in, pulling the skin of his cheek taut. He tutted. It was definitely a zit. It would need a dab of foundation before he went out tonight.

In the late-afternoon sun, Jimbob continued walking down the hill, passing the Sidewinder pub and a new place selling hideous retro furniture. Ahead of him, a police car was parked up on the pavement. He crossed the road to avoid the officers getting out of it.

On St James's Street, the crowds were gone. Kemptown was being reclaimed by its workaday denizens: bag ladies, addicts, queers, crims. Jimbob ignored the smashed-in faces of the junkies. As he walked, he scoped the pretty faces of Kemptown's boys. Oversized sunglasses, geometric hair, tight urban clothing – they were all looking fine. A lot of them knew him, too. Jimbob was young, just turned nineteen. With his floppy, peroxided hair, he was something of a talisman round here. He got plenty of nods and smiles.

The Red Roaster café was at the bottom of St James's and it was Jimbob's favourite place for coffee. When cash was short, it could also be a fair place to pick up trade. Glancing around at the other customers, Jimbob went and ordered at the counter. Then he took his cup and plate over to a table near the door.

Before he sat down, Jimbob took an already-opened letter out of the back pocket of his artfully ripped jeans. He slapped it down on the small, circular table, placed his mocha next to it. Outside, yet another police car went crawling up the hill. Something was definitely up.

Jimbob sat in one of the chairs. He stirred lots of sugar into his coffee, took his first bite of the Danish. The letter stayed there in front of him on the table. Sipping his drink, Jimbob tried not to look at it.

Jimbob's father hadn't contacted him in years.

By the time he'd reached the top floor of the Kemptown station, Beckett was sweating and he had to stand on the landing to catch his breath. He didn't want Chief Superintendent Roberts to see him like this. Through the window in the door, Beckett glimpsed the corridor leading to Roberts's office and its wood-panelled wall lined with trendy black uplighters. More tarting up, Beckett thought. More money wasted on his vanity. Tom Beckett's own career had stalled in the middle ranks a long time ago, and by his age that was a very uncomfortable place to be,

16

dumped on from on high at the same time as taking all the flak from below. Well, if it's promotion Minter wanted, Beckett thought, he was welcome to it. Steeling himself, Beckett was just about to grip the door handle when he stopped dead.

It had been going on for weeks now. Every night he lay awake in bed and every morning he woke up with the same sick feeling of dread inside his stomach. It was the undercover operation; it was Roberts going on at him; it was Minter being foisted on the team. Then it hit him. It wasn't any of these things that had been gnawing away at Tom Beckett worse than any stomach ulcer. It was today's date, a date that had been burrowing unseen through the pages of his diary for months. Letting go of the door, Beckett leaned back against the wall to rest his head. How could he have been so stupid? How could he have been so selfish, so wrapped up in his work that he hadn't even realised that today was 4 August? Beckett swallowed hard, choking back his tears. 'I'm sorry,' he gasped. 'I'm sorry.'

A year ago today, Tom Beckett's wife had died of cancer.

In front of the main entrance to Kemptown Station, television crews and press photographers jostled each other for the best position. When a female PR officer in a dark suit emerged from the building and came down the steps, there was a surge towards her.

'We're right up against deadline,' yelled one of the journalists. 'When are we going to get the statement?'

The young woman felt a little overwhelmed by the sheer number of reporters. This kind of thing didn't happen every day, even in Brighton. Taking a deep breath, she held up a hand for silence. 'Thanks for being patient, guys,' she said. 'We're going on the record about the shooting in a couple of minutes.'

'Who's coming out?' asked another reporter.

'Chief Superintendent Roberts is just finishing up a meeting now,' said the PR. She paused to let their pens scribble down the name.

'Who's he when he's at home?'

'Chief Superintendent Roberts is the commanding officer in Kemptown,' said the PR.

'Where's Tom?' said one of the local scribes.

'DCI Beckett is leading the manhunt,' said the PR. 'As I'm sure you can appreciate—'

But they weren't listening to her anymore. Roberts had just emerged from the station and was standing at the top of the steps by the entrance. He was a tall man with a hatchet face and dark hair. His immaculate dress uniform had announced his seniority. The journalists all hurried over.

Roberts surveyed their upturned faces with well-concealed distaste. He could control virtually everything about the situation this afternoon, but he knew he couldn't control them and that always made him uneasy. 'Good evening, ladies and gentlemen,' he said grimly. He looked down at the typewritten statement he was holding in his hand. 'At three thirty-four this afternoon,' he began, 'a man was shot dead at Kemptown Racecourse. We can now name that man as Detective Sergeant Ray Tyler.' A ripple of surprise ran through the crowd of reporters. They had thought that the murder was the latest violent turn in the war between rival drug gangs. 'DS Tyler was an undercover police officer working for Sussex Police,' Roberts continued. 'Ray Tyler was an experienced officer whose job required immense determination. He was a brave man who put himself deliberately in the way of harm in order to protect the public.' Roberts located the nearest BBC television news camera and stared straight into it. 'We will all miss him,' he said. Roberts looked back at the statement. 'The perpetrator of this appalling crime is well known to Sussex Police. His name is Alan Day. He is a notorious drug dealer with a history of violence. We will not rest until we have hunted this man down and brought him to justice. A substantial reward has already been made available for information leading to his arrest.' Roberts ran his eyes over the pack. 'Thank you, ladies and gentlemen. That is all I have for you at this time.'

Roberts turned away smartly and went back into the building. The PR scurried after him. She caught up with Roberts in the reception, where a small group of police officers and civilians had gathered to watch the press briefing.

'I'm going back to Division now,' Roberts told her. 'I believe you have my direct line.'

'Yes, sir,' said the PR. She hesitated.

'What is it?' said Roberts.

'I just wanted to say,' said the PR, 'that I thought what you told them – I mean about undercover work – I thought it was highly appropriate. It even got to the hacks, you know. They were moved, I could tell.'

Roberts nodded. 'Good,' he said. He fixed the young woman with his beady eyes. 'It's just a pity you didn't do your job so thoroughly, isn't it?' Roberts said, thrusting the statement back into her hands. The PR looked puzzled.

19

'There's a spelling mistake in the second paragraph,' Roberts told her. 'Check your bloody press releases before you put them out next time. That *is* what you're paid for.'

Roberts turned away.

A few moments later, in the underground car park beneath the station, Roberts had ensconced himself in the back seat of his official Jaguar. 'Division HQ,' he told the police driver.

They hit traffic as soon as they left the car park. The rush back home had started. Exhausted, sunburned, shopped out, all the day trippers were driving back to London. A lot of them – the ones who'd gone to the races, or taken the air along the seafront – wouldn't be returning in a hurry.

The Jaguar crawled down St James's. This part of town was an open sewer, Roberts thought, as he watched the freaks and misfits coming out for the evening's festivities. By the time morning came, there would be needles in all the gutters and the pavements would be slippery with blood. God knows why Minter wanted to come back here, the super thought. The whole lot should be swept into the sea.

Roberts drummed his fingers on the armrest. With time to kill, he tried to find the upside to this afternoon. He'd been around a long time. He was a consummate politician. There was always an upside to be found.

Two of them, in fact. The first was Detective Sergeant Minter. When he'd been up at Division, Minter had been a protégé of the chief superintendent. It was against Roberts's advice that the ambitious young sergeant had transferred to SOCU. But at least it meant Roberts had a man on the inside now. Minter could tell Roberts all about the failings of the Crime Squad.

And there was DCI Beckett, too, of course. For a year now, Chief Superintendent Roberts had been looking for an excuse to get rid of the troublesome middle-ranking officer. The disaster at the racetrack presented the perfect opportunity. Roberts was going to deal with Beckett once and for all.

# 2
. . .

From his hiding place in the forest, Alan Day watched the Land Rover come to a halt on the other side of the quiet country lane. It was a Discovery XK sports turbo, not one of the crappy new saloons. The engine purred for a moment before the driver cut the ignition and got out.

Day had never seen the man before. He was late twenties, with short, thick, black hair and ruddy-looking skin. Hidden among the tall, close-standing trees, Alan Day grasped the handle of his Tokarev a little tighter.

Standing in the middle of the road, the man from the Land Rover took a good look around. He approached the car Day had left in the layby. He looked in at the windows. Then, standing up straight, he turned round to inspect the screen of trees. 'Alan?' he called out. His deep voice sounded Eastern European. 'Rita asked me to come and get you.'

There was a crackle of twigs. The man's eyes went straight to them. His hand still on the Tokarev, the muzzle pointed down, Day emerged from the forest and stepped out onto the side of the road.

The man looked at him. Unperturbed by the firearm, he smiled, showing his crooked teeth. 'Hi,' he said. He turned back towards the Land Rover. 'We should get going.'

The Eastern European opened the boot of his car and took out a heavy-looking rucksack. 'Come with me,' he said, slinging the bag up over his shoulder. Wordlessly, Alan Day followed him into the wood.

The man from Eastern Europe was a fixer, Day thought as he trudged along behind him. So Rita is looking out for me now.

Alan Day had only met Rita a couple of times, but everyone knew how well Rita was connected. Even better than Russell Compton. Things were looking up. For the first time in hours, he allowed himself to think that he was going to get away with it. It was quite a buzz. Alan Day was going to get away with offing a cop.

After five minutes' walking, the woods ended and they came out into open countryside. The heat of the day had gone and in the soft evening light Essex was nothing like Day thought it would be. At the bottom of a large field, there was a wide estuary and on the horizon, where it met the sea, there was a bristle of masts.

The man saw where Day was looking. 'That's the marina,' he said. 'You will sail from there.' He looked at his watch. 'It is half past six now. The boat will come after dark and you must be at the end of the harbour wall, where there are some steps. That's where you'll board.'

'How will they know me?'

'They will know you.'

Day nodded. Everything looked kosher; everything looked sweet. 'Where you from?' he asked.

'I am Tajik,' the man said. 'From Tajikistan.'

It meant nothing to Alan. It might as well have been the moon. The Whitehawk housing estate, the Brighton seafront – those were the twin poles of Alan Day's world.

They were walking side by side now, following a wider track that skirted the field and led down to the water's edge. The Tajik moved more quickly over the open ground, his shoulders rolling easily inside the shiny brown leather jacket. 'You could have gone from Harwich, of course, but no doubt the police already have the ports locked down. So you pick up a small craft here and you'll be at the Hook of Holland tomorrow morning.' He glanced back at Day. 'I hope you are a good sailor, because your North Sea gets choppy at night.'

Day kept walking towards the estuary. He didn't care about a little bit of seasickness. 'Where to after Rotterdam?'

'Up to you, my friend,' said the Tajik. 'There's money in the bag. Enough for a few months. Just stay out of the cities.' He walked on for a minute. 'It's very flat in Holland. Very boring. But safe. Get somewhere isolated. A farmhouse. Then you will be able to see who is coming.'

They trudged along in silence. Day imagined the dull and watchful life he was about to start living. He wondered when Rita might consider bringing him back.

At the end of the track, the Tajik scrambled down a four-foot bank. Day hurried after him. The two men faced each other on a beach of fine white sand. The evening breeze was carrying the sound of the halyards tapping on the masts in the marina.

The Tajik dropped the rucksack and squatted down on the sand, taking a yellow cloth out of his pocket. 'Give me your gun,' he said. Alan Day handed over the Tokarev. Carefully, almost reverently, the Tajik placed it inside the cloth, folding over the edges and putting the package back inside the pocket of his jacket. He started taking things out of the rucksack. 'Here,' he said, handing Day a small jerry can. 'Wash.'

As Day took off his shirt, he watched the Tajik laying out fresh clothes for him. There was a new pair of jeans, a T-shirt, a windproof jacket. From the front pocket of the rucksack, the Tajik took out a passport and a roll of crisp euros done up in a red rubber band. Once he was done, he looked up. Day was bollock naked. 'Rita asked me to take good care of you,' the Tajik said, his face splitting open into another smile.

Day grinned back. He unscrewed the lid of the petrol can and held it high over his head, pouring the stinking fuel over his body. When he was completely doused, Day put down the can and began rubbing the petrol in all his crevices, cleansing his body of every trace of gunpowder residue. Day closed his eyes against the petrol fumes. The next moment, he smelled the singeing of his eyebrows and when he opened his eyes, his entire body was engulfed by a sheet of yellow flame. He heard a full-throated laugh. Enraged, Day walked towards the sound, reaching out with his hands for the man who had set him alight. Still laughing, the Tajik backed away quickly along the beach.

Day was in agony now. His skin was starting to peel, curling away from his body. Blind, his hands grasped at thin air. He stumbled over the rucksack, falling to his knees on the sand. He could hear the crackle of his own combustion. Day was tallow, his fat whistling. Somehow, he forced himself back to his feet. He turned towards the estuary, taking one slow-motion step after another. At last, his ankles felt something soft. He let himself fall forward into the shallow water.

Day got to his knees, his smoking torso red and blistered, his lungs screaming. Through lidless eyes, he saw the bright diamonds of light playing for a moment on the surface of the water. Then a bullet from a silencer thudded into his brain.

On the Downs behind Brighton, the chalk path was a white line across the landscape. It chased up the side of one hill, then disappeared near the summit, only to re-emerge on the hillside beyond. Running across the flat was a solitary figure in a dark blue tracksuit.

Minter kicked hard, his stride widening as he accelerated. Hill running had made his body tough and lean, stripping it of every ounce of fat. He'd already run seven miles over the Downs this evening, but he still had another ten to go, with a target time of less than eight minutes for every one. Time was Minter's obsession. At home, he pored over his training log, a hard-covered A5 notebook with ruled columns littered with metrics on his weight, nutrition, distances and times. When Minter lined up for the start of a marathon, he might recognise a handful of his fellow runners, but he would rarely exchange a nod, let alone a word. Like the other guys – and it was mostly men who fell into rank on these occasions, fiddling with their training watches, anxiously checking their supply of energy bars – Minter was really racing against himself.

Minter settled into an easy rhythm. To his left, the red

sun was beginning its descent into a sea the colour of iron and all around him the shadows were filling in the folds and dips of the land. The only sound he could hear was the steady in-out of his own breath and the distant evensong of a bird. It felt good to be out here again.

For the last two weeks, Minter had trawled through hundreds of intelligence reports about Windmill. They helped him get up to speed on the operation, helped him understand Russell Compton's network of heroin dealers – its players, its hierarchies, its history. Compton's organisation had its weaknesses, but from where Minter was standing, it looked like Operation Windmill had a whole lot more. All along Compton had been one step ahead of the police – the intelligence suggested as much and now Ray Tyler's murder had put it beyond doubt. But for the moment, the violence and the detail and even Minter's doubts about DCI Beckett were all forgotten in the simple act of running. Slowly, the sinuous rhythm of his stride began to take over and every step cleansed more of the day's detritus from his mind's eye. Minter entered that silent, private zone only long-distance runners know. He loved this landscape that seemed to be turning under his heels and he loved this feeling of solitude.

Suddenly, a crackly sound came into Minter's mind, setting ripples going that disturbed his hard-won peace. It was the distorted sound of the audio recording from the wire Ray Tyler had been wearing at the racetrack and it was followed a moment later by the two questions Alan Day had asked before he shot the undercover cop in the face: *Who are you, Ray? Where you from, Ray?*

They were questions Minter couldn't answer any more

27

truthfully than Tyler could. Minter had been taken away from his mother when he was just six years old and he'd grown up in a succession of children's homes. Some of them were good, and some of them were bad, but the worst of all was Hillcrest.

Minter had been ten years old when a social worker drove him there for the first time. His stomach felt small because he was on his way to yet another home, with new rules to learn and new children to try and befriend. Sitting in the car, Minter looked out of the window as they drove out of the city he knew so well and on into the countryside. It was the first time Minter had ever seen the Downs.

The social worker's name was Pam. She wasn't a bad person, just rushed off her feet, with more kids to interview and endless paperwork to complete once she'd dropped Minter off and gone back to the office. Glancing in her rear-view mirror, Pam saw a good-looking lad whose blond hair had still not completely turned to mousy brown. He had a round, attractive face with delicate features and quick blue eyes that followed the rise and fall of the hills intently. 'You ever been out here before?' she asked. Minter glanced at Pam's reflection in the mirror and shook his head. 'When I retire, which, please God, won't be long, I'm going to get a little cottage somewhere out here. You know, the good life and all that?'

Minter had no idea what she meant, so he returned to staring out of the window at the South Downs.

'Don't say much, do you?' Pam remarked. She couldn't help feeling sorry for the glum-looking lad on her back seat whose latest foster placement had just come to an end. Given what was in his file, it wasn't surprising that Minter was uncommunicative and didn't relate well to adults. His father had disappeared years ago and there wasn't the remotest possibility of a reunion with his mum, not given the state she was in. 'Most of the kids at Hillcrest are a little bit older than you,' Pam said, glancing in the mirror again. 'Still,' she added, looking on the bright side, 'it'll be nice living out in the countryside, won't it?'

Out on the Downs, Minter leaped up onto the next hill. It was the steepest climb on the entire run and within just a few strides his calves ached and the sweat fell in a curtain. Shaking the beads away from his brow, Minter kept the toes of his running shoes chipping away at the chalk, climbing the white steps cut into the side of the hill. Halfway up, the muscles in his legs had dried completely and his breath came in short, ragged bursts. His whole body was running on empty and he cursed himself for not giving up the ciggies. Minter's lungs were on fire, and when he raised his head, the hill above him looked vertical. But despite its steepness and despite the bad memories that dogged him, Minter still rose, still made progress. There was no way he was going to just give up and start to walk. He'd run these hills many times before and he was going to run them now, run them even quicker, in fact.

In his bedroom on the attic floor at Hillcrest, Minter sat down on the bed. On the blankets next to him, there was a pair of striped pyjamas, the colours faded and the material worn from endless washing. It was a small, gloomy room with a cracked washbasin in the corner and eaves crowding down over the bed from the ceiling. A hundred years ago, it would have been where the servants slept. The house father, Mr Clements, a seedy-looking man in a cardigan with fingers stained by nicotine, closed the door behind him. Minter heard his footsteps retreating down the winding back stairs. He'd been too late for tea and he was going to go to bed hungry.

Minter picked up his battered suitcase from the floor and rested it on his lap, using his thumbs to push the latches up. He opened the lid and took out his little bundle of clothes, laying them on the bed beside the pyjamas. At the bottom of the suitcase, there was a ball of tissue paper and Minter took that out, too. He glanced around the room. Some of the children's homes he stayed in had provided foot lockers where the kids could store their valuables, but not Hillcrest. It seemed that Mr Clements didn't care about security any more than he did about providing the children with a few creature comforts. In Minter's bedroom, apart from the washbasin, there was just the narrow bed and a single wardrobe. Even the carpet on the floor didn't go right up to the walls.

Carefully, Minter opened out the tissue paper and looked at what was inside. The St Christopher's medal and chain was a cheap thing, really – a thin piece of stamped gold bought for a few pounds from a cut-price high-street jeweller – but to Minter it meant everything. He looked down at the famous scene of a well-built man carrying a boy on his shoulders across a river. As St Christopher waded towards the shore, he was bent almost double by the weight on his back and the swollen waters of the river in spate. When his mother gave it to Minter, she had told him that St Christopher was named the patron saint of travel because

30

of his act of ancient kindness. Ever since, on all his sad journeys, Minter had carried the gift with him. Over all the years, he had kept believing that, as long as he had it in his possession, he would one day find her again.

Hearing the front door open and some voices from outside, Minter laid the medal back in its nest of tissue paper and went over to the window. Down below, having said goodbye to Mr Clements, the social worker walked across the gravel towards her car. Just as she reached it, she turned round and looked up at the house, a look of consternation on her face. Minter took a step away from the window in case she saw him spying on her, and by the time he looked out again, she was in her car and starting the engine. Minter fought a sudden urge to bang at the window, to call her back, to plead with her to take him away. He had spent enough time in children's homes to know that, at Hillcrest, things weren't as they should be.

At last, there was a breath of wind on Minter's face. He'd made it to the top of the hill. Straight away, he reached a hand across to his Suunto training watch and froze the speeding digits. He glanced at the chunky watch face. He was running an average of seven minutes fifty-three seconds. Despite the training runs he'd had to miss because of Windmill, he was still in pretty good shape.

On the horizon, the sun sank into the sea and, almost immediately, a breeze scoured the hilltop where Minter was standing. Far below, Brighton was laid out on its lozenge of land between the Channel and the foot of the Downs. Lights were winking on all over the city as families settled in for the night and friends went out to meet with friends. Turning

31

away, Minter pressed the button on his Suunto stopwatch function and ran across the top of the hill. Gravity yanked him down the other side so quickly he had to hold both hands out to stop himself falling.

At Hillcrest, Minter was still standing over by the window when the door to his bedroom opened. The boy who came in was a lot older than Minter, about sixteen or seventeen, almost old enough to leave care for good. He had sharp features and long, lank hair and a pair of shiny Doc Martens on his feet. 'I'm Charlie,' he said, walking into the room. 'You must be the new boy. Clements told me you'd arrived.' His eyes darted around the room. 'What you got?'

'Nothing,' Minter said.

Charlie was standing close to him now. He had an earring in his left ear and a tattoo on his neck. 'You must have something. Money? Eh?' Minter shook his head. 'Fags? Weed? C'mon, everyone has something.'

'I don't have anything.'

But Charlie had already caught sight of the glint of gold from the bed. He bent down and snatched it up. 'What's this, then?' Turning the medal over, he frowned at the tiny hallmark. 'This'll do for a start.'

'Give it back,' said Minter.

Charlie was spinning the medal on its chain round his finger. He flicked his wrist so that the whole thing landed in his palm. 'Fuck off, you little runt. It's finders keepers round here.'

'Give it back!'

Charlie chuckled. 'Oh, hard man, are you?'

Minter grabbed Charlie's hand with both of his own,

32

trying to prise the fingers open. Charlie shoved him with his other hand and Minter fell against the side of the bed. Getting up, he flew at Charlie again, this time with his fists raised. He landed just one punch on the older boy's shoulder before Charlie laid him flat out on his back. Lying on the floor, Minter could taste his own blood on his lips from where he'd been hit. His ears were ringing and he could see Charlie standing over him.

'You know,' Charlie said, his voice suddenly quiet, 'I'm going to enjoy hurting you.'

He was as good as his word. The next day was a school day, but Minter hadn't got a place yet at the local primary school and Mr Clements went straight out after breakfast. Charlie was too old to go to school, so at half past nine, the door to Minter's room opened again and he came back inside. 'C'mon,' he said. 'Clements told me to show you round.'

Charlie led Minter down the back stairs and out of the children's home. They crossed the courtyard and went into a brick-built hut where the old-fashioned boiler had been installed. It can't have been working very well because that morning Minter had washed his face with stone-cold water.

It was dark inside the boiler house and Minter cowered on the cold, soot-covered floor, watching Charlie use a match to light a couple of the candles left out on a shelf. Minter watched the shadows leap up the bare brick walls and over the hulking, rusted metal tank of the boiler. Charlie lit a cigarette with the last flame of the match. The orange flare illuminated the menacing leer on his face. Charlie took a couple of huge drags, saying, 'Don't want to waste a good fag.' Holding the cigarette up, he blew hard on its end so that embers streamed off the chiselled tip. They went through the air like tracer bullets, a few landing on Minter's cheek, making it sting. 'Take your shirt off,' said Charlie.

Minter sat there, terrified. 'I'll tell Mr Clements when he gets back.'

Charlie laughed. 'Do you think Clements gives a toss about you?'

'He's the house father, isn't he? It's his job to look after us.'

Charlie shook his head. 'You've got no idea.' He stared down at Minter. 'I'm waiting.'

Minter pulled his T-shirt up over his head. He sat there shivering on the floor, his skin ghostly white. Charlie squatted down, the leather of his Doc Martens creaking as he did so. He held the cigarette close up to Minter's face, rolling it between his fingers. Charlie pushed Minter's head back against the wall, grinding the side of his face against the brickwork to hold him still. 'My record is fourteen burns with just one ciggy,' he said. The needle of heat came closer to Minter's chest. There was a singeing sound and the smell of burning flesh.

When it was over, Minter lay face down in the black dust, his entire body trembling. He heard Charlie blow out the candles one by one and go outside, leaving Minter to the darkness.

Anything under eight minutes per mile was race time. Tonight, for the whole seventeen miles, Minter had averaged less than seven minutes forty. It was his best ever time, but tonight it didn't seem to bring him any satisfaction. He had too much on his mind for that.

Minter jogged through the backstreets of the city to the quiet road in Hove where he lived in a one-bedroom flat. It had high ceilings and a patio garden where he could sit out in the summer, and although there weren't any knick-knacks or photographs on the wall, and there was no one to come home to when he finished work, it was the first place he had ever owned.

Most children who grew up in care did badly in life. They toiled at dead-beat jobs or drifted into a life of petty crime and ended up living on the streets, addicted to drink or drugs. But Minter was different. He'd done well for himself, especially after he got the job with Chief Superintendent Roberts up at the Park.

The Park was the nickname given to the new Private Finance Initiative-built Division headquarters on the out-skirts of one of Brighton's leafiest suburbs. Minter had sat in a well-lit, open-plan office, surrounded by the pleasant hum of administration. The whirr of photocopiers, the murmur of phone conversations, the whisper of the air-conditioning, everything was calm and orderly, a different world to the hustle and bustle of Kemptown. Now, jogging through one suburban street after another, Minter wondered how much of a mistake he'd made by transferring from the Park into SOCU. Minter wanted to work crime because he'd had enough of all the bureaucracy up at Division and he wanted to do some real police work for a change, but this afternoon DCI Tom Beckett had made it abundantly clear that Minter wasn't welcome at Kemptown.

Standing on the doorstep of his flat, Minter fumbled a little with his keys. The irony of what Beckett had said almost made him smile. SOCU looked after its own, that's what Minter's new boss had told him this afternoon, but Minter wasn't part of the family. Then again, Minter thought, he'd never had a family before, so how could he even know what that meant?

# 3
...

In the Kemptown restaurant, DC Vicky Reynolds took a sip of her red wine. It was only her second drink of the evening. The boys were way ahead of her.

'D'you know Dixie Harper?' DC Connolly almost shouted. The restaurant was filling up with a younger, pre-club crowd. There was a crush of people at the long bar and old-school house was belting out from a DJ deck set up in the corner of the room. 'Dixie's an evil-looking bastard,' Connolly said. He was sitting across the table from Vicky, but he wasn't addressing her directly. Of course he wasn't. He was talking to DS Kevin Phillips. Connolly gestured towards his own face. 'Got a great big spider's web tattoo all down his neck?'

Vicky looked away. One of Connolly's nasty little anecdotes was the last thing she needed at the moment. She was a fast-track graduate whose career in the Force had come to an abrupt halt in SOCU, where she was still just a detective constable. Vicky was tall, with dark hair and a fair complexion that needed little or no make-up. Statuesque, some might have called her, although it would have to be someone with a greater command of the English language than Sean Connolly.

'Anyway,' said Connolly drunkenly, 'I was riding on the Van last Friday when we get a call that this kiddie was taking a right fucking pasting off one of the bouncers at Madrid.' The cavernous club was the biggest and the busiest in Brighton. The Van was the Rapid-Response Unit, also known as the West Street Taxi, because it was along West Street that things kicked off every Thursday, Friday, Saturday. 'This guy'd been thrown out for being leery with some girls,' Connolly was saying, 'but instead of just swallowing, he starts mouthing off at the bouncers in the street. So they drag him into the side entrance and slap him a few times – nothing terrible – then they chuck him back out onto the pavement. But the silly boy still won't give it up. Starts giving them the verbals again in front of everyone waiting in line outside the club. So they take him back inside for another go, but this time they *really* lay into him. Yer man Dixie's one of the bouncers and he gets carried away. When we get there, the ambulance crew has already arrived and they're giving the kid oxygen. Could've died. Dixie's had it on his toes, of course, but we run his name and we find out how tasty he is. By the time we get to his house, we are mob-fucking-handed.

'Harper must have heard us coming,' Connolly went on. 'When we pull up outside his flat, all the lights are off.' Connolly grinned. 'Only, as soon as I get out of the Van, I can see his little face bobbing up and down at the window. He is one worried fucker, I tell you that. I try knocking, but there is no *way* he is going to let us in. So I talk to him through the letterbox. "It's all right, Dix," I'm saying. "No one's going to hurt you." But he just won't come out to play.' Connolly finished off his double brandy with a flourish. 'It takes half an hour of this crap before I finally get permission to break the door down.'

Vicky looked away again. In her mind, Ray Tyler had tumbled out of the locker she'd tried to stash him in. The scene was becoming even clearer in her memory now. She kept seeing the dark edges of the pool of blood soaking into the dusty ground of the car park.

An hour ago, once the Windmill team had finally accepted that Alan Day was not going to be found, at least not tonight, they had decamped to the snug bar at The Moon Under The Water, the police pub near the station. After a couple of drinks, the mood had changed from vengeful to sober. Most had made their excuses and left early and now Vicky wished she'd joined them. She didn't want to be here, listening to Connolly blather on, but she hadn't wanted to go home, either. Vicky didn't want to be on her own. Not tonight.

A waitress came to their table and squatted down to tell them about the specials. She was wearing a T-shirt emblazoned with a trumpet, which was the restaurant's logo. As she spoke, Connolly stared down at her ample chest. Vicky saw the lust in his eyes. It disgusted her. The waitress noticed it, too. Moving away from Connolly, she stood up to finish speaking.

Vicky picked up her glass and gulped at the red wine. Slowly but surely, the realisation had been dawning on her that joining the police had been a mistake. She woke up every morning with the same sense of unease. And, in the last couple of weeks, as Windmill drew to its violent climax, her unease had developed into full-blown fear.

Three years ago, Vicky Reynolds had passed her LLB (Honours) with flying colours. She had secured a place at one of the London law schools, but then, out of the blue, she turned it down. Vicky had decided she didn't want to practise law after all. She wanted to do something useful instead. Something real. So, the evening following her final exam, Vicky announced her decision to her fellow students. There were seven of them sitting in the back of a rented limousine, on their way to an upscale hotel for the Law Society Ball. Vicky remembered how, in their dinner jackets and bow ties, the boys had been preening themselves when she dropped her bombshell. One of the girls – like Vicky, she'd spent hundreds on her gown for the evening – had admired the degree of social conscience involved in Vicky's decision, but the overwhelming reception was one of mystification, even pity. Boys and girls alike, they'd all soon be earning top dollar in various commercial law firms in London. They couldn't understand why Vicky would be interested in being just a cop.

In the Kemptown restaurant, the waitress was asking Vicky if she'd made up her mind yet. Vicky looked down at the menu. After a moment's blank indecision, she ordered the tagine. Phillips chose the steak. 'And I'll have the duck in plum sauce,' said Connolly.

Vicky picked up her glass again. She'd given up the law to do something useful. Something real. Well, the racetrack was pretty bloody real all right. So real, in fact, that she couldn't stop her hands from shaking.

Connolly barely waited for the waitress to leave before he

started up again. 'So the door goes in. It's a maisonette type of thing, with stairs leading up to Dixie's flat, but he's only built this fucking barricade at the bottom of the stairs. It's chock full of chairs and shit. Not only that, as soon as we set foot inside the place, Dixie starts chucking things down at us from up top. Saucepans, plates, anything he can get hold of – they all come raining down. Then one of the glasses he lobs hits one of our mob. Hits him right in the face.' Abruptly, Connolly's tone took a serious turn. 'Our guy's out cold on the floor. There's blood everywhere. But still Harper's chucking stuff. So we take the uniform out of there and regroup on the doorstep.'

Pausing for effect, Connolly leaned back in his seat and waited to be asked. Vicky Reynolds wasn't going to give him the pleasure. She looked straight past Connolly towards the scene outside, where a steady stream of people made their way under the iron streetlamps of St James's and down towards the seafront. Vicky wished that she was with them, not stuck in here with Connolly.

'Well,' said Kevin Phillips, although even he sounded a little bored, 'what happened?'

Connolly leaned forward, lowering his voice to a conspiratorial whisper. 'Dixie Harper comes out all meek and mild,' he said. Vicky glanced down at Connolly's fist, which he was clenching and unclenching. 'At fucking last.' Connolly's fingers came to rest and Vicky noticed all the little scabs on his knuckles. 'Let's just say,' he told her, 'Dixie Harper did an awful lot of resisting arrest in that van on the way to the station.' He winked. 'An awful lot.'

*

41

It was early yet. The Aloha cabaret bar was far from crowded. Just a few hard-body queens at the bar, various piercings straining at the fabric of their T-shirts. At the rear, round a table next to a small stage, Jimbob McFarland sipped his drink. That afternoon, after leaving the Red Roaster, Jimbob had run some errands around Kemptown before heading back to his flat on Lower Rock Gardens for a kip. Now, refreshed, and having found some spot concealer and put on a bit of lippy, Jimbob was out again, sitting in his favourite bar with his flatmate, Terry Sampson, and their dealer, a man called Michael Lambert.

'I'll do you it for forty, Terry,' Lambert was saying, talking quietly and keeping an eye on the street door. Lambert was in his late forties. He had short, salt-and-pepper hair and a grizzled beard, and he'd been selling heroin in the Aloha for as long as anyone could remember. 'I'm telling you,' he insisted to Terry Sampson, Lambert's most voracious customer, 'there's nothing around at the moment. It's all dried up. I could walk into town right now and knock this same deck out for fifty or sixty. In fact, if you keep dithering around, Terry, that's exactly what I'm going to do.'

An Alice band was pulling Terry Sampson's long, black hair away from his forehead. With the tips of his chipped, black-painted fingernails he scratched thoughtfully at his cheek. 'OK,' he said at last. 'Done.'

The pellet of heroin was duly passed under the table from Lambert to Terry Sampson.

Bored, Jimbob McFarland glanced over to the bar. A small cheer had gone up at the arrival of a drag queen in a leopard-print miniskirt. When Jimbob turned back to the table, he was confronted with a tatty ten-pound note. "S'all I've got,' Terry explained, holding the note up in front of Jimbob's eyes. Terry shrugged, smiling ingratiatingly.

Jimbob shook his head. 'No way am I fronting you the money, Terry,' he said. 'I've got to work tonight.'

'Come on, mate,' Terry cajoled. 'You'll have more trade than you'll know what to do with at the weekend. Give Mikey here the money and we can go and bang it up.'

'I told you,' Jimbob said, 'someone's got to pay the rent. I've got an important punter coming over. I need to be at my best.'

'Well, you'll be flush again after, then, won't you?' Terry wheedled. 'And what's thirty quid to a successful young entrepreneur like you?'

Jimbob stared at his friend and former colleague. Terry's cheeks were hollow and the skin on his face was waxy. The tights he was wearing under the ripped jeans had seen better days. It wasn't a good look. Just grubby, unhealthy. Terry was starting to fall apart.

The drag queen reached their table. She was an amateur. 'Hello, boys,' she said, giving the yellow plastic bucket she was holding a good shake to make the coins in the bottom rattle noisily. 'Collecting for Pride,' she said. 'Terrence Higgins Trust.'

Terry glowered at her. Ignoring him, the drag queen looked Jimbob up and down, taking in his sweet face and his wedge of peroxided hair. 'I don't suppose,' she said, angling her head coyly to one side and fluttering her long and heavily made-up eyelashes, 'you'd consider doing something *else* for *charidee*?'

Despite himself, Jimbob smiled. 'As a matter of fact,' he

told her, pulling out his wallet from the back pocket of his jeans, 'I already am.' Looking at Terry, he raised his eyebrows. 'Although this one's probably a lost cause.'

Jimbob peeled off three notes. He gave the top two – a twenty and a tenner – to Terry Sampson. Then he dropped the other tenner into the drag queen's charity bucket.

'Thanks, darling,' said the drag. 'See you over the weekend ... I wish.' With that, she minced back towards the bar.

'Sweet,' said Terry, putting Jimbob's money on top of his own note and passing them all over to Michael. 'There you go, mate,' he said. 'Forty.' In one gulp, he finished the vodka and tonic he'd been nursing for the last half-hour. Then he looked back at Jimbob. 'You not coming, then?' he said.

'I told you,' Jimbob replied, 'I'm working.'

'I'm going for a slash,' said Connolly. A little unsteady on his legs, he stood up from his chair. 'If that waitress comes by,' he said to Kevin Phillips over his shoulder, 'tell her I'll have another brandy.'

'We've got the bill, Sean,' Vicky Reynolds protested.

But Connolly was already lumbering through the crowd. He waved away Vicky's objections and yelled over his shoulder, 'A double!'

For the first time that evening, Kevin Phillips and Vicky were left on their own. When Vicky had arrived at the Kemptown station a couple of years ago, Kevin Phillips had taken her under his wing. Kevin was still in uniform back then, but he was already making a name for himself. They were both bright, ambitious and good-looking. Everyone at Kemptown said they'd make a great couple, but for one reason or another it had never happened. And then Kevin met Fiona, a web designer with a taste for the Brighton high life. Within a year they were man and wife and then unto them a daughter was born. Just five months after the ceremony, if Vicky remembered rightly.

Kevin Phillips watched Connolly pushing his way through the crowd. 'He's not a bad lad.'

'You mean Connolly?' Vicky asked.

'He can get a little overenthusiastic.'

'Overenthusiastic?' said Vicky. 'Kicking the shit out of a suspect hardly counts as youthful exuberance, Kevin.'

Phillips looked at her. 'And this Dixie guy didn't have it coming, then?'

'By the sounds of it, he probably did. But in the courts, not in the back of a police van.'

'Still a solicitor at heart, eh, Vick?' Phillips said.

Vicky Reynolds had graduated in law and none of the SOCU officers would ever let her forget it. 'You've changed a lot, Kev. The Crime Squad's got to you. The cop I knew in uniform wouldn't have stood for that crap from Connolly.'

Picking up his bottle of lager, Phillips swirled the three inches of beer round and round the bottom of the glass. 'That was a long time ago, Vicky. A lot of things have changed.'

There was regret in his voice. Vicky wondered if he was talking about married life as well as his career. It sounded that way, at least.

Before she could ask, Phillips changed the subject. 'You got to Ray Tyler first, didn't you?' His voice had changed. It was gentler, less sarcastic – something of the old Kevin, the one Vicky used to know. She nodded.

'Must have been bad,' Phillips said.

'Tyler was alive when they put him in the ambulance. He was still breathing.'

Phillips looked down. 'It's different when it's one of your own. But give it time, Vick. It'll go away.'

She looked at Kevin. She could tell that he was sincere. 'Thanks.'

Sean Connolly pushed his way back towards the table. He flopped down in the seat opposite. 'That waitress been yet?' he asked.

Phillips shifted his body away from Vicky a little. 'Not yet,' he said.

Connolly leaned forward and clapped his hands. 'Right, boss,' he said, looking at Phillips, 'where we going?'

'We're not,' said Vicky, picking up her bag from the bench beside her and shoving her purse back in it. 'At least, I'm not. I'm all done in.'

'Yeah,' Phillips agreed. 'I've got to get back, too.'

'Your turn for the night feed, is it, Kev?' Connolly said.

'Your turn will come, mate,' Phillips told Connolly. 'Your turn will come.'

'I doubt that very much,' said Connolly. Sitting back, he regarded Phillips coolly. 'Must be hard for you, Kev.'

'What's that, Sean?' Phillips asked, expecting just more banter.

Connolly looked serious. 'Working with that arsehole,' he said. 'Someone gave me the nod. About Minter.'

The waitress returned. Picking up the saucer and looking at the bill, she started counting up all the notes and coins. She gave them all a big, Antipodean grin and said, 'That's great, guys. Have an excellent night.'

Vicky smiled up at her. As soon as the waitress was gone she turned to Connolly and said, 'What are you talking about?'

Connolly looked at her. 'Didn't you know?'

Phillips was already on his feet. 'Shut up, Sean'.

'Minter was in uniform back then,' Connolly told Vicky. 'He was in on a SOCU drugs bust. Fucker only went and made a statement after, didn't he. He told the panel that Kev here was alone in the front room, just before the Drugs Squad found the stash. Minter's statement stitched Kev right up.'

Vicky looked at Phillips. 'Is this true?'

Despite passing the detective exam, Kevin Phillips's first application to become a DS had been rejected. The second time, apparently, he only got through after Tom Beckett had intervened.

Phillips turned to Vicky. 'The complaint was dismissed by the panel. The perp went down. End of story.'

Lifting his brandy glass from the table, Connolly finished the dregs. Standing up, he swiped his jacket from the back of his chair. 'Maybe so,' he said. 'But the way I heard it, Minter could have just blanked it. Said nothing.' He shrugged on the jacket. 'You have to sort each other out, don't you? I mean, no one else is going to stick up for us, are they? Not in this fucking job.'

For the first time in her career, Vicky Reynolds found herself wanting to agree with something DC Sean Connolly said.

What would DS Tyler's widow get? A pension, yes – and maybe, after the application had trailed its tiresome way through all those committees, a plaque on the ground at the racecourse where he fell. But she was also left with two kids to bring up on her own, and a sick feeling in her stomach every time she passed a police officer in uniform.

So normally Vicky would have damned Minter like the rest of the team and thought no more about it. But Minter was clever, and clever was what SOCU needed right now. They were on the back foot. They'd tried brute force and ignorance and neither of them had worked. If they hadn't been so gung-ho about things, then maybe Ray Tyler would still be alive.

'Let's go,' said Kevin Phillips.

Outside, the night was still warm. Arm in arm, two men passed them by. 'Fucking Camptown more like,' Connolly remarked under his breath.

'Expect you'll be going to Pride, then, Sean?' Vicky said pointedly as they started walking down St James's.

'You what?' Connolly asked her.

'Haven't you heard?' Vicky said. 'There's an association of gay and lesbian police officers in Brighton and Hove. They're taking a float in this year's parade. Maybe it's time you got real, Sean. You know, came out.'

Connolly grinned back at her. 'They should never let nonces become coppers.' He paused to light a cigarette. 'They're a fucking security risk.'

A long queue of people were waiting at a cashpoint. To get round them, the three police officers had to step off the pavement. On the other side, they came to a halt. A young woman was lying in the gutter. She was face down, the cleavage in her buttocks revealed for all to see by the handkerchief of a skirt she was wearing. Two other women were reeling around her, both of them waving half-empty bottles of supermarket vodka and laughing like drains. The woman on the floor had her legs wrapped round a woggle – the kind of long foam tube that kids used in swimming pools. As she dry-humped the purple flotation aid, she moaned in mock-ecstasy.

Vicky crouched down on the pavement. Slowly, the girl's eyes focused on Vicky's face. She was in her early twenties. She was drunk, but her pupils weren't dilated.

'Hello,' the girl drawled, grinning inanely.

Vicky stood up. 'I think your mate needs to get home,' she told one of the other girls.

The young woman waved her bottle of vodka in Vicky's general direction. 'And who the fuck are you to tell me what to do?'

Vicky took a step forward. 'I'm a police officer, that's who the fuck I am. And you and your friend here are causing an obstruction. So if you don't clear off, I'm going to arrest you.'

One of the girls looked at her. 'OK, OK,' she said.

But Vicky was already helping the other girl get up from the gutter. It wasn't easy. 'Come on,' she said, taking hold of the girl's arm and dragging her to her feet. As soon as she was up, the girl linked arms with her friends and they all staggered off into the night.

'Dogs,' said Connolly.

Vicky rounded on him. She'd had enough. 'Don't you ever shut up, Sean Connolly?' she said. 'Ever?'

Connolly grinned into her face. All this madness was just water off a duck's back for him. The pissed girls, the psychotic bouncer at Madrid, Ray Tyler – it was all the

49

same to Connolly. Shaking her head, Vicky walked off down the hill.

'Wait up, Vick,' said Kevin Phillips as he set off after her.

A minute later, Vicky, Phillips and Connolly were standing at the traffic lights at the bottom of the hill. On the other side of the Steine, a row of tinted floodlights had transformed the Royal Pavilion into a luminous, rose-pink palace. The city was getting in the mood for Pride, too.

'C'mon,' urged Connolly, turning towards the seafront. 'I know the doorman at the Funky Buddha Lounge.'

'Sean, mate,' DS Phillips replied, 'I think you've had enough.'

Down the steep stone steps to the basement flat. Dark now. Stuck door the landlord still hadn't fixed, but a little shove and Jimbob McFarland was home.

He skipped quickly round the flat, making up time.

Oil burner. Where is it? Oil burner. Where the fuck is it?

He found it in the bedside cabinet.

Almond oil dropped – one, two, three – into a little puddle of tap water. Very fussy, very precise about what he wanted, this client. A tealight next, and it had to be unscented. A match struck inside the shadowy room.

The burning oil gave off such a heady smell. Made you want to go to sleep. Would be no bad thing.

Candles, too, of course. Just cold rinds of wax at the bottom of the dish. Stubs in the drawer. They'll do, though. Gold and red. They looked cute. Like Christmas.

Closing the thin curtains, pulling them shut so nothing could be seen from the street above.

Terry'd left his works out on the dressing table again. Sweep them into the bin. Such a wanker. All those smackhead mates of his. Well, Terry was on his way out in more ways than one. How the tables have turned, my old mucker.

Lights off and the room, the room looks beautiful. And just in time because there goes the doorbell.

One o'clock in the morning. A clear night and a cold one. Terry Sampson made a face at the young man leaning against the wall. The other rent boy was an old adversary, and someone else Sampson owed money. He sized Terry up for a moment, contemplating the ruck. Then he thought better of it. Terry was violent. He was diseased, too. A queen on the way down. With a contemptuous little laugh, the boy pushed his back away from the bricks. He sloped off into the darkness of the alley.

Terry breathed in the night air. He'd taught Jimbob how to stand like that. Jimbob had been a quick learner. He took to it like a duck to water – how to ask for the money upfront, when to insist on a condom. Good-looking, too. Jimbob was only fourteen when he and Terry hooked up. Terry taught him everything. And now Jimbob was treating Terry like shit.

An old car rumbled its way into Edward Street. It slowed and stopped.

The rent boy pulled open the car door. A middle-aged trick leaned over to inspect the goods. In the light that had come on over the dashboard, Terry saw the sweat glistening on the old guy's top lip. Terry had seen him somewhere before. Not as a trick, though. First-time punter, then. Just a few minutes and he'd be gone, Terry told himself. Then he could buy another deck from Michael.

'Where's Jimbob?' the man asked.

'How the fuck should I know?' Terry said angrily.

The man reached out a note. 'Give him this for me,' he said.

Terry took the note and stuffed it in his pocket. He slammed the door and the car moved off from the side of the road.

The tiny basement room smelled of sex and almonds. There was a man sitting at the end of Jimbob's bed. His back was turned to the naked rent boy, the sound of his breathing mingled with the hissing of the oil in the burner. The candlelight threw the man's shadow up the wall as he stood up to put on his shirt.

Lying on the bed, Jimbob felt his own cock stiffen a little. Despite the man's bulk, there was something arousing about him. None of his other regulars – men for whom Jimbob felt some small piece of affection – had quite the same effect.

The man was standing next to Jimbob. He gazed down at the rent boy and smiled. Jimbob put his knuckles up towards the headboard and stretched coquettishly, pushing his slim hips against the mattress. As he did so, the skin on his thigh tightened a little. The fresh bruise began to hurt.

The man watched him for a few moments. Then he reached over and lifted his black leather jacket from the chair by the bed. It was an expensive jacket. The leather was heavy and supple.

Jimbob knew the luxury in which this man lived. Many

times he had imagined what it might be like to have him as a daddy. Someone who would take him off the street once and for all. Someone to look after him.

The man pulled a couple of fifty-pound notes out of his wallet and laid them on the nightstand. 'For old times' sake,' he said.

Then he was gone.

In the middle of the night, two men stood in a clearing in a wood. Between them, a third man was hanging upside down, suspended by his feet from the lowest branch of the oak tree, his hands bound together behind his back with a length of electrical wire. They'd used the same kind of flex to tie a hood over his head.

In his left hand, Russell Compton held an offcut from a scaffolding pole, its chunky metal collar still attached. Russell bent forward until his own face was level with the head that dangled a few feet above the ground. He hadn't done this kind of thing himself for years, but with Alan Day gone, he had no choice. If he had to get his hands dirty, at least he was going to enjoy it.

'And those phones you sold us,' Russell told the man quietly, 'the Nokias? Well, we've got techies, too, Dave, and our guys rumbled those phones weeks ago. So all those conversations the filth were listening in on, all that crap Alan was telling them about moving the gear to a different stash house? Well, you know something, Dave? That was exactly what we fucking well *wanted* them to hear.'

Russell Compton's shoulders were broad and powerful like a boxer's and he took a step back. 'For twenty years I've put food on your fucking table,' he said, his temper rising into his throat. 'I even married that cunt of a sister of yours. And now you think you can sell me out, do you?' Russell swung his arm up in a high arc. 'Think you're smart enough for that, eh, Dave?' When it came down again, the metal offcut smacked against bone, making a whacking sound that was like a driver clipping a golf ball. Gillespie's elbow shattered immediately. He started to scream, but Russell Compton ignored it, drumming the offcut over Gillespie's body – stomach and shoulders, back and legs, the pole breaking bones wherever it went. Russell avoided the head, though, because he wanted Gillespie alive.

In the white beam of the torch he'd put on the ground, Chris Compton watched his father go to work. Chris was nearly a grown man, but next to his father he still felt like a puny kid.

At last, there was a pause. Russell bent down again, listening for the sound of Gillespie's breathing. Satisfied Gillespie was still conscious, he said, 'I treated you like family, Dave, and you grassed me up.' Gillespie started to whimper. 'But it wasn't just you, was it? It was you and that other wanker, Ray Tyler. Or, rather, Detective Sergeant Ray Tyler. A grass and a u/c, working together. That's how it all comes down, isn't it? Piece by fucking piece. Well, Tyler's well undercover now, isn't he? Under the fucking ground, in fact.'

Russell Compton took careful aim. He hit Gillespie on the side of the face. The screw on the collar split the man's cheek clean in two.

Using what was left of his jaw, Gillespie began to beg for his life. Breathing heavily after all his exertions, Russell stepped back and listened to the pleas for a minute, maybe more. Then, running his hand through his light-coloured hair, he began to laugh. 'Don't make yourself ridiculous, Dave,' he said.

Russell turned towards his son. 'Get the stuff from the boot.'

'Hasn't he had enough, Dad?' Chris said.

Russell Compton took a step closer to his son. 'What's the matter, boy?' he asked, raising the scaffolding pole a little. 'Lost your bottle?'

Chris hesitated. 'No,' he said. 'It's just ...'

'Go and get the stuff!'

Chris walked towards the open boot of the car his father had parked at the end of the farm track. As he went, he could hear the gentle sound of Gillespie sobbing.

When Chris returned to his father's side, the taut bundle held gingerly in his hands, Russell pointed to the earth underneath the hanging man. 'There,' he barked. Russell fetched a Stanley knife from his pocket and slid out the blade. Chris put the bundle down and started to unravel it. Russell reached up to cut the rope and Gillespie's body crumpled on top of the barbed wire. Russell kicked Gillespie a few times until his body lay right along the width of the roll of wire. Then, still using the thick sole of his work boot, Russell began to wrap Gillespie up in the barbed wire. He turned the guy over and over, carefully encasing him, every now and then pausing to stamp his foot down on the wire, keeping the folds snug. All the while, Gillespie's flesh was being shredded.

'You're my princess, Dave,' Russell roared. 'My princess in a fucking carpet!'

*

There was still a little time before dawn. When a sleepless Tom Beckett left his house, the Hove seafront was cold and misty.

The promenade was at the end of the road where he lived. Behind it, there was a children's playground and, in the grey half-light, the empty swings and deserted climbing frames looked desolate. Standing still, Tom gazed across at the bench in the far corner. He wondered if Julie had ever sat there to listen to the high-pitched chorus of the running, jumping children. Another grief, then, to add to his own infinite store. Julie's grieving for the children she never had, the children he'd never given her. Tom walked over to the bench and sat down. He surveyed the empty playground. He never knew there would be so much pain to get through. It was like some kind of terrible banquet.

Beckett was living in a sort of interregnum, in the narrow gap of time between two deaths – Julie's death, his own. He was just waiting for it to be over, for the space between them to be swallowed up.

Suddenly restless, Tom Beckett stood up. He walked away from the playground and down the steps to the beach itself. He trudged along the pebbles to stand by the water's edge. There was nobody else about on the beach. The sea was inert, the same pencil-grey colour as the sky. As a child in East Brighton, Tom Beckett had scampered by the sea for hours: rock-pooling or swimming or crabbing off the sea wall. As an adult, the sea would calm him down. When he was living in Hove and work was tough, Tom Beckett would bring his troubles to this little stretch of beach. It belonged to him. He would cast his worries out upon the waves and watch them disappear. Gone.

Not anymore, though. Now, the sea was spoiled for ever. Only terrible things came out of it.

They'd come down here on the day Julie got the final diagnosis. She'd been silent, registering the shock. Beckett had talked, of course. 'You'll get better,' he'd said. 'The doctors know what they're doing.' He promised Julie he'd take retirement the following year. He sold it to her well that day. He said he'd make it up to her for all those evenings she'd spent on her own at home, not knowing when he was coming home, or if he was coming home at all. Julie would get better and he'd leave the Force, Tom said. Then they'd have the life they'd always dreamed of. Yes, that's what they would do. They'd spend their savings and the generous pension on holidays in the sun and doing up the house. 'We'll enjoy their bloody money,' he told her.

'Yes,' she said. 'We will, won't we.'

Tom Beckett sat down on the shingle. On every pebble there was a smattering of dew. All of them were cold to the touch. Every one felt like a recrimination. Tom shivered. It was time for him to remember. Time for him to take out the memory that he'd been pushing away for all those weeks.

It had been midnight when the ITU nurse called the house in Brighton. Tom had just got back from a late-night meeting about Windmill. Julie had been sedated for more than two weeks and in that time the infection had spread all over her lungs. Every time Beckett visited – and he visited for hours every single day – she lay there, unconscious, surrounded by the machines that sustained her life. Nothing seemed to be happening. It had all settled into a routine. Beckett was astonished how even something like this could become just another routine.

It was midnight and Beckett was exhausted. In the end, the nurse had to come right out with it on the phone. 'Tom,' she said, interrupting his ramblings, 'Julie's dying.'

On his way out of Brighton, Beckett ran every red light. He drove like a madman through the small-hours traffic of central London. At the hospital, the nurse was still in the side room in intensive care. She was standing by the window, behind her little console. Above Julie's bed were the familiar green and red displays. Julie's breathing and heart rate were just about holding up.

'It's not when we add more machines,' the intensive-care consultant had told Beckett when Julie had been moved here from the ward. 'It's when we start taking the machines away, that's when you have to worry.'

Looking around now, Tom realised that that was exactly what had happened. The only machine that remained was the one that helped Julie breathe. All the others had disappeared. The doctors were in retreat. Beckett sat down in the chair by the bed and took Julie's hand in his.

It was over the course of the next few hours that Tom Beckett made the treasure hoard of his memories. He searched the complicated pathways of their marriage for those precious moments when they'd been most themselves. One by one, he fixed them in his mind. The day they'd met in Brighton. Their first kiss on the pier. The places they'd been to on holiday. Their wedding.

Those last few hours were Julie's final gift to him. It was as if she was trying to stay alive just long enough for her husband to harvest the memories that would light up the darkness to come.

'What are you thinking about?' asked the nurse.

Beckett looked up. The nurse had brown hair done up with a tortoiseshell comb. Later, she became like a pilot, steering Julie into harbour. She was an angel.

'I saw you smiling,' she said to Beckett.

'By the sea,' said Beckett. 'That's where we were happiest. Just walking by the sea.' He looked at Julie. 'I loved her so much then.'

At three o'clock in the morning, Tom gave them permission to turn off the last machine. Almost immediately, on the little screen above her head, the numbers started to decline slowly at first, then accelerating.

When it was time, Tom got up from his chair. He leaned over the bed and took Julie in his arms. 'I've got you,' he whispered into her ear. 'I've got you.' The nurse had already left the room. When Julie died, Tom was still holding her close.

'Oh, my darling girl!' he cried out, over and over again.

On Brighton Beach, Tom Beckett wept.

# 4

# ...

It was early in the morning and Minter was smoking his first cigarette of the day as he drove along the circular road that funnelled down through Whitehawk. The council estate nestled in a fold of land east of the city. The first houses had been built in the 1930s, when Whitehawk was known for its wide roads and big back gardens leading straight onto the Downs. Back then, people clamoured to be rehoused here. After the cramped, unsanitary tenements in the centre of Brighton, Whitehawk was the Promised Land.

Over the succeeding decades, though, things had changed. As the city's population grew, the council kept adding new parts to the estate. The worst of them were built in the 1970s. High-rise tower blocks had already gone out of municipal fashion, so the planners laid out a rabbit warren of tiny houses and higgledy-piggledy streets that were perfect for the drug dealers who thrived there in the following decade. Soon, Whitehawk was notorious and bus drivers refused to go there after dark and even fire crews on 999 calls insisted on a police escort.

Four years ago, when Minter was first in uniform, this part of the estate had been his beat. He'd taken the trouble to get to know the people. He realised that most of them were decent enough, just trying to get by on the meagre hand that life had dealt them, doing what they could to avoid the predations of the likes of Russell Compton.

Minter turned right into a cul-de-sac. He pulled his car up onto the side of the pavement. He cut the engine and rubbed his eyes. He'd sat up into the early hours last night, going through the Murder Book again with a fine-tooth comb. There were at least two significant clues that the investigation into Anna's death had glossed over.

The year Tom Beckett first became a detective, the Police and Criminal Evidence Bill was just a twinkle in the eye of some home secretary. Now, in the era of painstaking police intelligence and public accountability, Beckett was a throwback. He was out of date, a dinosaur and as far as Minter was concerned, the sooner he went the better.

Minter got out of the car. He locked it and the boom of a sound system suddenly filled the air. Minter glanced behind to see a souped-up Audi come skidding round the corner. It swept past him, the heavy bass line throbbing from the back, where the seats had been ripped out to make room for the speakers. Minter could feel the vibrations in his teeth.

At the other end of the cul-de-sac, there were some locked gates and a single-storey building. The Audi screeched to a halt just in front of the gates and stayed there, its engine still grumbling. Minter walked towards it. He was wearing a dark suit. Round here, he would stick out like a sore thumb. The young man in the Audi glowered at him in the rear-view mirror. The teenager gunned the engine, but keeping his eye on the driver, Minter stepped off the pavement.

The Audi's tyres squealed. The car reversed, missing Minter by a couple of feet. It turned round and came to a halt alongside him. The driver gave Minter the finger. Underneath his Burberry baseball cap, there was a set of pasty, hard-bitten features Minter didn't recognise. In Whitehawk, the faces were changing.

The youth spun the wheel again and the car lurched forward. Minter watched it roar away and disappear back along the main road.

Turning round, Minter took a closer look at the building behind the gates. It had a modern-looking, wave-shaped roof and there was a small, circular window on the first floor, where the crest of the wave had created a loft space. The blue-painted timber cladding on the front elevation emphasised the nautical theme. It made Minter think of Noah's Ark. There was a sign above the door. In funky, multi-coloured lettering, it read, *Kidz Klub*.

As Minter walked through the gate, he allowed himself a smile of satisfaction. When he and Irene Shaw had started up the youth club, it had been housed in an old Portakabin near some waste ground on the other side of the estate. Two years ago, when Minter had left Whitehawk to take up his new job at Division, Irene and he had just submitted the application for lottery funding to build something more permanent. Now here it was, right in front of him. The dream had become a reality.

Except last night, someone had trashed it.

Standing by the front door, Minter looked down. There was a large, round hole in the wood where a pair of bolt-cutters had been used to take out the Chubb lock. When Minter pushed the door with his hand, it swung open on its hinges. Inside, there was a small reception area and on a desk was a signing-in book for members. Minter ran his finger down the list of names. He recognised one straight away. The name spelled trouble.

'What do you want?' said a woman's voice from behind him.

Minter turned to see Irene Shaw standing in the doorway. She was a diminutive woman with short, blonde hair and a determined expression. She had lived on Whitehawk all her life. She'd raised her kids here. 'Minter!' she said. 'I didn't know you were coming.'

'I saw the report online,' said Minter.

'It's good to see you,' Irene said, walking over to Minter. Without hesitating, she gave him a big hug. Then she stepped back to admire the prodigal son.

'Have the plods been yet?' Minter asked.

'What do you think?' said Irene. 'This is Whitehawk, Minter. They've got far more important things to do.' She paused. 'Anyway, where you been hiding all this time?'

'I'm sorry I missed the opening.'

'That's all right,' said Irene. 'It was just a load of boring speeches and a few prawn vol-au-vents. Although,' she added with a sly smile, putting on a posh voice, 'the minister said he was jolly impressed.' Irene looked at Minter's suit. 'You a detective now?'

Minter nodded. 'I'm working crime,' he said. 'It's a big

case. We're going after the city's most important heroin dealer.'

'About bloody time,' said Irene. She frowned, remembering why Minter had come. 'I'll show you what happened.'

Irene led Minter into a little internal hallway, then through a door on the right. It was a large room, about thirty feet long, with a ceiling extended right up into the roof.

It was impressive, very impressive, a long way from the Portakabin. A huge mural of the New York skyline had been painted on the back wall, there were expensive-looking planks of wood on the floor, and in the far corner a big sink and shelves stacked with poster paints and modelling clay. In the middle, there was a brand-new pool table and on a workbench behind it a line of ten Apple Macs. 'This is the Activities Lounge,' said Irene. 'It cost a bloody fortune. Now look at it.'

The mural must have taken someone weeks to paint, but the vandals had ruined it in seconds by throwing paint up the walls as well as all over the floor. They'd ripped the plush green felt of the pool table to shreds and they'd smashed up all the Macs – the computers were lying upturned on the bench, their pristine white casings mangled and split, the circuit boards poking out at crazy angles.

'The office is even worse,' said Irene. 'They tried to start a fire in there. We're lucky the whole bloody place didn't burn down.' There was a look of utter bewilderment on her face. With the palm of her hand, she wiped away a tear. Irene had given everything she had to Kidz Klub. Twice now she'd remortgaged her own house at the top of the estate so that she could pay the bills. 'Why did they do it?' She said, looking at Minter for an answer.

Seeing Irene's distress, Minter wanted to go to her, to comfort this feisty, big-hearted woman as spontaneously as she had just embraced him, but he couldn't. No matter what he felt for Irene – and Minter felt a lot – he couldn't go to her. It was as if the space between them had become an immense, unbridgeable gulf.

A telephone started ringing from somewhere else in the building. 'I better get that,' Irene said.

When she was gone, Minter took out his mobile. If he couldn't help Irene with what she was feeling, then he could certainly protect her from the danger she was in. As Minter made his calls, he walked around the room, inspecting the damage more closely, although he already had a fairly clear idea of who was responsible.

'That was your lot,' Irene said, coming back into the lounge. 'They'll be here in a few minutes.'

Minter put his mobile away and nodded. 'Good. Now we've got to make sure this doesn't happen again. There's a locksmith coming over to put new locks on all the doors and windows. He'll put in a burglar alarm, too, one that rings straight through to Kemptown Station. And he'll install a proper CCTV system.'

'I can't afford all that,' Irene objected.

'He's a police contractor. He'll be sending the bill to me. I'll find a place to bury it.'

Irene smiled. 'You have gone up in the world.'

Minter looked around. 'You're going to have to replace all this equipment. I'll see what I can do about tapping up the police fund.'

'Thanks, Minter. You're a good friend.'

'I was,' Minter said ruefully. At first, when Minter

started working at Division, he still made time for the youth club he helped to start, coming down here on club nights to lend a hand and helping Irene as best he could through all the complex stages of the planning application and the new build. But Chief Superintendent Roberts soon put a stop to all that. Minter had more important things to do now than social work, the super used to say. The afternoon of the opening, Minter had been at his desk up at the Park, putting the finishing touches to a report for the HMIC, a report that Roberts had told him was both urgent and important.

Now Minter looked around at the wreckage of the club. 'Kids didn't do this, Irene,' he said.

'What do you mean?'

'There's a turf war starting up between the dealers on the estate. You know who Russell Compton is, don't you?' Irene nodded. 'There's a new mob moving onto the estate. They call themselves the Hangletons and they're a nasty little crew, even nastier than Russell Compton was when he started out.'

Irene made a face. 'I doubt that very much.'

'It's true,' Minter said. 'The Hangletons want to supply every dealer on Whitehawk as well as on the seafront, and one of their soldiers is a regular at Kidz Klub.'

'Who?'

'Dean Carver.' Minter nodded back towards reception. 'His name's all over your singing-in book.'

Irene looked doubtful. 'Dean's just a kid.'

'I've seen the intel. Believe me, Irene, sixteen's plenty old enough.' Minter thought about the young man in the Audi. 'This Carver, does he wear a Burberry cap?'

Irene nodded. 'That's him.'

'Every night he's down here is another night he's not out there, flogging Hangleton skag. It's the same with the other kids who come here: the gang wants them out on the streets, buying off them or selling their gear, not in here playing pool and listening to iTunes.' Minter looked at Irene. 'The Hangletons want Kidz Klub shut down. Only I'm not going to let that happen.'

The motorcycle cop's heavy boots rapped against the country stile. The officer lifted himself up onto the flimsy wooden platform, then lowered himself to the chalk footpath just the other side. Standing up, he pocketed the keys to the powerful Kawasaki motorbike.

In front of him, the land dipped away into a hollow. It was a lonely and obscure part of the Downs, covered in brambles and scruffy-looking coppices and not a single dog walker or rambler on any of the surrounding hills.

The officer took off his helmet. Immediately, the stench of warm leather was replaced by buckets of fresh, cold air. He breathed deeply. It had been a good run out here, open throttle over deserted roads.

The motorbike cop descended through the first line of trees. On the other side, he saw the first of the tyre tracks in the dried-up yellow mud of an old bridle path.

The officer began his tricky descent of the hill, holding on to branches to steady himself and leaning back to keep his balance. The last hundred yards or so he had to clamber down sideways.

At the bottom of the hill, there was a dog leg of land. As soon as he turned its corner he saw the car. The flames had popped the glass. They had incinerated the moulded plastic of both wings. All that remained this morning, hunkered down in a pool of sooty grass, was the bare and blackened metal.

He looked back. There were no scorch marks on the hillside. They must have rolled the car down here before setting it alight at the bottom. He imagined them scrambling down the steep slope in the dark. It seemed an awful trouble to take, just to make a moody insurance claim.

The carcass of the car was still smoking. Leaving his padded gloves on, the motorbike cop walked round to the driver's door. The metal creaked loudly as it fell open on a single hinge. He leaned inside. The dashboard had melted, fusing with the metal engine casing. The skeletal seats were empty.

Closing the door again, he walked round to the back of the car. The lock on the boot had gone; it sprang open at his touch. At first, he didn't know what the thing inside was, but there was a smell that wasn't charred metal.

Black, dried-out, the irregularly shaped object in the boot had been wrapped up in wire of some kind. Five swollen bumps were set around its edges. The officer caught a whiff of it again. 'Jesus Christ,' he breathed, recognising one of the stumps – the one stretching out towards him – as the burned remnant of a human arm.

Minter parked his car on a side road near Hove Park. It was only ten o'clock, but the sun was already high in the sky and if he walked this way to the flat, he had time to finish his cigarette. Trish Yates's mother had called. Trish had returned home this morning. She'd picked up a new boyfriend recently and last night she'd stayed at the guy's flat in Peacehaven. She was having such a good time she'd forgotten to call in sick at the restaurant and she hadn't even cancelled her mum for babysitting. Trish's little girl had been with Trish all night and when she'd been interviewed this morning, Trish had said she hadn't seen Alan Day for months. No doubt, thought Minter, as he walked along the road that skirted the park, the news would please DCI Beckett a lot. It would give him yet another reason to disregard Minter.

In the playground, yummy mummies slathered their charges with Factor 50 and Minter watched one of them fussing over her toddler's sun hat. Leaving behind the shade of the lofty plane trees, he crossed the road and turned up the Drive. Plenty of respectable ways to make money in Brighton, he thought, gazing at the neat front gardens and the mock-Tudor houses and envying the quiet and contented family lives that must go on inside, the kind of life that he had never had. The traffic noise had ceased, replaced by the swish of a sprinkler and the buzz and whine of a lawnmower.

Ever since Minter had found the cold case file, he couldn't get Hillcrest out of his mind. As he walked along the quiet street, he remembered the day he'd met Anna May.

Charlie couldn't bully him whenever Minter was at school, but he could as soon as he got back. So every afternoon around four o'clock, still dressed in his school uniform, Minter would slip out of the gate at the bottom of the back garden and into the open countryside beyond. He wasn't planning on returning to the big house until it was time for tea. Closing the gate behind him, Minter looked out over the patchwork of green and bronze fields, each one separated by a hedgerow or a dry-stone wall. In the distance, a tractor inched its way across the horizon, seagulls wheeling and diving all about it. Skipping down the gentle slope, Minter crossed the stream at the bottom using the two long planks of wood some of the kids had put there long ago. On the other bank, there was a copse of trees and thick hazel bushes, and congratulating himself on the success of his plan to evade Charlie, Minter sauntered along the path behind them.

After a minute or so of walking, Minter glimpsed something hidden in among the bushes. He stopped and retraced a few of his steps. There it was again – a flash of red and black, a shirt that he recognised. Leaving the path, Minter walked under an oak and paused, peering through the twigs and branches and heart-shaped leaves of the hazel thicket to make sure that it really was Anna May.

Anna was fourteen years old and her bedroom on the attic floor of Hillcrest was just across the hallway from Minter's. A couple of nights after he arrived, she'd come into his room after lights out, saying that she couldn't sleep. Anna had sat on the end of Minter's bed and they'd chatted for a while about their families and about how awful Mr Clements was and it was then that she caught sight of the bruises on Minter's back. She lifted the jacket of his pyjamas and winced.

'Charlie wears those boots,' Minter explained, 'the ones with the steel toecaps.' He told her how Charlie had stolen his St Christopher's medal. It seemed that, if anything, he was more distressed about the loss of his mother's gift than he was about the terrible beatings. Perhaps that was why when Anna said goodnight, she leaned across the bed and kissed Minter on the cheek.

'You're a brave boy,' she whispered, 'and I promise it'll get better.'

Now here she was again, sitting on the grassy bank with her shoes by her side and her legs dangling into the stream. She had strawberry-blonde hair down to her shoulders and she was wearing a denim skirt, in the lap of which was a letter. Slowly, Minter edged his way into the little clearing.

Hearing a twig snap on the ground, Anna turned round. 'Oh, it's you,' she smiled, looking pleased to see him.

Minter hesitated. He shouldn't be here.

'How was school?' Anna asked.

'It was OK.' Already this afternoon one of the other boys had asked Minter where he lived. Not for the first time, Minter had wished he was a better liar. 'Why don't you ever go to school, Anna?'

'I'm what they call a school refuser.'

'What does that mean?'

'It means that me and teachers don't get along.' She patted the long grass. 'Sit down. I'm glad you're here, actually. I've got something for you.' It was snug inside the little den and Minter felt safe when he sat down next to her. Anna rooted around in her canvas satchel. 'Here it is,' she said triumphantly, pulling something out of her bag and holding it up so that Minter could see. The gold of the St Christopher flashed in the sunlight. 'It's the right one, isn't it?'

'Yes!' Minter said. He was up on his knees, reaching out for the medal. 'That's it!' Minter put the chain round his neck and tried to do up the tricky little clasp. When it was finally secured, a thought struck him. His expression changed

71

immediately to one of worry. 'Did you steal it from him, Anna? What if he finds out?'

'No,' Anna laughed, 'I didn't steal it. I told him to give it to me.'

Minter was too busy slipping the medal under his shirt to wonder what Anna had given Charlie in return. 'Thank you,' he said. 'Thank you.'

'That's all right,' she said, but now she looked unhappy as well.

Minter looked down at the handwritten letter she'd been reading. 'Is that from your brother?'

Anna bit her lip. 'Pete's foster parents want to adopt him.'

Minter knew that Anna's brother lived in a children's home in another part of the country. 'What about you?' he asked. 'Does it mean that you're going to leave?'

'They don't want both of us, just Pete.' Anna looked across at Minter. 'You look like him, you know.' She put her hand up to ruffle Minter's hair, but he flinched.

In the quiet Hove suburb, the noise of the lawnmower had stopped. Minter turned round to see a balding man retreating into an open garage, pushing the mower in front of him, his lawn green and striped in the broad sunshine.

All those years ago, Minter had flinched when Anna reached out to touch him. She'd just needed something to remind her of her brother, Pete, who was being taken away from her, but Minter hadn't been able to give her even that. Just like at Kidz Klub this morning he hadn't been able to give Irene comfort at the moment of her distress. Taking off his suit jacket, Minter continued up the road.

72

The block of flats from which the surveillance operation against Russell Compton was carried out was a couple of streets away. Minter had seen the Windmill financials: the rental on the luxury apartment was another upscale budget item. There was a swimming pool and a couple of tennis courts in the grounds, which none of the SOCU officers ever got the chance to use, boiling their way through long shifts on the ninth floor instead.

Minter entered the flats through the back door. He didn't want to be here this morning. He'd rather be on the seafront. The bust on Sillwood Crescent was SOCU's first opportunity to hit back against Compton, but Beckett hadn't involved Minter at all. He'd told him to come here instead. Minter took the service lift up to the ninth floor, found the right flat and rang the bell. When it was Vicky Reynolds who answered, he was pleased.

'Minter,' Vicky said. 'What are you doing here?'

'My name's on the roster,' Minter said. 'Surveillance for the next two hours.'

'I'll be glad of the company,' said Vicky, although she still sounded a little unsure.

Minter followed Vicky down the hall, passing a large, open-plan living area with bare walls and deep carpets. The equipment had been set up in a tiny room at the end of the hallway. Inside, a young man was sitting at a long desk, his back to Minter. On the desk itself were two Sony Vaio laptops. The screen on one of the laptops showed some pre-recorded night-time footage and the other was streaming live from one of the many covert surveillance cameras surrounding the Compton mansion. This angle covered the garden and the back of the house. The colour image was top-notch. Minter could see the ripples of light on the surface of the huge blue swimming pool.

Vicky looked across at Minter. He had high cheek bones, full lips and short brown hair. When he glanced shyly back at her, the light in his blue eyes seemed to be in constant dazzling motion. There was something penetrating about his gaze as well, something that cut through all of her misgivings about him. Pulling her eyes away by main force, Vicky sat down next to the techie and carried on giving instructions about the editing of the infrared footage.

Leaving them to it, Minter walked over to the window. On the other side of Dyke Road, Russell Compton's red-brick pile appeared in all its tasteless glory. There were three floors in all: plenty of leaded windows and gabled roofs as well as a triple garage, a clock tower and a pair of rampant lions on the gateposts. Chateau Chav, as DC Connolly had referred to it this morning in the briefing.

More significant than the architecture, though, were the steps Russell had taken to make his house safe. It was set a long way back from the road, behind tall iron gates and a high perimeter wall and a wide expanse of block paving, where Russell's Shogun and his wife's BMW Z4 were parked. Close to the house, three raised flowerbeds had been planted with palm trees and high-wattage security lights. On the roofline, Minter counted three separate video cameras, one of them turned away from the property towards the flats where Minter was standing. It was difficult to say who was watching whom.

The sun had moved round and the fans on the laptops were kicking out heat into the cramped room. Minter draped his jacket over the vacant chair and looked at Vicky

Reynolds. 'So Beckett didn't need you at Sillwood either?'

Vicky glanced up from the laptop screen. Without his jacket, the leanness of Minter's torso shadowed the seams of his white work shirt. There didn't seem to be an ounce of fat on his whole body.

'I think Drugs Squad can handle it,' Vicky said.

Feeling a little flustered, she looked back at the computer on the desk. Vicky liked to give people the benefit of the doubt – that was another reason why she was still a DC – and she had to admit that Minter was very good-looking, but now she reminded herself what DS Phillips had told her last night after the restaurant.

Minter nodded at the footage playing on the Sony. 'What's that?'

Vicky looked back at the computer. 'I'm putting together a sequence from last night's CCTV.'

'Anything interesting?'

'Show him,' Vicky told the techie, a little reluctantly.

A few keystrokes later and the image on the laptop changed. The time signature at the bottom of the frame read, *23.06:22*. On the grainy footage the front door of the Compton house opened and a man whom Minter recognised straight away as Russell Compton stepped out onto the porch. Even at this distance, he looked enormous.

As soon as Russell stepped out onto the block paving, the image on the screen flashed to white as all of the security lights came on. The surveillance camera automatically adjusted its aperture and Compton strode towards his Shogun. On the screen, a much smaller figure appeared behind him.

'That's Chris Compton,' Vicky said.

75

'I know,' Minter replied.

There was a jump cut. Another video clip began playing on the laptop. It was the same shot, though. The front of the house. Minter looked at the clock again; Russell had made it home at 2:15:22. The electronic gates were swinging open and Russell turned the Shogun off Dyke Road and parked in front of the house. The door of the 4x4 opened and the same bulky figure stepped down, followed by his son. They both walked quickly to the front door.

Vicky Reynolds's initials were on the bottom of an awful lot of the intel reports from the surveillance. For such a bright officer, she was spending far too much time up here. The footage was good, especially the way she had cut it. The tape would stand up in court. 'Russell's wearing a different jacket,' Minter commented.

Vicky nodded. 'That's right. It's leather, the same style, but the one Compton's wearing in the second clip is slightly longer.' She looked at Minter. 'Whatever it was that Russell and Chris were up to, they had to change their clothes afterwards.'

'Where did they get to last night?'

'We don't know.' Vicky turned back to the techie. 'Can you burn a copy of the edit onto a DVD?'

Nodding, the techie reached across to where the shrink-wrapped blanks were kept in a storage box.

'What about the mobile surveillance unit?' said Minter. 'I thought Compton had a tail 24/7.'

Vicky picked up a clipboard from the desk. 'You're in intelligence, Minter. Take a look for yourself.'

Minter accepted the events log from Vicky Reynolds. The badly photocopied form at the top was covered with a spidery handwriting. DC Carver had taken his turn last night. Minter scrutinised his notes. He turned back a page, making sure he understood. Minter looked at Vicky. 'Eleven o'clock is when our drivers change shift.'

'A few seconds' head start,' she said. 'That's all it takes.'

Minter gave the events log back to Vicky. After Trish Yates, he wasn't in a hurry to jump to any more conclusions. 'Maybe Russell got lucky.'

'Maybe,' said Vicky. 'But it's the fourth time it's happened this month.'

'We need to change the drivers, then,' said Minter. Every station leaked, and an organised criminal like Russell Compton would have his own intel operation to take advantage of them.

Vicky nodded. 'That's what I told the SIO a couple of weeks ago.'

'Did Beckett do anything?'

Vicky hesitated. 'No.'

'Compton can't just come and go with impunity. God knows what he did last night.'

Vicky shrugged. 'I suppose it wasn't a priority.'

Inside the house, Jacqui Compton sat down on a bar stool. She put her cup of coffee down on the butcher's block in the middle of the huge kitchen. Behind her, an acre of slate flooring stretched away towards the floor-to-ceiling windows and the sunny back garden.

With her long, auburn hair and her striking, deep blue eyes, Jacqui had been a looker once, but now she was the wrong side of forty and the ciggies and the vodka had begun to take their toll. She was getting heavy in all the worst places.

From the hallway came the sound of loud rock music. Jacqui put her hand to her forehead and groaned. This morning's hangover was a bad one. She didn't remember how she'd got to bed.

The music was coming from the den. It was where her husband, Russell, spent most of his time these days pacing and plotting. Whenever he had a phone call to make, Russell cranked up the CD. It was the same pounding White Stripes album over and over again and it was driving Jacqui mad. She didn't know how much more of this she could take.

Jacqui glanced down at the Boucheron watch on her wrist. The diamonds on the face sparkled prettily. It was eleven o'clock. With the fingers of her other hand, Jacqui stroked the baby-pink alligator strap. Most days now, she went out as soon as she could. Showered and dressed and left. When Russell was in this kind of mood, it was a lot safer than staying in.

She looked up at the sound of footsteps to find Chris standing at the bottom of the stairs near the front door dressed in a pair of shorts and a T-shirt. These days no one in the Compton household got up early.

Jacqui folded her silk dressing gown more modestly round her ample chest. 'Morning, Chris,' she said. She'd been aiming at a breezy tone, but her voice just sounded croaky.

Grunting, Chris walked over to the sink. He filled a glass with water from the tap and drank it down in one.

He was getting taller, Jacqui thought, but there was a tuft of hair sticking up at the back of his head that still made him look boyish. Jacqui hoped he was growing out his crop. She tried again. 'Did you go somewhere nice last night?'

Chris reached across and switched on the ghetto blaster on the worktop. Dance music blared.

Jacqui put her hand up to her forehead again. 'Turn that thing off,' she said.

Chris turned round. 'You forgotten about the cops listening in?'

'For God's sake, Chris, I only asked you where you went.'

Chris left the music playing. He looked at her. 'How do you know you heard me going out last night?' he said. 'I mean, you were pretty fucking pissed.'

Jacqui looked down. 'I had a couple of drinks,' she said.

'A couple of drinks, was it?' Chris sneered back at her. There it was. The snide look. The one Russell always gave her. 'You were spark out as usual, Mum, snoring away, empty bottle on the floor.'

'Look,' said Jacqui, reaching out a hand across the table, 'why don't you sit down. I'll fry us some bacon.'

Chris shook his head in disgust. 'I'm going out,' he told her. 'Places to go, people to see.' Turning on his heels, Chris left the kitchen to go and get dressed.

Alone again, Jacqui forced herself up off the stool. She went over to the counter and turned off the stereo. She put the kettle on for more coffee. After that, she thought, she was going to get the hell out of the house.

The club always made Jacqui feel better. There were young girls in tunics to minister to her with exotic-smelling wraps and facials. In the spa, the steam room would soothe her head and she could float away in the Jacuzzi's warm, forgetful waters.

The kitchen phone went off. Thinking it might be her brother, Dave, Jacqui hurried across to pick it up off the counter but the ringer went silent before she could. Russell had got it from his den.

Minter and Vicky Reynolds were alone in the surveillance flat. The techie had gone outside for a cigarette break. It had been twenty minutes since Chris Compton had left to go to Sillwood. Since then, Minter and Reynolds hadn't heard a thing from the officers waiting on the seafront. The house over the road had gone quiet, too.

'Why didn't you take the bar exams?' Minter asked Vicky. 'You'd be on serious money by now.'

'I suppose I wanted to make a difference.' Vicky glanced out of the window at the bright blue sky. 'Silly me.'

'There's nothing wrong with being idealistic,' said Minter. 'We all need a reason to come to work in the morning.'

Vicky nodded. She looked unsure, though. The truth was she had been going round in circles about her so-called career and she didn't even know if she wanted to stay in the police at all. Vicky was still young and knew that lots of people these days made a false start before retraining to do something completely different. She had a friend in Brighton who worked as a project manager at one of the Lloyds offices. She never quite figured out what Michelle did, but she finished work most nights at six and had weekends free to do as she wished. Vicky knew, too, that Michelle earned enough at the bank to be able to afford a flat just off the seafront, where her sexy Italian boyfriend stayed over whenever he was asked to.

So, right now, leaving the police seemed the smart thing to do. But there was a competitive streak in Vicky that was at least a mile wide. She didn't want to let the boys have it all their own way.

Minter seemed to intuit some of what she was thinking. 'Did you go for the DS post last year?' he asked.

He was very well informed, Vicky thought. 'I did.'

'And?'

'Beckett didn't even interview me. Said I didn't have enough experience on the squad as yet.'

Minter glanced at the clipboard on the desk, the one that recorded how easily Compton had slipped his tail. 'Another one of Beckett's mistakes, then.'

Vicky looked at him warily. Before she joined SOCU, she was on fast track. She should have been the DS, not Kevin, so she didn't owe Tom Beckett anything. But there was such a thing as loyalty. 'Windmill might have its problems, but they're not Beckett's fault. He hasn't been given the resources.'

There was another reason why Vicky didn't want to share with Minter what she really thought about the way Windmill had been run. Last night in town, as Vicky had been waiting with Kevin Phillips in the queue for their respective cabs, Phillips had told her something else about Minter. 'You better be careful, Vick,' he said. 'Minter might not be up at the Park anymore, but he's still working for the super. Minter is Roberts's boy. He's here to dish the dirt, Vick. And not just on me this time. It's Beckett that Roberts wants.'

'And,' Vicky said to Minter, 'Beckett's been under a lot of pressure.'

Inside the over-warm surveillance flat, Minter shrugged. 'Pressure is what Beckett's paid for.'

81

'Did you hear what happened to him last year?' Vicky said, a touch of anger in her voice. Minter shook his head. 'His wife died. Stomach cancer.'

'I didn't know.'

'It happened at the same time Windmill was launched. You know what it's like at the beginning of a major investigation. We had to hit the ground running. The whole team was working ten days straight, twelve hours a day. Double shifts sometimes, too. And Tom Beckett was doing more hours than any of us.' Vicky shook her head at the memory. 'I don't know how he did it.'

'I had a briefing from Roberts about the case,' said Minter. 'He was very thorough. He didn't mention anything about Beckett's personal life.'

A cloud of suspicion passed over Vicky Reynolds's face. It was the same look Minter had seen from every other SOCU officer in the last few days.

'Tom Beckett can retire next year,' she said. 'He's done his twenty-seven years. Don't you think he deserves to be cut some slack?'

'By who?' Minter asked. Vicky hesitated. 'By who?' Minter asked again.

She looked at him. 'You tell me, Minter.'

There was a silence. 'I'm here to give Windmill an intelligence edge,' Minter insisted. 'That's all.'

The exchange apparently over, the tension between them left hanging in the air, Vicky busied herself by updating the events log for the umpteenth time and Minter returned his attention to the window. Every now and then, though, Minter would glance back at her. He always had Tom Beckett down as something of a timeserver, a job-sick DCI waiting for his pension to arrive, but now he knew that last year had been very hard on Windmill's SIO and things started to make a different kind of sense. Beckett cared about his team and about the operation – that much was obvious from everything he did and said. So maybe Vicky was right. Maybe he did deserve to be cut some slack.

'I want to speak to Rita,' Russell Compton said into his phone. In his den, music was still roaring out of the quadraphonic speaker system, concealing his words from the listening devices he knew the police were using.

'Who's Rita?' came the bad-tempered reply down the phone. 'I don't know any Rita.'

Compton's fingers drummed on his desk. 'Yes, you do. And just in case you need telling, this is Russ Compton speaking. I've had nothing for two weeks. I'm getting tired of waiting.'

There was silence for a moment. 'Can't hear a word you're fucking saying, mate. Turn the music down next time.' And he hung up.

Russell threw the mobile across the room where it smacked into the far wall, gashing the oak panelling. 'Fuck you,' Russell said under his breath. He'd made that bastard rich, paid for his flat, his cars, now the little prick was hanging up on him. Well, there'd come a time for payback.

The seafront was crying out for gear and Russell couldn't get any. Which meant one thing: someone else would move in. The Hangletons were making the first move. Scum, Russell thought. Little cunts with their machetes and mopeds. Until now, the quality of Rita's gear had blown the Hangletons off the seafront, limiting their territory to the chicken-shit estate they came from, but Russell would bet his Lexus all that was changing fast. He could almost hear their little motorbikes buzzing around the Steine, the junkies queuing up to buy their bags. No loyalty, of course. Not an inch, not in this business. None expected, either.

Think, he told himself. What's the next move? Take out one of the Hangletons? The psycho with the scar on his cheek. Make it very public, too. But who would do it for Russell now that Alan Day was gone?

Russell spared a thought for his former business partner. It wasn't a long thought, just something along the lines of needs must, because Alan Day might have been a great streetfighter and the best enforcer Russell had ever employed, but he was still just a kid. And Alan Day had gone too far by offing that cop at the racetrack. The police would have caught up with him pretty soon and then they would have turned him, just like they did his brother-in-law, David Gillespie. In no time at all, Russell would have ended up facing Alan Day across the sunken floor of a crown court – Day in the witness box, Compton in the dock. It was a shame it had to happen, but needs must.

The thought of taking out one of the Hangletons appealed to Russell. It would be some kind of retribution, at least. But that wasn't the point. The point was that the machine had to be fed. He had to get hold of some gear. A big slab of it. There was the stuff in the woods. That would keep them going for a week or so, but he needed a bigger deal. Ten kilos at least. Then he could flood the seafront, undercut the Hangletons, get the dealers and the punters back. Special offers, two for one. Any fucking thing. And getting that kind of weight meant face time with Rita, who needed reassuring. Yeah, sure, things were touchy at the moment, but steps had been taken, steps that would ensure Russell was still Mr Punch in Brighton.

His thoughts were interrupted by a soft knocking at the door of the den. After a moment without a reply, Russell's wife, Jacqui, opened the door. She was wearing the short dressing gown, the one that showed far too much of the cellulite dimples on her thighs for Russell's liking.

Jacqui hovered at the open doorway. She knew that Russell didn't like to be interrupted in his den. 'Russ,' she asked him gently, 'do you think you'll be needing my car this morning?'

Russell Compton hadn't heard what his wife was saying. He was too busy taking apart another stolen mobile. Without looking up, he said, 'What you going on about?'

'The Beemer?' Jacqui repeated, still hesitating by the door. 'You won't be needing it today? Only you said you might.'

'No, I won't.' A thought occurred to him. 'Where you going?'

Jacqui looked at Russell. She was very nervous of him. There were still two red marks on her neck left by his fingers a couple of days ago.

Russell glanced up. 'Fucking hell,' he said. 'I'm only asking.' He looked her up and down. On Jacqui's legs, the blue, spidery lines where the veins had popped were beginning to join up.

'I'm going to the club,' Jacqui replied. 'I was just checking you didn't need my car today.'

Sighing, Russell pulled the BMW keys from his pocket.

Jacqui took a couple of small steps into the room. but rather than wait for her, Russell lobbed the keys across the room. She reached for the enamel fob, but as he had intended her to do, she missed. Jacqui had to bend down to pick the keys up off the floorboards.

Those floorboards cost a ton a piece, Russell recalled, watching his wife's bottle-auburn hair falling untidily around her head. By the time Jacqui stood up, Russell had turned his attention back to the SIM card in his hand.

'I'll go and get dressed,' Jacqui muttered, but she stayed where she was.

Russell looked up at her. 'What is it now?'

'Do you know where Dave is?' she asked.

Russell snapped the cover back onto the telephone. 'No idea,' he said. He stared at Jacqui knowing very well where her brother was. Last night, Russell had spent sixty-five minutes smashing every bone in David Gillespie's body, but he still hadn't quite sorted out what he was going to tell his wife about her brother's disappearance.

'I can't get hold of him at all,' Jacqui said. 'I've been ringing and ringing.'

'What you asking me for? Dave's your fucking brother.'

The new mobile sprang to life in Russell's hand. Immediately, he started dialling a number. When he was finished, he looked up, daring Jacqui to ask him another stupid question. Closing the door gently behind herself, Jacqui left the room.

As the call connected, Russell reached across the large desk and took a Sobranie cigarette from the pack, sparking it with his chunky desk lighter. Jacqui'd got him into these ciggies, he remembered. She thought they were sophisticated.

There was no reply. Russell rapped the phone down on his desk and puffed on the dark brown ciggy. If it all came on top, he thought, he had no doubt he could get by. He was ready to clear out of Brighton once and for all. Plenty of other places to go, maybe foreign ones at that. He didn't need the house, and he could certainly do without all the poncey gear Jacqui had stuffed it with. Russell had money that even the dodgy lawyers didn't know about. Real folding stuff you could pick up in your fist. Money to start all over again.

He could do it. No problem. But Jacqui couldn't. This house, the club, the boy. They'd nailed her here, once and for all. He'd have to leave her behind.

Good riddance, then.

He glanced across the room, towards the bank of television sets connected to the cameras on the front of the house. On the furthest screen, the iron gates swung open and a moment later, Chris's Mini joined the traffic heading towards the city.

Russell smiled. He was still Mr Punch.

On the promenade, a man on roller blades, pads on his outstretched knees and elbows, went swooping between the pedestrians. Behind him, the English Channel, the city's watery perimeter, lay very still, as if stunned by the heat.

Inside the liveried BT van parked on Sillwood Crescent, DS Kevin Phillips sat on a narrow metal bench between two Drugs Squad officers. It must be even worse in that get-up, Phillips was thinking, watching a trickle of sweat running under the leather chinstrap of the crash helmet worn by one of them. Phillips glanced down to where the hem of the officer's bulletproof vest all but concealed the dull metal of the holstered pistol at his hip.

Phillips shifted in his seat until he could see out of the tiny window behind him. He watched a car go slowly down Sillwood, hunting for a parking space. He turned round again and leaned back against the side of the van, tapping his foot against the bare floor.

The other Drugs Squad officer, the older one sitting on the right, leaned forward and grinned. 'You nervous, mate?' he asked. You didn't have to be clever to join the Drugs Squad. You just had to like smashing things up.

Phillips shot him a glance. 'No,' he rejoined. 'I'm bursting for a pee.'

The first blue-clad officer put his finger to his earpiece. 'Not now you don't,' he said. 'Looks like your man's here.'

Sure enough, Chris Compton's black-and-yellow Mini appeared at the top of Sillwood Crescent. It passed the BT van, heading towards the seafront.

'He's parking up,' the Drugs Squad DC narrated. There was another pause. 'Looks like we're on.'

Keeping his head low and his footfall light, Phillips got up and moved to the other side of the van. Out of the smoked window, he could see Chris Compton coming up from the direction of the sea. He was on foot now. Despite the high sun, he was wearing a sweatshirt and his hands were stuffed deep inside its pockets. That's where the cash will be, Phillips thought. He watched Chris Compton walk lightly, confidently, up to the front door of the narrow Regency townhouse.

Adrenaline began to chase round Phillips's body. Chris Compton would not be getting away today, the DS told himself grimly. Not like Alan Day had got away yesterday. It was like Beckett had said at the briefing. This was family business. This was balancing the books. You take out one of ours, we'll take out one of yours.

The Drugs Squad officer flung open the doors of the van and heavy boots thumped the tarmac. In the blink of an eye they were across the road, ramming the heavy front door with a two-foot length of iron bar. The lock gave way at the first, expertly aimed impact and they were inside.

Speed was the thing. Get to the gear before it could be flushed down the toilet. Upstairs, another smack against a doorjamb and the officers hurled themselves into the flat, Phillips just behind them.

Rat-faced Jeff Walters stood transfixed in the middle of the hallway. He raised his hands immediately, but it made no difference. The leading Drugs Squad officer marched forward, planted a leg behind Walters and shoved him in the chest. Walters crashed to the floor. 'Face down, scrote!' the officer screamed at his sprawled figure. 'Face fucking down!' Walters rolled over as quickly as he could.

The second officer, the metal pole still in his hands, strode past his colleague and disappeared into the bathroom.

Chris Compton appeared at the end of the hallway. Phillips pounded towards him. 'All right!' Chris called out, his hands held up in front in a gesture of surrender. Phillips smacked into the drug dealer and they both fell backwards into the lounge. The SOCU officer was first to his feet, spinning Chris round while he was still on the floor and wrenching his arms behind him. Phillips cuffed Chris Compton and pulled him to his feet, glancing around the room as he did so. There were loads of electronics and expensive gizmos – exactly the kind of place a one-kilo guy like Jeff Walters would live in. There was a huge cracking sound followed by the noise of falling water. The cistern in the toilet was getting smashed up and one of the Drugs Squad dogs was barking enthusiastically. Phillips pulled Chris Compton to his feet and shoved him onto one of the leather sofas.

'Fuck you,' Chris snarled at Phillips.

'Yeah,' Phillips snapped back. 'You, too.'

DCI Beckett walked into the room and came straight over to where Compton junior was sitting. 'Save us the bother, Chris,' he said. 'Tell us where the gear is.'

'What gear?' Chris asked.

Beckett bent down. 'Think you can get away with killing a cop, do you? You little fuck.'

Chris Compton said nothing, just stared at the floor. He was remembering the tricks his father had schooled him in.

On the other side of the room, Phillips was using a tyre iron to wrench a flat-screen TV off its wall bracket, one of the uniformed officers giving him a hand. Beckett's mobile trilled. The unit posted at the rear of the building reported in. They'd seen nothing. No one had come down the fire escape. Nothing had been thrown from the windows.

Beckett bent down again. With both hands, he grabbed Chris Compton by the scruff of his sweatshirt and yanked him to his feet. 'Look at me, you bastard!' He slapped his cheek – once, twice. 'This isn't a fucking game!' he yelled.

Finally, the teenager turned his face towards Beckett. Their eyes met as he asked, 'How's your wife, Tom?'

Beckett punched him hard in the stomach, an upward blow that winded him and bent him double. There was more to come, but at that moment the senior Drugs Squad officer appeared in the doorway, a sledgehammer held between both his hands. He watched Chris Compton crumple to the floor. Unsurprised – it was just SOCU doing the kind of thing they did best – the Drugs Squad guy told Beckett, 'There's nothing here. Fuck all.'

Beckett tried to rein in his temper. 'OK,' he told the other officer. 'OK. You lot can get off.'

As the officer went back along the hallway, DS Phillips picked Chris Compton up off the floor and put him back on the sofa. 'Stay there.'

Beckett and Phillips inspected every other room in the flat one by one. They'd all been ransacked, turned completely upside down: if anything had been there, the Drugs Squad and their dogs would have found it for sure.

'So what the fuck was this all about?' Beckett asked Phillips once they were back in the hallway, but all Kevin Phillips could do was shrug. 'Get Chris Compton down to the station, Kev.'

'What's the charge?'

'I don't know,' said Beckett. 'Non-payment of fucking council tax for all I care. I'm sure you'll think of something on the way.' As Phillips went back into the living room, Beckett shook his head. He'd been wrong about the bust this morning and he'd been wrong about what he'd just said to Chris Compton. This *was* a game. And right now the Comptons had Tom Beckett just where they wanted him.

Little Preston Street was a narrow, seedy-looking alley just off the seafront. One side of it was made up of the tatty rears of houses whose frontages had been turned into the cheap restaurants and takeaway shacks that made up Preston Street itself, where clubbers stopped late at night to refuel with food. Very few people ever walked down Little Preston Street, though.

The Major Incident Vehicle was disgorging a couple of Scene of Crime officers at the top of the road. Both of them toted orange satchels and were dressed in white suits. Behind the MIV lorry, a private ambulance was pulling onto the pavement.

Minter ducked under the police tape. In front of him, the street was lined with the bright green garbage trolleys Brighton City Council gave to restaurants for their food waste. About halfway down the street, Home Office pathologist Dr Iain Hunter was emerging from a small marquee. He was followed out by a plain-clothes officer Minter recognised from the time he spent in East Brighton. The two men nodded to each other as Minter reached the tent.

Dr Hunter put something in his pocket and said, 'Good of SOCU to show up at last.' A Welshman living in Haywards Heath, Hunter was notoriously bad-tempered.

'There's an operation this morning,' Minter explained. 'DCI Beckett is tied up on that.'

In truth, Minter was very glad when he got the call. He didn't want to spend the entire day holed up in the surveillance flat.

Hunter rolled down one of his latex gloves and Minter noticed the dark hairs tumbling over the edge of his shirt cuff.

'Was the body moved here after death?' Minter asked.

Hunter looked at him. 'Almost certainly, Sergeant,' he said. The pathologist was a stickler for rank. 'He was killed sometime yesterday afternoon, I'd say. I'll give you a more exact range in the preliminary.' Hunter looked at his watch, sighed. 'I'd cleared the decks for some paperwork, but I suppose this one takes priority.'

'If possible, sir,' Minter said exchanging a sly smile with the DC. At this point, it wouldn't have been a good idea to inform the pathologist that another body was already winging its way towards his lab. And that Dave Gillespie's corpse wasn't a pretty one.

'I'll meet the cadaver at the mortuary,' said Hunter. 'The preliminary post mortem will be online around three.' With that, Hunter bade farewell.

Minter looked up and down the narrow street. 'It gets packed here at night,' he said, 'Someone should have seen something.'

'We've started the door-to-door,' the DC replied.

On the other side of the road, a woman with dark hair and impassive features was watching the scene from an upstairs window. 'You might need some translators,' Minter suggested. 'You could give the Brighton Chinese Society a call.'

The DC nodded. He turned away from Minter and waved at the uniformed officers standing near the police tape to let the coroner's men through.

Minter pushed aside the tent flap. The air inside was dank. In the middle was one of the refuse trolleys, its hinged lid flung open, its interior stuffed with bulging bin liners. The fetid smell that swamped the tent was coming from them rather than the body.

Hunter was right, Minter thought, turning his head slightly to get a clear view of the gunshot wound in the victim's left temple.

'One of the bin men found him,' the DC said from behind Minter.

In death, lying naked on his side on top of the bags, his legs folded neatly underneath him, Alan Day was still at last, his burned features just about identifiable from his picture book. Up at the Park, crime had become abstract for Minter. It was all a matter of statistics: of calculations and percentages. Now, staring at Alan Day's flayed body, it had suddenly become very real.

'I hope the bastard suffered,' said the DC. 'I hope the fucker burned alive.'

Sweating buckets, Terry Sampson headed down Lower Rock Gardens. At the end of the street, a green-blue sea rocked queasily up and down in the sunshine. Terry's body thermostat had blown up months ago. Sometimes, all it took was the slightest exertion and he'd be chucking up like this. At other times, he was a block of ice.

Ahead of him, on the other side of the street, an elderly woman emerged from one of the terraced houses. Terry came to a stop to let her go, but she took her time, fussing with her handbag and her keys, locking the door behind her and then testing it out just to make sure it was secure. Carefully, slowly, with agonising caution, she reversed down the steps outside her door.

Terry glanced behind. No one was following him. The old woman was making steady progress towards the seafront now. But she stopped again. She patted one of the pockets of her coat. Who the fuck would wear a great big heavy coat like that in this weather?

'Come on,' Terry muttered. 'Come on.' He was dressed

in the clothes he'd slept in, the street-hustler uniform of skinny jeans and dirty T-shirt. Under his long, black, badly crimped hair, his scalp was crawling with moisture, but the rest of his skin was drying up. It felt like he was shedding it.

Need to get well again. That was all that mattered. The brick was in the flat somewhere, stuffed deep inside his old wash bag, along with his works. It was huge. Massive. Number 4. The solution to all his problems. The answer to his prayers.

He could cook up a hit then and there. No fucking worries – the sickness gone just like that. But he couldn't bang it up yet, could he? Not yet he couldn't. He'd have to cut it with something first. He didn't want to end up like Jimbob.

Now the old cow was looking in her handbag. 'For fuck's sake, help me, God,' whispered Terry. 'For fuck's sake, help me.'

It was stupid to go back to the flat, he knew that. The cops might turn up at any minute. But it was far too early for trade, and none of the dealers would give him credit anymore, so he had to get his hands on that brick. It was that or nothing.

At last, on the other side of the street, the old girl ambled forward. 'Thirty fucking pounds,' he muttered, hobbling towards the sea at a pace that wasn't a whole lot faster. The fucking fuss Jimbob had made over thirty notes.

Jimbob was nothing when Terry had met him. Just a ragged-arse little chicken, flogging blow jobs for a fiver in the cottages. So who the fuck was Jimbob to talk to him like that? Thirty fucking notes. That was all Terry wanted.

95

It was Terry who took the young boy under his wing. If it wasn't for Terry, Jimbob would never have made it off the streets. He'd have been dead a long time ago. Jimbob used to know that, too. He used to be grateful. They'd been good together, way back then. They even loved each other, sometimes.

Suddenly, Terry was outside the flat. He snatched another quick look up and down Lower Rock Gardens; then he threw open the gate. In his eagerness, he almost stumbled down the stone steps to the basement. On the wall, the familiar number was outlined against the cracked plaster in a twisted length of rusty old iron. Someone, at some time, had been house-proud. The flat itself was still locked up, just as Terry had left it. There was no sound coming from inside so he keyed the lock and pushed the door hard.

Standing in the hallway, he recognised the musty smell. The place was always damp, even in summer, and in winter they'd be sponging mildew off the walls. To his left, the door to Jimbob's bedroom was open. Terry hurried past it.

He made it through into the tiny, grubby kitchen and from there into the windowless back bedroom. The mattress on the bed was covered by a soiled sheet. Terry walked past it, up to the second-hand chest of drawers where he kept his works. The drawer squeaked in protest as he yanked open the top drawer, but the wash bag wasn't there. 'Fuck!' Terry cried.

He stood up straight, his mouth bone dry and his stomach cramping something rotten. He swept the jumble of cheap cosmetics off the top of the chest. His best lippy rolled by his foot and disappeared under the bed. Terry turned round and fell to his knees. Maybe his works were under there.

Terry shoved his hand under the bed, his palm brushing against the dust and scraps that had collected on the thread-bare carpet. Something grabbed his fingers. Something clammy. 'Shit!' Terry yelled, pulling his hand out quickly. He sat back on his haunches to try and get away from whatever it was. 'You're fucking dead!' he screamed at the darkness that seemed to be spilling out from under the bed. 'Stay fucking dead!'

Drawing up his hand, Terry stared at his palm. He was deep in cold turkey now and beginning to hallucinate. The skin was pale, mottled, sickly-looking and it rippled like something was moving underneath. He shook his hand, trying to rid himself of the feeling. It was only then that Terry remembered where he'd left the gear. It was in Jimbob's room. That was where he'd fixed up last. There was no other choice. He'd have to go back inside the room.

Getting to his feet, Terry hurried through the kitchen and down the hall. He stood in the doorway, trying not to look at Jimbob's corpse. Gathering his courage, he walked over to the dressing table under the window. Jimbob's necklace was draped over the corner of the mirror. It was a cheap thing, just pieces of coloured stone threaded through a leather thong. Jimbob didn't wear it anymore but that first summer they were together, he'd worn it all the time. He thought it was cool.

The yellow plastic wash bag had fallen off the edge of the dressing table and landed in the waste bin on the floor.

'Yes!' Terry cried, bending down and grabbing it, his hands were shaking as he unzipped the bag. Inside were the needle, spoon and the fat lump of pure.

Standing up, Terry glimpsed Jimbob's body reflected in one of the bevelled mirrors propped up on the dressing table. His skin was pale, so pale, and his eyes were open. They seemed to be watching him.

Terry wiped away some snot with the back of his hand. 'I had to do it. I swear.' He sniffed. 'I'm sorry mate they didn't give me any choice.'

When Minter walked into the charging area of the Kemptown station, the custody sergeant was standing behind his desk, his pen moving slowly across the surface of a form. The sergeant was a tubby man but no matter how hot it got outside, he always wore the same blue serge jumper with the pips on the shoulder. After painstakingly finishing off his notes, he looked up at Minter.

It paid to be on the right side of the custody sergeant. This was the skip's area. Everything that happened here was down to him. So, a few jokes later, the sergeant was telling Minter what had happened at Sillwood Crescent. 'Not a sausage,' he concluded. 'The whole flat, clean as a whistle.'

Minter nodded. 'Is Chris Compton still in custody?'

'For the moment,' the sergeant said, straightening the corners of the release papers on his desk. 'In fact, DCI Beckett is upstairs with his brief now.' The desk sergeant enjoyed a good gossip. He considered Minter for a moment before confiding, 'There's been a little complaint, you see. About an injury Compton sustained during the arrest.'

Minter tutted. 'That's all Beckett is going to need,' he said. 'And which interview room is Compton in?'

'Four,' the sergeant said. 'I'll buzz you in.'

Minter turned towards the locked door leading to the custody suite.

Looking at Minter closely, the sergeant nodded. 'See you later,' he said, reaching for the button underneath his desk. There was a buzz: the electronic lock was thrown. Minter opened the door and walked into the corridor on the other side.

A modern custody centre had opened last year at divisional headquarters, so now Facilities felt free to neglect the old interview rooms at Kemptown. In the corridor, the paintwork was chipped and peeling. The high windows were filthy. Minter knew he shouldn't even be here, but what he'd found out up at the surveillance flat had whetted his appetite. He wanted to talk to Chris Compton about what had been going on the night before.

Windmill was going belly up. It was obvious. Everywhere Minter looked there were loose ends and bad decisions. It wasn't just ExCal – even the surveillance regime was unpardonably lax. And arresting Chris Compton might help the squad's morale, but it showed far too much of the police's hand. If this was the best SOCU could do, Minter thought, no wonder Russell Compton was in front.

Interview Room 4 was at the end of the corridor, on the corner of the building. Minter opened the door to find Chris Compton sitting on his own on the other side of a metal-legged table. He looked up only briefly when Minter walked in.

Minter sat down opposite Compton and put an A4 Manila envelope on the table. He glanced around, scanning the predictable litany scrawled on the walls by bored or despairing suspects. Such-and-such an officer *is a wanker*. So-and-so *is going to die. Seagulls.* Directly above the empty tape recorder, someone official had sellotaped a typewritten sign to the wall: *It is illegal to smoke in this room,* it read.

Chris's frame was a lot slighter than Russell's, just as it had appeared on the surveillance footage, but he still had his father's bull neck. He had inherited Russell's obstinacy, too. His gaze remained fixed on something invisible just over Minter's shoulder. Chris Compton was ready for the next round.

Minter let the silence in the room fester for a little while longer. Then he pulled a pack of Benson & Hedges and his lighter from the side pocket of his suit jacket. He turned the golden rectangle round and round in his hand before fishing out the last two cigarettes. He held both of them up in front of Chris.

'You the good cop, are you?' said Chris Compton.

'If you like,' Minter said. He put the first cigarette in his own mouth and lit it. He put the other one down in the middle of the table, placing the open packet down beside it to use as an ashtray. 'Shouldn't take a moment to sign the papers,' said Minter. Sitting back in his chair, he exhaled. 'Then you'll be on your way.'

Chris Compton looked at the cigarette. 'Two hours,' he said. 'That's how long your boss kept on with the questions. Do you think you can do any better?'

Minter nodded. 'Like father, like son, eh, Chris?'

Compton's eyes found Minter's face. 'Yeah,' he said. 'That's right.'

Minter smoked his own cigarette. He nodded at the other one on the table. 'It's only a ciggy.'

Chris fixed him with his eyes. Without looking down, he reached out his right hand and snatched the Benson & Hedges. Minter lit it for him. As the nicotine reached Chris's brain, his shoulders dipped visibly.

'I just popped in to see if you remembered me, Chris,' Minter said. He made a show of looking around the poky room again. 'I think it was next door.' Chris's brow furrowed a little. 'Interview Room Three,' Minter explained. 'I was in uniform then, of course.' He smiled at the hatchet-faced young drug dealer. 'I had no idea I had such a celebrity on my hands. You must have been – what, twelve?'

Chris flicked invisible ash from his cigarette. Minter could tell that he remembered.

PC Minter had been called to a fight at a house party in Whitehawk. Chris Compton had been at the party. He was one of the youths thrown into the van and taken to Kemptown. When Chris turned out his pockets at the desk, there was enough skunk on him to stop an army.

'Of course,' Minter said, 'you've changed a lot since then. Grown up and all that. You're a big man now, aren't you, Chris.'

The memory of that earlier interview squatted between the two men. Minter didn't have to spell it out. Both of them remembered how Chris had cried, begging the uniformed constable not to ring his dad, ashamed about getting caught, scared witless at the thought of what Russell was going to do to him when he finally got home.

Minter looked at Compton, wondering if there was any of that vulnerable twelve-year-old left at all. 'Big enough man,' he said, taking the glossy, full-colour photos out of their envelope and laying them side by side down on the table, 'to do this.'

Chris Compton stared at the photos of the burned corpse.

'That *is* your uncle, isn't it?' Minter said. 'Uncle Dave?'

Chris looked away. He remembered how the scaffolding pole had risen and fallen against the night sky. He recalled how the flames had started to lick around the boot in the moonlight. It had been then that Dave had started to scream.

'No,' Minter insisted, tapping at one of the photos with the end of his finger. 'Take a good look, Chris.'

Compton did as he was told.

Minter took a drag on his cigarette. He turned his head so that he could get a better view of the photo. 'Body's unrecognisable, isn't it,' he said. 'But we know it's your uncle Dave. We found his wallet nearby. That was careless, wasn't it, Chris. Now we've just got to establish a time of death. My money is on somewhere between eleven p.m. and two fifteen a.m. That was when you and your dad went out.'

Chris Compton turned his cold eyes on Minter. 'No comment,' he said.

Minter leaned back in his chair again. He had to hand it to Chris – the boy was good. Minter leaned forward. 'Did your uncle Dave use to play with you, Chris? When you were a lad, I mean.' But, once again, Chris didn't bat an eyelid. 'Like father, like son, eh, Chris?'

No doubt Chris would know that he and Russell had lost

the mobile surveillance unit on their way out to the Downs last night. They would have swapped cars at least once, as well as burning all their clothes on the way home. Chris didn't have a lot to worry about.

Minter tried another tack. 'I've just come from the seafront,' he began. 'They found Alan Day's body, too.' A falter in Chris's steely concentration told Minter that he didn't know that Alan Day was dead.

Minter had seen the intel. At one time, Day was Chris's best mate. For a while, they'd knocked around Whitehawk together. 'Alan's body was dumped last night,' Minter said. 'They chucked him in a bin, along with all the rancid kebabs.' He shook his head. 'Dave *and* Alan. Not bad for twenty-four hours work, is it, Chris. Even for your dad.'

'My dad didn't kill Alan,' Chris said tersely.

'Really?' Minter asked casually.

Chris knew he'd made a mistake. Furiously, he stubbed his cigarette out against the cardboard of the Benson & Hedges packet. Red embers scattered across the tabletop.

There was a snatch of conversation from the corridor. The custody sergeant walked into the room, followed by Tom Beckett and a man in an expensive but conservative suit.

'About fucking time,' Chris Compton told his solicitor, getting up from the table.

The desk sergeant looked at Minter. He nodded at the sign sellotaped to the wall. 'Can't you read, DS Minter? There's no smoking anywhere in the station. I know you're new to this nick, so I won't be writing out a Reg 9 this time, but don't let it happen again.'

'Never mind about all that,' Beckett told the sergeant. 'Just get Compton out of here.'

Chris Compton grinned at Minter and Beckett in turn. 'See you,' he said to the latter, before following the sergeant and his solicitor out into the corridor.

The door closed behind them. Last night, Beckett hadn't slept a wink and this morning's operation had proven to be yet another disaster. He turned to Minter and said, 'What the fuck are you doing here? I told you to stay up at Dyke Road.'

Minter put out his own cigarette against the cardboard carton. 'Yes, sir,' he said, 'but DC Reynolds had already been assigned that duty and it was getting kind of crowded.'

'Don't get sarcastic with me, DS Minter,' said Beckett. 'I'm the SIO, remember. If I tell you to spend a whole fucking week on surveillance duty, then that's exactly what you'll do.' It was only then that Beckett caught sight of the photos of Dave Gillespie's burned corpse on the table. 'Where the hell did those come from?' Beckett looked at Minter. 'I know your game. You're sniffing around for Roberts, aren't you?'

Minter stood up. This time, he wasn't going to let himself be intimidated. 'Was Dave Gillespie the source for this morning's raid on Sillwood Crescent?'

'That's between me and the guy who runs the informant,' Beckett said. '"Sterile corridors", Minter. That's one of your phrases, isn't it?'

'As Windmill's senior analyst,' Minter said, 'I should be up to speed on all covert operations. U/c, CHIS, everything.'

'I don't give a shit about your job title,' said Beckett.

Minter said, 'Did you know that Gillespie was dead *before* you ordered Drugs Squad to break down the door of Walters's flat?'

Beckett waved a finger in Minter's face. 'I warned you yesterday about telling me how to do my fucking job.'

'Because if you didn't, sir, then I'd say that was a tactical mistake. Compton was way ahead of us on Tyler and now he knows about Gillespie being an informant, too. This operation is full of holes. It can't even run surveillance properly.'

'What are you talking about?'

'The Comptons lost their tail again last night. That makes it four times in as many weeks. If they hadn't, maybe Dave Gillespie would still be alive. It's just not good enough, sir. But then again, you're not used to running tight operations, are you?'

Beckett grabbed Minter by the lapels of his jacket. 'One more fucking word,' he said. 'Just one more fucking word.'

'Anna May, for example.'

Beckett's right hand flashed back. His fist caught Minter on the left cheek, the punch sending him sprawling over the chair. Minter landed in a heap on the floor on the other side.

Beckett kicked the chair away. Reaching down, he grabbed Minter's jacket again, dragging him to his feet. 'You're trying to fuck me over, aren't you, Minter!' he screamed. 'Just like you fucked Kevin Phillips over!' Beckett slammed Minter against the wall, cracking his head against the brickwork. 'Well, you're not going to do that! I'm not going to let you!'

Suddenly, something inside Minter snapped. He was back in the boiler house again with Charlie. But Minter had spent a lot of time in the gym since then and despite his wiry frame, the muscles in his body were very powerful. Very powerful indeed.

Minter punched Beckett in the stomach. The older man crumpled straight away. At the same time, Minter brought his knee up. It smacked into the centre of Beckett's face. There was a crunching noise as Beckett's head shot up and he staggered back across the floor, his nose streaming blood.

Minter moved in for the kill. He shoved Beckett against the opposite wall with the palm of one hand. 'Don't ever fucking touch me again!' he yelled, raising his other hand high above his head and making a fist.

The door flew open. 'What on earth is going on in here!' yelled the desk sergeant from the doorway.

Minter and Beckett froze. This was still the desk sergeant's territory. The skip looked from one to the other. He was surprised to note that Beckett had come off worse. 'It's bad enough with all the crims in here,' he scolded, 'without you two idiots kicking off.'

Minter and Beckett separated. Beckett took a handkerchief out of his pocket and held it to his nose to stop the bleeding.

'Sorry, Skip,' said Minter.

'That's better,' said the sergeant. He looked at Beckett. 'Your suspect is waiting to be released, sir. Any time you're ready.' With that, he walked out of the room.

The sergeant's footsteps squeaked back down the hall. Humiliated, Tom Beckett turned away from Minter. He stared outside the window. Behind the frosted glass, a

106

blurred pair of feet was hurrying along the pavement. Suddenly, the adrenaline that had kept Beckett going these last few days had all gone. He felt exhausted.

Minter's hands were still shaking. 'Listen to me,' he said. 'You've got it wrong, all of you. I'm not here because of Roberts. I'm not here to set anyone up. I just want a chance.'

But Beckett wasn't listening. His telephone rang eight times before he fetched it from his pocket and answered it.

Beckett had a muted conversation with the police despatcher then he put the phone back inside his pocket and stared out of the window again. 'You want to do some D work, do you, Minter?'

'Yes, sir,' Minter replied.

Beckett just wanted him out of the room. 'Forty-two Lower Rock Gardens,' he said. 'Take care of it.'

# 5
· · ·

By the time Chris Compton had come through the front door of the house in Dyke Road, his father was waiting for him in the hallway. 'All right?' Russell asked his son cheerily.

'Yeah, fine,' Chris replied. 'It was good.' He moved towards the stairs, but Russell stepped further into the hall, blocking Chris's path.

'You see,' Russell said, 'I told you I was right. About that other thing. That thing the other night.' Russell assumed that the police overheard every conversation that happened inside his house. He always spoke in this strange way, avoiding any nouns that might later be used in evidence.

'Yeah, Dad,' Chris said. 'You were right.'

Russell searched his son's face. 'Come on, then,' he said, turning round. 'Come and tell me all about it.'

Chris had no choice. He followed Russell into the den. 'Sit down, mate,' Russell said, pointing to the nearest sofa. Each on his own Chesterfield, father and son faced each other across the lacquered coffee table. Russell offered Chris a cigarette.

'No, thanks,' Chris said. He'd had enough of fags for the day. In the car, he'd had time to think over his conversation with DS Minter. What he'd said had been a mistake. A bad one.

'Okey-doke,' said Russell taking a Sobranie from the pack for himself. 'You know, Chrissy-boy,' he said, 'you're right about these fags. Can't taste a thing.' He snapped off the gold-coloured filter of his ciggy, then put the other end to his lips. Never taking his eyes off his son, Russell lit the Sobranie and scooped the remote control from the coffee table. He pointed it at the CD player and the White Stripes album leaped in volume. 'I just got off the phone to the lawyer we sent down to Kemptown,' Russell began, raising his voice a little. 'He told me you played a blinder with Beckett.' Russell puffed on his ciggy, holding it in the crook of one of his thick fingers. 'Well done, mate,' he said. 'Nice one.'

'Just like you said, Dad,' Chris replied. 'No comment.'

Russell smiled broadly. 'That's the stuff, boy. Don't even admit you're alive.' Chris looked at his watch. Russell narrowed his eyes, wondering if Jacqui had been having words with the boy. 'God,' Russell laughed, 'you *and* your mother. No one's got a moment to spare me today.'

'It's not that, Dad,' said Chris. 'It's just that I'm going into town with some mates this afternoon.'

Russell nodded. 'That's OK, son,' he said. 'That's fine. Just leave tomorrow free. I've got a little thing I need you to do.'

Chris nodded. He was glad there didn't seem to be any

more questions about the police interview, but he wondered what his father wanted now.

Russell sat back. 'I saw which way the wind was blowing a long time ago,' he began. 'This Windmill shit has been going on for more than a year now. A few months back, I decided to take out a little insurance policy.' Chris nodded again. His father was always a few steps ahead. 'Every time I got a big score, I'd rake a little off. It all adds up. It's not in one of the stash houses, though. It's somewhere different, somewhere the filth are never going to get their hands on it.' He looked at his son, checking his understanding. 'I need it now, Chris. I can't supply any of my dealers without it. But the thing is, mate, I can't fart without a cop appearing at my back. Especially after Tyler.' He leaned forward again, and smiled.

The implication was clear. 'I'm not sure, Dad,' said Chris. 'The police are probably watching me as well now.'

Russell opened his arms innocently. 'Why should they? You've done nothing wrong. You just paid a social call to Jeff Walters, that's all.' But he could see the boy wasn't convinced. 'Chris,' he said, a little bit of annoyance creeping into his voice, 'you've got nothing to worry about, mate. The cops will be following *me* tomorrow. To Sainsbury's, as it happens. And, just in case, I've even arranged a switch of car for you in town.'

'What's the weight?' asked Chris.

'It doesn't matter what the fucking weight is!'

'I don't know, Dad,' Chris equivocated.

Russell started to rub his thumb against the side of his index finger. 'Fucking hell, Chris,' he said, 'it's child's play. I tell you where the gear's buried. You go and dig it up.'

He stared at his son. 'Look, mate, I'm sorry if the police had a pop at you this morning. I told you about Beckett. He's a chippy little cunt. But we all get pinched every now and then. It's a fact of life. You got to learn how to cope with it.' Russell picked a shred of loose tobacco from his lower lip, flicked it away. 'Anyway, I'm not asking you. I'm telling you.' He tapped the ash from his cigarette against the side of the heavy glass ashtray. 'Why you bottling it, Chris?' he said quietly. 'You did *do* a no-comment interview, didn't you?'

'Yeah, of course I did,' Chris said. 'Ask the lawyer.'

'I told you,' said Russell. 'I already have.' These days, Russell was paranoid, but he was right to be paranoid. SOCU and the Hangletons – they *were* all out to get him. And he could see it all over Chris's face. Something had happened. 'Come on, Chrissy,' he said, 'you can tell your old man. What did you say to the filth?'

'Nothing, Dad,' Chris said. He was scared now, a lot more scared than he had been by Beckett. 'I swear, Dad, they'd stopped taping.'

Russell's hand flashed across the table, catching Chris hard on the face. 'You fucking twat!' Russell exclaimed. 'Why would you go and say something off the record? There's no such thing as off the record. Not when the brief's out of the room.' Russell got up. He went to stand over his son. 'You better tell me exactly what you said.'

'N-noth—' Chris stammered. He hadn't stammered like that for years. Not since he was a kid.

Russell hit him in the face again. This time, though, he used his fist. It was a light blow, a glancing one, but it drew blood from Chris's lip. 'Stop yammering, yer fucking retard and tell me what you said!'

Chris put his hand up, partly to protect his face, partly to hide from his father the hot, secret tears of his own terror and humiliation. 'It wasn't Beckett,' Chris managed to get out.

'Who the fuck was it, then?'

'M-Minter,' said Chris. 'He was called Minter.'

Russell bent down. He put his face as close to Chris's as it had been to David Gillespie's the night before. Chris could smell the stale smoke in his father's lungs. 'This Minter,' Russell hissed in his ear. 'SOCU, was he?'

Chris just about managed to nod.

'And what did you tell this cunt Minter?' Russell asked.

'I said,' Chris began. 'I said—'

'Spit it out, boy!'

'I said you didn't do it, Dad.'

'Do what, boy?' roared Russell. 'Do what?'

Chris's voice sank to a whisper, but even the whisper caught in the back of his throat. 'K-kill him.'

'Oh, you fucking tosser!' Russell shouted. 'Kill who?'

'Alan.'

Suddenly, the White Stripes stopped. Apart from the two men's ragged breathing, there was silence in the room.

Russell picked up the remote control and started the album again. If that was the worst of it, he thought, then maybe it wasn't too bad. He'd thought for a moment that the cops had got Chrissy talking about Gillespie. This Minter was new to him, though. Russell could list the names of all the SOCU officers on Operation Windmill. He knew a lot about some of them as people, too. Personal stuff. But he'd never heard of Minter. There was another thing, too, and it was worse. Minter might be new, but pretty soon, Rita would get to hear about what Chrissy had told him. Rita heard about every fucking thing in the end. You couldn't keep anything from that cunt. And that would make it even harder for Russell to swing another deal.

Russell went to sit back down on the other sofa. He lit another cigarette and looked over at his son. The boy's downcast face was red and crumpled and Russell hoped he hadn't gone too far. He couldn't afford to make an enemy of him. Not for the moment. Chris's punishment would have to wait.

'You know, Chris,' Russell began again in a calm voice, 'we're in the shit, son. Up to our necks in it. Look at me when I'm talking.'

Chris raised his face towards his father. Over Russell's shoulder he glimpsed the low, curvaceous shape of his mother's BMW stopping outside the tall iron gates that protected the Compton house. A moment later, both of them heard the gates opening.

'I'm trying very hard to get us out of it,' Russell continued, 'but it ain't easy, Chris. I'm having to fight for it, mate. Every inch of the way. I'm not just fighting for me, Chris. You know that, don't you?' He lifted both hands in a gesture that took in the entire house. 'I'm doing it so we can hang on to what we've got, what we've worked for. You know, you're going to end up running the whole show, Chris. That's why I'm showing you the ropes. So you're ready to take it on. 'Cos I've got faith in you, Chrissy-boy.' The front door opened and closed. Jacqui Compton was back from the club. 'Just you remember that, boy,' said Russell. 'In here, babe!' he called out.

A moment later, her hair still wet from swimming, Jacqui's face appeared round the den door. 'What is it, Russ?' she asked.

Russell waved her forward. Jacqui hesitated, wary of disturbing Russell's conference with Chris. 'I'm not going to bite you,' Russell said. 'Get in here.'

Coming round the sofa, Jacqui caught sight of the spot of blood on Chris's lip and the red slap mark on his cheek. 'You all right?' she asked him. Chris wouldn't look at her. He felt ashamed because he'd been crying and now Jacqui felt ashamed because she hadn't been able to protect her son.

'That?' Russell said dismissively. 'That's nothing. A little father-son bonding. We've got something much more important to tell you.'

Jacqui looked at her husband. 'What is it?' she said.

'You know you were going on about Dave this morning?' said Russell. Jacqui nodded. 'Well, now we know why he's slipped off the radar.'

'Where is he?' Jacqui asked. 'Where's Dave?'

'I don't know, but I do know one thing, babe. I know your brother Dave's a grass.'

'What you talking about, Russ?' said Jacqui. 'Of course Dave's not a grass. He's my brother, and he's been running the stash houses for years.' Jacqui knew that Russell had his suspicions about Dave, especially after one of the stash houses got busted last year, but Russell was suspicious of everybody.

Russell looked across the table at Chris. 'Go on, son –

tell your mum where you've been all morning.'

Chris didn't have his father's talent for lying. He couldn't bring himself to look his mum in the eye. 'I've just come back from Kemptown Nick. I went to Jeff Walters's flat in town this morning. The police were waiting for me.'

'I don't understand,' said Jacqui. 'What's this got to do with Dave?'

Russell got to his feet again. If it kicked off, he wanted to be able to shut Jacqui up. 'I got the word last night,' he said.

'What word?' she asked. 'From who?'

'Never you mind,' said Russell. 'But I didn't go steaming in, Jax. I tested it out first, to see if it was kosher. I met up with Dave at the weekend and I gave him a spiel about the deal I was putting together with Jeff for five kilos. I told him I was sending Chris over to Jeff's flat to pick up the gear today.' Russell paused. He looked down at Chris. 'Go on,' he said. 'Tell her.'

'I'd just turned up at Sillwood,' Chris said. 'I was sitting with Jeff in his flat when the Drugs Squad kicked the door in.'

Jacqui looked from her son to her husband. 'They arrested Chris?' she asked. 'You let them arrest Chris?'

'Of course I fucking didn't,' said Russell. 'Because there *was* no deal.' He took a drag from the Sobranie. 'But Dave didn't know that, did he. As far as he knew, Chris was there to pick up five kilos of heroin. If you're caught with that kind of weight, Jax, it's a 'piracy charge and a six-year jail sentence.' Russell took another drag. 'Your brother sold us out,' he said. 'He sold out his own flesh and blood.'

115

'He couldn't have,' said Jacqui. 'It must have been someone else.'

'Who?' said Russell. 'No one else even knew that Chris was going into town this morning.'

'What about Jeff?' said Jacqui, clutching at straws now.

'Even Jeff didn't know,' said Russell triumphantly. 'We didn't tell him anything. He thought Chris had turned up for a chinwag.'

Jacqui shook her head. She couldn't believe what was happening. 'Dave was scared, Russ. He wasn't blind. He knew you didn't trust him.'

'Turns out I was right, then,' Russell said.

'That doesn't make him a grass, though.'

'Don't it?'

'Please tell me where Dave is,' Jacqui pleaded. 'Please say you haven't done anything to him.'

'I told you. Dave's skipped. The cops must have told him about what happened at the bust. Believe me, Jacqui, I've done the ring-round already. No one knows where the cunt's run off to.'

Jacqui turned to Chris. 'Do you know anything about this?' He looked away. He couldn't bring himself to meet her eyes, although this time it was a different kind of shame, more akin to guilt. The memory of what he and his father had done to David Gillespie was far too fresh in his mind. 'Chris, Dave is your uncle.'

Russell had heard enough. He stepped over to Jacqui. 'Yeah. That's right. And Chris's uncle just tried to get him sent down for six fucking years. How's *that* for family loyalty? Now piss off out of my den. Me and Chris have got work to do.'

116

Jacqui looked helplessly from Russell to Chris and back again. Both of their expressions were stony and unrelenting. She had no choice. She left them to get on with it.

Minter pulled his car into a residents-only parking space on Lower Rock Gardens. It was a safe but down-at-heel neighbourhood, where the red-brick Victorian suburbs met the seaside stucco of Georgian Kemptown.

As soon as he got out of the car, a text clanged onto Minter's phone. It was from Chief Superintendent Roberts ordering him up to the Park for an urgent meeting. The slaying of an undercover police officer at the racetrack was still all over this morning's newspapers, including the nationals, and the text Roberts had sent sounded urgent. The super wanted the inside track on Operation Windmill.

A uniform was standing outside number 42. As Minter slipped on his overshoes and smoothed on a doubled pair of gloves, he exchanged a few words. 'Young lad,' the constable told him. 'Looks like a straightforward OD.' Minter walked down the steps to the basement flat.

The half-glazed front door was unlocked. In the hallway, Minter noticed a liverish smell. Lying on the rickety old hall table were a couple of letters. The first was contained in a handwritten envelope. It had already been opened. The other, still sealed, was a bill from a utility company. The name on both envelopes was the same. Minter's mobile rang. It was the Brighton and Hove despatcher. She told Minter that the pathologist would be busy all day. Alan Day's post mortem had been finished, but there was Gillespie to do as well. Minter wondered how much death one day could hold. He asked for a police surgeon to attend instead.

Then he read out the name on the envelopes and asked for a PNC check. He cut the call. To his left, there was another open door.

Inside the bedroom, the curtains were partly drawn and the room was in heavy shadow. From the doorway, Minter caught his first sight of the body. He took a few paces into the silent room. The deceased was lying on the unmade bed, naked from the waist up, his chest was sunken and pale. The lower part of his body was still entwined in the bedclothes, although his left foot was sticking out from underneath the sheet and his body was twisted, as if he'd been making an effort to get out of the bed when he finally slipped into unconsciousness. The young man's left arm had fallen over the side. It extended almost to the floor. One of the fingers pointed accusingly at a blackened spoon on the threadbare carpet. His face was turned towards Minter, the sleepless eyes looking down.

The dead man was young, like the uniform had said. Little more than a child. About eighteen or nineteen, Minter reckoned. There was a purple-blue swelling under the cheek that was pressed against the pillow. Minter recognised hypostasis: the blood cells sinking into the parts of the body nearest the ground. Gravity keeps on working, he remembered, even after you're dead. Outside, the seagulls started to shriek. The weather was beginning to break at last and they were heading out to sea.

Minter made a search of the room. On the table beside the bed, there was a tube of lubricant and a large pack of condoms, most of them missing. He walked over to the wardrobe and opened its sagging door. Underneath a few hanging clothes, there was a square plastic storage box.

Inside that was an assortment of sex toys – outsized dildos, butt plugs, plastic beads. A rent boy's stock in trade.

Minter turned. He looked down at the track marks along McFarland's arms. Not too far gone, then, he thought, that the young man couldn't still find a good vein. Minter's mobile rang again. The police surgeon would be there in a couple of hours, the despatcher informed him, and the occupant of the flat was known to the police, too. Eighteen months ago, James McFarland had been arrested on suspicion of soliciting. 'It didn't go to court,' the despatcher continued, reading off the screen. In the background, Minter heard the tapping of a keyboard. 'CPS knocked it back for lack of evidence.' Tap, tap, tap. 'He's a runaway with two convictions for possession.' Tap, tap, tap. 'All a bit predictable.' A sigh. 'Anything else you want to know?'

'No,' Minter said. 'Thanks.' He ended the call.

Dirty hits and accidental overdoses, Minter thought as he pocketed his mobile phone and looked at the body of the deceased. In Brighton, they happened at least once a week. Minter looked around the room again. It all added up – the contents of the cupboard, the needle on the floor – and the despatcher was right: everything about James McFarland's short life was grimly predictable. A rent boy and a junkie, McFarland was a person on the edge of the light, an outcast from both his family and society, the lowest of the low. Flotsam and jetsam, his death had happened such a long way downstream of Russell Compton that it would be easy to pass it by, just like Beckett had passed by Anna May. No one had ever been charged for Anna's murder. She didn't have any tearful parents to keep her death in the public eye and the police team on its toes. Anna was an orphan, a nobody.

Right now, Minter was aware that he was holding Tom Beckett's future in his hands. What Minter had found out about Windmill this afternoon was enough to put an end to the SIO's career. It wasn't just the stuff Vicky had told him about the flawed surveillance regime up on Dyke Road; it was something much more worrying than that, something that went straight to the heart of the whole operation. If Roberts were to find out about it, he would shut down Windmill immediately and Tom Beckett's police service would finish in ignominy and disgrace. Perhaps that was what it deserved.

A noise drew Minter's attention away from the bed and towards the window. Through the gap in the curtains, he glimpsed a grey suit coming down the steps towards the basement, and a few moments later, Detective Constable Connolly appeared in the doorway of the bedroom.

'Minter,' he said sounding surprised.

'Good to see you, too, Sean,' Minter replied sardonically.

Connolly smiled. 'I picked up the call from the car.' He glanced at the dead body on the bed. 'There's a little bit of pure knocking about at the moment. Thought I'd take a look-see.'

Minter explained who the young man was. 'The police surgeon could be a while, he's in Chichester.'

Connolly paced around the room. He opened the door of the wardrobe and looked at the box on its floor. He wrinkled his nose in disgust. Pushing the door to again, Connolly went over to the bed and picked up the spoon in his gloved hand. 'Well, then,' he said, putting it back down on the worn carpet. 'No point us both standing here twiddling our thumbs. Why don't you get off?'

Roberts was waiting for Minter at the Park. The super hated officers who failed to be punctual. 'You sure?' Minter asked Connolly.

'Yeah, yeah, Like I said, I want to follow up on the pure. Put the word about. I'll finish up here; then the uniform can do the babysitting until the doc arrives.'

Minter hesitated. When he glanced down at the corpse for the last time, it was as if James McFarland was trying to tell him something important. He hesitated. 'I want to sign off all the paperwork – scene-of-death report, the autopsy, the coroner's papers, all of it. I want this done properly.'

Connolly looked at Minter. 'What makes you think it won't be, DS Minter?'

Minter looked at him. 'No reason.' He took his car keys out of his jacket pocket. 'Thanks, Sean. I owe you one.'

Connolly grinned. 'I'll hold you to that,' he said.

# 6
· · ·

'I have lots of different names,' said the big man in the
pinstriped suit. He glanced to his right where four
terracotta-tiled church steeples rose high above the cobbled
streets of Tallin Old Town. It could be in Italy, thought
the fat man in the suit. 'But you can call me Rita.' Evening
was coming on and there was a distinct chill in the air. They
were definitely in northern climes and Rita was glad he'd
worn this suit, a handmade by Gresham Blake, Brighton's
most fashionable tailor, whose shop was in the Laines. The
dark cloth had a wide chalk stripe running through it, just
like Rita had Brighton running through him. 'Thanks for
lunch,' he said, his mouth still tainted by the slimy fishiness
of the eels. 'It was' – he considered how best to describe the
Estonian delicacy – 'nutritious.'

The two men were walking through a little park. Young
couples still dallied on the grass, and someone was playing
a guitar. Ahead of Rita, at the water's edge, a giant roll-on-
roll-off passenger ferry was sliding out of the narrow channel
into the Baltic. Rita glanced across at Emile. The other man

was thin, with fair hair and red-raw patches on his cheeks. In another life, Emile would have been a good fuck, he thought – a little bony, but lithe and loose-limbed all the same.

'You have docks like this in Brighton?' asked Emile.

'No,' smiled Rita. 'We do have piers, though.'

'What is "piers"?' asked Emile.

'It's an English peculiarity. We build them for our amusement – they have bars and funfairs, games arcades, that kind of thing.'

'Arcades,' Emile repeated. With his right hand, he made the shape of a gun and pulled an imaginary trigger. 'Shoot-'em-ups.'

'That's right,' Rita said.

'I am looking forward to my visit.' Emile's mobile went off and he answered it, talking quickly in Albanian to whoever it was on the other end of the line. Rita had heard nothing like this language before. Albanian sounded half European and half Asian, but Rita was used to being neither one thing or the other, so he could relate to that. Emile closed his phone. 'Alan Day is dead.'

In the movement of Rita's eyelids, there was the hint of a flutter, but he nodded courteously. 'That was very efficient.'

Emile waved a hand. 'Our guy was in the UK. But this other man at the racetrack, this Tyler, he was *polizei*?' Rita nodded and Emile's expression hardened. 'So they are close to your organisation?'

'The sadly missed Alan Day used to work for a man called Russell Compton. This Compton has become the target of Operation Windmill and ever since he became a

123

police target I've had nothing to do with him. Russell Compton is on the way out.'

'But Brighton is a small city and that means the police know something about you.'

'No,' Rita insisted, 'it doesn't mean anything of the kind. Believe me, I know a lot more about the police than they know about me.'

Emile looked at Rita. The Englishman had a domed head that was entirely bald and in his left ear he sported a silver earring. Emile didn't like him at all – if it was up to him, he'd butcher the fat pederast right here and now and slew his guts into the cold sea. But Emile's bosses had instructed him to cut a deal and there was a lot of heroin to offload in a very short period of time. 'Good,' he said. 'But police interest increases the risk for us, and that increases the price.'

'Really?' said Rita. 'After what happened in Amsterdam, I thought I was the one taking the risk.'

Emile waved that away. 'Holland is finished for us. The route has too many middlemen and too many arrangements to make, which shrinks the quantities. No, Rita, we are looking for wholesalers who can take big amounts in just one delivery.'

'But the Balkan route has risks of its own. There'll be new border guards and new drivers. How do I know the heroin will even get into Europe?'

Emile nodded at the scene in front of him. 'Because it's already here.'

The huge red-and-black hull of the container ship loomed out of the water, its name written on the prow in Russian, its immense, flat deck absolutely empty. On the dock alongside, two lines of articulated lorries were waiting to start loading their containers. The drivers at the back, knowing they were going to be some time, had got out of their cabs and were standing on the tarmac, smoking cigarettes and chatting. A burst of laughter and the sound of another Eastern European language fluttered over on the breeze to where Rita was standing.

Rita smiled back at Emile. 'Then I'll be in Scotland to greet it.' Right on cue, one of the seven cranes lining the dockside groaned into metallic life.

Of all the drug-dealing gangs, the Albanians were the most feared, their vendettas the stuff of underworld legend. Even the Yardies Rita dealt with in London were afraid of the Albanians. They weren't just vicious, though; they were smart, too, and that was why Rita was so keen on dealing with them. The Albanian smuggling gangs never deadheaded. On their way up the Silk Road, some of the lorries parked on the Tallin dockside would have stopped off in the former Soviet republics to pick up illegal immigrants. They'd have taken them to the cities of northern Russia, where they were worked as forced labourers or put straight into the sex trade. In Moscow, the trucks would have been reloaded with the white heroin en route to Western Europe from Afghanistan. Now the trucks were here, idling by the Baltic, ready to load their precious cargo onto a ship bound for Scotland.

'Tell me about the money,' Emile said.

'Six and a half million euros will be in your offshore account tomorrow morning, the other half as soon as we've unloaded the ship.'

'OK,' said Emile. 'It is agreed.' Behind him, on the open

125

sea, another giant passenger ferry was turning into the port. Even at this distance, they could hear its chugging engines. 'In five years' time, Tallin Port will be twice this size and that park will be another dry dock. We have ambitions, Rita, and we want you in on them.'

Rita nodded. He watched the crane swing the first container off the truck. When they left the docks here, the trucks would pick up Russian guns to sell back to the Afghan warlords who had sold the white heroin to the Albanians. It was a slick operation and nicely diversified. Narcotics, migrants, weapons, the three most valuable commodities on the planet and the things that made the world go round. 'I've got ambitions, too, Emile,' said Rita. This one deal was going to make him the biggest heroin wholesaler in the entire UK market. Overnight, he was going to quadruple his money.

On summer evenings, Brighton people began to live outside. New Road, once a narrow, congested street in the heart of the city, had recently been paved over in two-tone grey brickwork to create a kind of elongated piazza. The Pavilion stood on one side of the newly pedestrianised street, the elegant, eighteenth-century Theatre Royal on the other. In the middle, all the bars and restaurants had set up tables. Waiters in starched white aprons buzzed around taking food orders.

Minter was standing on his own outside the Mash Tun pub. He'd come here straight from his meeting with Chief Superintendent Roberts, who had asked him lots of questions that Minter had tried to avoid answering. The super was an

126

intelligent officer, though. He could see straight away that Minter was being evasive.

Next to Minter on New Road, a table full of office workers laughed at an in-joke. On the other side of the street, a boy dressed in a pair of Bermuda shorts, his skateboard tucked under his arm, greeted his friends in a series of high-fives. Minter looked up the road towards Church Street, where Vicky Reynolds said she'd be parking her car. It was Vicky's suggestion to meet up for a drink when they both finished their shifts, but she was nowhere to be seen. It surprised Minter how much he wanted to glimpse her tall figure coming through the crowd towards him.

He'd just rung Irene at Kidz Klub. The locksmith had been and gone, there were three new cameras, inside and out, and the alarm system had been rigged up. Irene sounded a lot happier now that Kidz Klub was going to be open in the morning as usual.

Minter thought about the two long years he'd spent working at HQ after leaving Whitehawk. It had started small – just a few figures missed off the end of the calculations of the weekly crime stats. He thought it was a mistake and brought it to Roberts's attention, but was surprised to be told to let it go through to the final report. After that, he learned not to question such things, shunting the figures around to make them add up the way the super wanted. Later that year, Brighton and Hove was awarded its third star on the basis of improved performance. The super was given an even larger office and more staff, and on his personal recommendation, Minter was made a sergeant.

Occasionally, Minter got bored with what he was doing and he continued to have his qualms about it, too, because he knew the figures were beginning to tell a very different story from what was going on at street level, but every time he requested a transfer Roberts turned him down. Minter was far too important to the Force, the super said, for him to become just another grunt. All along, Minter realised now, Roberts had been playing him, leading him by the nose of his own ambition. The super had given Minter exactly what he needed: patronage and promotion and, above all – or so it seemed to Minter at the time – protection.

When Minter looked up from his thoughts, Vicky Reynolds was standing right in front of him. 'Hi,' she said. 'You look like you're miles away.'

'Yeah,' Minter said. 'I was just thinking about Windmill.' He gave Vicky the glass of red wine. 'The bar's heaving, so I took the liberty of getting us both a drink.'

Vicky took the glass. 'Thanks.' With her free hand, she pulled out a DVD in a clear plastic case and gave it to Minter. 'I had the surveillance tapes from Dyke Road enhanced, and I've reminded Beckett to rotate the drivers.'

'What about the Shogun?' Minter asked. Russell Compton's car had been hauled in this afternoon and given the onceover by Forensics.

'*Nada*,' said Vicky. 'They must have switched cars on their way up to the Downs. Both Chris and Russell have got cast-iron alibis for the early hours.'

Minter nodded. 'No surprise there, then.'

'What about you? Anything to report?'

'I got sidetracked. Beckett sent me to an OD in Kemptown. Connolly thinks it might have been some of the pure that's knocking about at the moment.'

Vicky nodded. There'd been lots of rumours about

Number 4 heroin coming into Brighton for the first time. 'You partnered up with Sean, then, Minter?' The police force attracted a lot of men like Connolly – ignoramuses who got turned on by the uniform, by the tribal thing – but Vicky already knew that Minter wasn't like that. The only thing was, she wasn't sure what Minter *was* like. 'Seems an unlikely combination.'

Minter smiled. 'Connolly's not the sharpest tool in the box.' Changing the subject, he asked, 'You worked Kemptown, didn't you?'

Vicky nodded. 'Last year.'

'Did you ever come across a heroin dealer called Michael Lambert?'

'Lambert's been part of the Kemptown scene since for ever. He's small-time, though. What are you interested in him for?'

Minter explained. 'I'm doing a new Target Profile for Russell. The picture of the dealing network is fairly complete. Lambert's in there, all right, but he's something of an anomaly.'

'How do you mean?'

'He doesn't fit with the prevailing culture of the Compton organisation. Apart from Lambert, all the dealers are of a piece with Russell Compton himself. They're white working class and they've all got convictions for violence. Michael Lambert's none of the above.'

Vicky Reynolds nodded. 'You mean he's queer?'

When Minter smiled again, his piercing blue eyes softened a little. He had a sense of humour after all. 'That too. And older. No matter how sophisticated the criminal organisation

129

gets, in the end it's still just a gang.' He drank some of his orange juice. 'A bit like SOCU is a gang.'

Vicky stuck to the point. 'Kemptown's a village. It's nothing like the seafront. It's the Pink Planet up there. Lambert knows it well – he's been on the scene a long time and he knows the clubs and the punters. So maybe Russell just lets him get on with it. The only thing that counts for Russell Compton is the money he gets from the deals.'

Minter nodded. 'You're probably right.'

But Vicky's interest had been piqued as well. 'This Kemptown OD, was it something to do with Lambert?'

'Maybe,' said Minter. 'The deceased's name was James McFarland, aka Jimbob McFarland. He probably bought gear from Lambert.'

'Name rings a bell,' said Vicky, wracking her brains for details of the case. She couldn't find them, though. 'A lot of the rent boys are users.'

For some reason, Minter went quiet. Just like in the surveillance flat, there was something inaccessible about the new DS, something locked down, cut off. 'What's wrong, Minter?'

Minter wasn't used to people asking him questions. 'I had another row with Beckett.'

'About what?'

'I interviewed Chris Compton.'

Vicky laughed. 'Is that all? You're a detective now, Minter. You're getting stuck in. Good for you.'

'It was after the formal interview had finished and Chris Compton's brief wasn't in the room. I didn't get the SIO's permission, either.'

Vicky raised her eyebrows. 'I can imagine what Beckett thought about that. So why did you do it?'

Minter shrugged. 'I'd met Chris years ago when I arrested him for possession. I suppose I wanted to see if I could get a line across.'

'And did you?' In the surveillance flat, Vicky had spent a lot of time listening to Russell knocking seven bells out of his son. Chris Compton was still only seventeen, so there was hope for him yet, but if his dad carried on treating him that way, Chris would just become vicious.

Disappointed, Minter shook his head. 'Not a sniff.'

Vicky still couldn't blame him for trying. 'You know, what you just said about SOCU was right, Minter. It *is* a gang. And sometimes it's hard getting accepted.' She looked down into her glass. 'I'm afraid word's got round about you. Everyone in the squad knows about Kevin Phillips.'

Beckett must have told the other officers, Minter thought. Windmill's SIO had been blackening Minter's name right from the get-go. 'That's all I need.'

'Is it true?' Vicky asked. 'Did you make a statement to the panel?'

'I told them the truth. That's how it's supposed to work, isn't it?'

Vicky looked at Minter. There was a time when she had seen things in black and white like that, but not anymore; now everything had turned a dirty shade of grey. 'Kind of. But what *did* you see at that drugs bust, Minter?'

'I saw the Alsatian dogs go into the room. They came out a couple of minutes later with nothing. Not a single thing. Then Kevin Phillips goes into the bedroom to take a look for himself, and when he comes out, he tells the dog handler to put the Alsatians in again. This time, it's a different story, because this time the officer emerges from the room with a plastic bag full of rocks. You tell me, Vicky. How could that have happened?'

Vicky hesitated. 'It was a raid, Minter, and raids are chaotic at the best of times.'

'I was an observer, Vicky. It was my job to notice what was going on.' He paused. 'Beckett talks about the SOCU clean-up rate being the best in the division. Perhaps now we know why.'

Vicky shook her head. 'I've been in SOCU a lot longer than you have. Kevin's not like that. He wouldn't plant evidence.' She remembered Connolly's story about the bouncer from the Madrid nightclub. 'There might be one or two cowboys on the team, but I've never seen anything corrupt.'

'There's something else,' Minter said.

'What?'

He hesitated, wondering if he could trust her, wondering, in fact, if there was anyone he could trust in Kemptown. 'It's ExCal. Something's wrong with the database.'

'You're telling me,' Vicky snorted. 'Bloody thing's always offline.'

'It's more than just a teething problem.'

'What is it, then?'

'The ExCal passwords give SOCU officers different priv-ileges,' Minter explained. 'The intelligence they can access depends on the level of their security clearance. The CHIS module is very heavily restricted, for example.'

Vicky nodded. CHIS stood for Covert Human Intelligence Source, the part of the database that should have been the most secure of all because it was where the details of every informant were stored, along with the intelligence they provided and what they expected in return. 'Go on,' said Vicky.

'I need to talk to IT. It might be just a glitch in the software, but some of the officers in SOCU are able to make enquiries on restricted parts of the system – areas they shouldn't be able to see at all.'

Vicky shrugged. 'So the database doesn't work properly. Report it and get it fixed.'

'But think about the implications,' Minter said. 'Dave Gillespie was a CHIS and that's where the intel about Sillwood was kept. Gillespie is dead and Sillwood went belly up. And then there's Ray Tyler – don't forget he was a CHIS, too. If this is as bad as it looks, it might be that Tyler's cover was blown before he even set off for the racetrack.'

'So whose fault is all this?'

'DCI Beckett was responsible for the implementation of ExCal. It was Beckett who assigned the wrong passwords.'

'But who's making the enquiries? Do the records show that?'

'A few names come up more than most,' said Minter.

'Who?'

Minter shrugged. It seemed that he couldn't – or wouldn't – say. Vicky shook her head. 'Beckett's crap at computers. He can hardly work his laptop. Maybe this is just an honest mistake.'

'I hope it is. Because that's a whole lot better than the alternative.'

Vicky hesitated. 'Beckett's not a techie, but he's a hell of a good SIO. Tom Beckett's got policing in his bones.' For the first time, though, she felt scared. A leak from the mobile surveillance units was one thing. All it would have taken would be for one of the drivers to tell his wife the shift pattern and for her to then tell someone who she shouldn't have. But this was something else. The whole operation was compromised and Ray Tyler's wife had lost her husband, his two kids had a lost a father. 'That was why you spoke to Chris Compton without telling Beckett, wasn't it?' Vicky asked Minter.

'That's right,' he said.

Vicky shook her head. 'This is huge. You can't just keep this to yourself. You've got to tell someone, or your neck will be on the line.'

At his meeting with Roberts, Minter hadn't breathed a word about the potential security breach. If he had, Roberts would have pulled the plug on Windmill and before that happened, Minter wanted to be sure. 'I have told someone, Vicky. I've told you.'

'This is way above my pay scale, Minter. Don't get me involved.'

'Don't you want to find out why Windmill's such a mess?'

'Of course I do, and believe me, I want to send Compton down as much as anyone does.'

'So what do you think?'

'I think I need another drink,' said Vicky. She glanced down at Minter's orange juice. 'I think you need a drink as well. A proper one.'

'I'll have a pint of Harveys,' Minter said. It was his

favourite tipple, a beer brewed just a few miles away in the county town of Lewes.

'Harveys it is,' said Vicky, taking Minter's glass and going inside the pub.

The bar was as busy as Minter had said it would be. The crowd were a little bit alternative, but good-natured with it. There were a few crusties and a smattering of goths. Feeling hopelessly overdressed in her black skirt and jacket, Vicky took up a position near the end of the bar, where a young woman was doing her best to serve the crush.

The barmaid got to her early. Vicky ordered the beer and another Merlot. 'Sure,' said the young woman breezily, fetching the bottle from the rack behind her. Vicky watched the wine pouring into her glass, thinking she was beginning to develop too much of a taste for it. If it was true that SOCU was a gang, then it was also true that the cost of entry was high. Waiting for the drinks, Vicky thought about Minter. He wasn't like Connolly, that was for sure. Minter was clever and perceptive and his only blind spot seemed to be the way his colleagues saw him. Minter seemed to care about what he was doing. There was something in his expression when he talked about the OD that reminded Vicky Reynolds of why she'd decided to join the police force. There was a determination to discover the truth, and there was something else, too, something that looked suspiciously like compassion.

'There you go,' said the barmaid, putting down the wine and the pint of beer on the counter.

'Cheers,' said Vicky, wondering if she was developing a taste for Minter as well as Merlot.

When she'd been in uniform, Vicky had dated one or two

of her fellow officers. They were good guys for the most part, but none of the relationships developed into anything because the men just didn't interest Vicky enough: they were too limited. So she promised herself that her next boyfriend would not be a serving officer, but that had been over a year ago now and so far she'd met no one.

Outside, Minter watched the workaday crowd disperse with quick waves goodbye and a few jokes thrown over shoulders. Then they went their separate ways to the bus or to the train. It was the time of day when the beachfront was at its best. The magic hour, photographers called it, when the sea was calm and the light was the colour and softness of vanilla ice cream. Minter imagined what it would be like to sit on the beach with Vicky, that light sculpting her features. After work on summer evenings, that's what couples did – take a bottle of wine down to the beach and sit there watching the waves and the sunset. It had always seemed like such a simple thing to do. Minter slipped a finger between two of the buttons on his shirt and touched the St Christopher he was wearing and thought about Anna May and the child he'd once been.

At Hillcrest, Minter opened the gate at the bottom of the back garden. He felt happy, happier than he had been for a long time, and he flew down the steps two at a time and ran out onto the hillside. It was an even hotter day than yesterday and he took off the school jumper he was wearing and tied it round his waist. Three times now, Charlie had ignored him: once last night when the older boy was coming out of Anna May's room across the hall and bumped into Minter on the stairs; again this morning when Minter had been

136

brushing his teeth in the bathroom; and once again just a few minutes ago when Minter had stuck his head round the door of the office and found Charlie talking to Clements. Three times since yesterday Charlie had had the opportunity to do something to Minter and each time he hadn't bothered. It was Anna. Anna had done it. First she'd got Minter's St Christopher back and now she had stopped Charlie hurting him. Anna was a miracle worker and now Minter didn't have to lie awake in his bed anymore, dreading the thud of Charlie's boot on the top stair outside his bedroom. He didn't have to skulk around the house, trying to keep out of everyone's way, doing his best to make himself invisible.

At the bottom of the hill, Minter crossed the makeshift bridge and ran along the line of trees. He was going to thank her and he wasn't going to flinch away from her touch this time. He'd made up his mind that he was going to let her know exactly how grateful he was for what she'd done and how much he liked her.

Sure enough, through the same hazel thicket of branches and heart-shaped leaves, Minter saw Anna's red-and-black checked top. 'Anna!' he called out, pushing his way into the clearing.

She was lying asleep on the bank of the little stream, her back turned to Minter. In one of the shafts of sunlight that penetrated the trees, a dragonfly darted over the surface of the water. 'Guess what!' Minter said excitedly, kneeling down next to her and stretching out a hand. He shook her shoulder gently, not enough to wake her up but enough to roll her body over.

Anna's face was all but unrecognisable. There was blood all over it and the bones were smashed, an edge of splintered jaw showing white through her chin. Minter felt sick and he couldn't breathe properly. Not knowing what to do, he stood up and ran out of the thicket, the branches scraping at his face as he went.

Minter pounded onto the track that skirted the fields and he didn't stop running until he had reached the coast, three miles away. By that time, his clothes were soaked through with sweat. He stood on the top of the white cliff and gazed over the waves.

For the second time that evening, Vicky interrupted Minter's melancholy thoughts. 'There you go,' she said, handing Minter the pint glass.

Minter covered up the emotion he was feeling by taking his first sip. 'So tell me about Beckett,' he said to Vicky. 'What's Roberts got against him?'

'Roberts and Beckett go back a long way. As far as Beckett is concerned, Roberts isn't even a proper cop. He's just a jumped-up civil servant – a bureaucrat. On the other hand, Tom Beckett is the super's worst nightmare, because he never gets his budgets in on time, and when he does hand them in, the forecasts are always wrong.'

'There's got to be more to it than just the paperwork.'

Vicky nodded. 'Beckett's standing in the way of the reorganisation of the division. He's fighting it with the senior team tooth and nail.'

'Are you talking about the merger with Surrey?'

'If it goes ahead, Brighton and Hove SOCU will be disbanded and everyone will lose their jobs. That's you and me as well, Minter, not just Beckett. And for what?'

'The Crime Squads have to work across the borders. We can't be parochial anymore. Organised crime doesn't stay in one place, so neither should we.'

Vicky smiled. 'You have spent too long up at Division, haven't you, Minter? Sussex Police has got to cut five million pounds this year. That's what this reorganisation is all about – saving money and breaking down the old constabularies so the Home Office can exert even more control over us all. And try to imagine what the effect will be locally, Minter, when there's no Serious Crime Squad based in Brighton. What's that going to do to the city, especially now the Hangletons have started a turf war with what's left of Compton's empire?'

Minter could see what Vicky was saying – the body count was rising by the day.

'That's the real reason why everyone's so suspicious of you, Minter. They think you're here to give Roberts more ammunition for the merger. And come to think of it, this stuff about ExCal is just the thing he needs.'

After his meeting with Roberts this afternoon, Minter knew that it was true. In his office at the Park, the super hadn't asked a single question about the contribution intelligence was making to the success of Windmill. The only thing he was interested in was Beckett and the operation's many failings. 'I told you this morning, Vicky. Roberts might think I'm still working for him, but I'm not. I'm working for Windmill.'

'I believe you,' said Vicky, 'but it's not me you've got to convince. It's the likes of Kevin Phillips and even Sean Connolly.' There was a silence. 'Anyway,' Vicky said, 'tell me your secret, Minter. How come you became a DS at such a tender age?'

'I did the NIM training last year. Windmill's my first operation.'

'They certainly threw you in at the deep end.' It made sense, though. A lot of officers had kick-started their careers with the National Intelligence Model. It was the biggest Home Office initiative of recent years and at the time , there'd been plenty of seminars and conferences, plenty of promotions. Vicky was ambitious and if she'd been quicker off the mark, she'd have done the same thing. But with the cutbacks it looked like she'd missed that boat, too.

Minter looked up and down the street. He didn't want to talk about work anymore. 'Do you come from Brighton?'

'Close to,' Vicky said. 'Hurstpierpoint.'

Hurst, as it was known, was a comfortable commuter village on the other side of the Downs. 'Posh,' said Minter.

Vicky smiled. 'That's what people always say.'

'What did your parents think when you told them you were giving up law to be a cop?'

'I argued about it with my dad for months, but I won in the end. I'm stubborn like that.'

'He didn't like the police?'

Vicky laughed. 'Oh, no, Dad liked the police, all right. My father was a superintendent in the Met.'

'The Met, eh?'

'My dad came up the hard way. He worked a beat in Hackney for five years before he went into uniform. And he didn't pull any strings for me, either, if that's what you're thinking.'

When she was a little girl, Vicky's father was her hero. She loved the smart blue uniform he wore – the sharp creases in the trousers, the brightly coloured ribbon that ran across the top of the breast pocket of his jacket, the shiny peaked cap that he tucked under his arm. She knew that his job was to protect the capital city from crime, to make it safe for all the families that lived there. In a way, he wasn't just Vicky's hero, he was everyone's.

'Is he still around?' Minter asked.

Vicky shook her head. 'He had a heart attack, just after he retired.'

'I'm sorry,' Minter said.

'It happens like that, doesn't it?' she said. 'Dad always worked under such a lot of pressure. He never stopped. As soon as he retired, I suppose it all caught up with him.'

Minter wondered if Vicky had been so quick to defend Beckett because in some way Windmill's SIO reminded her of her father. 'He must have been proud of you, Vicky, when you joined the Force. You were following in his footsteps.'

'Yeah, deep down I think he was. You should have seen him the day I passed out of college. He couldn't keep the grin off his face.' Vicky looked at Minter. 'What about you? Do you come from a police family?'

It was the question Minter always dreaded and the one he usually sidestepped. This evening, though, he decided not to. 'I grew up in care. I haven't seen either of my parents since I was six.'

'I had no idea,' said Vicky. Suddenly, the reasons for

141

Minter's reticence had become clear. 'God, that must have been hard.'

'At times.' There were so many things Minter wanted to tell Vicky about his childhood. 'My mother had some kind of breakdown. They said she couldn't look after me anymore.'

'What about your dad? Wasn't he around?'

Minter shook his head. 'From what I was told, he got out as soon as he could.'

Vicky could see that Minter was uncomfortable. 'So what made you join the police?'

'When you're eighteen, they kick you out of the home. You're on your own and there's nowhere for you to go, with no routine and no one to look after you.' He shrugged. 'I'd done OK at school, so the day of my eighteenth birthday, I caught the train to Shrewsbury.'

Vicky nodded. She must have been at the police training college a year or so before Minter. She remembered all the orders and the marching about, the strict regimentation around waking and sleeping and even eating. After the comforts of her home and the freedom of university, it all came as quite a shock to her. For Minter, it seemed, things were different.

'I felt at home straight away,' he said. 'Everything about it was familiar. The dining hall and the dorms and the people always there to tell you what to. I loved it, in fact, and passed out top of my class.' He looked at Vicky. 'That's me all over, you see. That's my secret: I'm a conformist. I do what I'm told and these days that counts for an awful lot. It's why I did so well up at Division, although, in case

142

you're wondering, I didn't transfer into SOCU for the sake of my career.'

'Why are you doing this, then, Minter? Why *are* you here?'

Minter thought about it for a moment. It had something to do with feeling bad about all those crooked statistics he'd compiled for Roberts, and something about his nagging suspicion that Tom Beckett was a better officer than he seemed, but most of all it was because of Anna May. The teenage girl had stuck up for Minter when no one else had, but there'd been no one there to do the same for her. He'd found her by the stream, her face bloodied and her body broken, murdered by an unknown hand. Now Minter wanted someone punished for the crime. 'It's my conscience, Vicky. I suppose that's why I want to be in SOCU. Like you, I'm trying to make a difference.'

Exhausted, Tom Beckett arrived home that evening at nine o'clock. Climbing the stairs, he went into the bathroom, turned on the overhead light and looked in the mirror. There was yellow-black bruising beneath his eyes, and his nose was a complete mess, its swollen tip an angry red. Its nostrils were packed with dried blood, and when Beckett squeezed the bridge, the stabbing pain made him wince. Despite all this, the blow to his pride was far more painful.

Looking into the mirror again, Tom Beckett brushed his fingers through the hair around his left temple. About a year ago, he'd noted the appearance of his first strand of grey and it was still there now, although hidden by the old black. Wondering why the rest of his hair hadn't followed suit, Beckett took a closer look at the renegades. They weren't really grey; they were white. It was like something out of a fairy tale, he thought. The shock of losing Julie had actually turned his hair white.

Beckett switched off the light and left the bathroom. He crossed the blue-shadowed landing and went inside the bedroom he had shared for so many years with his wife. He went over to the window and looked out. The small lawn was surrounded by deep beds where, years before, Tom and Julie had planted out the rose bushes and azaleas and rhododendrons. The garden was in bloom now – the red dahlias, the tall yellow sunflowers – but when he took a closer look, Tom could see how withered they'd become under the day-long assault of the sun. The soil was parched and the lawn was overgrown.

Closing the curtains on his neglect, Beckett went to sit on the side of the double bed. Every man's life ended in failure; he had realised that a long time ago. He'd even reconciled himself to his strength diminishing, his ambition beginning to shrivel, but nothing could have prepared him for this last twelve months. There didn't seem to be any milestones in his grief. He didn't go through stages, like people said he would. For Beckett, every single day was the same. It felt like he was walking along the bottom of an endless sea.

He listened to the silence in the room. 'What am I going to do?' he asked it. Beckett sighed. 'I've made a mess of everything,' he said, staring down at the carpet. Outside, the birds had stopped singing, settling down in their nests for the evening. Tom remembered the day they'd taken Julie from her ward into intensive care. It had all happened so quickly. Now he wiped his eyes and said, 'You must have been so scared, but I never even talked to you about dying, did I? I let you down there as well.'

Beckett sat there for a minute or two, listening to what she would say. 'Yeah,' he replied. 'You were way ahead of me there, girl. Years ahead, as per usual. We should have had a baby. If we'd had a baby, maybe I wouldn't be so lonely.' The tears slid down Beckett's cheeks as he thought about what having a son would be like. 'Do you know what it was? Do you know why I was so against the idea? It was because I couldn't stand the thought of sharing you with anyone else. Yeah, that's the truth of it. That's how stupid I was, Joolz. A big, jealous kid, that's me.' By now, the room was dark. 'Yeah,' he said. Julie was always Beckett's conscience, always his better half. 'You're right about Minter, too. He's just trying to do his job. And maybe he's got something to offer.'

Anna May. That was the name Minter had used in the interview room at Kemptown. Beckett remembered the name very well. Anna was a murder victim, Beckett's first, and she'd been killed at a kids' home in Brighton. It had been a bad case, ugly and flawed.

There was a creak from downstairs. A wind started catching the door that led from the garage into the kitchen. Beckett must have left it open again. Let them try it, he thought. I can deal with a burglar at least. The wind moved the door a second time. In the silence, it sounded like the creaking timber of a ship lost somewhere far out to sea. There it was again. The sound, Beckett realised, was what he himself had become. A ghost ship, becalmed, adrift, waiting. Another long and sleepless night stretched out before Tom Beckett and he'd measure out every awful minute until, finally, the sickly grey light would trickle in through the gap in the curtains and tell him to rise again and begin the day.

'Did you?' Beckett asked the darkness. 'Did you know how much I loved you?'

# 7

## ...

T he next morning, Paul Dempsey strode into a beachfront bar and club. Passing all the empty tables, he walked up to the circular bar in the middle of the long room. A clink of beer bottles came from behind the counter. A head bobbed up. Young girl. Ponytail. She smiled. Then the smile disappeared.

At first, from a distance, it looked like Dempsey had just nicked a bit out of his eyebrow. It was the fashion. Close up, though, you could see the pale line left by the machete. The scar was still a little red at the edges and in cold weather it felt scratchy. It slanted across Dempsey's forehead, leaping the crevasse of his left eye socket, appearing again on his cheekbone only coming to a halt at the very edge of his lips. It was a mighty scar, like a crease in his face. It was as if he hadn't been born at all, just unfolded.

'Pint of Stella,' Dempsey told the girl. She was about to object that the bar wasn't open yet, that they were just setting up, when he shot her the glance. Obediently, she fished a glass out of the steaming washer.

As he waited for her to pull his drink, Dempsey listened to the low rumble of traffic over their heads. The club was housed in a tunnel running under the busy seafront road. He took a proper look around. The walls were grey-painted bricks and even this morning the sunlight struggled to reach the back of the room where the DJ hut had been built on a platform overlooking the dance floor. A lot of cash must come across this bar at the weekends, Dempsey thought. That was cash he could use to wash his new profits in. He could retail the drugs on club nights, as well, coke and pills, stuff that was new to him. You put your fingers in as many pies as possible. That was good business.

'Cheers,' he told the girl, picking up his pint from the bar. He replaced it with a tenner and walked away.

Dempsey was in an expansive mood. He was feeling good about the way things were going. He would do whatever it took and that was the other secret of success in his line of work, doing whatever it took. He strolled outside into the sunshine and, putting on his wraparound shades, walked onto the shingle, choosing the table closest to the shore. The sea glittered and the morning air was hushed and the world was Paul Dempsey's. As he sat down, a faint scream carried over from the rollercoaster and Dempsey's gaze tracked back down the length of the Palace Pier until it met the land at the Steine. On the other side of the roundabout, like a sentinel standing at the beginning of the road leading to Kemptown, the chrome and glass profile of the Van Alen Building rose up from the pavement. Sunlight bounced off its metal balconies, sending Dempsey's eyes even higher, up to the million-pound penthouse. That was where he was heading, he thought: straight to the top with nothing to stand in his way. He raised his lager in a private salute.

He lowered his gaze again, to where a couple of men were walking towards him along the boardwalk. Immediately, he recognised the loping walk of his cousin, and next to him was the spotty guy, the one with a face like a pizza, the one whose name Dempsey always forgot. He finished his beer. The business of the morning was about to begin.

On another part of the seafront, Tom Beckett was having his breakfast, too. He hadn't slept a wink. At four o'clock, he'd gone downstairs and made himself a pot of tea. At six, he'd sent a text message, and now, at the open-air café on the promenade near his house in Hove, he collected his mug of coffee and his round of white toast and went to sit at one of the tables near the back. Even though the tide was turning, the sea was calm.

Near to Beckett, a grand old lady of Hove was sitting in a fur coat, a spoiled-looking Chihuahua lapping milk from a saucer at her feet. At a table by the green windbreak, a white-haired man with a beard was holding court. Beckett recognised him straight away – there weren't many characters in Brighton whom he hadn't met during the course of all the years he'd been a police officer in the city. This guy owned a jeweller's in the Laines and he'd once furnished Tom Beckett with some valuable intelligence on one of Brighton's most prolific burglars. Sitting next to the jeweller was a woman in her sixties with sagging jowls and an expensive brooch; the ageing triumvirate was completed by a balding, doddery-looking man listening intently to every word the jeweller said. Perhaps that was what he'd do once he'd finally retired, Beckett thought: sit here at the café with a couple of cronies blethering on for hours. He turned away in time to see Minter walking towards him along the promenade from the direction of the pier. He kept his eyes on Minter all the way over to his table.

'I got your text,' said Minter, looking at the nasty bruise on Beckett's face. 'It sounded urgent.'

'It is,' Beckett said.

There was an awkward silence. 'I'm going to get a coffee,' said Minter. 'Do you want anything else?'

'No, you're all right. I'm sorted.' Tom Beckett was a proud man. He could count on the fingers of one hand the number of times he'd asked anyone for help.

All the way over to the counter, Minter could feel Beckett's eyes drilling into his back. As he waited for the filter coffee to be poured, Minter turned round to scope the place Beckett had chosen to meet. There was a lot of space between the tables, which meant their conversation was going to be very private. Minter remembered his conversation with Vicky Reynolds outside the Mash Tun. At the very best, the cock-up with the database was a piece of gross incompetence on Beckett's behalf; at the worst, well, the worst made Beckett a very dangerous man indeed. Perhaps, Minter thought, he would have been wiser to have come here this morning wearing some kind of wire.

He collected his coffee and made his way back to the table. Away from his natural habitat at the Kemptown station, Tom Beckett looked smaller and older, and along with the customary belligerence, there was a terrible sense of sadness in his face when he looked up at Minter. Just before they parted company at the Mash Tun, Vicky Reynolds had told Minter that Beckett was over the worst of his grief, but now Minter somehow doubted that was true. When he sat down, he couldn't stop himself from looking again at the damage he'd done to Beckett's face.

'I'm not going to be entering any beauty competitions,' Beckett said, noticing his stare, 'but you don't have to worry – my nose ain't broken.' Beckett ate the last corner of toast and rubbed his hands together to get rid of the crumbs. 'Phillips is interviewing Russell Compton at Kemptown now,' he said. 'It won't get us anywhere, but I just want to wind him up a bit, keep him on the boil.' Beckett took a sip of his milky coffee, put down the mug and considered the young man in front of him. 'We didn't exactly get off on the right foot, me and you.'

'No, sir, we didn't.'

'You were right about Sillwood Crescent, Minter. That drugs bust should never have happened. My problem is that I'm too Old Testament. It's still an eye for an eye, a tooth for a tooth. That's why I went after Chris Compton too, to get back at Russell for what they did to Ray Tyler.'

Minter nodded. 'They take out one of ours, we take out one of theirs.'

'That's right,' said Beckett. 'Stupid, really.' After the fight in the interview room, Beckett had done a little digging. He'd spoken to a couple of people he knew up at Division and he'd called Vicky Reynolds late last night. 'Tell me about Kidz Klub,' he said.

'I went there yesterday. Someone had trashed the place and I think it was the Hangletons, sir.'

Beckett nodded. 'Could be. But I don't want you to tell

151

me about the break-in, Minter. I want to hear about what you did to get the youth club off the ground in the first place.'

'I was beat officer on Whitehawk back then. This woman, Irene Shaw, she came to see me one day saying she wanted to do something for the kids on the estate. She had loads of great ideas for what the club would be like, but she didn't have any money or any contacts.'

'So what did you do?'

'I asked the football club if she could use the Portakabin on the playing fields. After they said yes, I got the council to fix it up properly – put in heating and windows. When Kidz Klub opened for business, we couldn't believe it. The youngsters came in droves.'

'There was probably nothing else for them to do on the estate,' Beckett put in.

'That's right. I put a knife bin into the Portakabin, and when I emptied it on a Friday, it was always full. We took hundreds of blades off Whitehawk that way, and even a few guns. After that, we started talking about a proper building, some kind of permanent base. It took two years, but we did it.'

Beckett was impressed. Whitehawk was the hardest place in Brighton to get results in, and there weren't any careers to be made out of policing the estate. 'There was me thinking you were just one of Roberts's bean counters,' he said.

'I didn't want to leave Whitehawk, but what was I going to do? Knock back the chief superintendent? Stay as a PC?'

Beckett nodded. There was a time when he'd been ambitious, too. 'Why did you pull the Murder Book on Anna May this week?'

It seemed like Beckett had a lot of friends in Kemptown. 'She died at Hillcrest,' Minter said.

'I know. It was July 1995 and she was beaten to death with a claw hammer. In 1995, I'd just been promoted to DCI. Anna May was my first murder investigation.'

'I've looked at the Murder Book, sir. There were over-sights.'

Beckett bridled. 'Name one.'

'The fibres on Anna's clothes.'

'There was a partial match with the fibres on a jacket owned by one of the other kids at Hillcrest. I interviewed him myself. An older boy, name of Charlie Banks.' Minter nodded. 'Nasty piece of work, Charlie was. I fancied him for it all along. Charlie had a beige Harrington. You know the sort – blouson jacket with a tartan lining on the inside, like the skinheads used to wear in the 1980s?' Minter nodded again. He remembered the type very well indeed. 'But at the time, jackets like that had come right back into fashion. They were in all the shops – there were thousands of them.' Beckett shook his head. 'We had a right go at Charlie Banks, but we couldn't find anything else to tie him in.'

'What about the semen Scene of Crime found?' Minter asked. 'Why wasn't that ever tested?'

'It was.'

'Why isn't the forensic report in the file, then?'

'It was seventeen years ago, Minter but believe you me, that sample got tested. It belonged to a man named Clements.'

Minter was surprised. He was sure that it would have turned out to have belonged to Charlie Banks. Giving the older boy sex, he'd assumed, was the way Anna had got

Charlie to stop hurting him all those years ago.

'Clements ran Hillcrest for the council,' Beckett said. 'Clements was a right nonce: we established that he was regularly having sex with at least one other underage girl at Hillcrest. Anna May had Clements's semen in her, no question of that, but it was at least a day old, and Clements had an alibi for the day of the murder as well. He used to moonlight running a business on Woodingdean High Street, a pet-food shop of all things. The day of Anna's murder, Clements was at his shop premises from the morning until mid-afternoon and a lot of people saw him or spoke to him. By the time Clements got back to Hillcrest, Anna was already dead.'

Minter thought about the way Clements used to leave the house shortly after breakfast. It seemed that Hillcrest was just another business he was running, another source of income. Minter thought, too, about the brand-new clothes Anna May always had, like the red-and-black checked shirt. Now he knew where Anna got them from.

Beckett finished his coffee. 'We prosecuted Clements for the sex offences and he ended up in Lewes Jail. Here's hoping he had a bad time.' He looked at the young DS. 'You must have been just a kid when Anna was killed.'

'I was. I was living at Hillcrest.'

Beckett sat back in his chair. 'You're full of surprises today, aren't you?'

'Anna May was kind to me,' Minter explained. 'She helped me through a difficult time. I owe her and I want to reopen the investigation.'

Beckett looked doubtful. 'Like I said, seventeen years is an awful long time for a case to go cold. You're going to have to find a new piece of evidence, something that wasn't available to me at the time.'

'I'll get the new evidence,' Minter said.

Beckett liked the determination he heard in Minter's voice. Minter was going to need that if he was ever going to be a real investigator. And Beckett had to admit he was more than a little drawn to the idea of finally nailing Anna May's killer. There was a host of new forensic techniques that hadn't been available to him back then, and now there was Minter, too. If it came to it, Beckett thought, he would do it on his own time. 'Tell me what you know about Charlie Banks, Minter.'

'Mr Clements was the house father, but it was Charlie Banks who really ran the home. He was Clements's eyes and ears when Clements was away. Charlie kept the kids in line.'

'How?'

'The usual.' Minter pulled a pack of cigarettes out of his pocket. 'Do you mind?'

Beckett realised that Minter had been another victim of Charlie's bullying and intimidation. 'Go ahead and smoke,' said Beckett. 'To tell you the truth, it's nice to know you've got one vice at least.'

Minter lit his Benson & Hedges and smoked for a few moments. On the other side of the promenade, the sea was all the way in, but the waves were still little more than ripples as they tumbled over onto the nearby shingle. 'I think there was something going on at Hillcrest. Something more than all the violence and abuse.'

'What?' Beckett asked. Even at the time, Beckett had a funny feeling about the case: he knew that there were things he didn't properly understand about the circumstances of Anna May's death. Then again, his copper's nose, that instinct Beckett had developed over time, could be a funny thing.

Minter shook his head. 'I don't know.'

'But you think that whatever it was has got something to do with Anna May's murder?'

'Yes.'

'You know, Minter,' he said, 'I thought you were fast-track-graduate stuff, the kind of geek who's ambitious to the point of being a right pain in the arse, but you came up the hard way. If anyone's got the right to feel proud of what he's achieved, it's you. I'll tell you something else, as well. I owe Anna May just as much as you do, maybe even more. That murder was my first case as SIO and no one ever went down for it. It's been riling me ever since, even used to keep me up at night. So I'm going to help you find out who killed her, Minter, but you've got to do something for me in return.'

Minter began to understand what it was about Beckett that inspired such loyalty in SOCU. 'What's that?'

'I'm not going to let Windmill crash and burn. Anna May was my first investigation and Windmill was meant to be my last, so I'm not going to draw a blank on this one, too. I'm going to put Russell Compton away for a very long time indeed.'

'What do you want me to do?'

Beckett leaned forward. 'You asked me yesterday if Gillespie was the source for the bust on Chris Compton at Sillwood Crescent.' Minter nodded. 'Well, he was, but Gillespie's always been on the money before.'

156

'So why did Chris Compton turn up carrying just a pack of duty-frees?'

'You've heard the surveillance tapes. Russell Compton has had his doubts about Gillespie for months, ever since we took down the stash house in Whitehawk. I think Russell was using the bust at Sillwood to test Gillespie out.'

Minter nodded. Beckett was thinking along the same lines as he was. 'Russell feeds Gillespie a little bit of gossip about a deal going down between Chris and Jeff Walters.'

'Then he sits back to see what happens.'

'Gillespie passes on the gossip to you,' said Minter. 'Then along comes the Drugs Squad, right on cue.'

'Bingo,' said Beckett. 'Now Russell knows that Gillespie's the grass.'

'But Gillespie was killed on Monday,' said Minter. 'That was *before* the raid on Sillwood Crescent.'

Last night, Beckett had had a lot of time to think it through. 'So for some reason Russell didn't need the proof, after all. Perhaps he got the word from someone else, someone who knew for sure that Gillespie was a grass.'

'If Gillespie was your source,' said Minter, 'who was Russell's?'

'That's what I want you to find out.'

'Why me?'

'The more I think about it, the more I'm convinced that we've had a leak at Kemptown for a long time. You're new to Windmill, Minter, and that makes you the only officer on the squad I can trust. You're smart, too, which helps – you know your way around the intel. But we don't have a lot of time to do this. I've got a meeting with Roberts up

157

at the Park this morning and I've got a very good idea of what he's going to say to me. He's been itching for an excuse to take Windmill away from SOCU and what happened at the racetrack gives him the perfect opportunity to do just that. Then Roberts is free to turn Brighton and Hove SOCU into another one of his efficiency savings – at which point, Russell will walk away and all that hard work on Windmill will have been for nothing.'

Minter had seen the duty rosters; he didn't need Beckett to tell him how hard the SOCU officers had been working on this operation, but these days that didn't count for much. The meeting of targets was what got rewarded now, the grim, bureaucratic charade as supervised by Minter's old boss, Chief Superintendent Roberts, for whom the piling up of amenable data mattered a whole lot more than the piling up of dead bodies. It was time for Minter to work out where his own loyalties lay – to his old boss or his new one, to Roberts, who had made his career, or to Beckett, who had just offered to help him track down Anna May's killer.

'There's another thing you should know before your meeting with Roberts,' Minter said.

'Oh, yeah?'

'Those crime statistics you detest so much. They aren't all they're cracked up to be.'

'What do you mean?'

'I mean Roberts fiddles them.'

Beckett sat up. 'You mean the crime stats that come out of Division are bent?'

Minter nodded. 'Like you said when we first met. Mangled.'

'Fuck me,' Beckett chuckled. 'Can you prove it?'

Minter thought of the rows of HMIC reports lining the bookcase in his office. 'Yes, I can.'

Walking down the hallway of the quiet house at Dyke Road, Jacqui Compton stopped outside Chris's room. The door was ajar, so she stuck her head round. When she saw he wasn't there, she went inside.

It was a big room, with fitted wardrobes along one wall and another wall with shelves packed with electronic goodies like an Xbox and a flat-screen Panasonic. Jacqui let Chris buy whatever he wanted for his room because it was her way of making it up to him. As she looked around, she tutted at the teenage lair, a plate or a glass on every single surface and clothes strewn all over the floor. Russell had sacked the Polish maid a couple of months ago because he didn't want any strangers in the house and this was the result. Chris wouldn't even notice the mess. He was just a big kid.

That stunt Russell had pulled on the seafront with Jeff Walters – there wasn't going to be a charge, but it would have been enough to put Chris in the frame with the police. Chris had had some scrapes with the law before – what boy his age hadn't? – but now he was involved with Russell, Jacqui feared for his safety. The violence inside the house was one thing. There'd always been fights between Russell and her and, far too often, Chris caught it as well, but all that was nothing compared to what occurred outside the house. Outside the house, people got killed.

Hesitating in the doorway, Jacqui wondered where her

brother, Dave Gillespie, was. Russell was capable of anything, especially if he thought Dave was a grass. That kind was the lowest of the low, way beyond the pale. Jacqui wasn't stupid. There were a lot of things she turned a blind eye to, but she knew very well there was a good chance Russell had been lying through his teeth when he insisted Dave had skipped town. And Jacqui had a good idea that Chris knew more than he was letting on about where her brother had been taken.

Jacqui walked over to the pile of clothes Chris had abandoned last night by the side of the bed. Fishing out a pair of jeans, she held them up in her hands. The denims were new on, still a little stiff from the washing machine, not soft and grubby like usual. Her hands trembling a little, Jacqui turned them to the light coming from the windows but couldn't find any marks anywhere, nothing to show where Chris had been the night before last. She slipped her hands in each of the pockets, looking for a scrap of paper with an address, or a mobile she could search for a number but all she found instead was a foil-wrapped condom and a pack of giant Rizlas. The shame of it was that Jacqui had no idea who Chris's girlfriend was. No strangers in the house, that's what Russell insisted on. Sighing, Jacqui put the condom and the Rizlas back in the jeans pocket.

Outside the room, Chris's light, barefooted steps padded up the stairs. Jacqui wasn't properly in the hallway by the time he made the landing and the jeans were still in her hands. Chris glared at her. 'What are you doing in my room?'

Jacqui thought about saying she'd been tidying it up, but

160

they both knew she wasn't that kind of a mother. 'You seen my sports bag, love?'

Chris walked towards her. 'No idea, and, anyway, what the fuck would it be doing in my room?' He pushed past her, not wanting to give her another chance to ask him about Dave, but Jacqui put a hand out to stop him, her fingers brushing against his chest. 'What?' said Chris. He hated it when his mum looked at him like that – the pleading, pathetic face.

'Please, Chris. Dave's family.'

Chris couldn't look at her. If he did, he might blurt out what his dad had done to Uncle Dave out on the Downs. 'I told you, I don't know where your brother is,' he said.

'I'm begging you, Chris.'

Stomping into his bedroom, Chris threw himself onto the bed and grabbed one of the Xbox controllers from the table where he'd left it. 'Look, Mum, I'm busy right now.' It was true. In less than an hour, he was supposed to be meeting Stevie Elliott in town. It was going off just as his father had said it would: there'd be another change of car; then Chris would drive up to the Downs on his own to dig up all the gear. Chris pointed the controller at the media cabinet and a moment later dark shadows started circling the television screen and sci-fi music dripped menace into the room.

Jacqui was standing over him. 'I just want to talk to you, Chris.'

A dustbowl planet somewhere in a distant solar system loomed out of the TV screen.

'We used to talk all the time when you were little.'

The game had started now and Chris's fingers were

pushing and prodding expertly at the controller.

Reaching down, Jacqui grabbed the contraption out of his hand. 'Listen to me!'

Outraged, Chris sprang off the bed and onto his feet. 'Fucking well give it back!'

'Please, Chris, I want to talk to you. I've got to talk to someone.'

Chris gave up reaching for the controller. 'Why do you *think* I never speak to you?' he yelled. 'It's because you're fucking pissed all the time, Mum. You can't even string a sentence together most days.'

Jacqui threw the controller down onto the floor and the little black box smashed into pieces. 'It's no wonder I take a drink every now and then. It's living in this house that does it!'

Chris laughed in her face. 'Now and then? That's bullshit, Mum, and you know it. You're a fucking drunk!' Jacqui raised a hand to slap him. 'Just you try it.'

There was a silence as Jacqui stared at her son. He was taller than she was and capable of hitting her, of beating her up, just like his father. And Chris was right about the other thing, too, about Jacqui being a drunk. Always had been and always would be. She put her hand out to touch Chris's face. At first, he flinched; then, as if it was for old times' sake, Chris let her fingers brush his cheek. 'You were such a lovely little boy,' she said. 'I told Russell he could do whatever he had to do, as long as it didn't involve you. That's the agreement we made, Chris, all those years ago when the money started rolling in. I've been a bloody awful mum since then, I know that, but I always did my best.

162

That's why I'm still here, Chris. That's why I put up with that pig.'

Chris was repulsed by his mother's hypocrisy. Since when had she ever tried to protect him from his father's temper, his father's fists? 'You don't have to worry,' he lied. 'I don't deal gear, Mum. A few bits and pieces to mates, maybe, at the weekend and that, but that's all.'

Jacqui shook her head. 'This isn't about a little bit of weed, Chris. Can't you see what it is that's happening? Russell's using you. Like he uses me to launder the money. Like he used Dave to hold the gear.'

'This is a family business. Dad needs my help.'

Jacqui smiled sadly. 'That makes you feel important, does it? Makes you feel like a man?'

Chris looked at her. 'Yeah. As a matter of fact, it does. I certainly don't need you looking after me.'

Downstairs, the front door opened. Russell was home from the police station. 'Anyone at home?' he roared up the stairs. The great Russell Compton hadn't been interviewed under caution for years. He'd be furious and there'd be a price to pay and Jacqui knew who was going to pay it.


Sunlight filtered down from the canopied roof of Brighton Station as the train from London Victoria came to a slow stop. There was a moment's silence before the doors opened and the platform filled with loud holiday voices.

A couple of young women got down from the last carriage. Both of them were wearing short skirts and crop tops, exposing their bodies to the hot, dusty air inside the station. The tightness of their skirts meant the girls had to step sideways, one leg at a time, down onto the platform. When they'd done it, they turned to each other and brayed with laughter before tottering off towards the turnstiles.

Stevie Elliott got off another train. His one hadn't travelled down from London – it was a local service from Portslade – and Stevie wasn't in Brighton for a good time. He'd come here to do a job of work.

One by one, the London passengers pulsed through the automated ticket barriers, the two girls waiting at the back of the throng. 'Fucking hell,' one of them said, reading the text she'd just received. 'He's only already here.'

Stevie was just behind them now and he could taste their cheap perfume in the back of his throat. He was twenty-seven, but he looked at least twice that age, his face pinched and his body emaciated. It had been years since Stevie had been with a woman and these days he couldn't even get a proper hard-on. The pair of girls wouldn't have even given him the time of day.

The one with the phone shuffled closer to the ticket barrier. 'Ocean Rooms tonight,' she said to her friend. 'It'll be well fucking kicking. Bar goes on till four o'clock.' A space opened up at a turnstile to the left of them. She grabbed her mate by the hand. 'Come on.'

Stevie didn't usually pay for railway tickets, but today was different. He didn't want to have to talk to anyone official, not even a poxy ticket inspector, so he'd bought a ticket. The metal machine snatched the thin piece of card and shot the barrier and Stevie was through. He walked under the stern Victorian clock suspended from the ceiling of the station and hurried on towards the exit.

Outside the station, the two girls from London stepped

into the strong sunlight. 'Fucking hell,' said the leader. 'I think we've got too many clothes on.'

Her mate gave a little laugh. 'Yeah, right.'

The first girl fetched her mobile out of her tiny handbag. She rang her boyfriend and grimaced. 'Oh, you are shitting me,' she said in disgust. 'Fucking message service, innit.'

The second girl was looking straight down Queen's Road. 'Wanker.'

The traffic lights changed and the two girls crossed the road as quickly as their heels and skirts would allow. 'Any idea where the fuck we are?' asked the one with the mobile.

'Not a clue,' said the other one.

The first girl said, 'I'm gonna fucking well kill him.'

Queen's Road had been doing this for decades, sucking people off the trains and propelling them giddily down to the sea. Arm in arm, the girls clattered along, passing estate agents with too many pictures in their windows, and recruitment firms with too few jobs in theirs. Finally, cresting a rise in the road, they caught sight of the sea. Just a lick of blue, that's all there was, framed by the Odeon and a hotel at the bottom of the hill.

A couple of hundred yards behind, having paused at the newsagent in the station to read the front-page story about Dave Gillespie in the *Argus*, Stevie Elliott had forgotten all about the girls. The Hangletons were taking over. For weeks now, Dempsey had been pulling small-time dealers like Stevie into alleyways, telling them to buy their drugs from him – and only from him – or to take the consequences. Now, with David Gillespie murdered, the stakes had risen yet again.

Stevie tucked himself closer into the stream of people

heading for the seafront and told himself he'd only be in the city for an hour or so, just long enough to pick the car up from the King's Road and drive it back to the multi-storey in the middle of town. Leave the keys in the ignition and piss off and that was all there was to it. He wasn't even breaking any law. A pub Stevie knew came up on the right. In the absence of skag, he thought, a drink might be enough to steady his nerves, so he went inside and walked up to the bar and ordered a Southern Comfort. He looked around. It was a dark, cavernous place, red leather sofas lining the walls, and apart from Stevie just a couple at the other end of the bar. The big fella's biceps were bursting out of his T-shirt. Stevie's drink arrived and he took a nip of the amber whisky. It was hot and sweet and turned his mind over. A couple of years back, Stevie Elliott had his own little thing going on. There were three of his boys punting it out on the streets, while Stevie stayed at home in Portslade, chopping away, skimming off the top. But Stevie hadn't been ruthless enough and he'd got too wrecked to keep an eye on how often his so-called boys were ripping him off, so now he was back on his own, and down to zero. Despite his years of addiction, he retained a little store of leftover loyalty. Russell Compton had always seen Stevie all right, even though Stevie stepped on his gear to within an inch of its life. He owed Russell Compton this one favour.

In the pub, the record changed. Nervously, Stevie pulled his phone out of his pocket, his hand shaking as he did so. He might not own much now – fuck all, in fact – but he still had a cool phone. Stevie wasn't carrying, but he knew he could score somewhere near here because if there was any skag at all left in the city, it would be on the seafront right now. He called a number, but it didn't answer. Stevie finished the Southern Comfort and walked outside.

Outside, the pavement was solid with people, all sliding down the hill, barely making room for Stevie to join them. The drink had only made things worse. His eyeballs felt peeled. The crowd swept past the Clock Tower and as they crossed the road into West Street, the weight of their numbers brought a long line of cars to a complete standstill. The group of lads walking next to Stevie had scrubbed up for the day, their hair freshly razored and gelled. They were cussing each other. At the bottom of the hill, most of the crowd turned left, heading towards the pier. Just a handful of people turned the other way with Stevie and soon even they had disappeared, leaving Stevie to walk on, almost on his own. The heat of the day was stacking up and not a breath of a breeze came off the diamond sea. Feeling more exposed than ever, Stevie quickened his pace. There was metered parking all along the seafront road and he tried to remember the registration plate he was looking for. It ended with a J and there were two fives. Stevie remembered that all right because five was his lucky number. At last, he found it. The door was open, like they'd said it would be.

Sitting in the driver's seat, Stevie reached up. The ignition key fell down from its hiding place in the vanity mirror, just like they said. It bounced against Stevie's knee, landing somewhere in the dark footwell. 'Fuck it,' he said, bending forward and groping on the floor with his hand.

The passenger door opened and Stevie sat up as a man got into the passenger seat. Straight away, Stevie recognised the long, livid scar running the length of Dempsey's face. 'Where we going, Stevie?' he asked.

'I been trying to ring you, Paul,' Stevie stammered.

Dempsey nodded. 'I'm not that hard to get hold of. I mean, I know my number's not in the book, but most people don't find it too difficult, not judging by all the calls I've been getting. Seems I'm very popular all of a sudden.' He turned to Stevie and grinned. 'You didn't call me, though.'

Stevie's bowels turned to iced water. 'No, straight up, Paul, I've had enough of Russell's gear. It's shit. I swear I wanted to see if you could put a brick my way. I've got the cash and everything.'

Dempsey reached up and scratched the scar that ran down the middle of his face. 'That's very nice of you, Stevie. It's always encouraging to see our customer base expand.'

Stevie's hands were shaking so much that the keys rattled and jingled. He was praying Dempsey didn't ask him about the motor. If he found out Stevie was running an errand for Russell Compton, then it really was all over. 'What is it about, then, Paul?'

'You're not the only worthless cunt who made the wrong decision about who to back in our little business dispute with Russell Compton. In fact, I think it's time someone was made an example of. So I'm going to throw a little party today, and do you know what, mate? You're the guest of honour.'

# 8
...

'Have you been in the wars, Tom?' Chief Superintendent Roberts asked Beckett.

In the super's office, the two men faced each other across the big desk in the middle of the room. 'You mean this?' asked Beckett, pointing a finger up at his own face. Roberts nodded. 'I fell off a ladder at home,' Beckett told him. 'Dangerous thing, hanging pictures.'

'I can see that,' Roberts said, examining Beckett's face more closely.

The chief superintendent began to peruse the report in front of him and Beckett took a moment to glance around the room. There was Scandinavian blond-wood furniture and beige walls. Blandly expensive or expensively bland – Beckett couldn't decide which it was – but modern, certainly. The super was the very model of a modern senior officer.

Roberts looked up from the piece of paper on his desk. 'Were you aware, Tom, that last month Windmill took up fifty-eight per cent of SOCU's total allocation of D time?'

'No, sir, I wasn't. But then again, Compton is this city's

most dangerous criminal, so fifty-eight per cent sounds about right.'

'Other SOCU operations are being neglected,' Roberts said.

'Then give us more manpower.'

'I already have done.'

Beckett smirked. 'Oh. That was what Minter was for.' He pantomimed looking at his watch.

Roberts sat back in his chair. He brought the tips of his fingers together and regarded Beckett over the arch. At their meeting yesterday, Minter had been surprisingly unforthcoming and Roberts had wondered if the young officer had fallen under Beckett's spell a little. 'Now you come to mention it, how is your new DS getting on?'

For a moment, Beckett studied the polished silver epaulettes on the shoulders of the super's uniform. 'Minter's doing fine.'

Roberts nodded. 'A senior intelligence analyst is a valuable asset, Tom. I hope he's getting to know the operation inside out.'

'I think DS Minter would agree that he's being stretched,' said Beckett.

'Good.' Roberts leaned forward. 'Let's talk about the murder of David Gillespie. How close are you to making an arrest?'

Beckett told him about the quality of the Comptons' alibis and about Forensics drawing a blank on the Shogun. 'We're checking CCTV from the roads out of the city.'

'That will take time,' said Roberts.

'We've got good tyre prints from Scene of Crime,' said Beckett.

'It's not a lot, though, is it, Tom? I mean, the car itself will have already been through a crusher. What's left is probably on its way to China.'

Beckett clutched at other straws. 'SOCO used the cooling of the chassis to establish the time of death. It looks bad at the moment, but we can turn it round.'

Roberts sighed noisily. 'I only wish I shared your confidence, Tom.'

The super's use of his first name was getting on Beckett's nerves. It was yet another of the affectations he would have learned at some crappy piece of management training, the same place he'd learned everything he knew. 'I've always delivered before.'

'Yes, I know,' said Roberts. 'Best clear-up rate in the division and all that.'

'It happens to be true.'

Roberts stared at the ageing, obstreperous DCI. 'The car pursuit of Alan Day from the racetrack could have been a disaster. The driver of the cab Day hit when he was trying to get away is still in intensive care and you were very lucky there weren't other casualties. It's Pride this weekend, Tom, and Brighton will be packed again. Remember that your first duty is ensuring community safety.'

'The community,' said Beckett, 'will be a lot safer once Compton is behind bars. And just in case you didn't notice, the racetrack *was* a disaster: we lost an officer.'

'I know that,' said Roberts between gritted teeth. He looked out of the window, trying to calm himself. 'This stuff about community safety, community cohesion,' he said, looking back at Beckett, 'it's all a foreign language to you, isn't it? You've never really adapted to change, Tom, and that's why you're still a DCI.'

Beckett could see he was being got at, but he couldn't help himself. 'I know exactly what community cohesion means. It means whatever the *Daily Mail* wants it to, and it means delivering peace of mind to the middle classes, a bit like Ocado does, only more expensive. And I'll tell you what else it means.'

'Oh, yes?'

'It means cooking the books,' said Beckett.

Roberts put his head on one side and looked at Beckett. 'What are you saying?' This was a lot more serious than Roberts had thought. It seemed that Minter hadn't just discovered an unlikely taste for crime-fighting, he was intent on damaging his old boss, too. Well, if the worm had turned, it would have to be crushed underfoot.

'Just a rumour, sir,' said Beckett, backtracking quickly. 'Something going round the canteen.'

Roberts's eyes narrowed. 'There isn't a canteen at Kemptown. I had it shut down, remember?'

'Oh, yeah. That "canteen culture" thing was bad for morale, wasn't it? We can't have officers actually talking to each other, or it might get in the way of all the paperwork.'

Roberts ignored the jibe. He'd deal with Minter soon enough, but right now it was Beckett's turn. 'I've got some news for you, Tom.'

At the end of a country lane stood a small, detached farmhouse. It was invisible from the road, hidden by several oak trees. Even now, when the sun was at its highest, their dense foliage cast impenetrable shadows over the scruffy-looking house.

To the side, there was a driveway where a handful of chickens clucked and strutted over the broken concrete. Their black, metallic eyes scanned constantly for food, beaks pecking furiously against the hard ground.

A fast-driven car turned up the lane and into the driveway. Squawking with alarm, the chickens flew up, scampering quickly into the undergrowth. The car engine roared as it was gunned past the side of the house and round the back, where it joined a collection of other big boys' toys. There were three mud-caked dirt bikes, two chunky-looking quads, a windowless Land Rover.

Upstairs in the house, in the middle of the small back bedroom, a naked Stevie Elliott was tied to a chair. The three Hangletons had bound his hands and feet, taped his mouth and gone to work, shattering his knees with a baseball bat and slitting his nostrils with a blade. Warming to his task, Paul Dempsey had taken time to gouge out the tattoo on Stevie's arm. *Mum*, it had read once. Now it was just a shred of coloured flesh lying on the floor.

Dempsey went over to the window. 'The car's here,' he said. 'Go and lend a hand.' The pizza-faced kiddie hurried out, leaving Dempsey alone with his cousin. Dempsey walked over to the chair. Looking up at him, Stevie Elliott started to shake. His bowels opened again. 'I know,' Dempsey coaxed, enjoying the extremities of his own art, interested to see just how far he could take this. 'I know, Stevie,' he repeated, watching the man's terrified eyes squirming in his face. 'I've heard it all before. And I believe you, mate, I really do. You're never going to buy off Russell

Compton again, are you?' Elliott shook his head desperately from side to side. 'From now on you're only going to score off of us, aren't you?' As quick as he could, Stevie Elliott nodded. He could feel his own blood gathering in his bound fingers. He heard a fat drop of it fall onto the floor. Blinking away the sweat, he looked up to see compassion shining in Dempsey's eyes. For the first time, Stevie started to believe that Dempsey was going to let him live.

'But it's like I told you,' said Dempsey. 'Your business isn't worth anything. Not a fucking thing. Most of it you shove up your own arm.' He looked down. 'Or into that pathetic little cock of yours.' From the corner of the room, Dempsey's cousin giggled. 'And what's left you cut with so much crap that no one wants it. Personally, mate, I wouldn't feed your skag to my dog.' Dempsey took a phone out of his pocket. It was Stevie's mobile. He pointed the viewfinder at Stevie Elliott's face and snapped a picture. 'And I don't even have a dog,' he added. He looked down to inspect the picture. Dissatisfied by the lighting in the first shot – it didn't show all the damage he'd done – he took a couple of steps sideways so he wasn't blocking so much light from the window and snapped another picture. 'You know, Stevie, I'm surprised that Alan Day let you get away with it. Alan must have been going soft for a long time now.' Dempsey looked at the second photo. It was much better. He smiled.

The door opened and the kid with the acne came back into the room. 'All ready,' he said.

Dempsey nodded. He turned to Stevie again. 'Cool phone, by the way.' Dempsey pressed a few more buttons, sending the picture to all the people on Stevie Elliott's contacts list. Russell Compton's name wasn't there, but someone would forward it to him. Stevie's mum's name was on the list, however. She'd be getting her copy straight away. Dempsey closed the phone. 'Let's go.'

The two other Hangletons advanced on Stevie Elliott. Bending down to untie the flex, they yanked him to his feet and dragged him from the room.

At the top of the stairs, Dempsey paused. It was good to have a place like this. Somewhere out of the city, somewhere private. But his boys kept it like a pigsty. There was crap everywhere, and the downstairs hallway was piled high with knock-off electricals. He'd have to tell them about that.

So many things to take care of, Dempsey told himself, as he strode outside the house. He patted the mobile in his pocket. Right now, everyone would be opening the photograph of Stevie Elliott. In all the shitty seafront bars where small-time smack dealers hid from the police, they'd be talking of nothing else. No one would want to cross Paul Dempsey again, that was for sure.

Outside, the pizza-faced kiddie and Dempsey's cousin had already stuffed Stevie Elliott into the car. Pizza-faced kiddie was leaning into the boot. He punched Stevie Elliott in the face. 'Cunt!' Stevie's head banged against bare metal then the kiddie hit him again for good measure. Dempsey's cousin was carrying a large cloth tool bag. He took out a household hammer and gave it to Dempsey, who had joined them at the car and was standing in the middle. The cousin took something else out of the bag, too, and gave it to Pizza-Face. It was a massive nail, an inch wide at the heft. Pizza-faced kiddie felt its weight for a moment before stabbing it into Stevie's shoulder. Dempsey brought the hammer down. With a sickening crunch, the pin went through the bone.

Stevie shrieked. The pizza-faced kiddie had to look away but Dempsey didn't. 'He's gone into shock,' Dempsey remarked dispassionately. He found moments like this interesting. 'Knees,' he said. 'Quick.' Pizza-faced kiddie took another nail from the bag and jabbed it into Stevie Elliott just above the knee. Dempsey whacked that one with the hammer, too.

'Where the fuck did those things come from?' Dempsey's cousin asked.

'The other knee,' said Dempsey. Pizza-faced kiddie did as he was commanded. 'It's railway gear,' Dempsey said. With the biggest blow yet, he smacked the head of the last nail with the hammer. He felt the tip of the spike bite deep into the metal of the chassis. 'They use them to lay down sleepers.' A low groan escaped from Stevie Elliott's lips. Dempsey stood back to admire his own handiwork. 'That'll do.'

Dempsey took the phone out of his pocket. Flipping the lid again, he captured another moment for posterity. He sent it, then slammed the boot shut. 'What time is it?'

'Two o'clock,' said his cousin.

Sweet, Dempsey thought. They had an appointment at the Van Alen Building at four. He had a good couple of hours to enjoy the racing.

By the time Vicky Reynolds walked into the Major Incident Room, most of the Windmill team had already gathered. There was no air-conditioning and the early afternoon sun was flooding in through the big windows. It was too crowded and too hot and instantly Vicky knew something was wrong. There was none of the usual ribald banter.

Vicky went over to perch on a desk beside Kevin Phillips. 'What's all this about?' she asked. 'Why the three-line whip?'

Phillips stifled a yawn. 'All I know is that today was my rest day. Martha's nine months old and in all that time I haven't had a single night's unbroken sleep.'

Vicky nodded. She looked around the room again. 'Where's Beckett?' It was an article of faith that the SIO was always first to arrive for briefings. One morning, not long after joining Windmill, Vicky had turned up at six o'clock to get some paperwork out of the way. DCI Beckett was already there, checking notebook entries from the day before.

Phillips shrugged. 'No idea.'

The low hum of the background conversation dipped as soon as the door to the MIR opened. It wasn't Beckett who came in, it was Minter. For an instant, his eyes met Vicky's. She looked away quickly, but Kevin Phillips had already observed the look that passed between them. 'Well, well, well,' he said under his breath, 'who would have thought it?'

'Don't be an idiot, Kevin,' Vicky said.

Phillips grinned. 'No, I think it's great. I think you'll be very happy together.'

'Anyone would think you were jealous, Kevin.'

Kevin Phillips looked at Vicky. 'Maybe I am.'

Vicky glanced away. Nothing, in fact, had happened last night. She and Minter had just finished their drinks and gone their separate ways. When she'd woken up this morning, though, Vicky had Minter on her mind. 'How's Fiona?' she asked Phillips.

Kevin smiled. 'She's good.'

Kevin had changed a lot since Vicky had known him in uniform – he was more cynical now and hard-bitten, as well as being patently less loyal to the woman who had become his wife – but Vicky still couldn't believe he was a bad man. She looked across to where Sean Connolly was standing near the door. With his short-cropped hair and hatchet face, Connolly looked a lot like some of the crims they talked about in here. If anyone in SOCU was corrupt, Vicky thought, it was going to be Connolly.

'Who the fuck's this?' Phillips said.

Another plain-clothes officer had followed Minter into the MIR. He was somewhere in his late forties and he carried a pot belly in front of himself and sported a goatee. Ten years ago, Vicky thought, that beard would have been considered racy. In full dress uniform, Chief Superintendent Roberts was next into the room. This was going to be important. Vicky looked across at Minter, who was standing in the corner, and wondered whether he had told the super about his suspicions after all.

The room settled down as the plain-clothes officer with the pot belly turned to face his fellow officers. 'Good morning, ladies and gents,' he began. 'My name is Detective Chief Inspector Slater. Geoff Slater.' Vicky cast her eyes about again and saw that Slater's first stab at making friends had not been successful. The reception got even more frosty when he announced, 'I'm from Serious and Organised Crime in the Surrey Constabulary, and I'm Windmill's new joint SIO.' Protests swept across the room – this was exactly what the SOCU officers had feared and Slater had to lift his voice above their noise. 'I'm bringing with me a team of five detective constables from Surrey to beef up the team. Now that the Hangleton gang has seen its chance, Windmill has gone critical. They're moving onto the seafront and Russell Compton isn't going to take that lying down. That's why we're taking pre-emptive action: we're going to hit the bastards hard before they get the chance to start a full-blown war. This afternoon, SOCU and Drugs Squad will be mounting joint operations in Whitehawk, in Kemptown and on the seafront. All of you are going to be involved. We're going to sweep the dealers off the streets.'

The rousing finish wasn't greeted with any enthusiasm at all. Next to Vicky, Phillips's hand went up. 'Yes?' said Slater.

'DS Phillips, sir,' the Brighton and Hove officer introduced himself.

'Yes, Kev?' said Slater. He'd done his homework, then.

'If you're SIO,' Phillips went on, 'where the hell is Tom Beckett?'

Chief Superintendent Roberts stepped forward. 'Unfortunately,' Roberts began, with an expression of pained regret stuck to his face like a tin badge, 'Tom Beckett has refused the offer of becoming joint SIO alongside DCI Slater. So this morning, I reluctantly accepted his resignation as Windmill's senior investigating officer.' Immediately, there was another outbreak of muttering and even, this time, some swearing. Roberts waited for it to die down. 'As you all know, Tom Beckett has been under intolerable strain this last year. I don't think he would mind me telling you now that I offered him a three-month leave of absence after the death of his wife. It's a measure of the man that he turned that down.' Looking round the room, Roberts fixed each and every Windmill officer in turn with his eyes. 'I know that losing Tom as your SIO will come as something of a shock, especially to those of you who have been in SOCU for a while, but perhaps it's time we all realised that even Tom Beckett has his limits. Beckett is still a DCI and is still on the Windmill team, but as you've just heard from DCI Slater, this morning sees a fresh start for the whole operation. With the arrival of the Surrey officers, I'm expecting a turnaround very quickly. You all have your part to play, so let's get on with it.' With that, he left the room.

Looking around, Slater could see the extent to which the chalice he'd just been handed had been poisoned. 'Right,' he said nervously. 'You heard the man. Let's get down to business.'

Back in his office, Minter drummed his fingers on the desk. He wanted to ring Beckett now, to offer him his help. Their relationship had begun in suspicion and argument and even a fight, but it was turning into something different now. It would have cut Tom Beckett to the quick to be forced to resign as SOCU's SIO. Last year, Beckett had lost his wife, and this year, it looked like his career.

There was already an email from DCI Slater waiting in Minter's inbox. He downloaded the list of the names and addresses of the targets Slater had selected for a visit this afternoon from the Drugs Squad. Most of them were already well known to Minter from the files, but none of them were major league. One or two were associates of Russell Compton, but as far as Minter could see, not a single one had links to the Hangletons, who were the real threat to public order at the moment. Arresting them wouldn't do any good at all. There'd be a decent photo in the newspapers tonight – the super standing behind a table spread with firearms and polythene bags of Class-A drugs – but clearing the seafront was a percentage game at best. It was the wrong call.

The door to Minter's office opened and Chief Superintendent Roberts came inside. 'Minter,' he said, carefully closing the door behind him. 'Glad you're here. Shame about Beckett, although, as you know, the SIO was way past his sell-by date.' Stepping over to the bookcase, Roberts ran his fingers along the thick bindings of the HMIC reports on Brighton and Hove's performance against Home Office targets. He chose one and pulled it out. It was last year's: the one that had earned the division its third star and the one that had earned Minter his promotion. Roberts flicked through the pages until he reached the back. He turned round. 'You drew up all of these appendices, didn't you, Minter?'

'Yes, sir.'

Roberts walked over to where Minter was sitting. Closing the cover, he flung the heavy report down on the desk, where it landed in front of Minter with a thud. 'You haven't heard any malicious rumours about your work, have you?'

'Rumours about what, sir?'

'About the robustness of the data you published in that report.'

Minter looked up at Roberts. At Division HQ, everyone had warned Minter that Roberts was a fearsome enemy to make. The super was ruthless, with a long memory and a stack of grudges he was working through very patiently. When the chief retired, Roberts wanted his job and he wasn't going to let anything stand in his way. So Minter knew exactly what the super was insinuating. He was saying that any manipulation of the figures was down to Minter. 'No, sir,' said Minter, 'I haven't, but you know what Kemptown's like.'

Roberts nodded. Gossip was what Beckett had blamed, too. 'Yes, I know what Kemptown's like. If you remember, Minter, I was the one who advised you not to come back here. I told you at the time that the really clever young officers – the ones with promising careers in front of them – avoided Crime Squads like the plague. But you chose to ignore me, Minter, although now I rather think that recent events have proved me right. Windmill is a basket case and someone's going to have to take the blame. If you're not careful, Minter, your brilliant career will be over before it's even begun.'

When Minter looked up at his former boss, he didn't blink for an instant. 'I'm not sure what you're trying to say, sir.'

'Let me tell you something, Minter. Everything you've ever heard about the real decisions being made out on the golf course, or over tea and biscuits at the chief constable's residence, well, all those rumours are absolutely true. No matter what the HR handbook says, that's how things get done round here and that's how officers like you rise and fall. So be careful what you say and who you say it to in future. Remember that I made you, Minter, and I can break you just as easily.'

The lime-green Mazda was in the front row of the cars lining up for the start of the Rookie Riot. The driver revved up the engine. The other cars replied in kind. All the drivers had their eyes fixed on the chequered flag.

Dempsey found a place in the crowd. Next to him was his cousin: Not because Dempsey liked him, but because he wanted someone riding shotgun now. It suited someone of his status. The dozen or so concrete steps of the terracing were rammed with stock-car fans, most of them dressed in T-shirts and baseball caps. Dempsey and his cousin were standing close to the track, on the second step of the terrace. The noise of the snarling engines from the dirt track was deafening.

'There!' Dempsey said excitedly, pointing out the Mazda. 'That's our car.' A large sticker had been placed on the side of the garishly painted stock car: 22, it read in big black numerals on a plain white background. Dempsey grinned. It was his age. A tribute. 'Nice one.'

The flag went down and the engines roared. The Mazda surged ahead of the pack. Its driver had a lot of experience on fast roads, but this was his first proper stock-car race. 'C'mon!' Dempsey yelled from the stand. 'Get in among them.'

As if the driver had heard, the Mazda slowed down. Straight away, the car behind him smacked into the Mazda's tail, shunting it forward. The Mazda stalled. A speeding Ford careered into its side, knocking it into one of the straw bales in the centre of the track. 'Fuck that! They didn't like him taking the lead, did they?' he said.

Back on the track, the Mazda was racing again, threading its way through a couple of the trailing cars. One of them swerved inward to try and sandwich the Mazda against the wall of tyres at the edge of the track.

The driver put his foot down and surged past them, dinking the tail of the Saab so that it spun off to the side. Then it drove straight into the back of a battered-looking Honda. A moment later, another car rammed its own backside. The three cars shunted forward together in an unbroken line. Then they jack-knifed one way or the other, before sliding into the path of the oncoming bangers. There was a series of loud impacts.

Dempsey wasn't interested in the race now. Instead, he was staring intently at the limping Mazda. That will have woken Stevie up, he was thinking. In his mind, Dempsey was playing with the dark and gleaming images of what was happening inside the boot of the car, as if they were stills from one of the films he liked to watch.

The Mazda had stalled again. It sat there helplessly in the middle of the dirt track. In revenge for the tricksy spin-off, the driver of the Saab accelerated into the back of the lime-green car. There was a huge thud. It bent the Mazda's fender in two, crumpled the bonnet. Then the Saab reversed and did it again.

After dropping off the intelligence reports with DCI Slater, Minter headed back for his office. He turned a corner on the fifth floor and saw Sean Connolly coming towards him with a piece of paper in his hand. 'Can you sign this, sir?' Connolly said, as the two men met.

Minter looked down. It was the sudden-death report of James McFarland, the rent boy whose body had been discovered in the basement flat at Lower Rock Gardens. Minter was the officer assigned and he'd asked to approve all the paperwork. 'Nothing to it,' Connolly said. 'Straightforward OD.' He glanced down the corridor behind Minter. 'You seen the boss?'

'You mean Beckett?'

Connolly grinned. 'You don't think I'm talking about that fat bastard Slater, do you?' That was Sean, always ready to see the funny side. 'Anyways, Minter, you going to sign that now? Only I wanted to get rid before I go out on the Van.' Connolly was looking forward to being back in action. 'Busy day ahead.'

'Leave it with me.'

Connolly went to protest.

'I told you,' said Minter, 'I want things done properly on this.'

Connolly shrugged. 'Suit yourself. I'll just get it off you tomorrow, then.' He turned and walked away.

In the corridor, Minter scanned the contents of the sudden-death report. The next of kin had already been informed of McFarland's death and first thing this morning the father had been taken to identify the body. The obligatory post mortem had already been done and the corpse was ready to be released, so everything was in order. Despite appearances to the contrary, it seemed that Connolly was an efficient officer.

When Minter got back to his office, the door was open and Tom Beckett was standing by the window, looking out over the city. There was a small cardboard box on the floor. Beckett had already packed up his office ready for Slater to move in. Inside the box, sitting on top of an untidy pile of stationery items, there was a framed photograph and Minter glimpsed a middle-aged blonde woman sitting on a sunny terrace.

'I guess you heard,' said Beckett.

'We all did,' said Minter.

'I'm not going to hang around taking orders from Slater,' Beckett told him. 'I wouldn't give the super the pleasure.'

'You've still got your rank, haven't you?'

'For what it's worth.' On the whiteboard in Minter's office, the diagram of the Compton organisation had been wiped off and in its place a street map of the Whitehawk housing estate was being projected from Minter's laptop. Beside the image of the map, he had written a list of six addresses. 'These Slater's targets?' Beckett said, walking over to the whiteboard.

'Yes, sir,' said Minter.

'Swamping the seafront with officers isn't going to change anything.'

'I know,' said Minter.

Beckett looked at him. 'If Russell Compton's going to survive, he needs to score big. He's going to have to show his hand, go outside his circle for once, and that'll be our chance to take him. Only we won't notice when it happens because we'll be running around the seafront, nicking every kid carrying a few five-pound bags.'

'You're right,' said Minter. 'But what can we do? We can't just sit here waiting for the war to start.'

Beckett dug his hand into his trouser pocket. 'I know,' he sighed. 'Here,' he said, taking a folded piece of paper out of his pocket and giving it to Minter. 'Talking of leads.' Minter unfolded the paper and read the address Beckett had written on it. 'I had a look at my own records,' said Beckett, 'and I made a few calls. If you fancy looking him up, that's where your chum Clements is living now.'

'Thanks,' said Minter, surprised that Beckett had found the time.

'I couldn't find anything on Charlie Banks, though. Seems like he's off the radar altogether.' He turned round and started studying the map again. 'There,' said Beckett, pointing at a particular street. 'That's where I grew up.'

'On Whitehawk?' Minter asked.

Beckett nodded. 'It was what they called a self-build scheme. Back in the 1950s, the council used to parcel out little bits of land for people to build their own houses on and that's what my dad did. Built the whole thing himself, in fact, every brick of it.' Beckett looked at Minter. 'He always said that it was the second proudest day of his life when we moved in.'

'What was the first?'

Beckett looked at Minter and smiled. 'The day I was born, of course.'

'Of course,' said Minter.

'Only child, you see,' said Beckett. 'Believe it or not, Whitehawk was a great place to grow up when I was a kid. It was safe then, not a car in sight, let alone a drug dealer.' He traced a few more streets with his fingertips. 'And there, that's where Russell Compton got started up.'

'Falcon Close.'

'Yep. The 1980s was when the council moved in the problem families, the people like the Comptons. They fucking ruined Whitehawk – in the end, my mum and dad were scared to leave the house.' Beckett shook his head. 'They just couldn't understand what had happened. Used to love it on the estate, they did.' He looked at Minter. 'That was another reason Windmill was so important to me: I wanted to make it up to my old man for what the likes of Russell Compton did to his home.'

'The whole squad is aware of what's happening, sir,' Minter said. 'We all know what Roberts is up to.'

'Then tell Chief Inspector Pendle what you know, Minter. Tell him about the dodgy crime stats.' Minter hesitated. 'All those numbers are beyond me, mate, so it's going to have to be you that does it.'

'Did you tell Roberts about the stats?'

Beckett shrugged. 'I may have dropped a hint.'

'Jesus Christ. Have you got any idea what you've just done?'

'Listen, Minter. You can't kick Kevin Phillips in the teeth just because he plants a little bit of dope on some two-bit fucking dealer, then stand by and watch as Roberts turns this whole place to shit.'

Minter hesitated. Blowing the whistle meant risking everything he had achieved – his rank, his flat, even his police career. He'd be on his own again, with nothing and no one by his side. 'I can't,' he said.

Beckett sighed. Bending down, he picked up the cardboard box from the floor and cradled it in his arms. 'I can't say I blame you. The job was important to me as well once. Not anymore, though. Roberts can stick it.' Walking out of Minter's office, he said over his shoulder, 'Just let me know how it goes with Clements.'

When he was gone, Minter went to sit down at his desk. He sat there for a few minutes, weighing his career against doing the right thing. On his computer, Minter opened the ExCal logs yet again. Down the left-hand column, the times of all of last Sunday's events appeared. Minter scanned the corresponding list of passwords, cross-checking them against the log-ons. There was no doubt about it – every time there was an unauthorised access, Windmill took a distinct turn for the worse.

Minter couldn't keep this to himself any longer. He made a few more changes to the spreadsheet then, with a covering note requesting an urgent meeting to discuss the anomalies it contained, emailed a copy to the Kemptown IT manager. *Message sent*, winked on the computer screen.

Looking down, Minter saw McFarland's sudden-death report where he'd left it on the desk. He reminded himself that accidental overdoses were ten a penny. McFarland's death was tragic, but it was nothing out of the ordinary. Vicky had already told him Michael Lambert was small time. Even if McFarland's death was connected to Lambert, it didn't mean an awful lot. As Roberts might have put it, this was a resource-deployment issue and right now, Minter had much more important things to do with his time. But something about the report kept nagging at him. Finally, he gave in and snatched the piece of paper off the top of the pile.

Minter saw what he was looking for on the second page. According to the report, Jimbob McFarland had lived alone. Minter pulled out of his jacket pocket the letters he had taken off the table in the flat at Lower Rock Gardens. One of them was a red utility bill – a final demand for payment for electricity – and there were two names clearly visible in the window of the envelope, a Mr J. McFarland and a Mr T. Sampson. People moved out of flats all the time, Minter thought, so perhaps McFarland had never bothered to take his flatmate's name off all the accounts, but he did a PNC on Terence Sampson all the same. There was a string of convictions for drugs and burglary, nothing particularly extravagant but still a running score and Lower Rock Gardens was there as Sampson's last known address. Someone like Sampson couldn't move around much without attracting attention.

Minter rang through to the Major Incident Room, but Connolly wasn't there and he didn't answer his mobile, either. Minter wasn't used to following hunches. He didn't trust them because they were just feelings disguised as detective work, but Minter knew what Beckett would do. It was time to find out a little more about James McFarland.

A lot of members were away on holiday. The health club wasn't busy. In the reception area, one of the beauty therapists was sitting idle, chatting with the girl behind the desk. When Jacqui came in, she turned round and smiled. 'Oh, hi, Mrs Compton,' she said. She was wearing a blue tunic and fake tan, and her make-up was immaculate.

'How are you, Emma?' said Jacqui. Unlike most of the members, Jacqui never spoke down to the staff.

'I'm good, thanks, Mrs Compton. Any treatments today?'

'No, thanks,' said Jacqui, 'but I have booked in for next week.'

'OK.' Emma smiled, showing her bright-white teeth. 'See you then.'

In the changing room, Jacqui slipped inside one of the private cubicles. She would have loved Emma to have given her a massage, or some kind of wrap, but she couldn't because there were bruises on her back from the fight she'd had with Russell. Looking down, Jacqui saw her hands tremble as they pulled her all-in-one swimsuit out of the bag. She hadn't had a drink this morning – there'd been no vodka left in the fridge, and Russell had been in a rage about some text he'd just received about Stevie Elliott. Jacqui had come straight here.

On the way out of the changing rooms, Jacqui checked her back in the wall mirror. There was just a small part of the bruise on show. It didn't look too bad, she decided, walking out.

Last night, Jacqui had begged Russell to spare her brother's life. She'd wept and pleaded for Dave, but Russell just kept on saying it was nothing to do with him. He said he didn't know and didn't care where Dave was. It had ended in a fight. A bad one.

In the spa area, Jacqui sank into the swirling waters of the Jacuzzi. She watched a solitary young woman making easy lengths of the swimming pool, the blue, sparkling water parting at her every stroke, the two patches of white skin on the underside of the woman's feet appearing and disappearing in the water. Then she settled her head back onto the tiles on the side of the hot tub and closed her eyes.

If Dave was a grass, she thought, there was no way Russell was going to let him just slip away into some Witness Protection Programme. She knew Russell's ire. His revenges would be terrible. Just the thought of what might be happening to Dave right now was making Jacqui feel sick.

Jacqui listened to the bubbling water. Slowly, the jets began to ease the tension in her neck. She could feel the headache loosening its grip.

Her memory took her the long way home. Not to the big

house on Dyke Road, but back to the house on Whitehawk. She was downstairs. She was nine years old.

'Mum!' Jacqui called up the stairs. 'Mum!'

Jacqui's mother was sleeping it off.

'Where's Davie's coat?' Jacqui called out. Again, there was no reply. Jacqui swore. She looked at her little brother, Davie, standing in the hall. It was raining outside and Jacqui couldn't find the hand-me-down coat Davie had been given by one of his cousins. It was Davie's first day at primary school, but he didn't have a school uniform and he was sobbing.

'Don't worry,' Jacqui said, trying to be the big sister. She glanced at her watch. It was a cheap LED thing. Red numbers on a black background. She'd nicked it the week before, but she hadn't given it to her mum, like she did all the other stuff that she stole to order from the shops in Brighton. Jacqui had kept the LED watch back. It was her birthday present to herself, the only one she'd be getting.

'Come on,' she said, almost pushing Davie out the door. 'We're going to be late for school.'

There was something about Davie that asked for trouble. He didn't mean it, she knew that. It was just the way he was. He was a spindly little lad. The gang of boys who roamed the playground at Jacqui's school would single him out in no time. That meant Jacqui would have to stick up for Davie, of course. With her sharp tongue and her bony little knuckles, she would do it, too.

In the Jacuzzi, Jacqui's back had started to hurt again so she moved across to the other side of the whirlpool, shifting her weight so that the jets didn't get at the tender part of the bruise.

Outside, in the sunny garden, three women were walking across the well-tended lawn from the direction of the tennis courts. They carried hooded tennis rackets in their hands and long, green tubes of Dunlop balls. Chatting and smiling, they gathered round a table on the patio near the pool house. After the briefest of consultations, one of their number went inside. Jacqui watched her sliding open the glass door that led into the bar.

The club's tennis coach approached the table where his other two pupils were sitting. There was an enormous sports bag stuffed with spare racquets slung over his shoulder. In truth, there was something seedy about him, Jacqui thought. He was a little too old to wear his bottle-blond hair in a ponytail poking through the back of his cap, but the women didn't seem to mind. As well as teaching them backhands, he was there for them to flirt with.

Dutifully, the coach stopped by their table to chat. As he congratulated them on their play, they gazed up at him, their eyes occasionally sliding down his body to his slender hips. Jacqui saw them laughing at the joke he made. She'd seen the women lots of times before. When they swam, they swam in a line three abreast across the pool, taking up its entire width, their neat bobs held out of the water as they vied against each other with titbits about holiday plans and their children's private schools. In the changing rooms, they shed their expensive, classy clothes with cheerful confidence. Nobody ever hit these women. They simply wouldn't put up with it.

Outside, the tennis coach gave his girls a final grin and walked off. Soon, Jacqui thought, they'd be coming in to swim, or to sit chatting in the Jacuzzi for ages. Reluctantly, Jacqui hauled herself out of the hot tub.

In the changing room, Jacqui's desperate need for a drink caught up with her. Forgetting about the Three Graces for a minute, she got dressed quickly and hurried out into the bar.

Shamefacedly, Jacqui ordered a Bloody Mary from the girl who was serving. Once it had been mixed, she took the highball to the table in the corner. There was a local newspaper on it, turned to the sports pages. The door from the garden opened. Laughing, still in their tight-fitting tennis tops with their sports bras underneath, the three women walked into the bar as if they owned the place. One of them plonked the tray of empty glasses down on the bar. 'Thanks!' she called to the girl behind the bar, giving her a little wave as well. 'Look,' she said to her friends, 'I must dash. Roger will have a fit if I'm not there to help him set up.' She kissed her friends on both cheeks.

'Good luck with the bash,' said one.

''Bye,' said the other.

Her head held high, the woman with the function to go to walked confidently through the bar, shooting Jacqui a disdainful little smile on her way out.

Jacqui turned over the *Argus*. It was today's. On the front page was the headline 'City Drug War Claims Next Victim'. Jacqui scanned the first couple of paragraphs. It didn't take her long to find her brother's name.

Number 29 Chester Street was a small end-of-terrace Victorian house. The white-painted stucco covering its front wall was badly cracked and weather-stained where the salt and the damp had got in underneath. When Minter opened it, the little garden gate squeaked on its hinges. He went up to the front door and rang the bell.

The image of James McFarland's dead body came back into Minter's mind as he waited on the doorstep. The corpse lay there in the silent basement, the skin pale against the soiled bedsheet. Minter had almost forgotten the humiliations that death wrought. Last night, he'd dreamed about Alan Day's blistered body, too. In his nightmare, Minter saw it folded up on top of the rubbish bags in the refuse bin. This time, the peeled, red features began to move.

Dead people didn't look like they were sleeping, Minter thought. They didn't look peaceful at all. He heard a muffled sound coming from inside 29 Chester Street. Footsteps came closer to the front door.

The man who opened it was in his sixties. He was small, with sandy hair and spectacles. Inoffensive-looking. 'Mr McFarland?' Minter asked.

The man peered down suspiciously at the warrant card Minter was holding up. 'Yes,' he said. 'But I've already spoken to your colleague.' It was a soft Edinburgh accent he was talking in. That figured, Minter thought. It went with the surname, the sandy hair. 'And I went to the mortuary, as requested.'

'Yes, sir,' said Minter, 'but do you mind if I come in?'

'I was having my dinner.'

'It won't take long,' Minter persisted.

McFarland sighed. 'Very well, then,' he said, moving to one side.

Stepping inside the house, Minter followed McFarland

along a gloomy, windowless hallway. They passed the first door on the left and went into the small back parlour where Alistair McFarland's meagre lunch – a couple of fried eggs, a mound of spindly oven chips – had been plated up on the small, square dining table. Minter looked around the room. The wallpaper was dingy, the mottled-glass lampshade peculiarly old-fashioned, its bottom speckled with dead flies.

As McFarland sat down to resume eating, quicker footsteps came clattering down the uncarpeted stairs in the hallway. A darting figure passed the open doorway. 'I'm off out,' a young man's voice called. The front door opened, then slammed shut again.

McFarland saw Minter's quizzical look. 'My lodger,' he explained.

The rented room would help McFarland make ends meet. The genteel poverty of its retired population was one of the things about Brighton that never seemed to change. Minter waited for the noise of the door to melt away, then said, 'I'm sorry for your loss, sir.'

Grunting, McFarland used his fork to spear a few more chips. When he'd been in uniform, Minter had encountered every kind of relative – the bereft, the maddened, the guilty – but he'd never met anyone so detached, so unruffled, as Alistair McFarland appeared to be.

'Do you mind if I sit down?' Minter asked.

McFarland nodded briefly, gesturing at the chair opposite with his knife. Minter took it. On the table in front of McFarland, there was a piece of paper and a biro. It looked like McFarland had been in the middle of writing a list. The handwriting was familiar. 'Can you tell me,' Minter began, 'when you last saw James?'

196

A truncated, sarcastic little laugh. 'Ages ago,' McFarland said.

'How long exactly?'

McFarland hazarded a guess. 'Two years, maybe three.'

'And you've had no contact with him ever since?'

McFarland cut up the first of his fried eggs. The soft yellow centre dribbled over the plate. He dipped a chip into the yolk and ate. 'None whatsoever,' he said.

The father's disdain for his own son touched a nerve in Minter. 'How old was James when he left home?'

'Fourteen,' said McFarland.

'How often did you see him after that?'

'He came round here asking for money a few times. When I refused, he stopped coming altogether. I can't say I was sorry.'

'Did you know he was a prostitute?' said Minter.

'Yes,' said McFarland. 'The police informed me, and social services. I told them there was nothing we could do.'

'Did you ever find out the names of any of the clients James had?'

'No, of course I didn't,' said McFarland. 'Look,' he went on, irritated by Minter's silence, 'I've told you. I've been through all this with the police officer who came yesterday. James was nothing but trouble. His mother tried. I tried. In fact, the only one who didn't try to change James's ways was the lad himself.'

'Is your wife still alive?' Minter asked.

'No,' said McFarland blankly.

'What ways were those?' McFarland looked at Minter. 'What ways did James have about him that were so difficult?' Minter asked.

197

McFarland sighed. 'All we knew was that he used to come home in the early hours of the morning, and sometimes not at all. It was only when you lot started fetching him back that we found out what was going on. His mother tried locking him in his room, but that was no good. He'd just jump out the window and shin down the drainpipe.' McFarland seemed to shudder. 'I knew this would happen one day. It was inevitable. That boy was wicked. The best thing I ever did was to throw him out once and for all.'

'Your son's dead, Mr McFarland,' said Minter. 'Don't you want to find out why?'

'I don't like your tone,' said McFarland. 'I haven't done anything wrong, you know. James made his own bed.'

Minter nodded. 'Can I ask you where you were last night?'

McFarland glanced up. 'I was here.' For the first time his voice faltered.

'All evening?'

'Yes, all evening.'

'Can anyone corroborate that, sir?' Minter asked.

'My lodger was in,' said McFarland.

'And his name would be?'

'Declan Scammell.'

'Where does Mr Scammell work?' Minter asked, glad that his interrogative tone was evidently getting up McFarland's nose.

'American Express,' McFarland told him. Minter stood up. It would be easy to ask the lodger to confirm McFarland's story. The credit-card company had an office close to Kemptown Station. 'Thank you, sir,' said Minter. 'That will be all, for the moment.'

McFarland didn't look at Minter. 'You can see yourself out,' he said.

A minute later, the garden gate squeaked again. Standing on the pavement, Minter thought about what he'd just heard.

*Low self-esteem.* That was how the criminologists would have explained it. For James McFarland to throw himself away like that – at such an early age, to find refuge in the dissolutions offered by heroin and prostituted sex – that must betoken a deep despair. Minter thought about it. To lose, you first had to possess. To despair, you first had to hope. In the countless children's homes he'd lived in, Minter had come to believe it was better to live without either of these things. He knew the other children hoarded old, cracked photographs of long-lost parents under their pillows and he knew how ardently they dreamed about being reunited. But Minter himself had renounced those compensations. There would always be just him.

Minter turned round to take another look at the house. The sun was behind it now. It cast a long, chilly shadow down towards Minter on the pavement.

He was a police officer now. He found people. That was what he did. It would be easy to find his own parents. To speak to his father and mother. To question them. Even if they weren't on any of the databases, there would be hospital records, especially for his mother. So why had Minter never tried?

Minter turned away from the shadowy house. Once again, he took the letters from Lower Rock Gardens out of his pocket. Underneath the electricity bill was a small envelope. On the front was the name of the addressee: *James*. It was written in the same spidery hand as the shopping list on Alistair McFarland's table. The same notepaper was inside, as well. There was a tatty edge at the top where it had been ripped from the pad. *29 Chester Street*, Alistair McFarland had written. Looking back at the house one more time, Minter wondered why McFarland hadn't mentioned the note he'd written to his son just a few days before he died.

'You really like it, don't you, Minter?' said a voice. Minter turned round to see Kevin Phillips crossing the road. 'You really like fucking police officers over. Last year, it was me, now it's Tom Beckett.'

'What Roberts did this morning had nothing to do with me,' said Minter.

Phillips was standing next to Minter on the pavement now. 'SOCU does the business. And what the fuck do you do, Minter? Grass up your colleagues, that's what.'

'I don't have time for this, Kevin,' said Minter. He pressed the remote on his car key fob and the locks flipped up. He opened the door.

Phillips slammed the door shut again. Minter spun round to face him. 'You shouldn't plant evidence, Kevin.'

'Fuck you. You saw the trial papers. That dealer was stone bonkers for supply. Like I said, we get the job done. Whatever it takes.'

'Yeah?' Minter said. 'Is that right? *Whatever* it takes?'

'What are you talking about?'

'If bending the rules of evidence is OK,' said Minter, 'I wonder what else goes on. And I wonder what it is you're hiding with this touching display of loyalty.'

The two men squared up to each other on the pavement. Something about the way Minter was carrying himself made

Phillips back down first. 'Roberts can't watch your back all the time, you know,' he said.

'Are you threatening me?' Minter asked.

'Of course not,' Phillips said. He looked up and down the road. 'I'm just saying that you've been stuck behind a desk for a long time, Minter. You're one of us now, one of the oiks and out here on the streets, things can get a bit out of hand. Who knows, someday you might need some assistance.' Phillips stared in Minter's eyes. 'Let's just hope it arrives.'

# 9

**. . .**

The boy watched the sports BMW turn off the main road and head on down the hill. Taking a quick look around, he bumped his bicycle down from the kerb and began pumping the pedals.

The road funnelled down through Whitehawk. Ahead, the tail of the car disappeared round the corner. Behind it, the boy reached up to pull his hoodie forward. He knew cars. The Beemer was the twin-turbo Z4 with the drop hard roof. Right one to have: not the rag top. Forty-five thousand pounds' worth of auto, with a top-of-the-range equipment list. He'd never seen the motor on the estate before. It was fair game.

The boy knew a short cut. He turned left into an alleyway. Fenced off, it run down a shallow incline for a good quarter-mile, taking him past the back gardens of a parade of shit-coloured semis. He was going fast now. A woman with a pushchair emerged from a side alley and had to press the side of the buggy into a broken section of fence to stop him clattering into her baby. She swore at him as he hurtled past. Not taking his eyes off the path, the boy waved a V-sign back at her.

A few moments later, even deeper into the estate, Jacqui Compton was pulling the BMW up onto the pavement of a cul-de-sac. She turned off the ignition and without getting out of the car, stared at the row of modern terraced houses. A long time ago, she'd lived with Russell and her baby in the one at the end. It was a narrow, off-white box and Jacqui couldn't believe how pinched it looked now.

Every Saturday night, Russell would come back here. In the kitchen, he'd empty all his pockets out, scattering grubby notes and coins over the chipped Formica tabletop. Jacqui would count it all up, every last penny, before using a bit of paper to work out the sums: two-thirds went straight back to Russell so he could buy the next brick, the rest Jacqui kept for the housekeeping. The division of labour, in fact, was the same now as it had been on Whitehawk, only on a much grander scale. Russell did the business, and saw off all his rivals, and Jacqui took care of the money. Over the years, she must have squirrelled away millions of pounds. Someone else washed the cash, of course – there was a whole team of them taking it in turns to go round all the betting shops and the bureaux de change – but Jacqui kept track of the clean money. She knew what went in where, and what came out.

In the small house, after divvying up, Jacqui would see to Russell's injuries. In those days, the dealers didn't have guns. There were lots of knives, but no guns. Jacqui used Dettol mixed with water to clean out Russell's wounds before they'd both start in on the drinking. As soon as they were good and pissed, the arguments would start. A single wrong word from Jacqui and Russell would kick off. Back then, Jacqui gave as good as she got and eventually the banging and crashing about would wake little Chris, but they'd leave him upstairs to cry in his cot because they were both enjoying themselves too much.

Jacqui got out of the BMW. Suddenly, standing there by the red car in her yellow Versace trouser suit and hundred-pound haircut, she started to feel very vulnerable. She glanced up and down the street. When she saw that she was alone, she bleeped the locks and left the car behind, walking down an alleyway and across a little park. It was a good couple of minutes' walk to the house where she had grown up with her alcoholic mother and her brother, Dave. That house was in the middle of yet another terrace, but it was just like the first one, the one the council had given her after Chris had been born. For the first three decades of her life, Jacqui had progressed from one poky little council house to another.

She stood in front of the house and looked up at the window of the bedroom she had shared with Dave. They had a single bed, that was all, and their mother often didn't have any money for the meter, so in winter it was freezing and Jacqui used to go to bed fully clothed, Davie snuggled up to her for extra warmth. How different, Jacqui thought, from the room where her own son now slept, warm as toast and stuffed with gizmos. Yes, these last ten years, the Comptons had certainly come a long way.

The boy cycled slowly past the BMW. He turned the bike round, coming to a halt in the middle of the road. The bike between his legs, he bent down to take a good look inside, admiring the tan leather of the seats, the orange detailing on the dashboard. When he grew up, he told himself, he was going to get one just like that.

He took a brand-new telephone out of his pocket. The phone was the bollocks. Touch screen and too many apps to count, let alone use. He dialled a number, told the man on the other end of the line about the car he'd found. He listened for a moment, then pushed the bike forward a few feet. He read out the sequence of numbers and letters on the Beemer's personalised plate. The man on the other end rang off. The boy stuffed the phone back into his pocket and cycled away.

The Hangletons were coming for Russell's old lady.

Minter pulled his car up outside Kidz Klub. This time, he wasn't going to let Irene down. Dean Carver, the Hangleton runt who had vandalised the youth club a couple of days ago, had paid another visit.

The gates to the car park were still locked. The door and all the windows looked secure. Everything was quiet. There were three cameras sticking out at different angles from the roof. The locksmith had been as good as his word.

There was no answer when Minter rang the bell. Then, from behind the building, Minter heard the spank of a basketball being bounced on tarmac. He walked round the side. Irene was there, sitting on the steps by the back door, watching a boy of about nine or ten throwing a basketball into a hoop attached to the wall.

As soon as she saw Minter, Irene got up. 'Thanks for coming over,' she said. 'I just didn't know who to call.'

'Is Carver still here?' Minter said.

'No. He had a go at me, but when I pointed out he was on *Candid Camera*, he drove off in a hurry.'

'Did he hurt you?'

'Just a load of verbals. He said he'd be back though.'

Minter pointed at the boy playing basketball. 'Who's he?'

'He's called Reece,' said Irene. 'He's nothing to do with Dean. He's just moved onto the estate. I didn't have the heart to tell him to leave. I don't think he's got anywhere else to go.'

The boy knew he was being talked about. He'd stopped playing and was staring over. He was scrawny, with close-cropped hair and a famished look around his eyes. On Whitehawk, there were plenty of children who went to bed hungry. 'Who are you?' the boy asked Minter suspiciously.

'This is Minter,' Irene said.

'What kind of a stupid name is that?' said Reece.

Minter shrugged. 'I didn't choose it.'

'It's a surname,' Irene explained. 'Even I don't know Minter's first name.'

'Man of mystery, are you?' said Reece. He bounced the ball to Minter.

Minter caught it in one hand. Basketball was one of his games. He used to play defence in the police team.

'Come on, then,' said Reece. 'Let's see what you've got.'

Glancing up once at the hoop, Minter launched the ball from where he was standing. It went straight into the string net without touching the backboard.

'Whoa!' said Reece, scrabbling to pick up the ball again and tossing it back to Minter.

This time, Minter laid up the shot properly. The ball sailed straight down the throat of the basket for the second time. Reece ran over to fetch the ball. Now he didn't give it back, winding himself up for a basket of his own. Minter was wise to that. Stepping forward quickly, he snatched the ball from the boy the moment before it left his hand. Minter grinned at Reece.

Looking angry, the boy stood up straight. 'You're supposed to let me win,' he said.

'Am I?'

'Yeah. You're the grown-up and I'm the kid. I need it more than you do. Don't you know anything?'

Minter laughed but he gave the ball back. 'Go on, then. Give it your best shot.'

Reece ducked past Minter to the side. He took two more steps and jumped. The ball flew through the air. At first, it looked a little too flat. It bobbed off the backboard, then trailed round the rim before finally going in. 'Yes!' Reece cried. He turned to look at Minter. 'In your face.'

'Beginner's luck,' said Minter. He collected the ball and threw it back at Reece. 'Try again.'

The boy swerved this way and that, but he couldn't get past Minter. Giving up, he took a step back and made to shoot. Minter could have easily grabbed the ball, but he didn't. For the second time, Reece made the basket. 'Skillage!' he exclaimed.

As Minter gave him the ball again. A look of understanding passed between them. Minter wanted to stick around and play, but he couldn't. 'I've got to go,' he said.

'See you later, Reece.' Turning round, he walked back over to where Irene was standing.

Reece watched Minter's retreating figure. 'Yeah,' he said, disappointed. 'See you later.'

Irene watched Reece start to play on his own again. 'You know,' she said to Minter, 'you should change your mind about mentoring.'

Kidz Klub ran a scheme. Once a month, an adult mentor would come and take out one of the more troubled youngsters. 'I'm a cop,' Minter said. 'None of them would want to be seen with me.'

'You'd be good, Minter. You know what it's like to have to fight for everything you've got.'

Minter glanced over at Reece. The boy was shooting hoops again. When he scored, he looked over, and when Minter nodded his approval, Reece held his gaze. It was a clouded look the boy gave Minter, but he could see what it was Reece wanted. The lad was looking for more than someone just to shoot some baskets with; he needed someone he could trust, someone who might help him with all the things he didn't yet understand, all the things he couldn't do. It made Minter think of Tom Beckett and the way he'd never given much thought to who his own father was. Minter looked at Irene. 'What's Reece's story?'

'I don't know,' she said. 'Not yet.'

Watching Reece darting round the empty car park, Minter wondered if he was qualified to give the boy at least part of what he needed. 'Am I a fighter, Irene? Am I that strong?'

'Of course you are, Minter. How do you think you survived?'

Minter nodded. 'When I'm finished with this case, if Reece is still around, maybe we'll spend some time together.'

'Just let me know when you want to start.'

Minter took his car keys out of his pocket. 'Come on. This place is secure enough now. I don't think Dean's going to come back. I'll give you both a lift home.'

Jacqui Compton turned away from the little house. She looked at her watch. It was the Boucheron, the one with all the bling.

It was getting late in the afternoon, but she didn't want to go back to the house on Dyke Road. It wasn't safe there, not with Russell like he was. Doing up the jacket of her trouser suit, Jacqui drifted into the scruffy little park and sat down on the bench to think about some of the families she'd known on Whitehawk. So many of the children never made it out of their teens. There was a time about three or four years ago when Chrissy seemed to come home from school every day with another story about how one of his old mates had got knifed or shot or chased out of town. At the time, Jacqui had turned a deaf ear to all she heard. By then, Russell had knocked all the fight out of her. Looking around at the tiny houses, Jacqui pictured the baronial place she lived in on Dyke Road. It was a monstrosity of a building, chock full of luxuries and drowning in cash. There was so much money, Jacqui had given up devising ways of spending it all, but somehow the essentials of her life had remained the same. Money and alcohol and violence, they were all still there, just like they had been in Falcon Close, just like they had been at the other house, the one where she and Davie grew up. As long as Russell was around, she'd never get away from any of them. Jacqui thought of little Chrissy, too, crying in his cot while his mum and dad knocked lumps out of each other downstairs. Well, Chrissy didn't cry anymore, either, because he was a big boy now. Just like his dad.

Jacqui looked down at her feet where the grass had been worn away to expose a little run of earth. All those young men dead, she thought, all those boys she had known on the estate who weren't here anymore, murdered by Russell – by Jacqui's husband, her provider – murdered for the drugs they had or just because they were in the way.

She looked up to see two youths enter the park and lope towards her across the grass. They had their fists in the pockets of their sweatshirts and one of them was wearing a Burberry baseball cap and for a moment, she imagined they were the spirits of those dead children, come to take revenge. Then Jacqui looked around the otherwise deserted park and the blind upstairs windows of the houses, and she realised too late how unsafe she had made herself sitting there in her designer gear with the keys to the Beemer in her trouser pocket. 'Shit,' she muttered, getting up from the swing.

The two youths started running. As best as she could in her two-inch heels, Jacqui turned and ran the other way, towards an exit from the park and an alleyway. Behind her, the two young men were getting closer by the second, whooping and cussing and calling her 'old bitch'. She heard their footsteps, then a laugh and the animal sound of panting and a hand shoved her hard in the middle of the back. Tripping over her own feet, Jacqui tumbled to the ground, winded. She lay there on her back, the two faces leering at her from above, silhouetted against the bright blue sky. One of them, the one with all the acne on his face, was holding a hunting blade with a set of deep serrations along the heft, turning it in the sunlight.

Minter dropped Irene off at home first and was on his way to Reece's flat in another part of the estate. The two of them were getting on well, chatting as they passed a red car on a side street.

The BMW didn't fit for a number of reasons. First up, it was too feminine: round here, power was always male; second, the kind of guys who could afford a motor like that would have bought a pimp-ride, not a little convertible. Minter pulled over to the side of the road and reversed, something else about the Beemer that rang bells in his head.

'What's the matter?' said Reece. 'Why have we stopped?'

Minter got out of the car. It was Jacqui Compton's BMW, all right. He'd only seen it yesterday, outside the house in Dyke Road. 'Stay here,' he told Reece. Minter walked down the narrow street. The doors of the BMW were locked and no one was inside.

A sudden burst of giggles spun him round as two young schoolgirls came out of the alleyway. 'Did you see her?' one of them was saying to the other.

'See who, girls?' asked Minter. Frightened, they looked at Minter. 'See who?'

'The woman,' one of the girls said, pointing to the alley. Minter glanced back at the Passat, where Reece was waiting. Turning round, he jogged into the alley. There was a scream and he broke into a run.

A huddle of three people were in the park, a woman lying on the ground, engulfed by two young men. One of them was raising a huge knife high into the air. 'Police!' Minter yelled, sprinting. The young men ran out of the park and into the alleyway. Minter dashed past Jacqui Compton on the ground, glancing down to check she was still conscious. All that training had to be good for something: in another couple of moments, Minter was out of the park himself and catching up with one of her attackers in the alleyway. The boy with the Burberry cap turned to face him, a kitchen knife in his hands. It was Dean Carver. 'Had enough of smashing up youth clubs, then, Dean?' said Minter.

'Fuck you,' said the teenage thug, brandishing the knife.

Ignoring it, Minter stepped forward. 'You're way out of your league, Dean. That's Jacqui Compton. You know, Russell's wife.'

'Think that fucking scares me, do you?' said Carver. Minter kept coming, so Carver lunged at him with the knife. Minter sidestepped, grabbed Carver's arm with both hands and swung the youth round, smacking his face against the wooden fence so hard that it splintered and the knife clattered onto the paving stones at Carver's feet. Minter wrenched Carver's right arm as high up his back as it could go and the youth cried out in pain. Taking hold of a fistful of Carver's hair, Minter banged his face against the fence. 'If I catch you near Kidz Klub again, I'll feed you to Russell myself. Do you understand?'

His eyes closed, Carver nodded. 'OK, OK.'

'Good,' said Minter.

A squad-car siren wailed from the direction of the park and tyres squealed on a road. It seemed that someone, at least, had been watching what was happening to Jacqui and had made a 999 call. Dragging Carver back to the park, Minter handed Carver over to the uniformed officer who was first on the scene, then walked over to where Jacqui Compton was standing. 'Are you all right?' he asked.

Jacqui's clothes were ripped, and her expensive haircut hung in shreds around her head. She had mascara down her cheeks, but she was all right. 'Who the fuck are you?' she asked.

'DS Minter, Brighton and Hove Police.'

'Never thought I'd be so happy to see a cop.' Jacqui looked over to where Dean Carver was being put into the car. She looked the other way, half expecting to see the other yob.

'They were two of the Hangletons,' said Minter.

Jacqui had heard Russell talking about his rivals, but she didn't realise how bad things had become. 'They're getting above themselves.'

'Looks like it,' said Minter. There was silence. 'I've seen the post-mortem notes, Jacqui. I know what happened to Dave.'

Jacqui nodded. The newspaper hadn't said a lot about the way that Dave had died. 'Tell me,' she said.

'Russell's Shogun left Dyke Road at just gone eleven, and it got back at quarter past two in the morning. Dave died at half past twelve. I can't say he didn't suffer.'

'Was Chris with Russell?' Jacqui asked. Minter hesitated. 'Was Chris with Russell when he left Dyke Road?'

'Yes.' Minter told her everything then: how they'd hung Dave up by his heels and broken his bones with a piece of metal pipe, how they'd wrapped him up in barbed wire and put him in the boot. 'There was smoke in David's lungs,' Minter said. 'When they torched the car, he was still alive.' Jacqui began to cry. 'You or Chris, Jacqui – one of you is going to be next.'

# 10

## . . .

A champagne flute poised delicately between his fingertips, Rita gazed out of the floor-to-ceiling windows
of his penthouse. In the late-afternoon sunshine, the English
Channel stretched out to the misty horizon in alternate rods
of jade and blue. In front of it, a tall silhouette in the middle
of the chrome and glass balcony, stood Paul Dempsey. The
boss of the Hangleton gang had his eyes clamped on the
crowded seafront, scanning the crowds far below him. He'd
gone outside in order to take a call and by the way his hands
were grasping the rail, it looked like bad news.

Rita had been doing business with Russell Compton for
seven years now, but the world was going to hell in a
handcart and he knew he had to move in the same general
direction. She had used the afternoon to take the measure
of Paul Dempsey.

Brighton's soon-to-be new heroin boss was certainly a
noxious cocktail – two parts psychotic to one part ruthless
businessman. Dempsey made Alan Day look like a model
of restraint. He was dangerous, altogether lacking that little

bit of patience and tact that Russell had developed. And Dempsey's rule would only last for a very short period of time. Russell had had seven good years. Dempsey would be lucky to have any more than one. The Hangletons would soon be devoured by their own violence, thrashing about in a cesspit of their own addictions and petty rivalries. It would be very easy for the next bunch – younger, wilder, greedier – to wrest the city from them.

In the meantime, though, the Hangletons' monopoly would make Rita a lot of money. A lot of money. Piece by piece, Russell Compton was losing his touch, losing control. The Hangletons, by contrast, were on the march. Their network had already spread both ways along the South Coast and Paul Dempsey had assured Rita that they could handle the kind of multiples that he wanted to bring in. Rita had already lined up wholesalers in Newcastle and Manchester, Glasgow and Liverpool but thirty kilos every month was a lot of skag even for him to offload. He needed distribution.

Rita turned round. In his penthouse, two other Hangletons had arranged themselves indecorously round the huge, open-plan living area. One was stretched out asleep on the cow-hide sofa. Dempsey's other lieutenant was younger and taller and yet more stupid, but he came from the same estate as Dempsey and from the same feral stock and he shared Dempsey's obvious taste for violence. This man was standing on the far side of the room, whispering something into his telephone. They weren't much of a crew, Rita thought to himself. It was only Dempsey who had the real potential.

Rita looked down at the glass-topped dining table. The coke he provided had got hoovered as soon as the talking was done. The handmade cake he'd ordered to celebrate their agreement was the only thing left for them to ingest and they set about it with gusto. Munchies or no munchies, it had been like watching feeding time at a zoo.

Of course, they'd shown no appreciation of the cake itself. Before he cut it, Rita had taken care to remove the six-inch figurine made of marzipan and icing. She was still there, on the table next to the Sabatier carving knife, perched on her little silver-foil platform. Marilyn Monroe in her most famous costume: the dress blown up above her hips, exposing her thighs. It was a miniature work of art, Rita thought, admiring the way the cake's maker had captured the folds of her billowing dress.

None of the Hangletons had noticed that the sugared Marilyn had been designed to match Rita's tribute. Rita, too, was wearing the legendary halter-necked dress. Their faces had been a picture, though, when they first encountered him in the hallway of the penthouse. The spotty Herbert couldn't help himself. He started to giggle, although Dempsey had put a stop to that with a single, fierce glance. Most of the time, though, Rita's dress – like the pancake make-up, the blonde wig – made the Hangletons feel desperately uncomfortable. It even put them off their predictable gangster patter. As indeed, Rita had meant it to.

He reached down. With his fingers, Rita broke off Marilyn's pendulous yellow breasts. He popped the morsel of marzipan into his mouth and let it slowly turn to goo, washing it down with more champagne.

Caught in the fog of his own ambitions, Dempsey continued to survey the street scene far below the penthouse balcony. He'd just been told that Jacqui Compton had got away. But not for long, he thought.

At the bottom of the Steine, people were sweeping across the road to get to the promenade. On the pier, the boardwalks were thick with visitors. The sound of the funfair at the end filled the air – tinny pop music, a loud klaxon from the dodgems, a scream or two from the big rides. Dempsey watched them all, watched their pathetic comings and goings, their cheap thrills. This was where he belonged, Dempsey thought. Up here where the air was clear. Dempsey looked at his watch. It was time to bid farewell to the fat queer.

Inside the flat, Dempsey's cousin was waking up the other kid with a quick slap across the face. Momentarily confused, the teenager looked around a couple of times before waking up properly and reaching instinctively for his glass of JD. Rita was standing there by the table, sipping champagne and watching them.

Rita turned round to the sound of the sliding doors. Dempsey entered the room, closing them again behind him. House-trained, at least, Rita thought.

'That's fucking good charlie,' Dempsey told him. 'Nice one, Rita.'

The importer nodded at the long-overdue compliment. To the Brighton dealers, he was known as Rita. It was the name of his heroine – the long-suffering, flame-haired Rita Hayworth but in the clubs and pubs of Kemptown he went by a different name. The Fat Man was an epithet that more accurately described his huge girth, as well as his lordly status. It was the wrong way round, of course. Queer Kemptown was where he should have gone under the drag name of Rita. And The Fat Man was the name of a legendary gangster, so it would have been more appropriate for the drug dealers to know him by that name instead of Rita. But that was OK. Rita liked everything the wrong way round.

'Plenty more where that came from,' he told Dempsey. 'Although we will have to talk about volumes, Paul. I need a commitment. For six months at least.'

Dempsey shook his head dismissively. 'It's not a problem,' he said.

'And there is something else,'.

'What's that?'

'Russell's been attracting too much attention to himself.'

Dempsey grinned. 'Now you're talking.'

'I think it's time we got rid of him once and for all.'

'With Compton gone,' Dempsey said encouragingly, 'I'll be needing at least twelve kilos every month.'

Rita looked Dempsey in the eye. He knew it was important to play to his associate's strengths, and the Hangletons' strongest suit was chaos and bloody murder. But Dempsey's presumption was beginning to annoy him. 'Do you think you can take Russell out yourselves?'

'Of course,' Dempsey insisted.

'He rarely leaves the house these days, and when he does, there's always a trail of police behind him.'

'Can you get us into the house, Rita?' Dempsey asked.

Rita considered. 'I can certainly help.'

'Sweet,' said Dempsey. 'We'll need some decent weapons, too. A whole fucking armoury, in fact. Russell's no push-over.'

'This has to be done carefully, Paul,' Rita warned, glancing over at Dempsey's colleagues. 'No fuck-ups.'

'Just tell us when,' Dempsey said.

219

The importer sipped at his Bollinger. 'OK,' he said. 'I will contact you, though. There's going to be a lot of heat in the city these next few days. I don't want you coming here, Paul, and I don't want you phoning my numbers, either.'

Dempsey stared back. He didn't mind the dress. Each to his own, as far as he was concerned. If that was what turned Rita on, he could dress up like Kylie Minogue and parade down the seafront, but that patronising fucking expression he'd been wearing all afternoon, it was beginning to get on his tits. 'What's it worth, then?' he asked.

'What's what worth?'

'Us offing Russell,' Dempsey replied. In truth, of course, nothing would give him greater pleasure. But Rita wouldn't have asked unless he needed it very badly. Dempsey had seen an angle. 'What you going to give us for that?' he said.

Rita chuckled. 'I think it's in your interest that Russell is taken out of the equation. After all, he's standing between you and greatness.'

Dempsey didn't bat an eyelid. 'No, Rita, I think it's the other way round. I think it's *you* that needs Russell out of the way.'

Rita and Dempsey studied each other carefully. It hadn't taken long for them to reach the first decisive moment in their relationship.

'If I do the slaughtering,' Dempsey went on, 'don't I deserve some of the meat?'

'What do you mean?'

'I know the margins you make, Rita. I don't want just the wholesale profits. I want a percentage of the import deal you're putting together.'

Rita nodded slowly. 'You're certainly an ambitious man,

Paul,' he remarked, taking another mouthful of Bolly.

'Yes, I am.'

Out of the gap between his front teeth, Rita forced a thin, continuous line of champagne. The pale yellow liquid arced through the air before splashing over Dempsey's chin.

Outraged, Dempsey took a step back, ready to retaliate but Rita picked up the carving knife from the table. The blade flashed upward, pressing against Dempsey's lips. 'Have you any idea,' Rita said quietly, 'who it is you're talking to?' He slipped the knife past Dempsey's lips. The cold metal rattled against Dempsey's front teeth. Rita slid it forward again. The heft disappeared into Dempsey's mouth. He could feel his skin begin to tear and sting. Smiling, Rita turned the knife's handle a little, forcing Dempsey up onto his toes. In a thick red curtain, blood was running down Dempsey's chin now and onto the floor.

Still Dempsey made no move. From out of the corner of his eyes, he saw his two minions walking over. With a wave of his hand, Dempsey stayed them both. Making a show of mastering his own pain, he held Rita's gaze. Slowly, his eyes bright, Rita drew the blade towards the windows. The heavy, single-piece Sabatier began to emerge, centimetre by centimetre, from the corner of Dempsey's mouth. 'One other thing,' Rita said. 'Leave Michael Lambert alone. Michael has my personal protection. Don't fuck with him. The rest of the dealers' – he shrugged – 'you can do what you damn well like with.'

Dempsey's bright red blood fell steadily onto the deep white carpet underfoot, but still he didn't move. A flash of understanding passed between the two men. Dempsey would do whatever it took. Rita could see that. Dempsey had no limits. No boundaries. Rita liked that in a man. With a flourish, he drew the point of the long blade out of the slit in Dempsey's face. With his other hand, Rita grabbed Dempsey's face and pulled him closer, kissing the dealer on the gashed mouth hard enough for both of them to taste the iron in Dempsey's blood and the lipstick Rita was wearing.

Stepping back, Rita replaced the stained knife on the table. He picked up one of the French-linen napkins and handed it to Dempsey.

Dempsey ignored the offered cloth. He smiled instead. As he did so, the blood pooled in the bottom of his mouth began to spill over the edges of his teeth and onto his lips. 'Let me know when you want Russell taken care of,' he said, sending flecks of blood all over the bodice of Rita's white dress.

There'd be another time with Rita, Dempsey told himself, a time when they didn't need him quite so much. For now, his torn mouth would be just another scar. Another trademark and another part of his burgeoning rep.

Turning round, Dempsey led his boys out of the penthouse.

DS Phillips yanked open the back door of the van. Inside, six Drugs Squad officers were sitting on the metal benches. 'You again?' said the one nearest the door.

Phillips recognised the sergeant from the disastrous bust on Sillwood. 'Yeah,' he said grimly, clambering up into the van. 'Me again.'

Sitting down on the bench, Phillips watched the sergeant fit a new cartridge into his American-made Taser X26. The key – the thick metal pole that the team would use to batter down the door – lay ready at his feet.

They were setting off all over the city. Vans crammed with officers in blue stab jackets and visored helmets. For the next twenty-four hours at least, the normal circulation of drugs in Brighton was going to come to a sudden halt. The seafront was being locked down. The estates, too. DCI Slater was getting off to a flying start.

Sean Connolly jumped up into the van behind Phillips and slammed the door. Before he could sit down, the sergeant banged on the roof and they lurched forward.

'Fucking hell,' Connolly said, almost falling over. Putting his hand up to the roof to steady himself, Connolly turned round and found a place to sit.

The Drugs Squad sergeant holstered his Taser. He looked at Connolly. 'SOCU got the intel right this time?' he said.

Connolly stared back at him. 'What's your fucking problem, mate?'

The van pulled out into traffic and accelerated. The officers in the back swayed with every turn. Phillips felt his stomach beginning to tighten. He started to think about his little girl. In three months' time, it would be Martha's first birthday. He thought about the presents they would buy her. He thought about how expensive it was going to be. Looking up, he surveyed his fellow officers. They were all up for it, every one of them. Two specialist firearms officers had been assigned to the unit. They wore the same protective clothing as the others, but their serials started with a different letter and they were both carrying large self-loading Glocks.

'OK,' said Connolly, assuming control. 'This is the biggest trophy of the day. When we're finished, the SIO is bringing in news cameras and all kinds of shit, so we're expected to find a lot of heroin, and a lot of cash. This is a Compton gaff we're hitting, so we're expecting firearms, which is why we're tooled up ourselves.' The van took the last corner too smartly. It jolted the men back against the metal sides. 'Maximum fucking prejudice,' Connolly concluded.

The van screeched to a sudden halt. The sergeant flung the door open and all the men piled out onto the pavement. Phillips recognised the house immediately from the photos in Minter's briefing notes. A small and anonymous Victorian terrace in a long and anonymous Victorian street.

The door went through. The SFOs were inside first. 'Armed police!' one of them yelled. 'Show yourself!'

Breathing heavily, Phillips plunged inside the house. There was a cramped hallway with stairs going up straight ahead of him. There was a blur of blue uniforms. Music was coming from the first floor.

'Show yourself!' the SFO screamed again.

A moment later, a man appeared at the top of the stairs. 'Arms in the air!' yelled the officer, his Glock pointed directly at the man's face. 'Arms in the fucking air!'

The man was in his twenties and looked terrified. He did as he was told. 'Come down the stairs,' the first SFO told him. 'Slowly.' The Glocks tracked the man's descent. As soon as he was within reach, the SFO grabbed him by the shoulder and pushed him onto the floor. Immediately, a couple of Drugs Squad officers fell on him.

Past the stairs, there was a living room and then a step down into what must have been a kitchen. It was from that direction that the sound of a flushing toilet could be heard.

The other SFO ran towards it. A moment later, two shots rang out.

Phillips was second into the kitchen. The SFO had already dealt with the shooter. He was a man in his thirties in a grubby black tracksuit and he was sitting on the floor. The SFO was standing over him, his Glock trained on the shooter's head.

The man sitting on the floor was staring down at his exploded knee. 'Shit!' he hissed. 'This fucking hurts, man.'

'You all right?' Phillips asked the SFO.

The officer nodded. He looked towards the floor, where the weapon had been dropped. 'Fucking thing blew up in his hand,' he said. Phillips followed his gaze. The gun looked like a drilled-out replica. He took out an evidence bag and bent down to pick it up. He dropped it in the zip-lock bag and stood up.

The shooter's left knee was burst open where the police officer had shot him. Through the burned, bloody fabric of his jogging bottoms, cartilage and bone gleamed sickly white. His left hand was badly messed up, as well. There'd be a lot of paperwork to fill out on this one. The kitchen was a state – the hob on the electric cooker was disgusting and there was a bad-drains smell.

The SFO was still pointing his pistol at the side of the perp's head. 'On your fucking back!' he said.

When the shooter looked up, his expression was desperate and he was breathing noisily. 'I told you,' he yelled in a high-pitched voice, 'the pain I'm in is fucking unbelievable. I'm not moving till I see a doctor.'

But the SFO hadn't taken kindly to being shot at. 'And I told you,' he screamed, 'to get on your fucking back!'

As best as he could, whimpering and cursing all the time, the man rolled over. Running out of patience, the SFO grabbed a handful of his hair and wrenched him down to the floor, lying him on his face. 'Now fucking well stay there!' the SFO said. Bending over his body, he cuffed the guy with a plastic lock strap.

The Drugs Squad sergeant came into the kitchen. He looked around, taking stock. 'Clear upstairs,' he said. 'One suspect in custody.' Another officer, this one carrying a sledgehammer, came past him on his way into the bathroom.

Outside, the ambulance was already waiting. The shooter was dragged out of the house first, carrying on about his knee the whole time. A uniformed PC shoved him unceremoniously into the back and climbed aboard after him. The perp who had surrendered on the stairs came next. Sean Connolly folded him into a squad car and turned back to the house.

In the sitting room, Phillips used a penknife to cut away the badly stitched lining of an upturned sofa. Once it was bare, he reached into the innards and started fishing out bag after bag of heroin. Soon, there was a pile of them on the floor. The police photographer came into the house and Phillips told him to get some shots of the bags. He put the knife in his pocket and walked back into the kitchen.

The Drugs Squad officer with the sledgehammer had emerged from the bathroom. In his other hand, he was holding a fistful of sodden wraps. He held up the BacoFoil twists. 'I managed to rescue these,' he said. 'There's more in the pipe outside.'

'Good work,' said Phillips. Things were going well. The

charges were stacking up by the minute. Now all they needed was the money.

Inside the bathroom, the cistern was in bits and there was a big pool of water on the floor. There wasn't a bath, just a shower cubicle in the corner. Phillips slid open the glass doors. The walls had been tiled right down to the edge of the tray, but there was no grouting at the join and nor was there any shampoo or soap on the floor of the shower.

Connolly appeared at Phillips's shoulder. 'Get me one of those small crowbar things,' he said.

'Sure,' said Connolly. A moment later, he was back in the bathroom. 'There you go,' he said, handing Phillips a small length of steel pipe with two long prongs at the end. The bathroom was so small that Connolly had to push the door closed so they could both get in. Phillips knelt down just outside the cubicle and ran his hand all over the bottom of the shower tray. It was bone dry. Not a drop of water had been left anywhere. It was loose, too.

'What you got?' Connolly asked from behind him.

'I don't know yet,' said Phillips, ramming the fork into the plughole. With a little forcing it went through the spars and found a purchase. Phillips pressed down on the other end and the whole shower tray lifted an inch or so.

Connolly got down on his knees next to Phillips. He put his hands underneath the lips of the heavy ceramic tray and together they wrestled it slowly up from the floor, lifting it onto its back edge and leaning it against the wall. Just as Phillips thought, there was no drain. Instead, in between the thick wooden floor joists, there were nine fat bundles of money, each one wrapped tightly in cellophane. Connolly whistled. He reached out and picked up one of the wads. It was about three inches tall and it looked like every single note was a fifty. He looked at the other wads and said, 'Must be about half a million quid there.'

From the hallway came the sound of the Drugs Squad trooping down the stairs and out of the house. They'd done their job and as far as they were concerned, the whole place belonged to SOCU now.

In the bathroom, Connolly and Phillips were still on their hands and knees. Phillips looked at the bundle of notes in Connolly's hand. 'What are you thinking, Sean?' he said.

'I'm thinking,' Connolly said, 'that no one's going to miss just one of these.' Phillips hesitated. It was enough to make Connolly change his mind. 'Put them in here, Kev,' he said, taking an evidence bag out of his pocket and opening it out. 'All of them.'

It was a suburb near the seafront newly favoured by the city's professional couples once they started having children. The houses all looked comfortable with bay windows, freshly painted woodwork and two new cars out front. A while ago, Minter thought, locking his own car and walking towards the sea, the street would have been festive with 'Sold' boards and there'd be skips in the driveways brimming with ripped-out old bathroom suites.

It was dusk and the light of a TV screen flickered in the front room of one of the houses. A woman was standing by the window, looking out for her husband, who was probably late home from work, and balancing a young child in pyjamas on her hip. Minter walked past. It was what he had never had: a home to come back to, a place where he was known and loved, a family.

After Anna's murder, Minter was sent back to a children's home in the city and it was from here each morning that he would set off when he wasn't at school. At the time, he didn't think he was looking for anything or anyone in particular; he was just wandering the streets all day long, observing the people of every neighbourhood and learning their routines. It turned out to be the perfect preparation for his chosen career. By the time Minter finally left care on his eighteenth birthday, he knew the city very well, from its elegant Georgian squares to its meanest alleys. There'd been so many homes by then that Minter had lost count of them, but he never took refuge in alcohol and drugs like the other kids, never shoplifted or broke up his room, never kicked against the traces. It was the encouragement of a handful of adults that got him through – however thin and frayed, what they told Minter became his lifeline. A couple of the carers, a few teachers, even one of Minter's social workers, they'd take a look at Minter's file and they'd raise an eyebrow, surprised to find such intelligence and ambition buried there. It was not the thing they expected from a lad with Minter's background. They'd look at the watchful, silent boy sitting across the table and smile. 'You're doing really well,' they'd say. 'Keep going.'

*Keep going.* They were the same words Minter heard out on the Downs, when the hills got steep and his lungs started burning. He never gave up. He might be alone, but he would finish the course.

Halfway down the street, there was a letterbox. Minter held the thick A4 envelope addressed to the crime correspondent on the *Evening Argus*. Chief Superintendent Roberts had forgotten Minter's characteristic thoroughness.

After that first time he had been told to doctor the crime figures, Minter had kept a copy of every email and every note the super had ever sent him, along with copies of the raw data. Everything was in the envelope, together with the amended versions of the statistics as they had appeared in the official Force reports. The full record might be enough to finish Minter's career, but it would end Roberts's reign in Brighton, too. Reaching out a hand, Minter let the envelope fall into the gaping mouth of the letterbox. It slipped down easily, bouncing a little on the metal grille inside.

Turning towards the sea, Minter started counting down the house numbers. There was one house he was looking for in particular. Knocking on doors, Minter thought, that was something else he hadn't done a lot of since he'd been working with Roberts up at the Park. In a funny kind of way, he'd missed that most of all. Being let in was one of those powers that made the job special, made you different from everybody else. Day or night, an officer had the right of entry.

After Ray Tyler had died, the entire Windmill team, including DS Minter, had trooped into the MIR where Chief Inspector Pendle was waiting to speak to them. Pendle was that oddity, a Yorkshireman who had made his way in the South, and he retained a reputation for plain speaking. He was a tough man and everyone in SOCU listened to him. He began by paying tribute to Tyler's bravery, describing the months of preparation during which Tyler had burrowed ever deeper undercover, living in a squalid little flat in Brighton, never seeing his family, taking bigger and bigger risks every time he met up with Alan Day. Then Pendle spoke of the terrible hole that Tyler's death had rent in the lives of his young widow and his little son and daughter. And finally, the chief inspector spoke of the police family. It was grieving, too, he said; it was hurting, missing one of its own.

Ahead of Minter, the backs of a row of green-painted beach huts lined the prom. Finally, he found the house number he was looking for. It took a couple of minutes for Beckett to answer. 'What the hell are you doing here, Minter?'

'There's been a development in Windmill,' Minter said. 'It's about Jacqui Compton.'

Beckett looked at the young man on his doorstep. 'This isn't another one of your hare-brained theories, is it?'

'No, sir.'

'What is it, then?'

'Jacqui's ready to make a statement. She wants to give up Russell.'

'Who told you that?' said Beckett.

'She did.'

After a moment Beckett opened the door wider. 'I suppose I haven't got anything better to do.'

Minter stepped inside. Beckett and his wife had lived in this house for a long time and the décor in the hallway was old-fashioned – dark green carpets and willow-patterned wallpaper. Looking down, Minter recognised the cardboard box filled with the things from Beckett's office. Only the photo of Beckett's wife had been unpacked, the rest of it untouched. Beckett walked into the living room and turned on the light. 'Come in here,' he said.

Minter went inside the homely-looking lounge. Sitting

231

down on one of the sofas, he took out his pack of Benson &
Hedges.

Beckett was old-fashioned enough to keep a glass ashtray
on the mantelpiece. He gave it to Minter. 'Did Slater tell
you to come here?'

Minter lit his cigarette. 'I don't work for Slater. You're
still the SIO as far as I can see.'

Beckett went to sit in his usual armchair by the fireplace.
'So what's this about Jacqui?'

'This afternoon, Jacqui Compton went back to Whitehawk. It was some kind of trip down memory lane. The
Hangletons got wind of Jacqui being there and they sent a
reception committee. If I hadn't turned up, Jacqui Compton
would be dead. She's all right now, but what happened
shook her up. She thought she and her family were untouch-
able, but now she knows that's no longer the case, she wants
some insurance.'

Beckett nodded. 'Protection for her and Chris, you mean?'

'Right. And she wants revenge on Russell for what he
did to Dave.'

'Does she now?' said Beckett, suddenly very interested.
'And how's she going to do that?'

'You were right about Jacqui doing the money laundering
for Russell. She knows all the financials.'

'So do we,' said Beckett. 'The problem is tying them to
Russell. We've had a forensic accountant working on that
for the last six months, Minter, and he can't get past Jacqui
to Russell.'

'Jacqui thinks she can get Russell's signature on some
papers.'

Beckett thought about it. 'Why are you telling me all this,

232

Minter? If you went to Slater with this lead, it could turn the whole game round.'

'Things need to be done quickly,' said Minter.

'Why?'

'Because Windmill won't be around after tomorrow.'

'What are you talking about?'

Minter told Beckett about the security breach with ExCal and he told him about the email he'd sent this afternoon to the IT manager. 'I couldn't keep it under my hat any longer,' Minter said. 'The whole operation has been compromised. Nothing recorded on ExCal is ever going to stand up in court. I didn't tell the techies everything I know because I wanted to buy us some time, but it won't take them long to work it out for themselves.'

'Shit,' said Beckett. Last summer, as well as getting Windmill off the ground, and going up to the hospital every day to see Julie, Beckett had to go to countless meetings with the computer boffins up at the Park, meetings that had sent his head to a point. 'This problem with ExCal,' Beckett asked Minter, 'was it my fault?'

'Yes. The implementation failed to follow CRAMM guidelines.'

'Plain English, Minter,' Beckett warned him.

'It was a mess, a cock-up from start to finish. The passwords were all given out with the wrong privileges. That's what confused me at first.'

'What will happen when the techies work it out?'

'They'll tell Roberts and the super will call in Professional Standards.'

Professional Standards was the national squad that looked into allegations of police incompetence and corruption. 'Shit,' said Beckett. He had spent the afternoon trying to come to terms with the end of his career as a DCI, but now it seemed he would be lucky to even get away with his pension. The loss of his reputation would be the hardest thing to swallow, though. Tom Beckett had a lot of famous scalps to his name and up until Windmill, even the likes of Superintendent Roberts couldn't take that away from him, but now it would be this one disastrous operation that everyone in Brighton and Hove would remember him for.

Minter could tell what Beckett was thinking. 'I'm sorry,' he said.

Beckett looked at him. 'It's my bad, not yours. I didn't exactly give you a lot of choice, did I?'

Minter leaned forward. 'Like I said, we've got a day at least to do this thing with Jacqui. And I think I know who's been selling Windmill out, too.'

Beckett perked up on both counts. 'Who is it, Minter? Give me a name.'

'Kevin Phillips or Sean Connolly. They've both been making enquiries in the CHIS module and the timings work out for both of them. I'll give their names to Professional Standards when they arrive. But before that happens, before Windmill grinds to a complete halt, I want to do something about Russell Compton.'

Beckett understood. 'Where's Jacqui now?'

'She's spending the night at home, just like normal. I'm going to meet her in town first thing in the morning.'

Beckett nodded. He could see just how far Minter was going out on a limb for this. 'And we're going to do this thing together, are we?'

Minter nodded. 'Looks like it.'

'Beckett and Minter, eh?' Beckett mused. 'Who would have thought it?'

It was the build-up to the Pride weekend and the Aloha bar was hotting up. There were no tables tonight because they'd all been taken out, just a small stage at the far end and a dance floor packed with men. As well as loud music, the promise of sex was everywhere. Somewhere near the middle of the room, a broad-shouldered man in a white singlet rooted greedily with his tongue in the ear of another man. He stopped. A look passed between them. Together, they traced their way across the dance floor. There was no aggression in their patient, gentle progress through the crowd. The Aloha wasn't like that. This wasn't like the seafront clubs, where the drink-fuelled fistfights were always on the verge of breaking out. Tonight in the Aloha, there was just touch and stare and desire. It was Pride.

At the end of the bar, there was a curtain. The man in the singlet paused in front of it to offer his more tentative lover a reassuring smile. He pulled open the curtain and for a moment the shadowy space on the other side was revealed. A low red bulb illuminated a collage of moving limbs. The two men went inside and the curtain fell behind them.

At the other end of the bar, there was a solid door and, behind this, a tiny dressing room where the Aloha's performers would prepare for their act. Inside, Rita was staring at his reflection in the mirror on the dressing table, his heavy frame engulfing the little stool he was sitting on. He took a drag from his cigarette, replacing it in the groove of the ashtray. He dabbed on the last of his pancake make-up before using a pair of giant tweezers to pick a set of false eyelashes out of the top compartment of the large make-up case he used on these occasions. One by one, the impossibly long eyelashes went in. Rita put his head back and blinked a couple of times, careful not to let the little tear in his eye dribble over the thick mascara. From outside, the music changed to a track that was big in the clubs at the moment, prompting a loud cheer from the crowd.

'It sure ain't the Gardens,' Rita drawled, slipping effortlessly into one of his familiar personas, 'but what's a girl to do?'

Standing behind Rita, Michael Lambert chuckled ingratiatingly. He jingled the loose change in the pockets of his grey chinos.

Rita fluffed up the curls on the cascading auburn wig draped over the milliner's dummy head on the dressing table in front of him. He glanced up at Lambert in the mirror. Rita was annoyed with him for coming backstage tonight. This was no time for complications. The gear was already on the seas and half the money was out of Rita's accounts. Everything in Brighton had to be ready.

Lambert took his own cigarettes out of the pocket of his leather blouson jacket. He shook a Marlboro free of the soft pack. 'Good luck tonight, Rita,' he said.

'Thanks,' Rita replied.

Rita Hayworth was itself a stage name, of course. In Hollywood in the 1940s, the film studio had given an unknown Hispanic woman called Margarita Cansino a brand-new identity. Out went her Mexican name and the years of abuse suffered at the hands of a particularly gruesome husband were deleted. Rita Hayworth was born in

Hollywood. Anxious, war-weary movie-goers were presented with yet another smiling, big-chested sex siren.

Brighton's Rita glanced up at Lambert again. 'What's troubling you, Michael?'

Lambert sucked in smoke loudly. 'I saw what the Hangletons did to Stevie Elliott. They're a bunch of fucking animals.' He looked at Rita. 'And then there was all that stuff on the TV news.'

Rita had seen it, too. The carefully synchronised drug raids had been the lead item on the local bulletin. 'It'll blow over,' said Rita, looking in the mirror to check his make-up one last time. 'The police are just trying to reassure the public. A little cup of cocoa to put them to bed with. You've got nothing to worry about.'

Lambert heard the scrape of impatience in Rita's last remark. 'I trust you, Rita, of course I do, but what about the Hangletons? They're getting out of hand.'

Rita teased out a curl in the wig with a comb. He'd seen the photos of Elliott, too. It seemed that Dempsey had some imagination, after all. 'The Hangletons are terrorists,' he said. 'They were looking for a *spectacular* and they found it in poor Stevie. But nothing's going to happen to you, Michael, because I've already told the Hangletons to leave you alone.' Rita got up from the stool and turned round. There was a clothes rail against the wall and Rita went over to it, flicking through a few of the costumes. 'So don't fret, Michael. I do so hate fretting.'

Rita unhooked his first costume from its hanger and pulled apart the Velcro tabs that were there because when he came offstage for changes, speed was of the essence. He glanced at Lambert, who was flicking ash nervously onto the floor. Michael Lambert had taste in lots of things that were important to Rita – drugs, travel, furniture, boys – but the Kemptown dealer was looking a little too frazzled. He shouldn't have come to the Aloha at all, and inside the cramped dressing room, it was becoming too hot.

'Now,' Rita said, the dress in his hands, 'a bit of privacy is needed.'

Outside, Lambert pushed his way to the bar. He'd only just ordered a drink when a man came over to him.

'Mikey!' the man greeted him, flashing a smile. He was wearing a peaked leather cap. It was retro, of course, but then every fucking thing in Brighton was one species of retro or another. The guy leaned in a little closer. 'You carrying?' Michael shook his head. The leather man looked at him sceptically. He was a regular punter: cocaine for clubbing and smack to mellow out with at the weekend. He must have a decent job because his purchasing habits had been constant for a while.

'Give it a couple of days,' said Lambert. The man understood. He nodded. 'By the way,' said Lambert, thinking of something else, 'you seen anything of Terry Sampson?'

The man laughed. 'Not likely. Terry's well poxed.'

Lambert nodded. He looked away. 'Come and see me in a couple of days.'

The guy clinked his bottle into Michael's. 'Nice one,' he said, disappearing back into the crowd.

Lambert sipped his lager. He could tell that he'd annoyed Rita. He would have to find a way of making it up to him quick. There were plenty of ways of doing that, he thought, surveying the writhing scene in the bar of the Aloha for a likely candidate to offer up to the importer.

At least Rita hadn't asked about Sampson, Lambert thought. Rita had entrusted the arrangements for James McFarland into his hands. They were trifles, but Lambert had managed to get that all wrong, as well.

The music stopped. The Aloha's manager climbed up onto the stage and stepped up to the microphone. His name was Charlie Brown and he tapped the mic to test it. 'Good evening, gents,' he said. He waited for a bit of hush. 'And ladies, of course.' There were a few cat calls. 'Tonight ...' he began to build ' ... and just for tonight ... the hottest ... hardest ... bitch is back in town.' There were cheers. 'I give you ... Lady Rita!'

The follow spot blinked on; its beam was directed at the doorway of the dressing room where Lady Rita was standing. She gave a wave to the crowd, lapping up their wolf whistles. With her right hand, she swept the train of her dress behind her and crossed the floor, pigeon-stepping on to the naked stage. All down her flowing, gauzy dress, the sequins spangled wildly in the spotlight. Putting her hands on her hips, Lady Rita let the audience get a load of her immense body. She blew kisses into the crowd, winking at one or two of the adoring boys. At last, as the applause and whistling started to die down, she reached up to the ceiling with one hand, her red-painted fingernails splitting the white light down the length of her body. Then her fingers started to twirl in time with the sinuous rhythm flowing out of the PA. A smoky saxophone introduced the tune and Lady Cansino rocked her voluptuous body from side to side. A snare drum cracked. She froze. In the sudden hush, a huge thigh appeared from the slit that went all the way up the side of her dress and Lady Rita took hold of the microphone in her pudgy hand. She caressed it, squeezing it tightly until there were a few moans from the crowd. Then, with a stern, wide-eyed stare, she silenced the room completely. 'Men go to bed with Rita,' her voice rumbled, 'but they wake up with me.' There was a roar of approval. 'Don't they get a big fucking surprise!'

The heavy, thudding disco beat of the first song started. The crowd burst into life as Lady Rita began to bellow the lyric into the mic. Delirious with pleasure, the boys danced. Lambert was there, too, lost in the middle of the crowd. It was going to be a long night.

# 11
· · ·

The next morning, in the living room of his flat in Kemptown, Michael Lambert was dreaming about falling.

A moment later, he sat bolt upright on the sofa. His head thumped and his mouth was dry. It had been an eventful evening and he hadn't got in until half past four. He must have fallen asleep on the sofa. Light was pouring in from the open French windows, where a gust of sea breeze moved the velvet drapes a little and the sun was just visible in the left-hand corner of a portion of blue sky. From the sun's position, Lambert could tell that it was still early, far too early to be awake, in fact. There it was again: the impatient thudding on his front door.

Frightened out of his stupor, convinced that the Hangletons had come for him, Lambert stood up so quickly that he almost fainted. Putting his hands out, he knocked over the wine bottle on the coffee table. The dregs spilled out onto the wood and the bottle rolled around. 'Shit,' Lambert whispered to himself, reaching out a hand to stop it making any more noise. He padded out of the room, clinging to the wan hope that they might just go away.

In the hallway, through the spyhole, he saw a tall, good-looking woman flanked by two burly police officers in uniform. 'Thank God,' he muttered under his breath.

'Michael Lambert,' the woman said through the door in a loud voice, 'I'm giving you a warning. If you don't open this door, we're going to have to break it down.'

Lambert slid the security chain over and turned the key in the mortise lock. He opened the heavy door. 'Are you Michael Lambert?' the woman asked. She was holding out a piece of paper and her police ID. He nodded. 'Good,' she said. 'Because I'm Detective Constable Reynolds and this is a warrant for your arrest.' Once inside, Vicky shepherded Lambert back the way he'd come. The uniformed officers began a thorough search of the flat.

The living room was quite something. It ran the entire width of the second-floor mansion flat. There was a huge fireplace on the far wall and a chandelier hung from an elaborate plaster rose in the middle of the ceiling. A chaise longue upholstered in gold brocade sat in front of the French windows.

Lambert went to sit on the barge-like chaise. He busied himself with a pack of cigarettes and a Zippo. Vicky glanced at the pair of silver cherubs fluttering on the wall either side of the fireplace. 'Bet you like opera, too,' she said.

Lambert lit his cigarette and coughed. Turning to the side, he stared wearily out of the window. As far as he was concerned, their conversation was over.

Michael Lambert had been careful. Very careful. He'd seen the way the wind was blowing so he'd cleared all the drugs and the drugs money out of his flat. There'd be residue everywhere if they got really picky but nothing that meant anything more than personal use.

Vicky stared down at Michael Lambert. With his elegant flat and his grizzled beard, it would have been easier to believe he dealt in antiques than narcotics. Like Minter had said, Lambert and Russell Compton inhabited different universes. Theirs was a very curious partnership indeed.

Vicky had checked Lambert's sheet before setting off. There was one charge of conspiracy that had never even made it to court. Other than that, just a single conviction for possession of cocaine was the best the police could stack against him, and even that had been a while ago. Someone was looking out for Michael Lambert.

One of the PCs poked his head round the door of the living room. 'Ma'am,' he said.

'Stay here,' Vicky told her suspect. She walked out of the room and pushed the door closed behind her.

'Anything?' she asked the PC in the corridor.

'Nothing,' he said. He was young, with clear brown eyes. 'Should we bring in the dogs?' he asked.

There was a van outside. Vicky had hoped it wouldn't be necessary. 'Go in the living room and wait with Lambert,' she said.

Vicky walked down the hall, going in and out of the rooms. All of them had been decorated with the same fastidious eye for detail. It was like an estate agent's fantasy of a Brighton period property, right down to the hyper-modern touch of the white Apple Mac sitting on a table in the master bedroom, where the second constable was rifling through Lambert's bedside cabinet. He took out a bottle of pills and read the label on the side. 'Prescription,' he told Vicky. 'Sleeping tablets by the look of them. Got his name on the label.'

Back in the living room, Michael Lambert was standing by the French windows, leaning down to stub out his cigarette in the ashtray on the lamp table. He glanced at Vicky quickly before turning his attention back to the Kemptown seafront. A jogger went by below him. A jam started at the traffic lights. 'Find anything you like?' he asked Vicky.

She gave him a long, contemptuous look before walking over to where he was standing. She picked up one of the roaches from the ashtray and smelled it.

'It's only a joint,' Lambert said. 'Just something to unwind with.'

'James McFarland,' Reynolds said. Like the tongue of a lizard, a flicker of recognition passed across Lambert's face. It was the last thing he'd been expecting her to say. Minter was on to something else, too. 'There's some pure knocking about, Michael,' Vicky said, covering her tracks. 'It's what killed McFarland.'

Through the French windows, another waft of sea breeze floated up into the room. 'I've got absolutely no idea what you're talking about,' Lambert said.

'OK, Michael,' Vicky said, 'you're coming with us.'

'So you've found a joint,' Lambert said. 'Big fucking deal. Why do I have to go to the station?'

'Well,' she said, 'the alternative is I bring in a couple of Alsatians and a few crowbars. That can do a lot of damage to a place like this. I'd hate to see the dogs crap all over that chaise, for instance.'

Michael Lambert sighed. 'Give me a minute to change my clothes.'

It was trying to be a church, Minter thought, looking around the large, empty chapel. Trying, but not quite succeeding. The high windows contained glass that was transparent rather than stained. Instead of a pulpit, the bald man at the front was standing behind a lectern on a platform raised up from the floor by a few scant inches.

Minter was sitting in the back row. He had come here this morning because he was curious to see who would turn up to say a last farewell to James McFarland. Apart from him and the officiator, it looked like there wasn't going to be anyone in the congregation. James McFarland's body had been released to his father at the earliest opportunity. No time had been wasted in arranging the boy's cremation.

The sound of the heavy metal latch echoed in the chapel. It was immediately followed by a high-pitch giggle. 'Shh!' someone hissed.

Minter turned to see three young men walk in. The foremost among them was wearing Aviator sunglasses. All three were wearing ripped, bleached jeans. It wasn't the conventional attire for a funeral. They walked past Minter and took three seats on the end of the middle rows of chairs. There were a couple more snorts of embarrassed laughter before they settled down.

The officiator, a sallow man in a dark suit, cleared his throat. He was just about to start speaking when the door opened again and Alistair McFarland hurried into the chapel. The first thing he saw was DS Minter's interrogative face. He glanced quickly away, nodding his apology to the man at the front and going quickly to sit down in the second row.

Finally, the officiator got the chance to say a few brief things. They were humane, consolatory remarks about friendship and the endurance of the family bond, but they were over almost too quickly to be decent. Then he stopped speaking and pressed a button on the side of the lectern and the coffin trundled forward on its rollers.

After a moment, there was silence. 'Is it over?' whispered one of the rent boys. The officiator looked over at Alistair McFarland and nodded.

That was it, Minter realised. That was the business that marked the passing of James McFarland's life. A handful of words, a low rumble and the coffin was delivered into the flames. There was a slight commotion as the three young men got up from their seats and headed for the exit. Stepping down from his platform, the officiator walked over to Alistair McFarland and shook his hand. The two men exchanged a polite word or two.

Minter caught up with McFarland before the latter could reach the door. The older man's forehead was a little glossy with sweat. 'What is it now?' McFarland asked.

Minter took the letter out of his jacket pocket. He showed the envelope to McFarland. 'Why did you lie to me, Mr McFarland? Why didn't you say you tried to contact James?'

McFarland looked down at the stone floor. Like everything else in his life, he had decided to keep the embarrassing memory of sending the ridiculous note firmly to himself. 'I didn't lie,' he told Minter. 'I told you I hadn't seen James in years, and I hadn't.' He nodded at the letter. 'That note was merely meant to remind James where I was living.

I never saw him. I was leaving it up to him to call me.'

The sudden-death report had stated that James McFarland had lived alone. Minter asked, 'How did the note come to be in James's possession, then?'

'James was a common prostitute. They have to advertise, don't they? I rang a few of the numbers I found in phone boxes and pretty soon I ended up speaking to his flatmate. It was distasteful, but...' McFarland left the sentence unfinished.

Minter could see how difficult it must have been for an outwardly respectable man like Alistair McFarland to make those telephone calls.

'I went to his flat a week ago,' McFarland went on. 'He wasn't there. I gave the note to his flatmate.'

'What was his name?' Minter asked.

'Terry something. I didn't know his surname.' McFarland looked towards the front of the chapel, at the purple curtain behind which his son had disappeared for ever. 'If he ever got the note, James didn't reply.'

'I spoke to your lodger,' said Minter. 'Mr Scammell told me you went out late on the night that James died. Where did you go, Mr McFarland?'

'I drove around Kemptown looking for him.' McFarland shook his head at the memory. 'I wanted to see him again, just the once. It was a foolish thing to do.'

'Did you find James?'

McFarland shook his head. 'People like James just don't know how to help themselves, do they? In your line of work, you must see that kind of thing all the time.' There was a silence. 'To tell you the truth, I wasn't even going to come today. I only changed my mind at the last minute. No matter what he did, no matter how he lived, James was still my son.'

Minter looked at the handwritten envelope, hoping that James had had the chance to read the note it held. Even if it was just an address, even if there was no message, he hoped James had understood how difficult his father had found it to reach out to him but how he'd tried nonetheless. 'Here,' said Minter, holding out the note to James's father. 'You should keep this.'

At first, McFarland didn't know what to do. Then he took the letter and placed it carefully inside his breast pocket. Minter watched him walk slowly down the aisle and out of the chapel, and a minute or so later, Minter left himself.

Outside, the sun was getting hot. Standing on the wide steps, Minter slipped off his black tie and stuffed it into his jacket pocket. In one of the parking bays, he watched McFarland getting into his old Ford and rattle off up the hillside. On the bright expanse of grass on the other side of the drive, the rent boys had gathered to smoke a cigarette. Behind them, the lawn swept away, dotted with giant blue rhododendron bushes. Standing around a plywood cross that indicated the area reserved for floral tributes, the boys looked out of place in their hustler mufti of ripped jeans and dyed hair. At their feet was a solitary bouquet of white lilies.

Minter walked down the steps and crossed the gravel. He looked down at the flowers. On the card attached was one word: *Jimbob*.

The man in the Aviators spoke up first. 'Can't you lot ever leave us alone?'

The policeman looked at the trio of sullen outcasts. They were putting on a dumbshow of defiance for his benefit,

Minter realised, hiding their vulnerability. Standing side by side, though, at least they had each other. And Jimbob had been one of them, too. So when he died, they'd bought him flowers.

Some kind of family, Minter thought. Any kind of family was better than none. 'Did you know Jimbob well?' he asked.

'Yeah,' said the man in the Aviators. 'We were his friends.'

Minter glanced at the others. 'If any of you are using, you should know that Jimbob's OD was because he was injecting pure. You need to be careful.'

When their leader took his sunglasses off, his features were gentler than Minter had expected. 'Thanks,' he said.

The sun climbed the sky. It was getting humid. 'Jimbob wasn't a heavy user, was he?' Minter asked.

The man shook his head. 'He couldn't fix himself,' he said.

'What do you mean?' said Minter.

'He hated needles. Phobic about them, he was.'

It rang true. The track marks on Jimbob's body were limited in number. 'So who fixed up for him, then?' It was the rent boy's turn to look at the lilies. 'Was it his flatmate?' Minter asked. 'Was it Terry?'

The rent boy didn't owe Sampson anything. Hadn't Sampson chased him off his patch twice last week? 'Yes,' he told Minter. 'It was Terry.'

'What's his surname?'

'Sampson. Terry Sampson.'

Minter looked the rent boy in the eye. 'What if it wasn't

an accidental overdose?' he said. 'Who might want Jimbob dead?'

As soon as he asked the question, Minter knew he had gone too far. It wasn't just the prohibition on speaking to the police that had fallen across the rent boy's lips, preventing him from saying anything more. It was fear.

As soon as Rita sat down at a table for a late breakfast at the Hôtel du Vin, the maître d' made his way over at a clip. 'Mr Ashton,' he said, 'so good to see you again. Are you well?'

'Very well,' Rita replied, leaning back a little so that George could flip out his napkin and settle it on his lap. Mr Ashton was the name Rita went by in the more salubrious precincts of Brighton. 'Just had my morning constitutional, so I'm feeling peckish.'

George nodded. He knew Mr Ashton's appetites very well. 'The full English?' he asked.

'Please, George,' said Rita. 'And Earl Grey.'

'Of course, Mr Ashton,' said George, giving an unctuous little bob before he scuttled off.

Most of the hotel guests had already left to begin their day. In the large dining room, there was just a sated-looking young couple sitting over by the window. Rita watched a waiter he knew traverse the room towards him. He was wearing a white apron tied French-style round his waist and was holding the silver tray above his head, balancing it delicately on his fingers. Arriving at Rita's table, he set down the silver teapot and Rita noticed the small bloom of condensation on the side of the warmed milk jug that followed it down onto the linen. 'Thank you,' he said.

'Thank you, sir,' said the waiter. When he left, his aftershave lingered in the air, the scent pleasingly floral in Rita's nose.

A moment later, Emile entered the dining room. Spotting Rita straight away, he came over. 'Good morning,' he said, putting a folded copy of last night's *Evening Standard* down on the table next to Rita's tea.

Rita glanced at the paper disapprovingly, then looked up at Emile. The Albanian looked rested and relaxed, but he was still too thin. Rita had decided that he didn't like thin men. 'Did you sleep well?'

'Very well,' said Emile.

Rita took his first sip of tea and dabbed at his mouth with his napkin. 'The food here is very good.'

Emile shook his head. 'I had breakfast in my room.' His gaze went from the Englishman's face down to the large ring on Rita's middle finger. He stared at the ruby for a moment before flicking open the copy of the newspaper. On the front page, there was a picture of a line of police officers outside a flat in Brighton. They were breaking down the door and the headline above the photo read, 'Seaside Cops Bite Back.'

'We are business people,' said Emile. 'We have to make a risk assessment.'

'I'm a business person, too,' said Rita, 'and you've got half my money.'

The waiter was approaching the table again, carrying a large plate of food. He put it down on the table in front of Rita, but this time Rita didn't thank him or even look at him because he was too busy imagining what it would be like to reach across the table and plunge the tines of his silver fork deep into Emile's impertinent fucking neck. 'These are local difficulties,' he said, cutting up some bacon instead.

With a distaste he didn't bother to hide, Emile watched Rita eat. 'When was the last time you supplied this Compton?'

Rita lifted the lid of the mustard pot and spooned some of the yellow condiment onto the side of his plate near the sausages. He knew that Emile would already know the answer to his question. 'Three months ago.' He jerked his beringed finger at the front-page story. 'That's why all this is kicking off, Emile. The new boys are taking their chance. Like I told you, Compton is history.'

Emile disagreed. 'Three months is not long enough to be safe. Three months is not history.'

Rita put down his knife and fork on the side of his plate. The Albanians were soldiers. A show of strength was what they wanted to see. He took his mobile from his pocket and rang a number and the call picked up on the second ring. 'This thing,' said Rita into his phone, 'it has to be done today.' Rita listened to Dempsey's demands. 'You'll have it.' There was another pause. 'Yes, everyone in the house, the whole fucking tribe.' Rita cut the call, put the phone back in his pocket and looked at Emile. 'Russell Compton will be dead before nightfall.'

Emile smiled. 'I can see you are a resourceful man, Rita.'

As Rita tucked into his breakfast, Emile studied the curious wall mural on the upper portion of the dining room. The painted figures were life-size. The man in the foreground was wearing an old-fashioned gabardine trench coat and a trilby hat. His skin had an unhealthy green tinge to it and his mouth was creased. Behind him, the bar scene was crowded with other figures. A brassy-looking blonde was chatting to a group of three sailors in old-fashioned bell-bottomed trousers. A girl in a red dress was talking to a smooth-shaven young man in a double-breasted suit.

Rita drank some more tea and put the cup back on the saucer. 'When does the ship dock?' he asked.

Emile turned back to Rita. 'At nine tomorrow morning. It's carrying drill parts for the oil rigs off Aberdeen. Big drills. The manufacturer is a Norwegian company called Myarstad. The gear will be well hidden.'

'Will we need specialists?'

Emile smiled. 'You're a clever man, Rita. I'm sure it's nothing you can't handle.'

Rita let the sarcasm go by. All that mattered now was the deal.

'And the rest of the money?' said Emile.

'The second instalment will be in euros,' Rita told him. 'Four million, as agreed, and it'll be in your accounts by close of play.'

Emile nodded. 'All is good, then.'

'Listen, Emile, whatever his faults, Russell Compton has been one of my best customers for years. I don't mind cutting him loose – he's finished, like I said – but I'm showing you a lot of goodwill by getting rid of him, so I expect something back in return. Next time round, it's twenty thou a kilo.'

'We'll talk again,' Emile replied, 'after we get the money.'

On St James's Street, two young men were gossiping to each other outside the Bona Foodie deli but as soon as Minter broke his stride to light a cigarette, they stopped. Vicky was right Minter thought: Kemptown was a village. Everyone here knew everyone else's business. But, like real villagers, they often kept what they knew strictly between themselves.

A Mercedes crawled past Minter, its driver peering down a side street, trying to sniff out one of the elusive parking spaces. The plates on the car indicated that it came from out of town. Kemptown was filling up for Pride.

On St James's Street, style lived next door to the down-trodden. In the middle of the next parade of shops was a Cash Converters and a shop selling accessories for pets called Doggy Fashion.

At the station this morning, Minter had bumped into Vicky Reynolds. They'd talked about Michael Lambert and Minter had told her about James McFarland.

According to Vicky, there were three types of rent boy. The lowest of the low were the hustlers who turned tricks out on the street and in the cottages. The hustlers were the ones most likely to be addicts and most of the time they were just looking for cash to buy drugs with. The money went hand over fist, from punter to rent boy to dealer. Street hustlers got beaten up and sometimes raped. They never lasted: if the hep or HIV didn't get them in the end, the dealers did.

Minter had read the post-mortem report on James McFarland. The boy was relatively healthy. He probably worked in the next division up from the street hustlers, turning tricks by appointment out of the flat on Lower Rock Gardens. He might have worked together with Terry, sharing the advertising costs, splitting the profits. At the top of the chain, there were the escorts and the strippers. The strippers liked to deny it, but they all sold themselves after hours in the back rooms of the clubs where they worked, or in the saunas along the Steine. Finally, there were the escorts who got called out to the hotels in Brighton – to the Metropole, the Hilton, the Grand. Of all the male prostitutes, the escorts earned the most. The lucky ones even got the chance to retire.

Minter checked his watch. It was eleven o'clock. He had to be quick. He was meeting Beckett in an hour. He looked down the next side street but the pub he wanted wasn't there so he crossed the road and kept going.

Minter came to another quiet side road. This time he glimpsed the pub sign he was looking for. The Queen's Head was halfway along. Minter paced quickly down the street and went inside.

A mirrorball had been suspended from the ceiling but that one detail aside, the place looked like any other upmarket drinking hole in Brighton. There were the same varnished floorboards, the same chocolate-coloured sofas, the same scrubbed wooden tables, at one of which a group of three businessmen had gathered. Behind them was a glazed door leading out into a small patio garden. It was nothing like the place Vicky had described. Perhaps things here had changed.

Minter ordered a St Clements from the barman, whose eyebrow was pierced by a sharpened slug of metal. When he asked for payment, Minter caught sight of another slug poking out of his tongue.

Minter sipped his drink. The door opened again. A nervous-looking man in his forties wearing designer jeans and a well-pressed shirt came in off the street and walked up to the bar. He ordered a brandy and looked around.

A minute later, the door opened again. This time, the newcomer was a man around twenty with close-cropped, peroxided hair and pencilled-in eyebrows. He walked up to the bar as if he was used to being the centre of attention. His arrival certainly perked up the man in the jeans.

The rent boy seemed to be ignoring his mark. He talked to the barman instead, paying for his spritzer before leaving the glass on the bar and taking his change over to the cigarette machine by the window, where he made a fuss of choosing his brand of cigarettes. Sure enough, the pair of jeans wandered over and there was a whispered conversation between the two of them. The rent boy nodded in Minter's direction. With a frightened expression, the other man turned round and quickly left the pub.

Cigarettes in hand, the rent boy returned to the bar. He picked up the spritzer and walked past Minter, going through the door and out into the tiny courtyard garden. He sat down at one of the picnic tables. Minter waited for a few beats, then followed him out.

The rent boy was sunning himself. He didn't open his eyes until Minter was sitting down on the other side of the table. He nodded at the St Clements. 'On duty, are you?'

Minter smiled. 'That obvious, is it?'

Scrutinising Minter carefully, the boy nodded.

Minter noticed that his once-boyish features were beginning to turn gross. 'Still escorting are you, Scott?' Minter asked. He might be no good as an undercover officer, but he had a great memory for names and faces. That was the advantage of being a senior analyst. All the records were open to you. 'Vicky Reynolds says hello,' Minter added.

Over Minter's shoulder, Scott Williams watched a seagull land on one of the terracotta chimneypots on the roofline of the houses behind the pub. 'Is Vicky well?' he asked.

'Very,' said Minter.

Scott took a drag on his cigarette. He looked at Minter. 'I don't give discounts for key workers, if that's what you're after. If it's not, let's make this quick.'

'Jimbob McFarland,' Minter said. 'You know him?'

'Everyone knew Jimbob.'

'You know he died this week?'

Scott nodded. 'Word gets round.'

'You sad about it?'

'Not really,' said Scott. 'Jimbob was well liked. He had a lot of regulars.' The sun came out from behind a cloud again. It caught the side of his face. The seagull flew off the roof. 'More punters on the open market. What's not to like?'

Minter nodded.

'What about Jimbob's flatmate?' Minter asked.

'Sampson?' Scott said with a snort. He had misunderstood what Minter was driving at. 'Not a lot of competition there. Terry Sampson couldn't pick up a newspaper.'

'Strung out?' Minter suggested.

Scott nodded again, this time a little more circumspectly.

'Where's Sampson now?' Minter asked.

Scott Williams thought about it. It was no skin off his nose. He'd had his fair share of fallings-out with that fucker. Everyone had. 'Try the London Road flats,' he said. 'That's where the skag boys go to die.'

'Jimbob's clients,' said Minter. 'Anyone important?'

For the second time today, Minter watched the edge of

fear creep across a rent boy's face at the mere mention of Jimbob's punters. Scott was braver than most. 'One or two rich ones,' he said.

'And one in particular that no one round here wants to talk about?'

'I told you Jimbob was popular. Especially a few years ago, when he was young. Good-looking lad, he was, so he used to get invited to all the parties.'

'Whose parties?' Minter was thinking about what McFarland had told him about the fourteen-year-old James McFarland shinning down the drainpipe to spend the night away from home.

Scott finished his spritzer in one big gulp. He stubbed his cigarette out in the ashtray. 'Believe me,' Scott said, 'you don't want to know.'

'Was it Michael Lambert's parties that Jimbob used to go to?'

Scott glanced behind Minter's shoulder at the quiet public bar. 'I've got to go. You're getting bad for business.'

# 12
## ...

In the charging area at the Kemptown station, no fewer than five bad-tempered suspects queued at the custody sergeant's desk, each one marshalled by his own uniformed PC. A commotion started up from the holding cell. The impatient young man who had just been locked inside was shouting and swearing at the top of his voice and hammering on the door with his fist. 'I told you already,' the custody sergeant yelled back from behind his desk, 'you'll wait your bloody turn.' Shaking his head, the sergeant turned to the line of other men. 'Right,' he said, lining up another charge sheet. 'Next!'

Whatever else it had achieved, Operation Clean Sweep was certainly taking people off the streets.

Along the corridor, Vicky Reynolds was sitting on her own in Interview Room 1. After a long and fruitless interview, she'd just released Michael Lambert. He'd spoken just the once, which was to put on record that the cannabis resin in his flat was for personal use only. At this point, the lawyer sitting by Lambert's side had nodded appreciatively and looked across at Vicky.

Most of the suspects this morning had been happy with the duty solicitor. Not Lambert. An upscale brief had hurried down to Kemptown as soon as he got word about his client's detention. Vicky recognised the firm's name on the business card. It had a large, plush office on the Steine, every bit as impressive as Michael Lambert's flat.

The half-closed door behind Vicky nudged open. Slowly, Kevin Phillips backed into the room carrying two large coffees in his hands. After the canteen at Kemptown closed, a vending machine was all the officers had. It dispensed coffee into the kind of thin plastic cups that scalded your hands.

'Skip said you were in here,' Phillips said, relieved to put the cups down on the table. 'Peace offering.'

'Thanks,' Vicky said. She picked up the sludgy coffee and sipped it. 'How's it going out there?'

'Shit,' said Phillips. 'The stash house was an early win. Now we're pulling in a bunch of deadbeats. No one's said a word about the Hangletons.'

Vicky nodded. 'They're scared stiff.'

'It's a waste of time,' Phillips said, pulling out the chair and sitting down facing Vicky. There was a pause. 'And what about you, Vick?' Phillips asked. 'You were upset at the restaurant the other night.'

Vicky shrugged. 'It's not so bad today.'

Phillips nodded. 'Sometimes you can think about things a little too much, you know.'

Vicky drank some more coffee. She'd already made her decision. Last night, when she got home, she'd downloaded an application form for the vacant job of family liaison officer. Vicky wanted to stay at Brighton and Hove, but she'd had enough of SOCU. Whatever happened to Windmill, it was time for her to move on.

There was another reason behind Vicky's decision. Ever since her father's death, Vicky's mother had lived all alone in an idyllic but isolated cottage near the West Sussex coast. The working hours in SOCU meant that Vicky only saw her about once a week. Her mother was never one to make a lot of friends and Vicky imagined her sitting on her own inside the house all day, just the old photographs and the ticking of the grandfather clock to keep her company. The thought pricked Vicky's conscience. If she worked office hours, she told herself, she'd visit a lot more often.

But Vicky had her doubts about that. She'd adored her dad, but not so her mum. Vicky's mother exuded an air of disapproval that clung to her like perfume. Like Coty powder, it rubbed off on Vicky whenever she tried to come close. The two of them never feuded the way mother and daughter were supposed to: raised voices were forbidden. As a result, now that Vicky was older, they rarely had anything to say to each other. So Vicky fled the house after an hour of stilted conversation, getting into her car with a palpable sense of relief, and breathing easily again only once she was well on her way back to Brighton.

In the interview room, it seemed that Phillips had something to feel guilty about, as well. 'I wanted to apologise, Vick,' he said.

'For what?'

'That thing in the MIR,' said Phillips, 'about Minter, it's

261

not up to me who you see. It's none of my business. Not now it isn't.'

Vicky laughed. 'Minter's not exactly boyfriend material.'

'Isn't he?'

This time, the silence was a little awkward. 'We've both moved on, Kevin. You're with Fiona now. You've got a baby.'

Phillips sat back in his chair. He sighed. 'Yeah. And everything after, as well.'

'What do you mean?'

Phillips drank some coffee. 'We're struggling to pay the bills, Vick. Wrong mortgage, you see. And there's no work around for Fiona at the moment.' Phillips looked at Vicky. 'I don't mean to saddle you with my worries. It's just that we were really good mates, back in the day. I suppose I miss talking to you.'

'We're still friends, Kev,' said Vicky. 'And things will get easier. Just hold on in there, mate. Remember that what you've got at home is worth a lot. It's what most people want.'

'What about you?' Phillips asked. 'Is it what you want?'

'Yeah,' said Vicky. 'It is. I'm looking for something serious.'

Phillips got up. 'OK, Vick, I hear you loud and clear. But like you said, we're still friends. Right?'

He'd been a little too quick to agree. It was almost as if he'd stopped by with the coffee to keep Vicky onside. 'Tell me about what really happened at that crack house.'

Phillips was irritated. 'Nothing. Nothing happened.'

'That's not what Minter says.'

'Fuck Minter.'

262

'He's as straight as an arrow, Kev. Why would Minter want to drop you in it?'

'You better ask him.'

'I have,' Vicky said.

Phillips hesitated. 'Did Minter tell you where those crack rocks came from?'

'No.'

'They came from the same dealer, Vick. Yeah, that's right, the toerag we raided that night when Minter came along as a so-called observer? Well, a uniformed officer from Kemptown took the rocks off of him at a nightclub on the seafront. That was just a few days before the raid. We couldn't use it then, of course. Rules of evidence.' He paused. 'So you see, Vicky, when we raided that flat, I was just returning the bag to its rightful owner. Now, I'm not proud of what I did, and it's not something I make a habit of, I promise you that, but what difference did it make? We got a conviction, and the perp got what he deserved. Where's the problem?'

Vicky shook her head. 'When you talk like that, Kev, you remind me of Sean Connolly.'

'I'm talking like a police officer.' Phillips leaned forward. 'Listen, Vick, sometimes you have to cut corners to get the job done.'

'So if you're talking like a police officer,' Vicky said, 'what does that make me?'

'I'll tell you one thing, Vick. Minter might not be boyfriend material, but he's sure messed with your mind. You've got to get your priorities straight.'

'Don't patronise me, Kevin. You're only a DS, remember.'

'For fuck's sake!' Phillips brought his fist down on the

table. It upset Vicky's coffee, sending a rivulet across the table and into her lap.

'Kevin!' Vicky yelled, standing up and brushing off the hot drink.

'Minter's got you believing it, too, hasn't he, Vick? You're just pumping me for fucking intel because Minter told you to.'

Turning round, Phillips stomped out of the room, slamming the door behind him.

Providence House was the end of the line, the last ditch. The ten-storey block of flats was marooned on a black pool of tarmac just north of the burgeoning New England Quarter. Day and night, five immense, nodding cranes used to hold sway over this part of the city. Rebranded and repackaged, the neighbourhood was once the high-water mark in Brighton's rising tide of redevelopment, but now all that had changed almost overnight. There was just one abandoned crane left above the bare girders, and during the day all the building sites were quiet. Work on the half-built apartment blocks had been suspended and Providence House had been reprieved from demolition. From his car, parked on a piece of waste ground above the flats, Minter looked at the rain-stained balconies. No, he told himself, there was nothing fortunate about Providence.

A lone figure crossed the sweating tarmac from the direction of London Road. The youth had a loping walk and even in the fierce sunshine, he wore the hood of his dark red top in such a way that the whole of his face was concealed from view. He was the third punter in less than an hour. Inside Providence House, someone was knocking it out.

The hoodie reached the back entrance, near the huge metal refuse bins. He looked carefully around the deserted car park before yanking open the graffiti-riddled fire door.

Minter waited a few minutes before he got out of his car. Leaving the Passat behind, he soon fell under the long, perpendicular shadow of the tower block. He opened the blue fire door at the back of the flats and stepped down into the narrow concrete stairwell. High up on the wall, the plastic cover of the security light had been vandalised. What little daylight there was filtered down unsteadily from the landing above.

The air inside the stairwell was rank. Rubbish was strewn all about and it stank of piss. From above, Minter heard the slow slap of trainers coming down the concrete steps. They halted, as if the person descending had stopped to inspect something. Then they started up again, getting closer. Minter walked as quietly as he could into the dark, dank corner of the stairwell.

The footsteps continued to echo down. Finally, the white jogging trousers appeared, followed by the red hoodie. Minter stepped forward quickly. Seeing his approach, thinking he was about to be mugged for the deck he'd just bought, the hoodie lunged for the fire door, grabbing at its metal handle. Before he could open it properly, Minter had kicked it shut again. He turned to confront the junkie.

'I'll fucking chib you!' the junkie yelled, his hand bulging threateningly inside the pocket of his hoodie. As soon as he saw Minter's suit, however, he shrank back.

'Put your hands where I can see them,' Minter snapped.

When they came out of the hoodie, the man's hands weren't holding a blade. 'Where've you just scored from?' Minter demanded.

'Dunno what you're talking about.'

'Tell me and you can keep the deck.'

The junkie thought about it for a couple of seconds. 'Third floor.'

'Which flat?'

'Nineteen.'

'You scored here before?' Minter asked.

The addict shook his head. 'Kiddie in the pub told me about the guy. He's new to me.'

Minter gestured back up the stairs. 'Show me where he is.'

By the first-floor landing, the junkie was clutching his stomach. By the second, he was doubled up. On the landing, a small, frosted-glass window had been set into the outside wall. In its smudge of light, Minter inspected the wretched self-pity all over the junkie's face. He stopped. 'I get to keep the deck, yeah?' he whined at Minter.

Minter jerked his head upward. Slowly, they started to climb the stairs again. By the time they reached the third-floor landing, the junkie was moaning.

Minter opened the stairwell door. He let the junkie in first, following him down the shadowy hall. Underfoot, the water-stained carpet had worn through, exposing the concrete.

The junkie came to a stop outside flat number 19. The unpainted plywood door would have given in at the first good kick. Instead, Minter walked across to the other side. He nodded his encouragement at the junkie. Reluctantly, the addict tapped softly against the hollow wood.

After half a minute, a low, suspicious voice came from within. 'Yeah?'

'It's Danny,' the addict said. This time, there was no reply. Minter nodded at him again and the junkie pressed his face against the door. 'You just weighed me out,' he half whispered, 'but the deal's all wrong.'

The door opened a couple of inches and Minter saw a slice of face. 'That fucking gear's—' Minter thrust his foot into the gap and rammed the rest of his body against the door. Before he had time to understand what was happening, the dealer was lying just inside, in a heap on the floor.

Minter stood over him. 'Terry Sampson?' he said. There was no denial.

There was movement behind Minter in the hallway. 'Hey!' Minter shouted at the retreating junkie. Minter glanced back to see the addict's reluctant face appear once more in the doorway. The junkie pulled his hood even closer around his own face, trying to hide himself from Sampson.

'That deck's no good to you,' Minter said over his shoulder.

'You said I could keep it.'

'A word of advice,' Minter said through gritted teeth, 'that gear is ninety per cent. If you bang it up without cutting it, it's the last thing you'll ever do.' Minter looked at Sampson. 'It's already killed someone,' he said.

Behind him, the junkie seemed to hesitate for a moment. 'Ninety per cent,' he said, looking down at the twist. He turned and ran towards the stairs.

Minter turned to Sampson. 'Get up!' The dealer did as he was told. 'Inside.'

Terry Sampson stood in the middle of the dingy living room. The prostitute-cum-dealer was wearing a torn black T-shirt and a filthy pair of combat trousers. His Alice band scraped his long hair back from his face and pulled the skin of his face taut. Sampson's skull bulged out alarmingly from behind his features, and the yellowy eyes matched the colour of his skin. There was a large, weeping abscess on the heel of his bare left foot that was already going septic. Hepatitis was in the process of grinding Terry Sampson into the dust. It wouldn't be long before he folded his ravaged body into one of the corners of the room and died. Minter wondered what he'd done to deserve that fate.

No matter how discoloured they had become, Sampson's eyes still moved quickly. As he weighed up the situation, his chest pumped up and down.

Minter circled the dealer watchfully, taking in the rest of the flat while he walked. In the bedroom, there was a small pile of possessions. The things he'd taken from Lower Rock Gardens, Minter assumed. The real item of interest was sitting on the table in the kitchen. A brown cube of heroin had been left out, next to a bottle of glucose powder and a cheap pair of scales.

Minter stopped in front of Sampson. 'Nice place.'

Sampson made a face. 'Funny,' he sneered.

'Let's start with the easy ones, shall we?' Minter let the silence stretch out inside the room. 'Tell me about Jimbob McFarland.'

'Who?'

Minter stared at him. 'You better start getting real, Terry. I know you lived with Jimbob on Lower Rock Gardens.'

268

Sampson's eyes went to the left – towards the window and the motionless crane. 'I rented a room off of Jimbob for a few weeks. So what?'

Minter put his hands in his pockets. 'I thought you and Jimbob went back a long way.'

Sampson shrugged. 'We were mates.'

'So when did you meet?'

Sampson had been interviewed a lot. He knew that the police rarely asked a question that they didn't know the answer to. 'Jimbob was hustling the toilets on the Level. A fiver for the little job, tenner for the works.'

'You gave him to Lambert, did you?' Minter asked.

'Who?' Sampson's chest had started to heave. He was in a panic.

Minter went back a couple of paces. 'So you rescued Jimbob, did you, Terry?'

'I took him in, yeah,' said Sampson. 'I had a little flat over in Hanover at the time. He came and lived with me.'

'And you set up in business together?'

Sampson nodded. 'Yeah. But I wasn't ripping Jimbob off. I helped him.'

Minter tried again. 'Tell me about Lambert.'

The hope that he might get through this was leaching out of Sampson now. 'Lambert gave us business.'

Vicky had told Minter about Lambert's drug deals, but the pimping was something new. Minter wondered why Sampson was throwing him this titbit. Was it to keep the cop away from the drug angle? 'Lambert brought you clients, you mean?'

Sampson nodded. 'He got a rake.'

Minter brought the discussion up to date. 'Tuesday night, when Jimbob OD'd, where were you?'

'I was in the Aloha,' Sampson said.

'With Jimbob?'

'Yeah.'

'What time was that?'

'About half nine. Then I left him. I went off to work.'

'And where did Jimbob go?'

'He went back to the flat.'

'Why?'

'He had some trade of his own,' Sampson replied.

'Who?'

'I don't fucking know,' said Terry. 'It's been a long time since me and Jimbob worked together. I mean, look at the fucking state of me.'

'What time did you get back to the flat, Terry?'

'I didn't,' Sampson said. 'I didn't come back until the next afternoon. By that time, you lot had arrived. There was a guy in dark shoes with a little notebook, knocking up the neighbours.'

Connolly, Minter thought. 'So what did you do?'

'It looked like Jimbob had been busted. Everyone's had a tug these last few weeks, so I headed back into town.'

'Who were you with that night?' asked Minter.

'Punters.'

'I'll need names, Terry.'

'How do I know their names? They're just tricks.'

'What about the regulars?' Minter enquired. 'You know who they are, don't you?'

Sampson stared at him. 'I don't have any regulars, not these days. I'm back on the streets now.'

'When did you find out Jimbob was dead?'

'Not until yesterday. By then, I was already here.'

Minter scrutinised Sampson. At some point, a very long time ago, Terry Sampson had jettisoned loyalty and conscience altogether. That much was obvious.

'Where did you get the smack, Terry?' Minter asked.

Sampson stonewalled. 'I bought it off some guy in Dr Brighton's,' he said.

Minter stared at Sampson. 'Someone like you, Terry, you couldn't scrape together the cash for that kind of weight. No matter how many blow jobs you do.'

An hour later, in an interview room at Kemptown Station, Terry Sampson was sitting quietly in the chair, his arms wrapped round his midriff, his head bent forward. He was sweating from every pore in his body.

Minter was sitting opposite him and Terry Sampson's signed statement was on the desk between them. The cassette tape in the machine hadn't stopped turning, though. For a moment, its whirring was the only sound in the room. Then Minter said, 'I can get you treatment, Terry. I can put you on a good methadone programme. Then the hospital can start treating your hepatitis properly. Who knows? You might even live.'

When Sampson looked up at Minter, his eyes were yellow. He shivered. All he could think of now was getting a hit. 'Fuck that,' he said. 'When's the doctor coming with my methadone?'

'All in good time,' said Minter. 'All in good time.' He looked down at the table. 'This statement you've just given me,' he said, 'it's full of shit. Just like you.'

271

Sampson shifted in his seat. 'I told you the truth.'

'No, you didn't,' said Minter. 'You didn't tell me anything like the truth.' He picked up the statement and scanned it. 'Let's start with you staying away from the flat all night. We have a witness who says he saw you entering the flat at just after one in the morning, which was around the time that Jimbob died.'

Sampson hugged himself even tighter. The pain in his stomach was worse. 'Well,' he said, sounding unconvincing, even to himself, 'maybe I got the time wrong.'

Minter shook his head. 'That's not good enough. I know you're trying to conceal something. Something to do with Jimbob.'

Terry rubbed at his cheek with the tips of his fingers. His nails were painted black and they were all chipped. They rasped against his day-old beard. He said nothing.

Minter looked at him. The junkie was on his last legs. In his state of health, he'd be unable to walk straight, let alone think straight. Someone else had been managing the situation at Lower Rock Gardens, someone who wanted Jimbob dead. 'Who told you to do it, Terry?'

Sampson stared down at the floor. Even in his present state of health, it seemed, he knew enough not to say any more.

The door to the interview room opened and Vicky Reynolds came in. She sat down next to Minter and gave a little nod. Looking at Sampson again, Minter said, 'Let's talk about Jimbob.'

'I told you about Jimbob,' said Sampson. 'There's nothing else to say.'

'I think there is, Terry. In fact, I found out a couple of

272

very interesting things about Jimbob this morning. I went to his funeral, you see. I talked to some of his mates.'

'Oh, yeah?' said Sampson bitterly. 'And what did they tell you?'

'They told me Jimbob was phobic about needles. They told me that whenever he wanted to fix, you had to inject for him. That's what you did on Tuesday night, wasn't it, Terry?'

'I've had enough of this,' said Sampson. 'When's that fucking doc coming?'

'We've got the needle from the flat,' said Vicky. 'Strange thing is, it's got your fingerprints on it, but not Jimbob's. Can you tell us how that could be?'

Sampson shook his head. He could almost see his lies draining away into the floor.

'Who was it who told you to OD Jimbob?' Minter asked. 'Who was it, Terry?'

Minter remembered Sean Connolly walking down the stone steps to the basement. He said he'd heard about the OD on the radio.

'Tuesday night, Terry,' said Vicky. 'You injected Jimbob with the same pure DS Minter found up at Providence House. That's in the lab reports, too. That needle contained white heroin, Terry. Number 4, the best a man can get. Jimbob's usual dose would have killed him in seconds. You knew that, Terry, didn't you? That's why you fixed it for him.'

Sampson looked her in the eye. 'Jimbob was a junkie, same as I am. What do you fucking care?'

Minter leaned forward. 'Jimbob might have been an addict and he might have been a prostitute, but that doesn't mean he deserved to die.'

273

Sampson had been holding it together for an hour now, all through the questions and the pounding junkie sickness when wave after wave of nausea had swept through his body. The worst of it all was the image of Jimbob's face that haunted his mind. Now, suddenly, when it returned yet again, Sampson couldn't take any more. Something inside him gave way. Covering his eyes with his hands, he cried out.

Vicky said in a quiet voice, 'Tell us what happened.'

When Sampson put his hands down, a single tear had left a little channel on his filthy cheek. 'I owed money,' he said.

'How much?' Minter asked.

'Lots,' Sampson mumbled.

'To who?' said Vicky. She and Minter were doing well. They'd fallen into a rhythm, each one seemingly knowing what to ask next.

Sampson pushed his hair away again. 'Everyone.'

'Michael Lambert in particular?' Minter suggested.

Sampson nodded. 'I was in trouble. I'm hardly earning these days. There was no way I could pay off what I owed him.'

Minter narrated it for him. 'Lambert offered you a way of writing off the debt once and for all.'

Sampson nodded.

They were nearly home and dry. 'Tell us exactly what happened on Tuesday night,' said Vicky. 'And this time, tell us the truth.'

Terry began. 'I bought the wraps of pure off Michael in the Aloha, as arranged. I was meant to go back to the flat with Jimbob straight away. The plan was to do it then and there, but Jimbob wasn't into it. He had a punter later on.

So I went home and fixed myself. I only had a taste – there was plenty left for him.' Sampson looked down. 'I left the heroin in the flat. When I got back later, Jimbob was there. He liked a bit of skag after doing the business, so I knocked on his door and asked him if he wanted to fix.'

'Who was the punter that evening?' Minter asked again.

'I never saw him,' Sampson lied for the second time.

Michael Lambert was a creep, but Minter knew there was someone behind him – someone a lot more important. For the moment, though, Minter let it pass. Right now, he wanted to know exactly how Jimbob McFarland had died. 'OK,' Minter told Terry. 'Go on.'

'It was way past midnight when I got back. It was quiet outside. Jimbob had some music playing softly in his room. He was in a good mood. We were chatting away all the time I was cooking up. It was like the old days. I used his lighter.' Sampson's voice had shrunk now. He was almost whispering. 'Jimbob was lying on the bed. I sat down. Jimbob gave me his arm. He wasn't like me: he had loads of veins left. The needle slipped in so easy.'

Sampson wiped away another tear. He was back in the flat now. He could see Jimbob's beatific expression as the first rush of the heroin lapped into his brain and the sweet oblivion began to break over his body. Just for a moment, Jimbob looked happy. Somehow, that made it simpler.

'We had plenty of bad times, me and Jimbob,' Sampson said. 'Times when we had no money and nowhere to go. We used to talk about OD'ing deliberately. That was the way to finish it, he said, if one of us got really sick. Fix up and slide away. A couple of good minutes at least. And that's what he did, right in front of me. Slipped away.'

275

There was a silence in the room. 'Stay here,' said Minter. Standing up, he gestured to Vicky.

Outside, they stood in the corridor. 'I don't understand it,' said Vicky. 'Why would Michael Lambert want Jimbob dead?'

Minter looked at her. 'Why don't you go and ask him?'

Vicky nodded. 'It'll be a pleasure,' she said. 'But what about you? What are you going to do?'

'I'm going to see the boss.'

'Which one? Roberts or Beckett?'

'Who do you think?'

# 13

· · ·

The Park Tavern was a very different kind of pub to the Queen's Head. Three miles back from the seafront, its bar afforded splendid views over nothing racier than the well-tended lawns of large front gardens. Instead of rent boys and their clients, the Tavern's patrons were drawn from the families who lived quiet, blameless lives in the houses nearby.

Tom Beckett collected his drink from the bar and went to sit at a table in the far corner. He hadn't come here because of the décor or the food. He'd come here because the Park Tavern wasn't a policeman's pub. None of Beckett's colleagues would be dropping by in a hurry.

A few tables away, a woman was having an early lunch. The plate in front of her was piled high with healthy-looking, multi-coloured salad leaves. She looked young and trendy, and every time she raised her fork to her mouth, the thick wooden bangles round her wrist rattled against each other. At the end of her table, there was a toddler fast asleep in a pushchair. Every now and then, she would look down to check on him.

Normally, Beckett wouldn't have given her a second look. She was just another Brighton mum, of the type who hogged the city pavements in summer with their attitude and their three-wheeler pushchairs. But today, for some reason, Beckett couldn't take his eyes off her or the boy in the pushchair at her side.

The sight of kids used to have the opposite effect on Tom Beckett. It used to make him feel younger, feel fortunate, even. It was *having* kids that aged you, Beckett used to think because, one by one, he'd seen it happen to his contemporaries. Lately, the same thing had even started happening to the younger officers Beckett had gathered round himself in the SOCU team he'd built. Kevin Phillips was one. Kevin used to go to the The Moon Under The Water every Friday night. Not anymore, though, not since his daughter had been born.

The little lad in the pushchair was beginning to wake up. Red-faced, his hair plastered to his forehead with sweat, his eyes flickered open. He yawned widely. The mother looked down. She hesitated for a moment, wondering if he might, by any chance, get himself back to sleep, leaving her to finish her meal in peace, but it wasn't to be. The boy started wriggling impatiently against the straps. His mother gave up. When she reached down to release him, Beckett could see how heavy the toddler was. The mother had to half lift, half drag him out of the pushchair and up onto her lap. Immediately, the boy clambered to his feet and turned round to face her.

The woman glanced across at Beckett. I must look a right

state, Beckett thought to himself as he looked away. He picked up his pint glass and drank, hiding his face from her scrutiny.

A young man in a stripy, open-necked shirt walked into the pub. A new-media type, Tom thought, noting the close-cropped hair and the cantilevered spectacles. The man moved briskly towards the table where the woman was sitting and straight away, the little boy in her lap started jigging about. 'And how's my little man?' said his dad, picking him up. He turned from the delighted little boy to his wife. 'Sorry,' he said. 'Got held up in a meeting.'

'I'm afraid I went ahead and had lunch,' said his wife, an edge of domestic resentment in her voice.

The man looked at his watch. 'We've still got time for that walk,' he said. 'I can grab a sandwich on the way back to the office.' He turned to his chuckling son. 'And you can have an ice cream.'

The boy clapped his hands delightedly as his mother gathered all her things together. Chatting non-stop, the little family made their way out of the pub.

It was such an everyday scene, Beckett thought, a couple and their baby taking a stroll in the park. Banal, really. But something like this, he realised, must have happened in front of Julie every single day. Round where they lived, the pushchairs never stopped. An entire generation of children went by their house, perambulated to and from the beach, ice lollies melting in their fists, and all the time, Julie would have been watching from the house.

A woman's need for a baby, Beckett thought, and a man's need for a career. Those were the things that made the world go round. On both counts, Beckett's life had turned out to be a disaster.

Beckett looked about him. With the family gone, the place was almost empty. There was just one old guy at the bar, bellyaching to the girl about the football. In a year's time, Beckett thought, that would be him. He looked down at the stain-ringed wooden table. Kids gave you hope; that was why people had them. If he'd had children, he might be able to see some kind of future for himself when, right now, he couldn't see any at all.

When DS Minter walked into the pub, he was carrying a large envelope. He came straight over to Beckett's table and sat down.

'What you got for me?' Beckett said glad of the distraction.

Minter took a few sheets of paper out of the envelope. 'There's a power of attorney here,' he said, spreading the documents out on the table so Beckett could see exactly what they were. 'And two deeds of transfer. They were drawn up in the last week. We got them from one of the many lawyers that Jacqui Compton uses.' On the front page of each document, Minter pointed to the names of the different companies. 'They're all nameplates with no visible connection to Russell himself. Jacqui runs them for money laundering. It comes to millions of pounds every year. Ever since we started getting close, Russell's been shifting a lot of assets. Every week, Jacqui brings the papers for him to sign. If he signs these papers in particular, he takes the businesses back into his name. With a bit more work and a lot of luck, we can connect him directly to the profit from the drugs deals.'

Beckett looked at Minter. 'How do you know that Russell's going to sign?'

'Jacqui's been taking care of the money side for years. These days, Russell just makes his mark and hands them back to her.'

Beckett nodded. It might just work.

'Tomorrow morning,' Minter went on, 'once these are signed and witnessed, we'll go before a judge in closed session. When we show him, he's bound to give us all the warrants we need. Then we can dismantle Compton's financial operation, top to bottom.'

Beckett read through the papers again. They all looked kosher. Kosher and complicated. Just the kind of thing Russell wouldn't bother with. Beckett looked up. 'You know, Minter,' he said, 'we'd have made a pretty good team. It's just a shame we'll never get the chance to work together again.'

Minter was puzzled. 'What are we doing now then?'

'I'm meeting Jacqui Compton in half an hour's time, just like we said, but I don't want you there. I don't want you involved at all, in fact, so you better find another way to explain how these documents came into my possession. I broke Windmill, Minter, and I'm going to fix it.'

'This was my idea, sir.'

Beckett nodded. 'Listen, Minter, I don't care about my career anymore. Roberts and Professional Standards can do whatever they like with me; it doesn't matter. I just wish I'd got out quicker, when Julie was still alive. But you're too young to take this risk. So this is down to me, and only me.'

'What if Russell tumbles something is up?' Minter said. 'You're going to need back-up.'

Beckett smiled. Now that he'd made his decision, a slice of the old self-confidence, the old swagger, had returned. 'I'll handle it. And don't forget there's armed response vehicles outside the house.' He started putting the documents back into the envelope. 'Now, if you'll excuse me, Jacqui Compton's waiting.'

For the second time that day, Vicky Reynolds found herself standing on the pavement outside one of the most elegant townhouses in Sussex Square. The heavy, gloss-black door was on the latch. She pushed it open and went inside, walking quickly up the grand staircase to knock on the door of the flat.

'What now?' said Michael Lambert after he opened the door to Vicky.

There were suitcases behind him in the hall. 'You going somewhere, Michael?' Vicky said. 'I hope you haven't forgotten that you're on police bail.'

Lambert looked at her. 'Have you really walked all the way up St James's just to remind me of that?'

'No,' said Vicky. 'I came here because we've got Terry Sampson in custody.' For the first time, Lambert looked a little worried. 'You better let me in.'

In the living room, Lambert sat on the sofa smoking a cigarette again. Vicky went over to the open French windows from where the sound of disco music was floating into the room. She moved aside one of the velvet drapes to see, on the other side of the gated gardens in the middle of the square, the Pride parade passing along the seafront. It was a nautical theme this year, and sailing atop a flatbed articulated lorry, the lead float had been designed to look like an ocean liner. Vicky could see the red funnels sticking out of the silver-grey hull. As it rolled on towards the city centre, the disco music faded. 'Thought you'd be down there, Michael,' she said.

'Chance would be a fine thing,' said Lambert, feigning disinterest.

Vicky looked at the various *objets d'art* lining the shelves of a display cabinet. Opening the door, she picked up a small bronze sculpture of a racehorse. The morning sun shone dully on the bronze of the heavy statuette. Walking over to where Lambert was sitting, Vicky said, 'I don't like horseracing, not since Ray Tyler got shot in the face.' Lambert looked up at her warily. 'Terry Sampson,' Vicky said, 'has just admitted that he deliberately fixed Jimbob McFarland with what he knew to be a lethal hit of heroin.'

'Shit happens,' said Lambert. 'Especially to junkie whores like Terry.'

Vicky nodded. 'True, but Sampson says you gave him the heroin.'

'He's lying.'

Vicky dropped the racehorse down on the coffee table in front of the sofa. Lambert's pack of Marlboro and his Zippo lighter both jumped as the metal base of the statue gouged a deep hole in the lacquered wood before falling off the edge. 'Whoops,' said Vicky. 'Butter fingers.' But she wasn't faking this. It wasn't an act, it was serious. For the first time, she was face to face with one of the men she knew was responsible for the murder of Ray Tyler. 'Terry

283

Sampson says you gave him the brick for services rendered,' she told Lambert. 'Constructive manslaughter is as good as murder, Michael. Terry knew Jimbob was going to die when he fixed him and so did you, as soon as you gave the gear to Terry.'

Lambert stood up. 'I'm going to ring my lawyer.'

Vicky shoved him in the chest so that the back of Lambert's legs knocked against the sofa and he fell backwards. 'Sit down,' she said. 'Let me tell you how it went, Michael. Jimbob was a runaway, fourteen years old, easy pickings for the likes of you. When Terry introduced you to Jimbob, the lad was cottaging, but in a few weeks they'd both made the big time. They were going to your sex parties and you were paying them a lot more than rent. They had a place to live and they had clothes and money for the drugs you started selling them. So we know about your sideline, Lambert. We know you've been pimping boys around Kemptown for years. And chicken that young and tender doesn't come cheap. Arranging child sex offences is another dozen years, Michael, and it puts you inside as a Category-A sex offender.'

Lambert was taking out his phone.

'Not yet,' Vicky commanded. 'First, you're going to tell me where you score from, Michael. I mean, Number 4 is still pretty rare in the UK, and as far as I know, it's never been sold in Brighton. That makes your supplier major league.'

Lambert shook his head. 'Grasses don't stay alive for very long in this town. Terry Sampson will never even make it to court.'

Vicky looked at him. 'Yes, he will. I can promise you that.'

'You thought Gillespie was safe, didn't you? What makes you so sure about Terry?'

'Because Terry Sampson told us about Rita.'

Lambert looked uncomfortable.

'That's right, Michael, we know all about the importer. And you're going to tell me where we can find him.'

In the surveillance flat, Tom Beckett was standing by the window. Behind him, a whirring began as the electronic fan inside one of the computers started up again.

On the other side of Dyke Road, Russell's mansion squatted behind its tall iron gates. Russell's car was parked out front. Jacqui's red BMW was nowhere to be seen.

Beckett lifted the two-way radio up to his mouth. He pressed a button and gave the necessary call sign. 'Still here, sir,' said one of the officers in the rapid-response vehicle parked a few streets away.

'You got the air-conditioning on?' Beckett asked.

'Too right we have.'

Beads of sweat had gathered in Beckett's eyebrows. He rubbed them with his finger. 'Wish I had some air-con in here.' The officer laughed. 'You keep on your toes,' Beckett admonished him.

'Yes, sir,' said the officer in the car.

Beckett put the radio back on the windowsill and turned round. The technical support officer's name was Trevor. When he found that out, Beckett had to stop himself from calling the guy Clever Trevor. From now on, though, Beckett was going to treat computers, and everything to do with them, with a little more respect.

'Hot in here, isn't it, sir?' said Trevor.

Tom Beckett nodded. He glanced at the copy of *Four-Four-Two* magazine lying on the desk. 'What chance do you think the Seagulls have got of promotion?' he asked. Over the summer break, Brighton and Hove Albion had lost their two best players. It was going to be a long season.

'No idea,' said the techie. 'Man U are my team.'

Beckett looked at him. 'Like to be on the winning side, do you?'

Trevor grinned. 'Something like that.' There was a pause. 'I thought all the detectives had been stood down from surveillance.'

'They have,' said Beckett. 'I'm just winding things up.'

Trevor nodded. It wasn't his job to question a DCI.

Beckett turned back to the window. The Compton house seemed to loom up at him. He wondered where Jacqui was. Maybe she'd bottled it, after all. Maybe Minter had been wrong about her.

When Beckett met Jacqui in town, the woman had been absolutely terrified. Her hand shook uncontrollably as she took the legal documents. Jacqui had been abused by her husband for more than a decade now. Ten years of victimisation, ten years of brutalisation. There were obvious compensations, Beckett thought, looking down at the house, but surely even that kind of wealth hadn't been worth it?

Beckett looked at his watch. 'Come on, Jacqui,' he whispered. 'You can do this.'

*

'Fifteen kilos,' Russell said quietly into his phone. He was sitting in his den. The White Stripes were playing on his stereo.

'Pure?' asked the voice.

'Seventy per cent,' said Russell. He was going out onto the Downs tonight himself. There was no point in waiting for Chris to dig up the stash. When Stevie Elliott never turned up with the car yesterday, Chris had high-tailed it home straight away. He never wanted to make the trip in the first place, Russell could see that when he asked him. Russell's own son was a long stream of piss.

'How much?' asked the voice.

'One hundred and twenty,' Russell said. It would be enough to pay his way, to keep him as he wanted to be kept.

The man on the other end of the line snorted with laughter. 'You're fucking joking, aren't you?'

Russell needed a deal for the whole weight. He reined in his temper. 'What's your best price, then, mate?'

'Ninety,' the man said.

'Now you're the one having a laugh,' said Russell.

'I'm not laughing. I'm not even fucking smiling. Haven't you heard? The pipeline's full of ninety per cent. It's going to be everywhere soon.'

Russell had heard rumours. Right now, Afghan white was the big score. He realised he'd been out of the loop for too many weeks. 'Make it a tonne and you've got a deal,' he said.

'I hate round numbers,' said the man.

Russell nearly told the guy to go fuck himself. For the

first time in years, though, he had to swallow. 'Ninety-five,' he said instead.

'OK,' said the man.

'I'll call you on this number early tomorrow morning,' Russell told him. 'You better be awake.' He pressed a button. The line went dead.

Russell rapped the phone back on the desk and glanced round the room. The hand-tooled desk, the French floorboards – he wouldn't miss any of it. None of it belonged to him now in any case. The title deed of the house had already been transferred to the ownership of the new offshore company that Russell's accountant had set up. One by one, ownership of all the legitimate businesses was being moved across, as well. It would take a few days for the paperwork to go through and then the whole lot was going to be sold, every little bit of it. Russell was cashing in. It was time for him to leave.

He took a Sobranie out of the packet and lit it. On one of the CCTV screens in the den, he watched the gates at the front of his house swing open. Jacqui was home.

'You getting this?' Beckett asked the techie, watching Jacqui get out of her car. The stack of papers was in her hand.

'Yep,' said Clever Trevor. He sounded bored. To him, this was all workaday routine.

'Check the mics,' said Beckett. 'All of them.'

From behind him, Beckett heard the quiet pawing of the keyboard. 'All OK,' the techie said, wondering why the DCI was so hot on the detail.

Jacqui was walking across the desert of block paving to the front of the house. Watching her, Beckett took a deep breath and uttered a silent prayer. This could all come crashing down so easily, and if it did, he would have just seconds to get inside the house. God knows what kind of scene he would find there.

Beckett wasn't scared, though, not for himself at least. He wanted to be gone, had done for a year now, ever since he'd lost Julie. If Beckett's life was going to end today, then that would be a good thing because it would save him the bother of eking it out any longer. He picked up the walkie-talkie from the windowsill. 'Forty-seven,' he said.

There was silence.

When Jacqui opened the front door, the first thing she heard was the rock music still playing loudly from the den.

The accountant had offered her a cup of tea, but that wasn't what she needed right now. She went straight along the hall and into the kitchen.

Jacqui yanked open the door of the huge American fridge. The new litre bottle of Smirnoff was lying on its side. She grabbed it, knocking over a couple of Russell's beer bottles as she did so. She let them rattle around on the glass shelf. Jacqui lifted the vodka bottle out of the fridge and unscrewed the cap. She drank a large measure straight down. It burned her throat and her empty stomach, but it gave her a little courage and it kept her topped up. She put the bottle back and closed the door of the fridge.

In Jacqui's hand were seven documents, five from the accountant and another two from DCI Beckett, whom she'd met in town on her way back from the accountant's house in Rottingdean. Looking down, she neatened the edges of the stack of papers. At least her hands had stopped shaking, she thought.

She could do this thing, Jacqui told herself. It wasn't the thought of sending Russell down that had made Jacqui stake her life on the outcome of the next hour or so, or even the prospect that Beckett had held out to her of reducing her own prison sentence. She was doing it for Chris. She was doing it to set him free.

One of the documents Jacqui was holding was printed on thicker paper than the rest. Someone had stapled a little cardboard collar over the top left-hand corner on which they'd printed the firm's name and address. There was nothing wrong with that, Jacqui told herself. Russell knew the firm. He dealt with it a lot. She neatened the edge of the pile again.

'You took your time,' said Russell from the doorway of the kitchen.

Jacqui couldn't bring herself to look Russell in the eye. He would see straight through her. She was convinced of it. 'Traffic was awful,' she mumbled, turning away from him and busying herself at the sink with the breakfast things. 'That Polish girl not coming back?' she said, trying to change the subject, trying to sound natural.

'You know she isn't,' said Russell.

Jacqui could feel his eyes on her back. She almost dropped the plate she was rinsing under the tap. It had been a mistake coming into the kitchen. *Don't go into the kitchen, Jacqui.* That's what Beckett had told her. *I can't hear you when you're in the kitchen.*

But Jacqui had needed a drink too badly.

She glanced over her shoulder. Russell was over by the

solid mahogany dining table now. He was leafing through the first document. 'Reggie done that games room yet?' he asked. He glanced over. 'You know, snooker table and all that shit?'

Jacqui put a mug down on the drainer. She shook water from her hands. 'Yeah,' she said. 'He showed me. It looks nice.'

'Give you the tour, did he?' said Russell.

For some reason, he was unusually talkative. Perhaps, Jacqui thought, he'd had some good news for a change. 'Yeah,' said Jacqui. 'Reggie was all right.'

Russell nodded. 'Reggie was all right,' he repeated. 'I should think he would be. I've made him a rich man.' He let the pages of the financials fall back into place. 'I probably paid for the entire house, in fact.'

Summoning up her courage again, Jacqui turned round. 'You gonna do those now, Russ?'

But she should have known better. Russell hated being told what to do. 'What's it to you?' he said.

'Only,' she said, 'the way Reggie was talking, it sounded like he wanted them back sharpish.'

Russell stared at her. The accountant better not have let anything slip about the money, he thought. Russell didn't want Jacqui knowing anything at all about his leaving. If she picked up any hint, she'd start in on the questions.

On the other hand, it would be good to get the numbers over with fast. The quicker Reggie got Russell's signature on the papers, the quicker Russell could be away. He scooped up the seven documents from the table. 'Tell you what,' he said, 'you can take them back after you've cooked me dinner.'

*

Five minutes later, sitting brooding in the den, Russell sniffed the air. It was frying sausages he could smell. His favourite.

Russell picked up his chunky Mont Blanc fountain pen from the desk and went over to the coffee table, where he always signed important papers. The table was hidden by the sofas. It was out of the way of even the longest telephoto lens.

The first paper didn't look like anything important, just something about a savings bond so he turned to the back page and started to scrawl his name on the dotted line. The ink wasn't flowing out of his Mont Blanc fountain pen. He looked at the gold nib to see if there was some kind of blockage. He held it out and shook it. He turned to the back page of the second document and signed that one, too. That was better. The ink flowed nicely. With some satisfaction, Russell looked down at the elegant signature.

When he got to the power of attorney, Russell stopped. He turned back to the front page and checked the name of the company concerned. He read the second and third pages carefully, taking his time over the complicated legalese. It was what it looked like: an attorney was to take the car dealership out of the blind trust it had been registered in for the last few years. There he was on the last page, named as the new beneficiary.

'Prick,' Russell said. Everyone was getting jumpy now. Even the usually pernickety accountant.

Russell took his mobile out of the pocket of his jeans. As he waited for the call to connect, he used the remote to start the music playing again. That was another thing he wouldn't miss. The White Stripes wasn't even his CD. It belonged to Chris. It was shite.

On the sixth ring, the call answered. 'Reggie,' Russell said, 'what you playing at? I know you're busy, mate, but I pay you well over the odds. I'm your number one fucking client and don't you forget that.' He listened to the protestations of the accountant. 'Yeah, I've got all those things,' Russell interrupted, 'but you've stuck in a right fucking moody. Who's got the log book at the moment?'

The log book was code for the car dealership in Portslade. Russell listened again. What Reggie was telling him about the arrangements he was making for the dealership didn't fit in with the power of attorney that Russell had in front of him at all.

'OK, mate,' Russell said. 'I understand what you're saying. You haven't spoken to Speccy Boy about this?' Speccy Boy was the solicitor. 'OK, mate. I'll get the others back to you this evening. You can crack on with the other thing then. And, listen, maybe I'll give you a game of snooker sometime.' With that, he ended the call.

A moment later, there was a quiet knocking. Jacqui put her head round the door and saw the papers lying all over the coffee table. 'Your tea's ready, Russ,' she managed to say.

Russell got up. He walked over to where she was standing. He had the power of attorney in one hand, his pen in the other. He held up the paper and said, 'Any idea where this thing came from?'

Jacqui shrugged. 'It's one of Reggie's, isn't it? I hardly look at those things now.'

'It wasn't from Reggie,' Russell said, throwing the papers in her face. As it fell to the floor, Jacqui stood there. She couldn't move. She knew what was about to happen.

He grabbed a handful of her hair. A big handful. He used it to pull her closer to him. 'So who fucking gave it you?' he demanded.

'Reggie did, I swear.'

'I don't believe you,' Russell said. He wound the thick tress of her hair even tighter round his fist. The roots tore. He pulled her down towards the floor.

Jacqui was on her knees. The tears were starting in her eyes. She raised her hands. 'Please, Russ,' she begged.

Like a dog playing with a toy, Russell shook her from side to side. She fell forward, but he still didn't let go. 'Are you and that fucking solicitor trying to thieve off me?' he said. 'Is that what this is? Did you think I wouldn't bother to find out what was happening to my fucking money?'

'No,' she said desperately. 'Of course not.' She tried to look up at him. 'Please,' she whispered.

Russell plunged the gold nib straight into his wife's eyeball. Jacqui screamed. 'Fucking tell me!' Russell bellowed, dragging her down onto the floor. 'You know I killed your brother, Jax. And I'll do the same to you as well, you cunt!' Russell stabbed at Jacqui's face again but this time she flinched and the point dug into her cheek. Russell jerked it upwards again. He bent down a little. There was blood all over Jacqui's face now. 'Was it the filth that put you up to this? You and Dave in this together all along, were you? The both of you?'

Suddenly, Jacqui shook her head with such violence that

her head came free from Russell's hand. Falling forward, she pounded the floorboards with her fists. 'You'll kill us all, you bastard! You'll kill us all!'

A thicket of Jacqui's hair trailed down from Russell's fist. He threw it over her, some of the strands catching the sunlight as they fell. 'Fucking right I will!' With the toecap of his Caterpillar boots, he kicked Jacqui in the side of her face. Her head snapped back and she rolled unconscious onto the floor. Russell took a step forward. He raised his foot again.

There was an almighty crash. This one wasn't from the stereo, though, or even Russell's boot. This one came from outside.

Beckett dashed over to the window from the computers where he'd been trying to listen in. The giant Land Rover was reversing into traffic on Dyke Road. The driver gunned the engine again and the tyres of the Land Rover squealed. Beckett put the radio to his mouth. 'Control to 47!' he yelled. 'Where the fuck are you!' There was another huge impact, then the sound of metal grinding against metal as the Land Rover struggled to extricate itself from the mangled gates.

Russell was watching it too now. For the moment, he'd forgotten Jacqui. He was standing over by the window of his den. The security gates had been a special order. They were made of reinforced steel. They might have buckled, but they hadn't broken. The bad news was that he could see the hinges poking out of the brick pillars either side. The gates were being wrenched right off. The door of the

Land Rover opened and a man jumped out. Russell recognised him straight away. It was the youngest Hangleton, the one with all the acne and in his hands he was carrying a machine pistol. 'Come to my house, would you?' Russell said, walking over to the long cabinet under the bank of CCTV screens and taking out a shotgun. He checked he'd left it loaded. He had.

Russell turned round. Jacqui was lying on the floor. He aimed the shotgun at her head.

In the surveillance room, Beckett watched the Land Rover crash full pelt into the gates again. The one on the right was almost bent double now. It toppled over, bricks falling onto the pavement. The radio in Beckett's hand crackled into life. 'Control, this is 92,' said a calm voice. 'What's the problem?'

'Where are you?' said Beckett.

'We're just clearing the city,' said the officer on Beckett's radio. 'We're not due there for another ten minutes.'

'Fuck,' said Beckett. It was just as Minter had said. The mobile surveillance units were fucked, like everything else about Windmill. Someone had arranged for them to be stood down. 'Are you armed?' said Beckett.

'Unit 47 is armed, sir,' said the officer, 'not us.'

Beckett watched two more men leap out of the Land Rover, both carrying guns. It was like an invasion and in a couple of minutes Jacqui Compton would be dead. Turning round, Beckett threw the radio onto the desk. 'Get everyone,' he told the techie as he dashed out of the room.

*

296

Boots and rifle butts drummed against the front door of Russell Compton's house. Like the gates, the door had been a special order. The pins were reinforced steel and the door itself was lined with lead. They could knock all they wanted, but they weren't coming in. The Hangletons caught on quickly, though. The door stopped shuddering. The next moment, there was a sustained burst of gunfire and the small window to one side of the front door went through, littering the hallway with fragments of glass. The head and shoulders of one of the Hangletons appeared through the hole. Pressing himself flat against the door, Russell squeezed the trigger of the pump-action shotgun. The blast decorated the hallway with the contents of the guy's head. Russell stepped forward and fired the other round through the window frame. He listened to the footsteps running into the passageway at the side of the house. There were two more of them. The guy who had tried to get in was jack-knifed across the windowsill, his blood making a puddle on the carpet.

'Won't have to worry about the zits now, will you?' Russell said.

Outside the block of flats on Dyke Road, the traffic had come to a standstill. The commuters were already taking cover, abandoning their vehicles and running away from the shooting. Beckett left the surveillance flat and ran down the stairs. He was back on street level now.

On the other side of the road, the Hangleton who'd been driving was just getting out of the Land Rover. He looked over to the house in time to see the body of his colleague tumble backwards onto the block paving. Things were not going according to plan. From down the hill came the sound of a siren.

Crouching down, using the stationary cars to conceal his progress, Beckett ran across the road towards him. The driver had taken out a pistol and as soon as the unmarked police car with the flashing lights had crested the hill, he aimed his gun and fired. The distraction was enough for Beckett to get closer. He reached the back of the Land Rover and squatted down. As the man started firing again, Beckett popped his head up. He could see the Hangleton through the window, his arm outstretched and taking aim. The police car had come to a halt a couple of hundred yards down the hill, the two officers taking cover inside.

Beckett rounded the 4x4 and charged at the shooter. He hit him as hard as he could on the side of his head, using both hands to maximise the swinging blow. The shooter sprawled to the floor and rolled over. Beckett was on him in a flash, kicking the gun away and kneeling on the man's chest in one swift movement. Beckett hit the shooter again. Under his knuckles, he could feel the guy's nose imploding.

Dempsey and his cousin were standing on the patio at the back of Compton's house. They both aimed their automatics at the plate-glass windows and fired. It was bulletproof, but everything had its limits. For a moment, the enormous panes hung in the air. Shivering, they turned frosty. They came down in an avalanche.

Russell was standing in the doorway of the kitchen. He blasted the patio with the shotgun. Dempsey's cousin took one of the shots in the head. He was thrown back onto the paving. Before he hit the stones, Dempsey had thrown himself into the dining area and rolled behind the massive table, from where he returned fire. Russell sank down behind the butcher's block in the middle of the kitchen.

Dempsey made his move. Leaping to his feet, his gun held at his waist, he ran across the open space. The bullets from his automatic strafed and shattered the slate tiles on the floor, eating their way into the butcher's block, turning the solid wood into matchsticks. Russell had time for just one shot. He moved to his left and loosed the shell.

Dempsey stopped running, all that wild energy suddenly thwarted by the blow. The Hangleton boss lay on his back on the floor of the kitchen. There was a huge crater in his stomach, but he was still alive. Russell walked over. Looking down, he wanted to do more things to Dempsey, to mark and change the man's body a little more, to tear and crush it, but he could hear the sound of the sirens and the faint chuntering of the helicopter rotor. He smiled to himself. The cops would always be too late. Russell picked Dempsey's machine gun out of the fragments of broken glass and looked at it approvingly. Reaching down, he placed the muzzle close to Dempsey's face, tapping the metal against the bloodied front teeth. Not only was the fucker still breathing, he was smiling back at Russell. Dempsey's legend was complete. Two years ago, he had bitten on the machete that had sliced open his face and yesterday he had bitten on the blade that Rita pushed into his mouth. Now he did the same to the perforated muzzle of the gun.

Russell looked Dempsey straight in the eye. 'Cunt,' he whispered as he emptied the rest of the magazine.

Beckett ran into the house, treading on the broken glass in the hall. 'Armed police!' he shouted. After the raucous burst of automatic fire, the massive house seemed suddenly quiet and deserted.

From the hallway, Beckett saw Jacqui lying in the den to the right. He ran into the room. It felt strange to be physically inside, having seen it so often on a screen. Beckett winced at the injuries to the woman's face. Checking her body over, he couldn't find any others. The pulse in Jacqui's neck was strong. Beckett stood up. From outside the house, he could hear the ambulances arriving.

Beckett went back into the hall. He knew the layout of the house very well and he walked into the kitchen, where the firing had just come from. Apart from the bodies, it was empty. Beckett had to ID Dempsey from the jacket he was wearing because the bullets had obliterated his face altogether. The other Hangleton was lying across the bottom of the patio doors, half in the kitchen, half in the garden, and all of him dead. Beckett stepped out under the striped awning and looked around the sunny back garden, finding, as he expected, no sign of Russell Compton.

In the middle of a manicured lawn was a large, kidney-shaped swimming pool. On the far side, there were wide steps going down into the water and the blue tiles in the bottom spelled out a large *R* and *C*. The letters were italicised and at various points they flowed into one another, like the fancy initials in a royal crest. No *J* for Jacqui or *C* for Chris, of course, just Russell's initials immortalised at the bottom of his swimming pool. The new owners of the house would dig out all those tiles, Beckett thought, because they wouldn't want any trace of the previous occupants to remain. They'd be respectable types – bankers or something. Beckett looked up. The helicopter was directly overhead now and the noise was almost deafening. It started to move. It could outrun Russell Compton easily, but it would have to find him first.

# 14

# . . .

F or the first time in years, Jacqui Compton was about to
wake up in a bed that wasn't her own. The sheets had
been tucked in too tight and she felt them pressing down
on her chest. It was like she was being suffocated. Jacqui
opened her eyes. One of them, anyway, because the other
was bandaged shut. She knew straight away she was in a
hospital bed. She glimpsed the little television on a wall
bracket and the tall, functional table by the side of her.
She knew it was the Royal, too: outside the window, she
could see a diagonal slice of the sky, the same bit she'd seen
when Chrissy had been born all those years ago. It was
black, so it was the middle of the night. Jacqui was wearing
a gown and she wondered where her own clothes were. That
life was over, she remembered then. There'd be no more
Valentino dresses for Jacqui Compton, no more Jimmy
Choos.

Feeling woozy, Jacqui struggled to lift her hand free from
the starchy sheets. They must have given her a sedative.
With the tips of her fingers, she began to explore her face,

feeling the rough stitches in her left cheek, discovering that the crêpe bandage covering her eye went round and round her head.

The door opened and a nurse came into the room. 'Ah,' she said, 'you're awake.' Before she closed the door, Jacqui caught sight of a police officer sitting on a chair outside the room with a machine gun on a strap round his shoulder. The nurse said, 'I've come to change your dressing, Mrs Compton.' She was Filipino. Small figure, wide cheekbones.

The nurse put the kidney-shaped silver tray down on the side table and took some things out of it. One by one, she arranged them on the tabletop. 'First,' she said, 'let's make you more comfortable.' Taking care, she helped Jacqui sit up in the bed and plumped the pillows. When Jacqui was propped up, the nurse reached behind her and snipped one end of the old bandage with a pair of scissors. She began to unwind it.

'What time is it?' Jacqui said.

The nurse glanced down at the watch face pinned to her uniform. 'It's two o'clock in the morning,' she said, unwrapping the last of the crêpe bandage.

With her good eye, Jacqui could see that the bandage had been soaked right through, stained red and yellow. 'Am I going to be blind?'

The nurse put the old bandage into the dish. 'The doctor doesn't think so,' she said. She leaned over Jacqui again. Carefully, she pulled the two little straps of tape that held the wadded Lanolin over Jacqui's eye. 'He'll be in to see you tomorrow morning,' she added, putting the dressing in the silver tray as well. When the eye was completely uncovered, Jacqui could see nothing but a smear of light.

The nurse placed a new dressing over Jacqui's eye and taped it into place. Then she took a new roll of crêpe out of its paper sleeve and wound it round Jacqui's head. 'You should try to sleep, Mrs Compton,' said the nurse, cutting the crêpe and tying off the end. She stepped back and gathered up her things. 'I'll see you later.'

Alone in the room again, Jacqui stared at the window where a pool of light from the bedside lamp was reflected in the blackness outside and Jacqui could see the new bandage round her head.

The door opened again. This time, it was a man who came in to see her. He wasn't a doctor; he was a policeman. Jacqui could tell by the badly cut suit jacket flapping around his pot belly. He introduced himself as DCI Slater, a native of Surrey and the new senior investigating officer of SOCU in Brighton. 'And how are you doing, Jacqui?'

Jacqui's voice hardened. 'I've been better. You got Russell?'

Slater hesitated.

'Fucking hell,' said Jacqui. 'Is there anything you lot *can* do?'

'It was chaos up at Dyke Road,' Slater said. 'In the confusion, Russell got away. He's gone to ground, but we'll find him.'

Jacqui looked at him. 'What do you mean, "chaos"?'

It was true, then, thought Slater, Jacqui had passed out before the attack had begun. 'Your house was attacked by the Hangletons. They made quite a mess and things didn't turn out too well. Three of them are dead, including Paul Dempsey and one of the men who attacked you in the park.

The other one's in custody.' He looked at Jacqui. 'Your husband's quite handy.'

Jacqui looked up at the ceiling, not sure whether to be proud or not about what Russell had done. So that was why she was still alive, she thought, not because Russell had spared her life but because he'd been interrupted by his rivals. 'What about the papers Beckett gave me?' she asked.

'You'll be glad to know that that worked out. Russell signed the bond. We can tie him into the drug money for sure.'

'What about my son?' Jacqui asked. 'Where's Chris?'

'He's not our suspect,' said Slater. He put his hands in his pockets. 'I know you're not feeling too clever at the moment, but I need you to make a statement tonight. A full statement. We're going in front of a judge first thing tomorrow morning and we'll be asking for a warrant for Russell's arrest on a charge of money laundering, although that will be just the start.'

'I'll help you put Russell away, but I want protection for me and Chris. It's the same deal for Chris or you'll get nothing.'

'I'll talk to the CPS right after we've seen the judge,' said Slater.

'You do that,' said Jacqui. 'I want it in writing, too, in writing and lodged with my lawyer.'

Slater nodded. 'We've got a car waiting downstairs, Jacqui. Anytime you're ready.'

Ten minutes later, dressed in borrowed clothes, Jacqui found herself walking through a dingy corridor in the basement of the main hospital building. DCI Slater was on one side of her, the armed officer from outside her room on the other. They exited through a fire door. Outside, it was dark and cold. In her T-shirt and jeans, Jacqui shivered. She turned to Slater. 'Who got me out?' she said.

'DCI Beckett,' said Slater.

'Where's he now?'

'DCI Beckett is no longer on this case.' Right now, in fact, Tom Beckett was being interviewed under caution, but Jacqui didn't need to know that.

The campus of the Royal was a rabbit warren. Jacqui and her minders turned left and right, skirting low-rise buildings used for offices and laboratories. In the darkness, with only one good eye and a head full of sedatives, Jacqui soon lost track of where they were heading, but she was grateful when they entered a covered walkway and got out of the cold. From somewhere up ahead came the sound of talking. A group of three nurses turned the corner and came towards them. They were huddled together, chatting easily but they stopped speaking when they saw the strange little party. As she passed by, the nurse on the left couldn't help staring.

Jacqui and the police officers came to the end of the walkway. In front of them was an access road. It went up a little and there was a car waiting at the top. 'That's it,' said Slater. He turned to Jacqui. 'You all right?'

Jacqui nodded. The driver was already inside the car and Slater helped Jacqui into the back seat, then went round the other side, where a uniformed officer was riding shotgun in the front. They left the hospital and turned right, heading for the dark seafront.

'Can I borrow your phone?' Jacqui asked.

'Sure,' said Slater, taking it out of his jacket pocket and giving it to her.

Jacqui knew the number by heart. It took a long time to answer. When it did, all she could hear was loud dance music. Jacqui raised her voice. 'Chris?'

'Yeah?' Chris didn't have the number on his phone. 'Who's this?'

'It's me,' said Jacqui. 'It's Mum.'

'What do you want?' Chris asked. He sounded suspicious. His mum never called him out of the blue like this.

'Have you been home?' she said.

'No!' he shouted over the din in the bar. 'What do you want, Mum?'

'Are you staying with your girlfriend tonight?'

Chris hesitated. As far as he was able, he kept everything about his life a secret. He didn't think that Jacqui even knew he had a girlfriend. 'Yeah,' he said. 'I'm in town.'

'Good,' said Jacqui. 'I'm glad. I'll ring you in the morning, then.'

'What's the matter?' Chris said. Something about his mother's voice was different. 'What's happened?'

'I just wanted to make sure you were OK,' she said. She paused as the police car stopped at traffic lights on the seafront road. A motorcycle pulled up behind it. 'I love you, Chris,' said Jacqui.

'Mum,' Chris said, 'are you pissed?'

Jacqui laughed. 'No,' she said. 'No, I'm not pissed. I just wanted to hear your voice.'

'Where are you, then?'

'Things are going to be different now,' Jacqui told him. 'I'm going to stop drinking altogether. I'm going to do the right thing by you now, Chris. You'll see. It's all going to be different. We're going to get a little place together, just you and me. It doesn't have to be big.'

'You sure you haven't been drinking?'

Jacqui chuckled through her tears. 'No, I haven't, I promise.'

'OK, then,' Chris said, sounding confused. 'See you later.'

Jacqui closed up the telephone and gave it back to DCI Slater. At least Chris was safe tonight, she thought. They'd make a new start tomorrow.

The motorcycle came alongside the car. Bending forward, the rider peered into the back. Then he pulled a gun out of his jacket and opened fire.

Vicky turned round and retraced her steps. On the pavement, her heels ground against builder's sand. She turned right, down a flight of unlit steps that led to another part of the development.

Minter was right about everything else, but he was wrong about Kevin Phillips, Vicky was sure of it. There was no way Kevin was responsible for Ray Tyler's death. He just couldn't be.

Like her stubbornness, Vicky got her sense of right and wrong from her father. The law was good because it made things very clear – it was all there in the statute books, all there in black and white. But sometimes, as her dad used to say, you had to trust the feeling you got in your water.

A couple of minutes later, the buildings started to look like they'd come out of an Ikea flat-pack. On the walls of the first block of flats she passed, there were two massive, toy-town sheets of primary-coloured cladding. In between, row after row of small, square windows mounted the eight floors. It was all faceless uniformity – a Soviet-style dormitory town. In between the flats, the developers had spliced in a few tiny courtyards, each one intended as a token of public space. It frightened Vicky a little to think that the demographic this place was targeting included urban singletons, people just like herself.

The density of housing reached its height in Eldon Lane. The address Vicky was looking for was part of a building that took up the entire block between the back of the New England Quarter and the scruffy end of London Road. It was an enormous, featureless, straight-edged box, twelve storeys high and riddled with street entrances. Already heavily sub-let, it was a slum for tomorrow. Pausing outside, Vicky checked the number. It must have been a year ago or more since she scribbled down Connolly's address one evening at the pub, but even at the time, she thought she'd never actually call. This evening, though, she'd been relieved to find the torn piece of paper again, lodged in between a couple of pages near the back of her address book.

Vicky Reynolds wasn't the only person interested in finding Sean Connolly that evening. Russell Compton was watching her from behind one of the hoardings protecting the unlit building sites across the road from where Connolly lived. Russell had got away from the chopper on Dyke Road and was on his way up to the Downs to dig up the last of the heroin he had stashed away in Brighton, but there was something he needed to do in town first. When Vicky was inside the flats, Russell left the shadow of the hoarding and came out onto the street.

Inside the silent lobby, Vicky walked straight over to the bank of three lifts and rode one up to the ninth floor and got out. The front door to Connolly's flat was open. It hadn't been forced – there was no splintering of the flimsy surround. Vicky pushed the door wider.

Inside, everything was dark and she hesitated on the threshold. 'Sean?' she called. 'It's Vicky.' Again, no response. 'Detective Constable Reynolds,' she added, hoping it might discourage anyone from taking her on. Hearing no response, she walked gingerly inside, feeling along one side of the wall for a light switch. The unshaded overhead bulb flashed on and the interior hallway sprang to life. On the other side of the hall were two doors, both shut tight, and a third, partly open door at the end of the corridor.

Connolly's bedroom was tiny and stank of stale cigarette smoke. The view from its uncurtained window was the brick wall of the flats next door and inside the room itself there was a bed, a single wardrobe and a chest of drawers, all of it utterly functional. Quickly, Vicky walked past the bed and over to the wardrobe. The rail was crammed with clothes; some of the jackets were still in dry-cleaning bags. She placed her hand in the middle of the rack and pushed half of the garments aside. There were lots of designer labels.

Vicky went back into the hall and into the main room. Immediately on the left, there was a galley kitchen decked out in trendy chrome. That would have been the picture in the brochure, Vicky thought cynically. But the sleek-looking

310

kitchen was given the lie by a pair of empty pizza boxes sitting on the counter. That's more like it, Vicky smiled to herself, thinking of the duck in plum sauce that Connolly had ordered in the restaurant on St James's. Beyond the kitchen, the sitting area took up the rest of the room. The walls were an inevitable shade of mushroom, and the floor had been laid with cheap laminate. It wasn't a lot, Vicky thought, looking around the cramped space, even for a bachelor pad. A giant plasma screen was bolted to the wall, though, a Sony Bravia, she noted, top of the range. On the other side of the room there was a Bang & Olufsen stereo. But so what if Connolly caned his credit card? He worked a sixty-hour week and was surrounded by the scum of the earth for most of them and all it had got him was this rabbit hutch of a flat and a takeaway pepperoni pizza on a Friday, so Connolly deserved the flash clothes and the boys' toys as compensation for his pains. Vicky was about to leave when she noticed a slip of waxy paper on a side table behind the stereo. Vicky walked over, but she knew what it was already – she didn't have to taste the white, powdery residue caught in the creases to know that the wrap had once contained cocaine. It proved nothing, she thought stubbornly. There was something else on the table. A slim piece of plastic. She took a closer look. Poking out of the junk mail was a key fob with a small, black-red logo at one end that was unmistakable. It was an electronic car key and it looked brand new. How many detective constables drove a Porsche? A car like that would have been Connolly's pride and joy, his biggest boast. They wouldn't have been able to shut him up about it. So why hadn't he mentioned it before?

It happened, she told herself. A young officer meets a guy in a gym. They have a few drinks and they hit it off. The next time, the guy tells the police officer about a mate of his who's just been offered a second-hand car. Only he can't make his mind up about it. 'No problem,' the officer replies, showing off just a little. On the Police National Computer, a Vehicle Online Description only takes a couple of seconds, so by the time they bump into each other the following week, the officer gives the guy the nod. 'It's a ringer,' he says. 'Cut and shut. Stay well clear.' 'Thanks very much,' says the guy, and he gets the beers in. The next time, it's more than a VOD, and the time after that, money changes hands.

Vicky had seen enough. She fetched her phone from her pocket and, punching in Minter's speed-dial, walked out of the room. Russell Compton was waiting for her in the hallway. He was a good foot and a half taller and for a split second she looked straight up into his eyes. 'Mr Compton,' she said, with an untimely sense of politeness. Compton punched her in the face, a right hook that broke the knuckle of his little finger and sent Vicky sprawling, her telephone clattered to the floor. 'Goodnight, darling,' Russell muttered, bending down to pick up the phone and looking through the call log to see if any of Rita's numbers were there. Finding none, he glanced at Vicky, wondering what to do with her.

Connolly hurried across the Steine. The lights at the entrance to the Palace Pier flickered once and were extinguished. He felt a trickle of cold sweat run underneath his arm. It was a quarter past one and he was already twenty minutes late.

In Kemptown, it was day for night. The Pride Parade was tomorrow, Saturday, and men had been arriving in the city from all over the country. The narrow pavements and even St James's Street itself were solid with revellers. Every streetlamp blazed; all the bars and restaurants were crowded. Some of the men even had the nerve to check Connolly out, then wondered what on earth this uptight straight guy was doing in Kemptown, tonight of all nights.

Stern-faced, trying to ignore them, Connolly pressed on up the hill. He hated Kemptown. It wasn't just the queers. It was the trendies, too. The people who thought this part of the city was all mosaicked garden benches and laid-back mezze lunches. They had no idea what it looked like in the morning.

That first cold winter in uniform – four years ago it had been – Connolly had taken the body of a junkie out of one of these shop doorways at dawn. The night had been so cold the seat of the guy's jeans had frozen to the step. 'Must have pissed himself,' one of the paramedics explained. 'Welcome to Brighton, mate.'

Ahead, just outside Café Polska, the crowd became worse. They were eight or nine deep, one side of St James's to the other, clustered around a carnival float that should have been parked up somewhere else, ready for the parade tomorrow morning. A cheesy track was flying out from the truck's PA. As Connolly came closer, he could see three young men dressed as cowboys on the back of the rodeo-themed float. One was sitting astride a fairground bullock, the sodium lights spangling the rhinestones of the waistcoat he was wearing over a bare, skinny chest. Two grinning cowboys were standing either side of him, both dressed only

313

in brown leather chaps and posing pouches. Above their heads they were spinning lassos in time to the music. As Connolly tried to get through the swell of noisy, excited men, one of the lassos flew out over the crowd. Accompanied by whistles and cheers from the spectators, the lasso snagged a man, whom the cowboys proceeded to drag up onto the back of the truck. They sandwiched his body tightly between their own and began to bump and grind.

Finally, shoving a drunkenly embracing couple out of the way, Connolly broke through the crowd around the truck. Then he stopped. In front of him was a uniformed police officer.

The sergeant was in his forties. 'You're SOCU, aren't you?' he shouted, recognising Connolly straight away. The plain-clothes DS had no choice about it. Connolly nodded. 'There's been a stabbing on West Street,' the sergeant yelled. 'I had to send four of my constables over to lend a hand.' He looked over the heads of the crowd to the top of the hill where yet another car had just been abandoned. 'We'll never be able to bring in an emergency vehicle,' the sergeant said.

Connolly knew he was being asked to lend a hand, but he couldn't afford to be any later than he already was. 'Are you in radio contact with Despatch?' he asked.

'Yes, sir,' the sergeant replied. 'I'm waiting for some more officers to be sent over from Hove.'

'When will they get here?' Connolly asked.

'Any minute now, I hope. Then we can start clearing some of these streets.' He glanced around. On the rodeo float, one of the cowboys was dancing stark naked. 'We're mob-handed tomorrow night,' the sergeant explained. 'It's never been this bad before on the Friday.'

'Contact Despatch every couple of minutes,' Connolly told the sergeant. 'Let them know exactly what's happening.' Ignoring the disappointed look on the sergeant's face, Connolly began to press his way through the crowd again.

A couple of minutes later, a breathless Connolly turned off Kemptown's main road into a narrow, unlit mews. The noise of the crowd melted away. At the end of the lane, he saw the familiar, smudged outline of the long, low car. He made his way over.

When Connolly opened the heavy door, the reek of cheap perfume and male sweat crawled down his throat. He slid reluctantly into the front passenger seat. With a solid *chunk* the door sealed itself back into the side of the Bentley. Despite himself, Connolly couldn't help admiring the sound it made.

The man in the driving seat didn't greet him, didn't even look across, just kept his eyes on the winged *B* standing a mile and a half away at the end of the bonnet. On the walnut console between the two front seats was a frothy blond wig.

Connolly turned round. In the back of the Bentley, in a halo of pale light thrown up from an open compact, Rita was inspecting his heavily made-up face. He was wearing a yellow miniskirt and a wing-collared white blouse. Without looking at the police officer, Rita delicately retrieved a small pair of tweezers from the cosmetics bag in his lap and used them to remove the set of false eyelashes he was wearing. 'Thank you for coming, Detective Constable Connolly,' he said quietly. Connolly glanced across at the other man sitting on the back seat. Beside the fleshy presence of the heroin importer, this man seemed small, almost childlike. He was gazing out of the window towards St James's. 'Don't mind Rudy,' Rita told Connolly. When he leaned forward, the remaining set of eyelashes made Rita's expression weirdly lopsided. With just the tips of two of his fingers, he tapped his driver lightly on the shoulder. Immediately, the man reached across Connolly to open the glove compartment. He fished out a pack of tissues and a thick, white envelope. He passed the tissues back, then dropped the envelope unceremoniously into Connolly's lap. From behind, Connolly heard Rita spit on one of the tissues. 'That's for the prompt information regarding dear old Jacqui,' he said, beginning to wipe foundation away from his cheeks.

The police officer opened the flap of the envelope. He riffled the edges of the red banknotes with the side of his thumb. The money felt good. It always did. But it had to stop now. 'They know,' Connolly blurted out. There was silence in the back of the car. 'They're talking about Professional Standards,' Connolly said.

The driver looked into the rear-view mirror. He seemed to receive some new kind of instruction. He leaned across Connolly again. 'It changes nothing,' said Rita. He resumed the removal of his make-up.

This time, it was a large felt bag that the driver took out of the glove compartment. As soon as he took it into his hands, Connolly knew that the bag contained a gun. 'By the way, Connolly,' Rita said casually, 'I hope you enjoyed the little treat we arranged for you at the weekend.'

Out of the corner of his eye, Connolly saw the driver's mouth split into a grin. 'Very nice, thanks,' Connolly replied, bemused but still polite. He took the gun out of the bag, feeling the weight of it in his hand. A piece of paper fell out of the bag into Connolly's lap. A photograph, too. The single sheet seemed to be a photocopy from an Ordnance Survey map but Connolly couldn't make out the picture.

'Natasha there,' Rita explained, 'can't speak a word of English, so she couldn't have told you how old she was. Even if you had bothered to ask her.' He reached forward from the back, shining the ghostly light from his compact onto the glossy surface of the 5x7 colour shot.

'Oh Christ,' Connolly whispered.

Rita sat back in his seat again. 'She was only twelve.' Through the one-way glass of the Bentley, he surveyed the silent mews. 'You lot are all the same, aren't you? Shag anything in a skirt.'

'I told you,' Connolly said nervously, 'it's over.'

'It's not over until I say it is.' When he leaned forward, the leather seat squeaked a little against his bare thigh. 'I mean, just imagine what you and Natasha there would look like on the front page of the *Daily Mail*. They'd blur up your cock, of course. It's uncut, I noticed. That's another thing I like about you, Connolly, by the way. But your face rather says it all, anyway, doesn't it?'

Connolly closed his eyes. There was nothing he could do about it. He belonged to Rita now. Absolutely and unequivocally, he was Rita's boy. Softly, almost affectionately, the powerful hand fell on his shoulder. 'Besides,' Rita said, 'I have one last thing I need you to do.'

'What is it?' Connolly knew it involved the gun in some way. 'Who do you want me to kill?'

'Tonight, Sean, you are going to become the hero of the city.'

Even Connolly realised he was being mocked. 'What do you mean?'

'You're going to kill Russell Compton. You're going to rid Brighton of its most dangerous drug baron.'

Connolly's mind was racing. Perhaps it wasn't going to be too bad after all, he thought. If he had to kill, then it was better it was someone like Compton. And if he was clever, it might even turn things round for him in SOCU. 'Go on,' Connolly said.

'Russell's going to have to skip town, but to do that he needs to get his hands on some cash. Which means his emergency supply, buried out on the Downs. You'll find the exact location indicated on the map you're holding. But you'll have to hurry, Sean.'

'What do I do with the gun afterwards?'

'Now that's the neat part,' Rita replied, excited a little by the cleverness of his own plan. 'That gun belongs to Russell. I took it off his quartermaster a couple of weeks ago. It's still got Russell's prints all over it. The last time that gun was used was on poor Alan Day. So you don't have to get rid of it. Instead, you'll say you shot Russell in self-defence. You wrestled the firearm off Russell and he was shot in the struggle. I dare say you can make the fit-up look convincing. You are a police officer, aren't you? And then Russell goes down for Alan as well as the drugs.' There was a silence in the car. 'Well,' Rita demanded, 'what are you waiting for?'

Connolly stuffed the envelope of cash into the breast pocket of his jacket. He put the felt bag in his side pocket, then opened the door of the Bentley. Within a minute, he was back on St James's.

If anything, it had become busier, noisier. An even bigger crowd had gathered around the carnival float and there were more dancers on the back. Connolly pushed through the cheering men. The sergeant was still there, standing in the middle of the road, trying to hear what was being communicated to him through his radio. The crowd to his left moved a little and suddenly DS Minter was revealed as well, standing just a few yards behind the preoccupied sergeant. Connolly was about to turn back when he saw Minter looking at him. Reluctantly, Connolly crossed the road to join his colleagues.

'Didn't know you were on duty tonight,' Minter said to him.

Connolly hesitated. Minter was exactly the kind of officer to check the roster. 'I'm not on duty.'

Minter looked around the delirious crowd.

'Is there something you've got to tell us, then, Sean?'

'Yeah, yeah,' said Connolly.

Minter was here because Tom Beckett had begged a favour from a DS he knew who worked on tele-communications. They'd traced all the private phone calls of both Connolly and Phillips, and at all the critical moments, it was Connolly who was making calls to the same unlisted number.

The sergeant had finished his radio conversation. He turned towards the two plain-clothes officers. 'Right,' he said, 'there's a van at the top of St James's and two teams in Edward Street. We're going to start dispersing people in the direction of the seafront.'

Minter nodded. He turned to Connolly again. 'So what *are* you doing here, Sean?' By themselves, the phone calls weren't enough to tie Connolly to the drugs gang. Minter and Beckett needed something else so the same DS had used GPS to track Connolly to Kemptown. Minter knew he wasn't here for the party.

Connolly had already put two and two together. He knew why Minter had been so interested in James McFarland, but he didn't know how much Minter had discovered about everything else. 'I had a call from a source,' Connolly said. 'He told me something interesting about your guy Lambert.'

Minter seemed to take the bait. 'What'd he say?'

'Seems you might be right about him, Minter. Lambert's much bigger than Beckett thought. He might even turn out to be the guy bringing the gear in. He's got a consignment waiting up on the Downs, ready for collection. I was going to check it out.' Connolly looked at his colleague. A glint of humour appeared in his eye. 'You busy here, Minter?' he asked. 'Fancy a bit of public order, or do you want to try for the big time?'

Minter hesitated. It was his last chance to get something to tie Connolly to the drug gang before Windmill went into meltdown. He decided it was worth the risk. 'OK. Where's your car?'

In the tiny hallway of Connolly's flat, Vicky woke up. She was a little groggy and her head was thudding. When she put her hand up to her head, she could feel the blood. It was already beginning to dry.

Vicky looked around. She saw her phone on the floor. She picked it up and dialled but Minter wasn't answering, just that stupid woman's voice asking her to leave a message.

She left the flat. A little wobbly on her feet, wondering what it was that Russell had used to strike her, Vicky took the lift down to the ground floor and hurried through the hall, stepping out onto the street and looking around nervously. When she couldn't see anyone waiting for her, Vicky started running back towards her car.

She was driving to Kemptown when the Bluetooth finally connected. 'Minter!' she said. 'Thank God! I've been ringing and ringing.' She could hear the engine of his car in the background. It got louder, as if he'd moved his handset to his other ear.

'I'm out of town,' said Minter. 'There's very little reception here.'

A tension in his voice told Vicky that Minter wasn't on his own. 'Is Connolly with you?' she whispered.

'That's right.'

'It's him. It's Connolly. I've been to his flat.'

There was a pause. 'I know. I'll see you in the morning, Vicky.'

In the car, Minter put his phone back in his pocket. He hadn't ended the call, though. He wanted Vicky to hear what was said next.

Connolly was suspicious. 'Who was that?' he asked from the passenger seat.

'Vicky Reynolds,' said Minter.

'What did she want?'

'Apparently, Slater's giving a briefing tomorrow morning. Eight o'clock at Kemptown.'

Connolly looked across at him. 'You and Vicky seem to be hitting it off.'

'She's a good officer.'

Connolly, bending down, picked up the heavy police flashlight Minter had fetched from the boot of his car. He turned the torch on and shone its beam against the palm of his other hand to test it. 'Funny,' he said. 'No one said anything to me about a briefing.'

Minter shrugged. 'It's probably a last-minute thing.'

Connolly switched off the flashlight and the car was plunged back into darkness. 'Yeah,' he said, 'probably.'

The country lane ended at a crossroads somewhere in the wilds of West Sussex. 'Where to now?' Minter asked.

'Take a right,' said Connolly. 'Head for Chanctonbury Ring.'

Minter hoped that Vicky had heard.

A couple of minutes later, out of the darkness ahead, the yellow beams of Minter's headlights conjured an end to the narrowing track. In front of a five-bar metal gate, he brought the car to a halt.

Minter looked around. Out here, there were no other houses, just fields rolling away from them to the left and to the right, the various shades of green turned monochrome grey by a decaying moon. Minter turned to Connolly. 'Guess the rest of the way's on foot, then,' he said.

As Connolly opened the door and got out of the car, the bulge in his jacket pocket was illuminated briefly by the beam of the courtesy light. The object was wrapped up in something soft that disguised its contours, but Minter knew it was a gun.

Minter got out of the car and the two men faced each other across the bonnet. Connolly switched on the flashlight.

This time, he shone it straight in Minter's face. 'Did Reynolds say anything else?' he asked.

The bright light hurt Minter's eyes. 'No,' he said, reaching up his hand. Connolly pointed the flashlight away. 'So,' Minter said, 'you going to tell me who your source is?'

Connolly tapped the side of his own nose with his index finger. 'Confidential, innit?'

Minter nodded his understanding.

Connolly got to the gate first. He slipped the metal latch. The gate keened a little as he swung it open. Minter followed him through.

The bridleway on the other side led sharply up to one of the high downs, its banks lined either side by thick bramble bushes. After a minute, the bushes were supplanted by trees whose overhead branches began to merge. Inside the steep tunnel, Connolly and Minter became invisible.

It was hard going. Summer had baked the rutted mud until it was bone dry and in the dark, both men lost their footing against the occasional unseen flint. As they climbed higher, Minter kept Connolly a few yards in front of him. Connolly had the flashlight in one hand and the other was swinging freely by his side. Minter kept his eye on that hand, expecting at any moment to see it reach inside Connolly's jacket for the gun. All the time, the yellow beam of Connolly's flashlight dashed crazily over the woodland floor. Somewhere high up in the canopy, a breeze stirred a few of the branches, making the leaves restless. Dawn was not too far away, Minter realised. As if it was shrinking from the approaching sun, the air turned even colder. The hill got steeper, the path through the close-standing trees more difficult to follow. Minter could hear Connolly's breathing becoming laboured. He was a lot fitter than Connolly and he knew these hills like the back of his hand. The longer this went on, the more the advantage shifted in his favour.

Minter glanced up to his right. Through the treetops, he caught sight of Chanctonbury Ring. The circle of trees marked the highest promontory on this part of the Downs and had been planted centuries before. The wind that always scoured the roof of the Downs had bent their trunks backward, making eerie shapes against the moonlight. As Minter and Connolly climbed towards the Ring, not a word passed between them.

It wasn't going to end here, Minter told himself. The best that he had hoped for had always been survival. For years, he had run these darkened hills and trudged the Brighton streets with no place to head to and no place that he was from. But now, as he walked up the path behind a man who wanted to kill him, towards another man – Compton – who had killed so many times before, Minter realised he wanted more from life, much more than it had given him so far. This time, when it came to it, he wasn't going to hesitate, he wasn't going to flinch.

They cleared the wood at last, emerging at the start of a track that ran westward along the top of the Downs. About a thousand yards away, the silhouettes of the tortured trees of Chanctonbury Ring touched the sky. Connolly extinguished the flashlight. A moment later, the faint beam of another torch appeared from the middle of the Ring. Instinctively, Minter and Connolly stood still as a small sound travelled over the deserted hillside towards them, the sound of a spade being thrust into the earth. Then the light was lost in the thicket again and the hill fell silent.

'It's him,' Connolly whispered. In the first light of the dawn, his grin was plain to see. 'You'll get your promotion all right, Minter. We can bust Russell with the gear.'

Minter hesitated. Ambition plain and simple, that was what all his colleagues believed provided his motivation. But, just like his colleagues, Connolly had got Minter all wrong.

'You're not scared, are you?' Connolly taunted Minter on the hillside. 'There's two of us, mate,' he cajoled. 'We'll be fine.'

Crouching low to the hillside, Minter followed Connolly towards the dense circle of trees. As they got closer, the light began to show more frequently and the sound of the spade grew louder. Soon the police officers were dodging from trunk to trunk, the hard ground working in their favour now because on the bare earth their feet made hardly any noise. Through a slalom of tree trunks, Minter saw him first. Russell Compton was about twenty yards away, in the middle of a clearing. He was squatting down, pulling something small from the hole he had just dug. When Russell stood up again, he looked enormous. Bold as day, Connolly walked forward. As he entered the clearing, Minter saw the gun in his hand.

In the semi-darkness, Russell peered at the dim figure. 'Who the fuck are you?' he demanded.

Connolly walked quickly towards him, raising the gun and putting his finger on the trigger to fire. 'No!' Minter called from the edge of the clearing. It was the only distraction Russell needed. He swerved his upper body to the left and the wayward bullet from Connolly's gun grazed the side of his head.

Before Connolly could fire again, Russell swung the bright-edged spade through the air. The flat of it smacked the side of Connolly's face, knocking him off his feet, throwing him to the ground. Minter ran towards them, but Russell got there first. He lifted the spade up over Connolly's head. 'I'm Rita's boy!' Connolly screamed, but Russell plunged the blade downward, bringing his work boot down against the top edge for good measure. The lip of the spade sliced through the skin of Connolly's throat, crunching through his windpipe, chipping his vertebrae.

The spade still upright, Russell stepped over Connolly's gurgling body. He picked up the gun and aimed it at Minter, bringing him up short. 'You filth, too?'

'Yes.'

'What's your name?'

'DS Minter.'

'Another DS?' Russell said. 'How many more of you people has that slag Rita bought?'

'Not me,' Minter told him. 'Rita doesn't own me.'

From behind Compton, Minter heard a sucking noise. Connolly was making a final, wretched effort to draw air down into his lungs.

Russell smiled. 'You come to arrest me, then, DS Minter?' He was close enough now for Minter to see his finger close on the trigger. Then, suddenly, it stopped squeezing. 'Chris?' said Russell. He was looking past Minter now, to somewhere on the edge of the clearing. 'Is that you, son?' Chris Compton was walking towards his father, and he was carrying a gun of his own. 'You're a bit late, aren't you?' Russell said. 'You should have come here yesterday.'

'Where's Mum?' asked Chris. 'I've just been home. It's a war zone, crawling with police. Where is she?'

Russell shook his head. 'Right now I've got no idea where Jacqui is, and I can't say I really care much, either.'

'Tell me the truth for once, Dad.'

Russell stretched out his arm, cracking Minter's temple with the butt of his pistol. His mind splintering, Minter's body collapsed onto the ground and he lay there, dazed. Russell turned back to Chris. 'Now, where were we? Oh, yeah, Jacqui. The cops took your mother away from the house, that's all I know. They've probably got her tucked up safe somewhere and she's probably getting ready to spill her guts, just like her brother.' In the silence that followed, Russell watched the indecision pass back and forth across his son's face. 'Tell me what you want, son. Tell me what you came here for.'

'I want some of the gear.' The golf-ball-sized packages of heroin were lying all over the clearing. Wrapped in cellophane, they gleamed in the short grass.

Russell took a step closer to Chris. 'You want what?'

'I don't want all of it, Dad,' Chris said, his voice wavering. 'Just enough to set me up. Then I'll go, I promise. You'll never see me again.'

Russell snorted. He'd always despised Jacqui and Chris for being stupid and spineless. When he stepped forward again, Chris didn't move a muscle. Candy from a fucking baby. 'That's a smart move, son, very smart. You've seen the opportunity that my situation has presented and you're going for it. I'd say that was laudable ambition.'

He took another step. He could almost reach out and touch Chris now. Russell's finger wrapped round the trigger of his own gun. 'I like that, son. It makes me very proud of you.'

'All I want is for you to leave me alone, Dad. I told you. I want out.'

Russell looked down at Chris's pistol. It was a drilled-out replica, but it could still do some damage. Chris's hand was shaking so Russell made his voice nice and gentle. 'OK, son, I know that. So why don't you put the gun away? If you put it away, then we can talk this thing through and come to some arrangement.' Russell looked straight into his son's eyes, deep into his heart. At the same time his massive fist closed around the muzzle of Chris's gun turning it away from himself. The boy felt as puny and helpless as he always did in the presence of his father. 'That's right, son, give it to me.'

Behind Russell Compton, Minter tried to get up, but he couldn't steady himself. 'Jacqui's dead, Chris,' he shouted. 'They shot her tonight.'

Almost nonchalantly, Russell's arm jerked backward. He squeezed the trigger twice, the first bullet ramming harmlessly into the dirt at Minter's feet, the second hitting him in the leg. As Russell turned back to Chris, there was a third explosion.

Russell Compton crashed to the ground beside Minter. He could see the damage Chris had done: from point-blank range, the gunshot wound had almost severed Russell Compton's arm at the shoulder. Russell's gun was still in his other hand and his eyes were open and, somehow, he was already beginning to lift himself up.

328

Chris stood over his father. 'You're a bastard, Dad! A bastard! You killed her, didn't you? Just like you killed Dave!' He aimed the gun at his father's head and pulled the trigger, but it jammed. It seemed that nothing would kill the man Chris Compton loathed and feared in equal measure.

Russell Compton was on his knees now, supporting himself with his good arm. 'You cunt!' he roared. 'You fucking cunt!'

'No,' Chris said, paralysed with fear. 'Please don't.' As Chris dropped his gun, Russell took aim with his. With all the might that he could gather, ignoring the shrieking pain in his leg and the blurred vision, Minter launched himself up from the ground. He crashed into Russell, knocking his aim. But Russell still got his shot off and Chris Compton fell backward.

Russell was on the ground, too, and he'd landed on his severed shoulder. 'Fuck!' he screamed. Minter scrambled up on top of him and hit Russell hard in the face. Supercharged by adrenaline, Russell didn't even seem to feel the blow. He was already bringing his own fist round and up; it struck Minter on the cheek, smacking into him with a terrible force, sprawling him back onto the ground. Before Minter could get properly to his feet, Russell was on him again. Taking a run-up, he kicked Minter in the head, flinging him backwards.

Looking on the floor, Russell bent down to pick up his gun. He was big, but Minter was quick – he was up on his feet in no time, and now he was holding the gory spade that Russell had used to kill Connolly. Minter swung it backward. The first blow broke Russell's knuckles and the gun fell from his hand. The second blow of the spade caught Russell square across the side of his face.

'Minter!' cried a voice. It was Vicky. The gunshots had brought her running from the crest of the hill and now she was standing at the edge of the inner circle.

Minter didn't hear her. He was picking up the gun from the ground where it had fallen. Russell Compton was kneeling on the ground in front of him, his arm hanging loosely by its scrap of skin and bone, his bloody face turned to Minter.

The final shot rang out.

Rushing forward, Vicky watched Russell's hand grope upward for a moment, as if he was going to try to pluck out the bullet lodged deep inside his brain. His eyes flickered and he gave up. Inch by slow inch, he sank down on the ground to one side and finally, he was still.

Vicky rushed over to where Minter was crouching, staring at Russell Compton, making sure that he wasn't going to get up again. The sound of police sirens rose up from the bottom of the hill. Minter saw the headlights piercing the gloom of the lowest part of the wood. 'Did you see what happened?' he asked.

Vicky nodded. 'Believe me, Minter, you don't want any crap about discharging that firearm. What I saw was a fight. Compton had the gun and he was going to kill you. You acted in self-defence.'

Minter looked around the little circle of trees. Despite what Vicky was telling him, despite his fogging brain, there was no mistaking what had happened. He didn't have to fire the gun. He could have made an arrest instead. 'He was on the floor.'

There were shouts from the woods now and the barking of dogs. They didn't have a lot of time to get this straight. Vicky fixed Minter with her eyes. 'You did the only thing you could do. Russell Compton was getting up and reaching for the gun again.'

On the other side of the little circle of trees, Chris Compton started to stir. 'You're going to lie for me?' Minter asked Vicky. 'Is that what you're saying?'

Vicky nodded. 'We have to stick together. That's how this thing works. We're family, Minter, and we look after our own.'

# 15

· · ·

The next morning, the press had gathered outside Kemp-town Station again. When Chief Superintendent Roberts came out of the double glass doors, they rushed towards him up the steps.

This time, Roberts wasn't flanked by the young PR and there was no official Jaguar to get into. Instead of being chauffeured back to the Park, Roberts was going to have to make his own way home.

'Has Chief Inspector Pendle made a decision yet?' shouted one of the journalists.

'No comment,' said Roberts, forcing himself through the gaggle of pressmen.

'Is it true you've been suspended?' called out another.

Roberts fixed him with his steely eyes, but there was nothing he could do. The super was, as old fashioned police officers used to say, bang to rights. Minter had made sure of it.

The press needed feeding. 'What do you say to the allegations that you've been fiddling the crime figures for over a year now?' said the woman from the *Argus*, who knew more than most.

Roberts pushed her so hard that she almost fell down the bottom two steps. There was some swearing from her colleagues and someone pushed Roberts back. Breaking free, he dashed across the road.

Upstairs, on the fifth floor, Minter and Vicky watched Roberts disappearing down a side street.

'He'll be back,' said Vicky. 'He's a slippery customer.'

'I doubt it,' said Minter. He winced. The bullet Russell Compton fired had gone straight through his calf, but the wound was still causing him a lot of pain.

'Are you OK?' said Vicky.

'It'll be all right, although I won't be doing any running for the next few weeks.'

Vicky couldn't say she was unhappy about that. She wondered why Minter was so sure about Roberts not coming back to haunt them. 'You seem to know a lot about everything.'

'I'm in intelligence,' Minter said. 'It's my job.'

Professional Standards had arrived in Brighton a couple of hours ago and they'd already set about slicing and dicing Operation Windmill. Minter and Vicky were waiting their turn to be interviewed. 'I saw Kevin Phillips coming in,' she said.

'How is he?' Minter asked.

'More than a little chastened, I'd say.'

The laxness of the ExCal passwords was one of many things that would be criticised in the final report on Windmill. In an effort to cover his tracks, Connolly had used

Kevin Phillips's password when he hacked into the CHIS module of ExCal.

'Kevin's told Professional Standards about something else, too,' said Vicky.

'What's that?'

'Yesterday, at the bust on the Compton stash house, Sean Connolly offered to split some of the drugs money with him. It was big wedge, tens of thousands of pounds. Kevin Phillips turned him down.'

'And how do we know that?'

'If Kevin kept the money,' said Vicky, 'why would he tell PS about it? Especially now that Connolly's dead.'

Minter nodded.

'You have to trust some people, Minter.'

'I just hope there's going to be no bad feelings between me and Kevin,' said Minter.

Vicky was surprised. She'd assumed that, job done, Minter would be back on his way to the Park. 'You staying in SOCU, then?'

Minter looked around the scruffy, overheated room. The working conditions might be terrible, but Minter was beginning to feel at home in Kemptown. That was why he'd turned down the job he'd been offered just this morning by the chief constable of Sussex. Now that Roberts had been suspended pending the investigation, the Force needed someone to steer the bureaucracy through the choppy waters ahead. As the whistle blower, Minter fitted the bill perfectly. If the public were going to believe the police were doing a good job, then the data had to be beyond reproach. Minter would have a corner office up at the Park with his name on the door and the rank of detective inspector in front of it.

It would be back to calm administration and steady progress through the middle ranks.

But it wouldn't be at Kemptown, and it would be very dull indeed. 'Like I always said,' he told her, 'I want to work crime.'

There was a pause. 'I'm not so sure SOCU is right for me,' said Vicky. 'In fact, when I get home this afternoon, I'm going to send off an application for another job.' From the look on Minter's face, she could tell that the possibility of her leaving Kemptown came as something of a shock. He didn't even try to hide it. 'It's still at Brighton and Hove,' she added quickly.

'Doing what?'

'Family liaison.'

Minter nodded. He could see the logic. 'Had enough of all the macho stuff, then?'

'You never know,' said Vicky. 'I might even end up doing someone some good. But don't breathe a word about it to anyone, at least not until I get an interview. *If* I get an interview.'

'They'd be insane to knock you back,' said Minter. He looked at Vicky. 'I'm sorry you're not staying, though. And I wanted to say thank you, too.'

'For what?'

'For putting me straight on the statement about the circumstances in which Russell Compton died last night.' He nodded towards the door. Professional Standards had set up base camp in an office along the corridor. 'It'll save a lot of trouble with this lot.'

'Not every *i* has to be dotted, Minter. Remember that. And, anyway, I'm sure you'd do the same for me, one day.'

'I would,' said Minter. 'Believe me.'

The door to the MIR opened and Tom Beckett walked in. He'd been in with Professional Standards for the past hour and it would be the first of many interviews.

'How's it going?' Vicky asked.

'Piece of piss,' said Beckett. It was typical bravado – Professional Standards hadn't made it easy for Beckett at all. They still held the problems with ExCal against him and they were suggesting he take early retirement as a way of sweeping the embarrassing episode under the carpet once and for all. But Beckett was no one's patsy and he wasn't signing any non-disclosure agreement just to get his hands back on his pension. Anyway, with Vicky and Minter on his team, Tom Beckett had two very good reasons to stay. 'Now,' he asked Minter, 'what about this Rita?'

After he'd found out what had happened to Russell and to Dempsey, Lambert had given Minter an address this morning. 'It seems that Rita's left town,' Minter told Beckett. Minter recalled the contents of the mirrored wardrobes in the master bedroom suite at the Van Alen Building. 'He's certainly a character.'

'He's got to be,' said Beckett.

'We know a lot about him now,' said Vicky. 'We'll get him next time round.'

'And where does McFarland fit in?' said Beckett.

'Lambert pimped him to Rita for sex parties,' said Minter.

'Pillow talk can be a dangerous thing,' said Vicky. 'Rita kept on seeing Jimbob McFarland for years, right up to the night he was murdered, in fact.'

'Jimbob was getting old,' said Minter. 'Maybe Rita had had enough of him, or maybe Rita had told him a little too

336

much about his business over the years. Either way, it seems Jimbob was a loose end Rita wanted tying.'

'It was the only mistake he made,' said Vicky.

Beckett said, 'And only you had the nous to spot it, Minter.'

The door opened again and a pale young man in a dark suit came in. He had Professional Standards written all over him. 'DC Reynolds,' he said, 'we're ready for you now.'

'Good luck,' Minter told Vicky quietly as she followed the ill-looking young officer out of the door.

Beckett turned to Minter. 'I'm not retiring after all, not now that idiot Roberts has gone belly up.'

Minter smiled. 'Beckett and Minter, eh? When do we start?'

'I've opened the file on Rita already,' said Beckett.

'No,' said Minter. 'I didn't mean Rita. I meant Anna May. We owe her, sir. Remember?'

# Epilogue

· · ·

The tall crane was built in sections. It swivelled from the hip. It looked like a jointed insect, Rita thought as the long arm of the crane swung out over the moored ship and its head jerked down into the hold. A moment later, there was a strange metallic kiss as the huge magnet latched on to the crossbar on the top of one of the containers. Rita watched the crane lift the rusty, brown box high up into the cold, Scottish air. The small figure in the cab looked down and waved. Everything was going well.

Rita had imagined a busier scene, but the other four cranes stood motionless on the dockside and there was just the one ship at anchor. He was a romantic at heart, picturing a pack of spring-heeled dockers, all hollow cheeks and slicked-back hair. Instead, there was nothing but this slow, mechanised grabbing. Bored, he turned away.

Rita had been told yesterday about the demise of Russell Compton and the massacre of the Hangletons and he couldn't say he was sorry about either. It hadn't taken long to find someone new to take over the distribution side of the South Coast business. They were queuing up for the chance to run it, in fact. A few phone calls and the arrangements had been made.

Now Rita had more important things on his mind. There were big deals to be done today all the way down the M1. By this afternoon, a lot of people were going to get seriously rich and it would all be down to Rita's alliance with the Albanians. The only downside was that he was going to have to leave Brighton. Not for long, of course, and he'd keep an eye on things from wherever he ended up, but for the moment he'd have to forsake the city he loved so much.

A small, low door had been cut into the side of the warehouse. Inside, it was a hive of activity. The gang scurried round the back of an articulated lorry, its engine already shuddering, filling the place with diesel fumes. As Rita walked over, the electric motor lifted the tailgate of the lorry up to the level of the interior, where row upon row of the packing cases had already been loaded, each one as tall as a man. A couple of hours before, Rita had opened the first of them himself, checking that the weight matched up with what he'd paid. It did, right down to the gramme.

The last of the cases safely in place, the men jumped back down to the concrete floor. They closed the doors and rammed the bolts home. 'I'll meet you at the rendezvous,' Rita told the men in the cab. Rita's boys were going to drive the lorry to a quiet industrial estate on the outskirts of the city, where they'd unload all the cases again and retrieve the heroin before bringing the reassembled drill bits back to the warehouse. Then the other lorry would be on its way south.

The doors to the warehouse were rolled back and Rita

followed the vehicle out onto the dockside. This was the most dangerous part of the trip. If the police were going to be waiting anywhere, it would be in unmarked cars just outside the port.

Rita watched the lorry pass a contented-looking security guard at the gates. In the sunshine, the city of Aberdeen looked pale. Even the churches were made of granite, Rita noted. The lorry turned the corner.

It would be a shame leaving Brighton, he thought as he walked over to the Bentley, but Rita knew he would be back on the seafront soon enough. After all, Brighton belonged to him.

Always had done, always would do.